ANTHEM'S FALL

S.L. DUNN

Prospect Hill Press

Prospect Hill Press
P.O. Box 9913
Seattle, WA 98109

www.sldunn.com

Anthem's Fall is a work of fiction. Names, characters, places, and incidents are a product of the author's imagination or are used fictitiously. Locales and public names are sometimes used for atmospheric purposes. Any resemblance to actual people, living or dead, or to businesses, companies, events, institutions, or locales is completely coincidental.

Cover Illustration by Tim O'Brien
Cover Design by Laura Duffy
Title Font by Leonardo Gubbioni

Library of Congress Cataloging-in-Publication Data:
Dunn, S.L.
Anthem's fall/ S.L. Dunn. –1st ed.
(Anthem series ; bk. 1)
Control Number: 2014908358

ISBN 978-0-9916224-0-5
ebook ISBN 978-0-9916224-1-2

First Edition

PART ONE

ANNIHILATION

CHAPTER ONE

Kristen

It had its certain comforts and learned familiarities, but New York had never felt like home. The initial novelty of Manhattan and all of its cultural and architectural grandeur had long waned, and what she once regarded with wonder, she now felt only a moldering cynicism. These days Kristen Jordan considered the soaring edifices and crowding streets to be the material shape, the substance, behind the insatiable and thoughtless ambition of the modern. Nudging her straw against the melting ice cubes at the bottom of an empty vodka tonic, Kristen looked about the shabbily decorated and dimly lit college bar. Glowing neon beer signs and television screens hung on walls that enclosed a dozen booths and tables. A distinct smell of stale beer and hot wings hung in the air, yet the nearby conversations of fellow academics, exultant and self-assured, ignored this atrophy.

Kristen studied genetics at Columbia, and her brilliance was unrivaled. Sitting quietly and gazing across the young faces of the bar, Kristen wondered if she stood out among her outwardly preoccupied and self-satisfied peers, or if they too were all carrying unspoken anchors of anxiety and doubt. On some level, though, she knew her general restlessness was an unfortunate byproduct of her intellect, and not an affliction shared by the masses.

From across the table her fellow graduate student Steve Armstrong had started rambling over the loud rock music, his hand clutching a perspiring glass of beer. "My point is that there's a difference between intelligence, or even consciousness for that matter, and awareness. They're two entirely different phenomena that are always lumped into the same category. Don't you think?"

Kristen Jordan groaned and rolled her eyes, which elicited a laugh out of another graduate student sitting beside her, Cara Williams.

"I don't care, Steve," Kristen said, her voice distracted and leaden. "I hardly think it's a topic worthy of lengthy discussion. There's no way of knowing for certain because that kind of technology doesn't exist."

"Are you kidding me?" Steve gulped his beer and glared at her, his words faintly slurred. The alcohol added a note of indignation to his tone. "You're saying we shouldn't consider how a new technology will operate?"

"Please not another booze-fueled theoretical science argument," Cara said. Steve and Kristen ignored her.

"No," Kristen said to Steve in her ever-composed manner. "I'm just saying this specific discussion is comparable to cavemen arguing whether a gas-powered or an electric-powered car is superior. It doesn't *matter*—a hybrid won't exist for thousands of years. You know? Yes, it's a worthwhile topic, but not at the present, and certainly not while we're out having drinks."

"I take it this is the type of conversation I should start to get used to around the Columbia crowd?" Cara asked.

Kristen nodded with a begrudging smirk. "Honestly, and shamefully, yes, this is pretty much par for the course. Professor Vatruvia likes to handpick re-searchers who are big on ideas and less caught up in practicality. The result is a strange group of argumentative theorists."

"And a staggeringly high ratio of undiagnosed Asperger's syndrome to boot," Steve added. Kristen laughed.

"Well, however Professor Vatruvia chooses his people, it clearly produces results." Cara said, leaning back as a waitress hurried by and plopped down a fresh basket of cheap chips and salsa. "I must say I'm a little intimidated to be working on the same research team that actually created the Vatruvian cell. Were you two working with Professor Vatruvia when he won the Nobel Prize?"

"I was," Kristen said, gratification in her tone. Her gaze moved across the table with a satisfied expression. "Steve hadn't joined us yet."

Cara regarded Kristen's youthful features with confusion. "Were you an un-dergraduate assistant?"

Steve chuckled, nearly spitting his beer. Nonplussed, Cara looked from him to Kristen. "I'm sorry I didn't mean to say something insulting. What's so funny?"

"Nothing, nothing." Kristen lifted a hand from the table and waved off Steve's amusement. "It's fine. I get that reaction a lot. No, I was on the *actual* research team when we invented the Vatruvian cell. I wasn't an undergrad. I was head geneticist."

"Oh, I didn't mean offense. You just seem a little young, you know, to be halfway to your PhD." Cara spoke with genuine surprise. "And I totally mean that as a compliment."

Kristen blushed. She'd heard it all before, but this reaction to her age still made her uncomfortable.

"Kristen Jordan here is the resident teenager of the research team." Steve spoke into his glass, taking some pleasure in Kristen's embarrassment.

"Yeah, I'm really a teenager." Kristen shook her drink, indicating the empty vodka tonic. "And I was overseeing the genetic sequencing for the Vatruvian cell while you were struggling to get accepted into graduate school and cheering your nerd friends through *World of Warcraft*."

"Wow, that's unbelievable. I had no idea you were that young," Cara said.

Kristen cast a wan smile at the hardened glass rings engrained into the wood of the table. "I'm twenty-one."

"If you hadn't already noticed it about her, Kristen's a genius who missed out on a childhood. It's a shame really—overambitious mindset, overbearing parents, closet insecurities, the works."

"And you have it all figured out, huh?" Kristen threw an ice cube at Steve, which missed its mark and fell to their feet under the table. She would not admit it, but her somewhat intoxicated coworker was not far from the mark.

Kristen was a biologist by degree, though she was well learned in several academic fields. Now in her third year of a doctorate program at Columbia, she had become the renowned Professor Vatruvia's right-hand colleague, more of an associate than a student. Technically speaking she was the youngest researcher on the team, though at the same time Kristen was also a leader within the team's ranks. She had been involved since the very beginning of the groundbreaking Columbia Vatruvian cell research project. No one could deny that—aside from Professor Vatruvia himself—Kristen knew more about the inner workings and nuances of the Vatruvian cell than anyone else on the research team, and therefore in the world.

Kristen's looks were a common source of discussion among the male portion of the laboratory teams. She never wore any makeup, not seeing the use in such vanities. Yet try as she did to avoid accentuating her looks, her discreet beauty penetrated through. Even though they were usually concealed behind her glasses and dark bags from late nights spent looking over DNA codes, she had enthralling green eyes and graceful features. Her dirty blonde hair was often pulled back, revealing her exquisite cheekbones and the soft skin of her neck. With the slightest bit of effort, Kristen could have been called stunning. Most of her acquaintances would have classified her as gorgeous regardless—her lack of cosmetic efforts only providing an air of refinement to her often-overworked countenance.

"How is it possible that you're so far along in your career at twenty-one?" Cara asked.

"Oh god," Kristen sighed and shook her head. "I'd need another drink for that tale. It's pretty unspectacular really. I graduated high school young because I skipped just about every other grade of elementary and middle school. I have my parents to thank for that one. Then I hurried off to MIT and graduated in two years. The next thing I knew, I was here at Columbia working with Professor Vatruvia. Basically the tone of my life has been a hurry with no clear purpose."

"Wow . . . I thought you looked young for your age . . ." Cara trailed off. "MIT in two years . . . that's unheard of."

"Yep," Kristen sighed, greatly desiring a change in subject. Her age had always been a touchy issue, having generally been the youngest individual in any given social situation since as long as she could remember.

After graduating from MIT at the top of her class, Kristen Jordan had been unsure which direction to take her career. She knew she wanted to continue in the field, though into which specific sector she could not say. Working for some faceless pharmaceutical company in a lucrative attempt to cure obesity or male pattern baldness seemed so mundane and fruitless. Medical school felt like a colossal waste of time and effort: to spend the majority of your days fixing people who were either unwilling or simply too lazy to fix themselves.

Graduate school seemed to be a logical progression, but in truth Kristen did not know how much more there was to learn from textbooks and lectures. Furthermore, graduate school was merely a mechanism by which to delay her inevitable career decisions. Kristen had been only eighteen years old, staring down the barrel of the settle-down-and-get-a-salary world, and she resented it deeply.

It was during this post graduation stagnation that Kristen received an unexpected email from a research professor at Columbia University, the renowned synthetic biologist Professor Nicoli Vatruvia. Professor Vatruvia had happened upon Kristen's senior thesis in an open-access journal to which she had uploaded it on a whim. The basic idea of her paper had stated that the DNA double helix was the most elegant model for an information network. Kristen had proposed further research into modeling computer and mechanical databases after natural ones, such as genetic codes. Most scholars had read her thesis and quickly shrugged it off as interesting, though purely theoretical. Even Kristen had thought it was a little lofty and out there, but nevertheless she had supported her data and presented an interesting case. Her professor at the time had given her an A, with a comment scribbled in red pen, *Laudable work, with points defended appropriately, though ultimately impractical.*

Evidently, the famous Professor Vatruvia had not agreed with her MIT professor, and Kristen was stunned one morning to see his name sitting amid the spam of her inbox.

Everyone in the upper echelon of academia and private sector research knew Professor Vatruvia of Columbia University. During the research for her senior thesis Kristen had read a number of his published papers. A few of Professor Vatruvia's works had even been noted in Kristen's lengthy citations section. Professor Vatruvia's research in synthetic biology was on the cutting edge of modern science, and his creativity eclipsed all other minds in the field. Many people held the belief that Professor Nicoli Vatruvia would prove to be a modern visionary: a Da Vinci, Newton, or Einstein of the twenty-first century.

After staring at the name Nicoli Vatruvia and the subject heading, *Let's Schedule a Meeting,* Kristen had clicked on the email.

Ms. Jordan,
I have read through your senior thesis and am very intrigued by your proposal. We should speak immediately. Please reply as soon as possible and we can arrange a face-to-face meeting. Got to run.
Best,
Dr. Nicoli Vatruvia

Kristen had read over the email a number of times in disbelief. It was surely a weird prank orchestrated by one of her friends. She immediately checked the email address: nicoli.vatruvia@ColumbiaU.com by opening up the Columbia website and performing a staff directory search for him. It was not a hoax. Why would an internationally renowned synthetic biologist want to have a face-to-face with her? Kristen sat back in her desk chair and gazed out her window with uncertainty. There she was, sitting amid the relics of her childhood bedroom, having moved back to her parent's home outside Boston. Beyond her window, the bleakly overcast November morning and naked tree branches mirrored her internal feelings. The excitement of a warm spring and a hopeful graduation day had since faded into a bare and discouraging autumn. Staring into the drab yard, she decided to take the trip to New York and meet Nicoli Vatruvia.

Later that same week Kristen anxiously sat by the sun-filled window of a Starbucks just off the Columbia campus in the Upper West Side of Manhattan. When they had spoken briefly on the phone, Professor Vatruvia had told her to meet him at that specific time and place. He had told her nothing else. Even as she sat in the busy coffee shop, Kristen had no idea what part of her thesis had piqued the celebrated scientist's attention so completely.

Knowing his face from various articles she had read about him, Kristen sat upright when the man she recognized as Nicoli Vatruvia opened the coffee shop door. She wondered if he could be considered a celebrity? In scientific circles it would certainly be true, but to the others in the coffee shop he was probably just another bookish intellectual.

Kristen swallowed hard and quickly suppressed her rising apprehension. She waved and smiled politely.

"Kristen Jordan?"

"Yes, hi, Professor Vatruvia."

Standing up, Kristen took his outstretched hand. For a moment Professor Vatruvia regarded her age with unmistakable surprise, before sitting down and taking out a packed manila folder from his briefcase. His looks did not demand attention, yet his features seemed inquisitive, and—although not youthful—he had a young way about him.

"Thank you for coming down to meet me."

"Of course," Kristen said, attempting to sound as polite as possible. The man before her was a superstar; a man so renowned that accomplished PhDs would be uneasy in his presence. Professor Vatruvia opened the folder and began flipping through dozens of loose pages as Kristen sat uncomfortably, unsure if she should engage the prominent synthetic biologist in small talk. People were shuffling in and out of line, and baristas hurried around taking orders for the customers.

"Are you from the Northeast?" Professor Vatruvia asked as he skimmed through many pages.

"Cambridge."

"Nice town . . ." He murmured with little interest. "Ah, here it is."

Finding what he had been looking for, Professor Vatruvia passed a solitary paper across the table. Kristen recognized the words at once. It was an excerpt from her senior thesis—the specific section that had caused most experts to write off her whole work as theoretical and bordering on science fiction. Kristen had spent many an hour in the MIT student library debating whether to include the section she was now looking at.

A knot tightened in her gut.

In short, the section suggested that the growing field of synthetic biology limited itself by researching synthetic cells only in terms of biological form and function. Kristen had proposed the idea of expanding synthetic biology to the next level of innovation, attempting to create not only improved synthetic cells in terms of their use by people, but also synthetic cells that differed in nature from all other cells ever studied. Now that a synthetic cell had been created—an incredible feat in its own right—it was now time to climb inside the double helix and see what new marvel could be created with this newfound control over genetics. Kristen had proposed that this extensive approach to a synthetic genome might give rise to new proteins, cellular functions, or perhaps something more. They were daring assertions, and she did not relish the notion of defending them against the world's preeminent thinker in the field.

"Do you really believe that?" Professor Vatruvia asked after letting her examine the page.

Kristen could feel her face flush. "Yes, on a theoretical level I do."

"A theoretical level?"

"Certainly, in theory." Kristen paused and sighed before begrudgingly pressing on. "But the number of potential DNA base pairs is practically infinite, and a means of testing all those base pairs to determine which could facilitate viable synthetic functioning would take forever. It's taken evolution millions of years to create the form of natural cells we already know, so I think it would be unrealistic to expect any drastic changes in a single lifetime."

Kristen's answer came out more smoothly than she had expected, which was encouraging. This was after all her thesis, and she had defended it against many hard-lined doctrinaires.

"I agree," Professor Vatruvia said after a moment, glancing with little interest through more pages of the manila folder. "But if it did exist—a means to code and test base pairs at a rate never before seen—and the theoretical of your thesis turned into scientific reality, what do you think could result?"

"That type of research has never been done, so it would only be speculation," Kristen said.

"And if it did? We aren't recording this conversation for journal publication Ms. Jordan. By all means, I am giving you permission to speculate."

"Well then, there is always the possibility, however unlikely, that these new artificial chromosomes and constituent parts could become . . ." Kristen tilted her head and trailed off. "I don't know."

"It sounds like you do know," Professor Vatruvia said.

"Speculation has no place in science."

"Indulge me. What could the artificial components create?"

Kristen sighed in resignation. "A functional cell."

"A cell?"

"Well, not in the natural sense. I imagine it would function in a similar fashion as a cell. But it would have to be designed and created in a laboratory using artificial means." Kristen shifted uncomfortably. "I am getting way ahead of myself here."

"Exactly." A thin smile surfaced on Professor Vatruvia's face as though he had won some sort of dispute. "You and I are thinking along the same lines. I believe we have both perceived of a similar vision."

Kristen maintained a noncommittal expression as she sipped her latte.

Professor Vatruvia sat back in his chair and folded his legs, regarding Kristen earnestly. "I am about to start a research project that will turn our individual visions into a reality. I'll cut right to the chase. I would like to formally ask you to come work for me."

Kristen choked and picked up a napkin to dab her chin. She shook her head emphatically. "Professor Vatruvia, I haven't applied to graduate schools yet, let alone to Columbia. In truth, I don't know if I *want* to go to graduate school. Thank you. Really, thank you. But I'm not ready to make any kind of commitment."

"Look, Kristen. None of that is an issue. I can get you accepted and taken on for the spring semester. Our program would be a good fit for you. You can start research in the lab as soon as possible. I desperately need a talented mind like yours on the research team I'm bringing together. We visionaries can't work alone, you know."

Kristen stared at him in absolute bewilderment. "I don't understand. What would I be researching?"

"The creation of your thesis." Professor Vatruvia smiled with an enthusiasm nearly childish in its exuberance. "We can unravel the mystery of this synthetic system we have envisioned."

In the months that followed, the research team Professor Vatruvia assembled was its own private research entity, barely affiliated with Columbia. The various minds Professor Vatruvia had drawn together for his research team were each brilliantly innovative, though from the very first day, the enterprise's youngest member, Kristen Jordan, always stood out as one of the most gifted.

As time progressed, it became increasingly clear that their research was going to foster a scientific breakthrough. Supercomputers were put to work and laboratory technicians were hired in droves. Never before seen laboratory techniques were discovered and implemented. Each day Kristen and Professor Vatruvia came closer to conceiving their synthetic cell; each month a new impediment was toppled. Then, in the early spring it finally happened. After a year of labor and toil, Professor Vatruvia along with Kristen Jordan and the research team successfully brought about the genesis of their technology.

The Vatruvian cell.

Some experts celebrated their invention as the greatest technological break-through not only of the twenty-first century, but of the entire history of science. Technology had given rise to a new and unique form of artificial life. In the process, Professor Vatruvia had earned a Nobel Prize. Kristen Jordan had even appeared in the background of a *Time* magazine photo of their laboratory. The world had found its modern visionaries to extol, and their creation, the Vatruvian cell, was like nothing even the most decorated academics could have foreseen. Many of Professor Vatruvia's peers correctly pointed out that his team had not created a form of life at all, because of the Vatruvian cell's inanimate structure and loneliness of relatives within the tree of life. On the contrary, a complex machine—they said—was a more appropriate classification for the Vatruvian cell. Man had not created life; he had created the most involved and complex machinery in existence.

Professor Vatruvia had further shocked the scientific community by pub-licly announcing that his research into their incipient Vatruvian cell technology was still in the blossoming stages. From news headlines, to magazine articles, to television specials across the globe, the mainstream world was waiting for the next breakthrough from Professor Vatruvia and his Columbia research team. To Kristen, the end goal of their research remained at best vague. Despite her close relationship with Professor Vatruvia and her integral hand in the Vatru-vian cell's creation, Kristen was beginning to feel in some ways as uninformed as the general public.

"What is your field of study again, Cara?" Steve asked over the rising noise in the bar.

"Molecular pathology. I started my lab work on the Vatruvian cell a few weeks ago." Cara said. "What about you?"

"Computer Science. Don't have much in common with you biology nerds."

Kristen looked at him doubtfully as she nibbled a chip with little interest. "Get real, Steve. You and I both know you're the biggest nerd at this table. Are you going to bring up artificial intelligence again? Or maybe discuss which dumbass superhero is strongest?"

"Yeah okay," Steve said. "How about we bring up the ethics of the Vatruvian cell again?"

"Are you *serious?*" Kristen said and turned to Cara, her voice abruptly turn-ing humorless and stern. Steve struck a chord he knew would resonate. "Unlike our shortsighted computer scientist here, I raised a perfectly valid question at the last research meeting."

"More like you called out Professor Vatruvia in front of the entire research team." Steve said.

"What do you mean?" Cara asked. "Called Professor Vatruvia out for what?"

"It was nothing," Kristen said.

"I wouldn't have called it nothing. Cara, you know the research meeting that's scheduled for tomorrow afternoon?"

Cara Williams nodded.

Kristen sighed with aggravation as Steve took a sip of his fresh beer, a layer of the thick head lingering on his upper lip. "At the last one, Kristen here asked—no *demanded*—Professor Vatruvia to tell the team the direction our research is heading."

This seemed to evoke some interest out of Cara, and she leaned forward. "What did he say? I've been wondering that myself since I started working with the Vatruvian cell."

"Absolutely nothing," Kristen said with a severe shake of her head. "Professor Vatruvia hasn't told us a damn thing. Evidently we're his mindless drones; we are to complete our work and not question a single aspect of what we're doing. It's shameful I didn't get more support from the rest of the team—a team of allegedly talented thinkers. When it comes down to it, everyone is a pawn who will do whatever he orders simply to be a part of the research."

"Don't look at me," Steve said with a ring of genuine defensiveness. "I just keep the computer programs running. I don't know the first thing about the Vatruvian cell. That's your department. The Vatruvian cell work is still way over my head."

"A little support couldn't have hurt," Kristen said.

"You know . . ." Cara began but fell silent, her brow creased. "I . . . I've been wondering the same thing, Kristen. I'm glad we're on the same page. In a weird way the Vatruvian cell kind of . . . freaks me out."

Kristen shot Steve a piercing look to prove to him she was not alone in her concerns, and took the last sip of melted ice from her glass. "Yeah well, too bad no one else feels the same way we do, Cara."

"It's been a few months now since the last meeting. Professor Vatruvia is probably going to make a big announcement," Steve said in an obvious attempt to subdue the rising tension between them.

Cara nodded. "I hope so."

Kristen turned and looked to the growing number of people gathering by the bar. It was primarily an undergraduate crowd—she could tell from the overly eager aura radiating from their slightly inebriated faces. As she watched their lighthearted exchanges, Kristen could not help but feel a sense of disconnection. There was a group of frat types waiting for pints of beer. The bartenders and servers were attractive girls with low-cut shirts and snug jeans. A line stemming from the bathrooms grew longer by the minute with buzzed students. Looming above them all, big screen televisions blared out the week's football highlights. Kristen's attention was drawn to two girls, giggling and leaning against a couple of guys. They were telling some mundane story about an off-campus party the other night. Kristen could only catch bits of the idiotic drunken narrative. But as she gazed at them, she could not help but feel somewhat envious of the carefree look of it all.

Kristen returned her attention to the late twenty-somethings sitting with her in the booth. They had an old, tired, and professional look to them. Steve had a receding hairline and a gut from spending too much time sitting at a computer and retaining a stellar attendance at weekly bar trivia nights. Cara was sporting a subtle diamond engagement ring. Certainly neither of these older colleagues would consider staying out late and enjoying a casual night of raging and forgetting about reality—and ultimately neither would Kristen. There was a full day of work in the morning, and that was all there was to it. The ever-present weight of work to be done was a force that had long since claimed authority of Kristen's life. Tomorrow, while all of these silly and simple peers would be sleeping off a long night, Kristen would be acting vanguard to a modern marvel of discovery.

An unsettling sensation of disquiet surfaced in the back of her mind as Kristen stared across the prosaic happenings of the bar and considered what had been nagging her for the past few months. What Steve had quipped about was partly true. She had made somewhat of a spectacle at the last research meeting with Professor Vatruvia. More and more as the weeks progressed Kristen was beginning to grow anxious about the Vatruvian cell, though she could not rationalize her concerns with any tangible justification. For the time being Kristen decided to keep her thoughts to herself.

"I'm going to head back to my place," Cara said at last, breaking the silence of their table and jarring Kristen from her thoughts. "It's getting late and way too loud in here for me."

"Okay. See you at the meeting tomorrow." Kristen smiled and rose from the table, allowing Cara to pass.

"Have a good night," Steve said to Cara, and after she left turned to Kristen. "Another drink?"

"Eh, I don't think so. I have to be up early tomorrow." Kristen said, not wanting to send even the slightest false impression of interest to the rotund computer scientist. She looked back to the undergraduates by the bar and noticed several of the more confident, or perhaps more intoxicated, guys attempting to catch her eye. Kristen took care not to meet their stares and grabbed her tion. But Kristen had noticed. She also knew the goal of the research had to be lofty, whatever it was. Kristen resented that he was hiding the truth from her of all people, considering she was one of the founders of the technology. Yet she could not help but wonder if her feelings were just misconstrued resentment at being sidelined from her vital involvement during the early Vatruvian cell developments the previous winter.

A growl in her stomach reminded Kristen that she had forgone breakfast, and she turned into a corner café. The door of the shop opened with the tinkling of a bell, and Kristen stepped in line behind half a dozen people. A television mounted on the wall drew her attention from the pastries. A CNN reporter was talking about an international flight over Canada. A commercial jetliner had undergone engine failure at thirty thousand feet. The anchors were stressing the bravery and quick actions of the pilots, who masterfully righted the plane and avoided certain catastrophe.

A passenger was talking into a microphone held by a reporter. "You aren't *listening* to me!" The man was exasperated, his face flushed. "The engines didn't start back up! I was sitting right behind the wing. I would have felt o-o-or *heard* them reengage. You know the roar of engines when you're behind the wing? Well there was no roar! They were puttering! Look . . . all I know is we fell like a rock for a whole minute. God, it was a nightmare. Oxygen masks dangling, luggage crashing out of overhead compartments. People were screaming. I remember my seatbelt digging into my stomach as it held me to my goddamn seat! And the passengers who weren't wearing seatbelts . . ." The man trailed off. "I thought we were goners."

"Well, we are all thankful the pilots were able to reengage the turbines and take control of the plane before any serious injuries occurred." The reporter chirped.

"No!" the passenger yanked back the microphone. "That's not what happened! The plane slowed to a stop in midair. It didn't *right itself*, and the engines didn't reengage. The plane *stopped*! I'm telling you, we were floating in the air all the way down to the ground. Look at the field where the plane landed, for god's sake! Do you see any landing tracks?"

A replay of a helicopter bird's-eye view depicted an enormous blue-and-silver jetliner parked like a beached whale in a cornfield. There was no indication of any landing. Surrounding the huge steel girth, tall corn stalks stood intact, the organized rows unmarked.

The broadcast returned to the colorfully decorated studio.

"Well, as you can see, the passengers are still in shock from the incident—no doubt shaken from the traumatic experience. Fortunately, the near disaster was safely avoided. Although crewmembers have declined comment, spokesmen for the airline have issued a statement that the engines reengaged at approximately fifteen thousa—"

"What can I get for you, sweetheart?" asked a café worker with a Brooklyn accent and cigarette smoker's growl.

Kristen shook her head and brought her attention back to the breakfast options.

"One of the blueberry muffins and a coffee. To go, thanks." Kristen said. She looked back to the television to see that the topic had moved on to a decline in European financial markets.

On the street, Kristen sipped her coffee and ruminated over a thick spiral notebook of her research observations she had pulled out from her backpack.

The Vatruvian cell. The *artificial* cell.

The possibilities of their new technology were nearly infinite, the potential uses and applications limitless. Far more limitless than the casual readers of various magazine and news articles, or the people who watched the *60 Minutes* special, or even most accomplished PhDs could grasp. Over the past few months Kristen had begun to realize her team had willfully entered a technological realm of unbounded promise. Sure the Vatruvian cell was microscopic in size and seemingly insignificant against the grand scale of most tangible technologies. Many authorities were even beginning to voice skepticism and proclaim that its initial significance had been greatly overvalued. But Kristen thought of a singular gamete—a sperm or egg cell—compared to the entirety of human existence. Those singular minuscule cells blossom into the full spectrum of what it means to be man: from skin and bone to intellect and creativity. Those individual cells, microscopic and unadorned as they are, give rise to *ideas*. Power of that magnitude was impossible to quantify. And now the incomprehensible capabilities of genetics had been harnessed by modern science. Harnessed, stripped bare, and reassembled by the whim of man. They had manipulated the altered blueprints of biological genetics to generate a distinctive wonder of their own: an artificial cell crafted by the human hand. Life, though on a microscopic level, had been twisted from the inanimate.

The Vatruvian cell balanced just on the imprecise threshold of what biology defined as a living organism. Most scientists equated the Vatruvian cell to a cancer cell or a virus: neither living nor dead, and containing attributes of each distinction. Having been one of the essential minds behind its conception, Kristen was familiar with how the Vatruvian cell had been constructed. She knew the mechanics and the novel proteins of the Vatruvian cell front to back, as well as even Professor Vatruvia.

"You're right, I suppose . . . one step at a time," Kristen said in an attempt to soothe his alarm, though she felt the complete opposite. "I have to get back to my transcribing. I'll see you at the meeting."

Kristen stood and walked to the doorway. At the threshold she paused but could not think of anything to say. There were far too many questions to ask just one.

"You're a very clever young woman, Kristen." Professor Vatruvia rotated his chair away from her and looked out of the window at the passing cars and people on the street below. "I'll give you that. Don't think I'm not aware of what you're thinking."

Kristen held her ground. "If you know what I'm thinking, then I'll ask it. Can the Vatruvian cell differentiate? Can it create complex systems?"

A wave of exasperation passed across his expression, as though he was beginning to see her as a nuisance. "Now you *are* getting ahead of yourself, Kristen. I think you better get back to your transcribing and rethink this knee-jerk reaction to our breakthrough."

Kristen was shocked with the brusqueness of his tone. With one last uncertain look in his direction, she stepped out of his office and shut the door firmly behind her. She walked through the hallway and down the stairwell toward her workspace, her mind reeling from the images of an animal Vatruvian cell replicating.

If the Vatruvian cell could replicate once, it could replicate a hundred times, a million times. Could it replicate itself enough to form tissues? If it could, then it was possible the Vatruvian cell could transform into a complex organism. One functionless cell incapable of division and floating in a Petri dish was one thing. A microscopic artificial life form with the ability to reproduce was completely different.

A chill ran through Kristen.

If the Vatruvian cell had the capability to diversify, it could transform into any cell type of a system—skin, bone, liver, or even a brain cell. If their microscopic wonder could harbor the genetics of template cells—and act as reproductive cells—the possibilities were monumental, and very corporeal. But that was only the very precipice of the rabbit hole, and Kristen felt certain the hole ran deep.

At noon, the research members departed from the monotony of their daily agendas and filed into the conference room on the second floor. The overhead lights were turned off, the blinds closed, allowing only a sliver of natural light to fill the large space. Twenty-odd chairs encircled a wide table in the center.

Professor Vatruvia was preparing a slideshow on his laptop to be projected on the large screen hanging front and center.

Kristen wordlessly entered the room and sat a few chairs from the nearest person. She had no desire for small talk. Steve Armstrong was sitting opposite her, engrossed in a conversation with another computer scientist. Kristen distractedly returned his wave as she surveyed the other attendees. As she glanced around the table, her gaze narrowed with incredulity. There were many faces she did not recognize. Outsiders had never been allowed to sit in on their private research meetings, though certainly not from lack of trying. Private corporations relentlessly jockeyed for an illuminating glimpse at the inner workings of Vatruvian cell research. Professor Vatruvia had always been disinterested in them, which Kristen had respected.

Evidently his sentiments had changed.

The half dozen tailored suits stood out among the unkempt dress of the overworked graduate students. Kristen's attention lingered on a man in a military uniform at the end of the table. He was wearing a light gray khaki shirt with an insignia on the left chest pocket Kristen did not recognize. His hair looked as though it had been buzzed that morning. The military man noticed Kristen's stare and nodded politely. Kristen did not return the nod. Instead she walked around the table and stood over him. He pulled out the empty chair beside him, offering her the seat. Kristen remained standing.

"Good afternoon, ma'am, this seat is not taken as far as I know," the man said, his voice kind enough.

"May I ask who you are?" Kristen tried to keep her manner as unassuming as possible.

"Certainly. Lieutenant Corporal Carl Worthen. Are you a colleague of Dr. Vatruvia's?" He raised his palm to shake her hand.

"Yes. I'm Kristen Jordan, a geneticist," Kristen said, meeting his calloused palm with an aloof skepticism. "May I ask if Professor Vatruvia invited you here?"

"He did indeed. I just got in from Washington. It's a great privilege to be among such a talented group. Very refreshing to see how young some of the minds are behind this amazing undertaking."

Kristen noticed Professor Vatruvia look at them from the front of the room as he prepared his presentation. Kristen eyed the rows and rows of multicolored decorations and medals on Carl Worthen's chest. "I take it you're in the Army?"

"The armed forces. Yes, ma'am. I'm here as a rep for the DOD"

"Department of Defense?"

"Yes, ma'am."

"What does the Department of Defense have to do with the Vatruvian cell?"

Carl Worthen tilted his head in misunderstanding. "The DOD doesn't have anything to do with the Vatruvian cell, as far as I'm aware. Dr. Vatruvia simply invited us here to sit in on a meeting. It would be improper to turn down a chance to see firsthand the people behind the most remarkable technology of our time."

Kristen sat in the chair Carl Worthen had offered. "Why would the Department of Defense even have interest in the Vatruvian cell?"

"Scientific intrigue, more or less. We like to stay up to date on burgeoning innovations."

Kristen was about to ask why a representative from the Department of Defense and not the Office of Science was in attendance when Professor Vatruvia's voice carried across the voices of the conference room. Carl Worthen raised his eyebrows in polite eagerness and shifted his attention to the projection screen. Kristen regarded the outline of his stern jaw for a moment. She held him in her gaze, disconcerted about the presence of the Department of Defense, before turning to face the screen.

The research presentation went exactly as Kristen had predicted. After a few minutes of logistical announcements and scheduling reminders, Professor Vatruvia clicked forward to the breadwinning slide. It was the microscopic images Kristen had seen earlier that morning, now blown-up on the projector. A singular Vatruvian cell was replicating, the stages of cellular division looking all the more disturbing to Kristen now that they took up the entirety of the projection screen. Those who were not biologists did not immediately recognize what the images depicted, and Professor Vatruvia provided a brief explanation of cellular division. Soon after, they too joined in the enthusiastic sentiment.

As Kristen had expected, the images were received with thrilled applause and even whistles of excitement by the rest of the research team. The whole conference room joined in celebration of Professor Vatruvia's advancement. Steve was one of the loudest clappers, despite being one who had required an explanation of the slides. Kristen surveyed the rising passion of the room and glimpsed the scientific zealotry smoldering beneath the communal fervor. Her coworkers were already considering how each of their own resumes would be regarded, having ridden the coat tails of the great Vatruvian cell. Ambition was blinding all of her otherwise brilliant colleagues, each of them only seeking to advance their future pay grades and academic prestige. For a brief moment she considered standing and drawing all of their attention to their obvious ignorance—or perhaps worse, indifference—to the dangerous ground on which they were treading. But Kristen knew she would be outspoken and made to look like a Luddite fool, just as she had been in the previous meeting for expressing a call for prudence.

"This is a large step in the right direction for our research," Professor Vatruvia said as the room quieted down. "We have infused another viable biological attribute into the Vatruvian cell. The cellular replication we have produced in our lab emulates animal cell replication with flawless mimicry. I must emphasize that the Vatruvian cell is still by all definitions *not* alive, and as such we can progress our research without getting caught up in painstaking regulations. However, our synthetic organism, the Vatruvian cell, can now replicate."

Another round of applause engulfed Kristen.

"This is of course thanks to the individual work of you all. You should be very pleased with yourselves. Let's keep up the hard work in the weeks to come."

Professor Vatruvia stepped away from the podium, turned off the projector, and flicked on the main light, filling the room with fluorescent brightness. Everyone was excited with chatter. Most of them made their way back downstairs to their respective workspaces immersed in fevered conversation. A handful remained, lining up with questions for Professor Vatruvia. Kristen noticed first in line was Cara Williams.

"Professor, I have a question," Kristen heard Cara say. Professor Vatruvia looked up, and upon seeing Cara, cast her an uncharacteristically acidic look. His expression took Kristen aback, and she pretended to check something on her cell phone as she eavesdropped.

"What field are we taking this research into?" Cara asked with a nearly hostile sternness.

"I'm afraid I don't quite follow you," Professor Vatruvia said, not looking up as he typed on his laptop.

Kristen feigned interest in her cell phone's home screen as she leaned against a whiteboard and listened.

"I mean what is the *intention* of our work," Cara said. "Is our goal to create artificial white blood cells, or something involving photosynthesis, or more efficient eco-fuel? I'm curious where we are taking all of this technology."

Except for Kristen, everyone nearby seemed oblivious to their conversation.

"You are getting ahead of yourself, Ms. Williams. It would be best to stick to the task at hand before we can even dream of applications for this technology. I shouldn't have to remind you of that."

Cara looked confused. "But it's a perfectly valid concern, professor. Especially considering what my latest test results have continued to show—"

"Cara!" Professor Vatruvia suddenly snapped, his face transforming away from his professional guise. He leaned in to her, talking in a low voice. "I am tired of going over this with you. Your results are *flawed*. You will find a way to correct them or your position on this team may be in jeopardy."

Professor Vatruvia looked to the few people waiting behind her and shifted his shoulders with agitation underneath his sportcoat. "Now please, Cara, I have to field the questions of these folks here. Talk to me when you correct your inaccurate and erroneous data."

Kristen pretended to shuffle through her bag, straining to listen to the conversation. Evidently, she was not the only one concerned with the applications of Vatruvian cell technology. Cara looked both hurt and irate as she turned from Professor Vatruvia and stomped out of the conference room. Kristen threw her bag over her shoulder and chased after her down the hallway.

"Cara! Cara wait!" Kristen called.

Having torn down the main stairs to the lobby and rushed past the metal detectors of the security station, Cara now turned, one arm holding the door to the street ajar.

"Hi, Kristen." Cara gave her a polite, tired smile. Her face was crimson with emotion.

Kristen hurried down the steps two at a time, and as she caught up with Cara, she noticed her colleague was on the verge of tears. "Where are you off to?"

"I, uh . . ." Cara cleared her throat and quickly composed herself. "I have to get out of here for a while and clear my head. There's a student debate today in the Legrande building. I told my friend I'd go to watch her."

"Want some company?" Kristen asked.

Although Cara looked like she would prefer not to have a conversation at the moment, she nodded calmly. "Sure, if you feel like it."

Kristen pushed through the doors and they started up the sidewalk toward campus. "I couldn't help but overhear your conversation with Professor Vatruvia back there."

"I wouldn't call it much of a conversation," Cara said. She craned her head back and looked up with frustration at their research building, her gaze resting on Professor Vatruvia's third-floor window. Reflected in the windows, a cover of gloomy clouds had moved in to conceal the sky from the morning sun. "He basically ignored my issue, my *serious* issue, and threatened my position on the team."

Kristen saw in Cara's exhausted eyes that they shared concerns. "For a while now I've been asking him the same question you just did. Over and over I've asked him. Professor Vatruvia always gives me the same vague answer—that he doesn't know or it's too early to say where our research is headed. It doesn't make any sense. There is no way, no conceivable way, that he doesn't know what the applications for Vatruvian cell technology could be."

"I know, it's insane."

Kristen nodded emphatically. She'd been waiting for someone else to recognize the implications of the Vatruvian cell. "I don't see how everyone isn't questioning Professor Vatruvia. The technology is expanding way too fast. Most of all I'm concerned about the ethics involved. The Vatruvian cell isn't *living* according to the regulatory definitions—"

"So in theory," Cara continued Kristen's thought, "the Vatruvian cell technology can develop without having to adhere to any scientific law."

"Right," Kristen said as they stopped at an intersection, the rich landscaping and dignified stone buildings of the Columbia campus sprawling before them. The sound of cars and taxis swallowed their conversation. "In truth we don't really know what the Vatruvian cell is. We know its physical properties and how it works. But what if the biology textbook definition of living isn't up to date with modern science. The Vatruvian cell could be outright dangerous. We're messing with a completely unknown and untested technology."

As the light signaled *walk*, Cara squeezed Kristen's shoulder. Kristen could feel the urgency in her touch. "Can I trust you not to tell anyone what I'm about to tell you?"

"Of course," Kristen said.

"I'm serious. No one. Professor Vatruvia explicitly told me if I tell anyone about my findings, he would have me released from my doctorate program." Cara relinquished her grasp of Kristen's shoulder. "My life would be over."

Kristen shook her head in confusion. "What is it?"

"It's big." Cara's face coiled in distaste; she sighed nervously. "It's really big. I don't know what I'm supposed to do. Professor Vatruvia said if I discussed my findings, it would give people 'the wrong impression' of the Vatruvian cell. He said the whole thing might be above my intellectual capacity and that he may have made a mistake in accepting me to the program."

"You're kidding me!" Kristen said, genuinely shocked, but mostly intrigued. What could Cara possible know that she did not? "I promise I won't tell a soul."

"Okay, I trust you. You're worried about where this research is headed and what the applications for the technology will be. Well, in truth, Kristen, you and the team don't even know *half* of the inherent risks of our research."

Kristen shook her head, her eyes unflinching. It was hard for her to believe she didn't know half of the dangers of the Vatruvian cell. It was her research that spurred this project, after all. "What on earth do you mean?"

"Over the past few weeks I've been performing stress tests on some of the Vatruvian cells. The specific cells I've been working with had their DNA transcribed from a single-celled bacterium. So, yes, the Vatruvian cells function and perform as most prokaryotes do. But get this . . ." They had come underneath an old elm tree. Cara leaned in to Kristen, bringing her voice to a whisper. "All the physical properties of the Vatruvian cell proved to be more resilient than the biological original. I'm talking *everything*. From physical environment requirements to subsistence levels, the bacterium Vatruvian cells were so much stronger than the bacterium cell templates that the two were almost incomparable."

Kristen stared at Cara, at a loss for words. It was more dire than she ever could have imagined.

Cara exhaled angrily. "And worst of all, Professor Vatruvia is insisting I made a mistake somewhere in the data recording. I didn't. Imagine not triple-checking data that showed a Vatruvian cell flourishing in a one-hundred-eighty-degree oven when the cell it was modeled after died at ninety-nine degrees. It's an insult! My data collection is meticulous. I graduated number one in my biology program at Stan—"

"Wait." Kristen held up her hand. "So what you're telling me is the Vatruvian cells have more robust physical characteristics than the original cells used to transcribe them? That shouldn't be possible. They follow the original cell's DNA blueprints—they have nearly identical genetics aside from some of the ones that code for structural proteins."

"I'm telling you what my data shows, what the facts show," Cara said. "What they continue to show over and over again."

Kristen took a deep breath. "Okay. First of all, I believe you. But if that is true . . ."

"It's true." Cara's eyes narrowed. "The Vatruvian cells are superior to their biological counterparts."

"Good lord." At once, Kristen understood the magnitude of Cara's discovery.

"That's exactly my point."

"But how could that be possible?" Kristen pondered the basic composition of the Vatruvian cell. "How could the Vatruvian cells have traits that differ from the template cells used to construct them? They're forged using mostly the same DNA."

"You tell me. You know the framework of the technology better than anyone on the team."

An undergraduate in sunglasses walked casually past them. Kristen ran a hand over her forehead, her gaze following his shoes as she waited for him to be out of earshot. Once his Sperrys were far enough away, she continued. "Aside from a few signaling hormones and structural proteins here and there, just about every aspect of the Vatruvian Cell is based off mimicry." Kristen stopped to consider the details. "I guess it's possible the synthetic composition could function at a more efficient capacity than the natural one. That could provide greater physical thresholds and strengths to a Vatruvian cell, but it runs counter to the whole foundation of our research."

"Well, I can tell you one thing that's absolutely certain," Cara said, her whisper staunchly matter-of-fact as they ascended the stairs to the Legrande building. "The Vatruvian cells *are* physically superior to their original cells—in every tested aspect. And Professor Vatruvia has explicitly threatened me against telling anyone about my findings. I have no idea what I'm going to do." They joined a small group waiting to enter the large auditorium.

"Unbelievable." Kristen murmured, stepping over the tall entry threshold into the bustling auditorium. Several hundred people were crowded into rows of seats.

"You're telling me." Cara sighed anxiously. She pointed to a poster by the entrance, where the Columbia student debate team's program schedule was listed in a flowery hand. "Fitting subject for us."

Kristen turned and read the first topic: *Ryan Craig, sophomore Anthropology major, and Alden Harris, consulting lobbyist for the Rijcore Company discuss the ethical principles in the ever-growing field of genetic engineering.*

"Oh boy," Kristen said.

They pushed through the standing crowd and sat in a pair of seats, Kristen still replaying the images of the replicating Vatruvian cell and all of its constituent parts in her mind. The Vatruvian cells were superior to their natural versions. Kristen had no doubt Professor Vatruvia knew this truth from the very beginning.

CHAPTER THREE

Ryan

Ryan Craig sat in silence at a circulation desk in the Columbia student library. Dark hair fell across his forehead in a controlled mess, unchanged since he rolled out of bed late that morning. The slight shadow of a beard—simply the result of forgetting to shave—spread from his neck to his high cheekbones. He was absentmindedly checking and rechecking status updates on his laptop, his eyes half dozing and his mouth agape. His mind was inundated by the tedium of his desk job.

Ryan was responsible for manning the circulation desk closest to the first-floor bathrooms. His sole job was to assist students or faculty members if they approached with questions, though no one had visited Ryan's corner desk since his shift had started that morning. He'd spent the stultifying hours observing young men and women as they entered and exited through the library's side door. He stifled a yawn and swiveled his chair to check the clock above the men's room. Quarter to one. The end of his shift, but the clock was set ten minutes fast.

Ten more minutes of mind-numbing torture. Ryan sighed and looked back to his laptop. He opened his homework for a class on globalization. It was a sham of an assignment: *Explain the conflicts that arise between capitalism and international human rights in two hundred words or less.* Ryan shook his head as he re-read the guidelines. The professor wanted him to take a topic that would normally require a hundred-page explanation, and do so in a few sentences. He grabbed his headphones and began constructing the essay, focusing more on the music than the words he typed. Although the particular subject was one he cared about intensely, Ryan was fairly certain this excuse of an exposition would never be read by anyone, his professor included. He would earn the universally recognized and ambiguous red check mark, as always. Turning up the volume, he began writing.

There is a fundamental conflict that arises between human rights as defined in the United Nations Declaration of Human Rights and the everyday practices of modern capitalism. The free-trade model of transnational capitalism leads to an inevitable disregard of the economic civil rights of citizens in third-world countries. Corporations depend upon a cheap global labor force to act as the backbone for inexpensive creation of capital goods. If one cannot charge the consumer more for a given product, one can pay the factory worker less for the creation of said product. Adhering to either approach, profits will increase. Companies in the global economy are dependent upon the exploitation of peripheral populations—

"Excuse me!"

An agitated voice rose over the bass and guitar riffs in his ears. Startled, Ryan looked up from his perfunctory typing. He quickly pulled off his headphones, silently cursing himself. Caught listening to music on the job again—luck was not on his side this afternoon. It was Janet McCreedy, the community taskmaster of the library supervising staff. The dowdy older woman glaring at him was short and stolid, her white hair pulled into a tight bun, which stretched her forehead. Janet McCreedy was Ryan's most critical and overbearing boss. She had threatened to fire Ryan on more than one occasion for what she called "poor work ethic," despite the fact there was rarely a speck of work to do. None of his other supervisors had issues with him, but the knowledge that others considered Ryan Craig a conscientious worker held no weight with Janet McCreedy. In fact, it seemed to irritate her.

Ryan wondered how miserable Mr. McCreedy must be.

"Hi, Mrs. McCreedy." Ryan forced a genuine-looking smile. If he acted oblivious, maybe she would forgo the tirade and write him off as a lost cause.

Janet McCreedy glowered down at him, her prickly demeanor masking any trace of warmth. "Ryan. Would you say I'm a reasonable supervisor? Mind you, I ask this question at the very same moment you sit and complete your own homework while simultaneously getting paid to work for me."

"I think you're a great supervisor," Ryan said. "I'm sorry. I won't wear my headphones again while I'm working at—"

"And you are aware at this very moment there are hundreds of books that need to be put back on their respective shelves?" Janet McCreedy regarded Ryan humorlessly. "Hundreds of books that easily could become your responsibility."

"I was not aware of that."

"Your duty at this desk is to help people with circulation questions. How can you answer their questions if you can't *hear* them? If you want to listen to music, you can be reassigned to shelving duty quite easily."

Ryan nodded noncommittally. Shelving books was the worst job in the library, by far, and everyone knew it. Endless and constantly growing stacks of worn books—often with infuriating broken bindings—requiring placement in one precise location on one of the hundreds of shelves. Shelving was a drudgery mainly relegated to incoming freshmen that did not know any better when signing up for the work-study jobs. Ryan had been on shelving duty last year, and he had no intentions of returning to it.

"You're right," Ryan said. "I won't put on my headphones again. Really, I promise."

"Oh, I know you won't. If I ever, *ever* see you wearing headphones at this desk again, you will be formally let go from your position. Is that clear?"

Ryan nodded. "Crystal."

"Good," Mrs. McCreedy said. "Since you've already been warned once, you can place this cart back onto shelves before you leave."

Ryan rose and leaned over the desk. She had pushed over a rickety steel cart filled with nonfiction books. It was a sight he knew all too well from his shelving days. He guessed from the size of the stacks that it would easily take an hour or more to place all of the books in their appropriate places.

Ryan looked up at her with resigned dismay. "Today?"

"Yes, I should think so. And don't leave until it's finished. Maybe this will remind you how easy you have it at this desk. I'm certain one of the freshmen would jump at the chance to have your position."

"But I have class at two." Ryan glanced to the clock. He would never finish the shelving in time.

"Do you?" Mrs. McCreedy checked her watch. "Well then, you had better get started."

Ryan sat down heavily and shut his laptop. She was mental if she thought he would skip class to shelve books for her. At the very least the clash between capitalism and human rights would have to wait until he got back to his dorm later that evening. He wrapped up his headphones with an assenting nod, tossing his backpack over the desk and onto the stacks of hard covers in the cart.

"Then I guess I better get to it."

"Very good," Janet McCreedy said. She turned and plodded toward the coffee lounge, stopping on the way to admonish a group of girls for laughing in a designated quiet section.

Ryan pushed the rusted cart of books, lurching it into motion. The front right wheel emitted a sharp squeak. Ryan smirked; Janet McCreedy was diabolical. He rolled the noisy cart through the otherwise silent library toward the nonfiction levels, causing many heads to turn and scowl. In return Ryan offered a self-deprecating shrug.

The windowless nonfiction levels of the library were a desolate place for the majority of the semester, excluding the days directly preceding midterms and finals. Long narrow aisles ran between cumbersome shelves and an endless treasury of enlightening texts. Faintly humming fluorescent lights cast the maze of shelves and immaculate tile floors in a harsh clarity.

With an apathetic sigh and a long stretch, Ryan began the task of organizing the texts. The daunting piles of worn books in the cart spanned an array of subjects, from *The Life Cycle of the Honey Bee* to *A Brief History of Italian Neorealism* to *Nero: A Leader Misunderstood*. Ryan knew the best strategy to deal with this task, as he was no amateur in the refined art of nonfiction shelving. He began to methodically organize the books into separate stacks by field: biology, history, music, film, engineering, geology, art, and so on. Shelving duty, although monotonous, had proven interesting to Ryan in some aspects. As he passed each book onto a respective stack, he decided shelving duty was not as bad as he remembered. It often exposed him to unusual or peculiar topics. While he had slaved away on these quiet floors the previous year, he had developed a habit of skimming through any book that featured a subject unfamiliar to him. Every volume he placed back on the shelves had been checked out of the library, and therefore every one of them was relevant to someone. He viewed his skimming as a constructive way of developing his basic knowledge of obscure subjects, a worthwhile pursuit. And since there was never a rush to finish shelving— because the job itself never ends—he had spent many isolated hours sitting cross-legged on the cold floor reading an array of topics and waiting out the clock.

Ryan was flipping through one such book presently. He had picked up *Legends of The Corn*, a worn hardcover tome with a withered binding. The pages were cracked and yellowing, and the book smelled ancient and musty. It was an old collection of Native American mythologies, and one particular narrative caught his eye.

The Legend of Mandamin says that one day, in the early days of the mother-world, the god Mandamin appeared out of a tall field of windswept grass and approached a village. His body was made of corn and he lashed out his deadly corn-arms at any brave warrior who approached him. The people of the village both feared and respected the living deity who stood before them. His voice spoke like the wind, and his gaze pierced like the sun and the moon. Mandamin challenged the warrior-chief of the village to battle—

The ringtone of his cell phone suddenly rang through the silent labyrinth of shelves enclosing him. Ryan raised his eyes from the faded words and looked down the long empty aisle, his only company the buzz of the lights and the lonely shelves. Finding him on a cell phone immediately after chastising him would surely be the last straw for Janet McCreedy. But getting caught on this barren floor was unlikely. Ryan pulled his phone from his jeans pocket and answered it.

It was Devon Richmond, Ryan's freshman roommate.

"What's up?"

"Ryan! Where the hell are you?" Devon's voice carried a youthful inflection even over the phone.

"I'm at the library. My boss is making me do a bunch of extra work, but I have class at two." Ryan balanced the phone against his shoulder and continued to read *Legends of The Corn*.

If he could not defeat the warrior-chief, the god Mandamin would present the chief's people with the gift of corn. If the warrior-chief proved unworthy and died in the struggle, Mandamin would leave the mother-world forever, and man would never learn of his gift.

Devon said something, but Ryan was not paying any attention. He mumbled something in return, his attention transfixed on the peculiar myth.

Mandamin and the warrior-chief fought in the open field from whence the mysterious god arrived. Mandamin thrashed his corn-arms, and the warrior-chief thrust his spear. For four days and four nights they clashed. In the end, the warrior-chief struck Mandamin in his husk-chest with his mighty spear. The god fell to the grass, and seeds of corn spilled and overflowed from the mortal wound the spear had hewn. His corn-body shook and writhed and transformed into countless seeds that were carried away in the wind, forever to be harvested by the village.

"Ryan! HELLO?"

"Yeah . . . I'm here, sorry." Ryan cleared his throat. "What is it?"

"Where the *hell* are you? The debate is going to start any second!"

The speaker vibrated against Ryan's ear from Devon's shout. Ryan jerked his head up. He swore aloud, panic overwhelming him. The debate had completely slipped his mind. "Oh god. I completely forgot."

"Hurry up! The place is packed!"

Ryan hung up and looked at the time, his body feeling abruptly hollow. The debate team's public forum started five minutes earlier in the Legrande auditorium. Ryan was the first student speaker in the lineup. He had chosen to discuss the ethics of genetically modified foods. A Columbia alumnus from Washington had evidently volunteered his time and taken the trip to New York to represent the interests of a biotech company. Ryan felt certain that this lobbyist—a career arguer—would be licking his chops at the chance to shoot down a bunch of disjointed, ill-conceived undergraduate perspectives.

Ryan groaned. How could he have been so unreliable? It was unlike him. He looked to the now diminished piles of books in the cart and decided he would return later and finish the shelving. If Mrs. McCreedy found the cart sitting here unattended, he would almost certainly be canned. But the debate was vastly more important. He replaced *Legends of the Corn* in the cart, taking care not to further damage the binding, and trotted down the aisle toward the main stairs. As he turned and jogged down the stairwell, he glanced at the time on his cell phone.

Six minutes late.

Avoiding the crowded main lobby, Ryan burst through a pair of double doors and into a narrow corridor that led to a side exit. As he ran, he cycled through the main debate points he had been preparing. The stance he had chosen was well constructed, but would it hold up against the scrutiny of an expert—and the packed crowd in Legrande? Ryan rounded a turn and crashed through the steel side doors, stepping into the cool air of a blustery overcast afternoon. Below a gloom of gray clouds, autumn was taking hold of the city. On the stone path, rich scarlet and bronze leaves rustled about his sneakers.

He headed toward the Legrande building. How many people would show for the debate? Ryan felt his heartbeat pounding as he quickened his pace to a rushed jog interspersed with sprints when no one was looking. Hustling past ivy covered brick-and-stone buildings, stately white columns, and trees drenched in warm autumnal hues, Ryan at last bounded up the granite stairs to Legrande three at a time and pulled open the thick oak doors to the auditorium.

His mouth dropped.

There were easily two hundred people sitting attentively in the ordered rows of chairs. The debate team had been expecting a minimal audience, not maximum capacity. The auditorium overflowed with the dull roar of their conversations. Ryan took in a breath of relief, seeing that they were still setting up microphones. The debate was behind schedule and he did not miss his spot, but the unexpected crowd still put him on edge.

Above the stage a projection screen reading *Fall Student Body Debate* separated two podiums. Behind the left stood a sharply dressed man in a black suit, surely the lobbyist. Ryan sized him up as he pushed past shoulders to make his way to the front. The lobbyist looked to be in his early forties, his features etched in haughtiness as he chuckled in conversation with a man sitting nearby. At once Ryan knew his predictions about the lobbyist had been right. It was obvious by this guy's self-important manner that he was looking forward to embarrassing a rudimentary undergraduate perspective on genetic engineering. The lobbyist was in for disappointment if Ryan had anything to say about it.

"Devon!" Ryan called as he approached the student presenters in the first row. Most were looking paler than usual, perhaps due to the unexpected size of the audience.

Devon Richmond shook his head. "Finally! I told them you were on your way, but I don't think they were going to delay it for another second."

"I know, I know." Ryan plopped down breathless in a reserved chair in the front row and nodded to the other presenters. "Sorry I'm late."

"Are you . . . prepared for this?" Devon asked. "You might want to let someone else step in—or bail altogether. I wouldn't normally say that, but this guy doesn't look like he's messing around."

"Nah, I'm fine," Ryan said. He pushed his backpack underneath the chair and waved to the debate team senior captain Julie Thorne.

Julie gave him a withering look, then stood and ascended the stage steps. Ryan rose and trotted up the steps himself, taking effort to maintain a calm and collected countenance. Public speaking made him nervous, but Ryan liked the challenge. He stopped behind the open podium and focused coolly at its wood surface, his expression a picture of concentration.

"Hello, everyone, and thank you for coming to Columbia's annual fall semester student debate." Julie Thorne spoke cheerily into the microphone over obligatory applause. Her anger toward Ryan seemed to have evaporated. "We are going to get our debates started right away. It is my pleasure to introduce you to an alumnus of Columbia, Alden Harris. Mr. Harris is a biotechnology lobbyist for the New York-based genetic engineering conglomerate, the Rijcore Company. To my left is sophomore Ryan Craig, an undergraduate student currently majoring in . . . ?"

Ryan leaned into his microphone, his voice echoing across the hall. "Anthropology."

The lobbyist smirked with a belittling chuckle.

Julie Thorne turned from Alden Harris to Ryan and cast a fake smile. "We welcome both of you to the stage! Our first topic of discussion will pertain to genetically modified organisms. More specifically, the recent controversy regarding genetically altered fish. I have no doubt you are all familiar with the Rijcore Company, which has devised a means of doubling the growth rate and adult size of the North Atlantic Salmon. They have done so by inserting foreign DNA segments into salmon eggs, which promote the permanent release of growth hormones. This innovation brings into question a pervasive ethical dilemma. Now we have quite a bit to plow through, and we are getting a late start, so we will have to limit each debate to five minutes. Ryan, we'll start with your position."

For a moment Ryan's tongue felt like lead as he looked into the sea of faces. He placed his palms on the podium and cleared his throat. "The issue of genetically modified organisms is one that—"

"Is nothing new," Alden Harris interrupted him, his voice carrying over Ryan's with practiced articulacy. "In fact, the concept of modifying our food at a genetic level goes back to the very roots of civilization. One could even say the altering of our food is what gave rise to developed society through the advent of agriculture and more prolific sources of crops. It is truly . . . *disappointing* . . . that a mainstream misunderstanding based solely in unqualified naivety is obstructing a perfectly innocuous technology. Furthermore I find it—"

"I'm going to have to stop you there, Alden." Ryan forced his own voice over Alden Harris's condescending tone. "The issue at hand is the insertion of foreign and *mutative* DNA into the heart of a species. You are inaccurately drawing a correlation between the adulteration of the North Atlantic Salmon's natural biology and the practices of selective breeding through time."

"I disagree," Alden Harris said. "Each case is merely a matter of fish being altered for a more efficient yield. They're both means toward the same end."

"No, they absolutely are not. The two means to which you are referring are so incomparable to one another that I can't allow you to suggest that point, or draw attention away from the main moralistic concerns that arise in this *specific* issue. If not, we'll fall into a debate over perspectives so philosophical that no ground will be reached. When we consider these genetically engineered fish, we aren't talking about a directional change through adaptation and selective breeding. We are referring to the alteration of a species' very identity, with countless pitfalls both seen and unforeseen, all in the name of increased productivity."

Alden Harris sighed and adjusted his tie. "There comes a point, Mr. Craigie—"

"Craig," Ryan asserted instantly, and heard a laugh move through the audience.

"Craig. Forgive me. There comes a point, Mr. Craig, where technological progress must be allowed to move forward. You just said we should avoid abstract philosophical perspectives in this debate. I couldn't have put it better myself. What justification does your opposition to this technology have if not a vague naturalistic nostalgia? There is no—I will repeat—*no* data that shows Rijcore Company's technology to be dangerous in any way."

"First of all," Ryan said. He turned his gaze from the audience to Alden Harris. "I would point out that what you contemptuously refer to as my *naturalistic nostalgia* is no less defensible than what I would in turn refer to as your reckless hunger for increased profits."

"Now wait one—"

"Further," Ryan raised a hand over him. "You mentioned data. Let's discuss that data. Your salmon grow twice as fast as a natural salmon and become an adult size that is double the size of a natural salmon. Is that correct?"

Alden Harris nodded. "Yes. And that is with absolutely no negative effect to their nutritional properties."

"I have no doubt when a company as immense as Rijcore undertakes a venture seeking only to validate its research in one single respect—in this case, nutritional value—it will succeed in that one respect. I'm not going to argue the nutritional value of your monster fish."

"Well, if you aren't going to present any actual data, what exactly is your point, Mr. Craig? And I hardly think *monster* is an appropriate word to be using in this forum."

"Very well," Ryan said, slowly with thought. "For the sake of argument, by an injection of mutative DNA into their genes, the fish grow double as fast, and reach twice normal adult size. That is correct? That's what your data shows?"

"Yes, Mr. Craig, I just said that is correct."

"Then you're right, monster was the improper word. Giant mutated baby fish sounds much more appropriate. I believe that name fits with all of your classifications."

That got a rise from the crowd, and Alden Harris gave Ryan an enraged smile. "Look. What we are dealing with here is a healthy method of producing larger quantities of farm-harvested fish without any detrimental side effect to wild fisheries. In fact, the larger production of farm salmon will put less of a strain on wild resources. If wildlife is not what you are seeking to protect with your position, I'm not entirely clear what is? The fact of the matter is that the Rijcore Company has created fish that are more efficient to produce with no excess risk or side effects."

Ryan stared at Alden Harris for a silent moment, only a few distant coughs breaking the silence.

"This discussion isn't about what people can have for dinner tonight. The argument comes down to a gratuitous exploitation of the very identity of a species for the cause of dollars and cents," Ryan asserted firmly into the hush. "What happens if and when these fish inevitably escape from their farms? What happens when, with their doubled size and accelerated lifespan, they can out-compete wild fish? As long as these mutated salmon even *exist*, the ecology of our waterways are imperiled on a global scale. Beyond that, the ecological side of my argument doesn't even bring into question the massive ethical concerns involved in this research. How long until pork, beef, and countless other food sources are mutated to the point of being unrecognizable? Your scientists at the Rijcore Company are ripping apart the natural world, and justifying their insatiable onslaught by stating their products are *nutritional*. It's madness."

"You're throwing so wide a net here, Mr. Craig, that I don't know where to contest." Alden Harris shook his head and shrugged in exasperation as Julie Thorne began to walk to the center of the stage.

"Well, I'm afraid we'll have to end that very appealing discussion there. Some interesting perspectives were brought up, and I thank you both for your time."

Ryan nodded in thanks to the polite applause that rose from the audience and left the stage as Julie Thorne introduced the next topic. Ryan sat down in front of Devon and rolled the tension out of his shoulders as he grabbed his backpack.

"Unbelievable, man," Devon whispered over the seat. "Are you leaving?"

Leaning back, Ryan spoke softly so he would not disturb the speakers. Things were not going well for the student. Alden Harris was spewing impassioned declarations over her meek objections. "Yeah, I have to go to class. I'll call you when I'm out."

Devon nodded. "Later."

Ryan slung his backpack over his shoulder and gave a thumbs-up to the rest of the debate team members assembled in the front row. A few returned his gesture, looking encouraged by his efforts against the ironclad lobbyist. He politely navigated through the spectators of the standing room to the side of the audience and out the back of the auditorium, receiving several whispered congratulations and disagreements as he went. Ryan shoved past the double doors into the breeze of the fall afternoon and began descending the pale granite stairs when someone called to him. He turned and saw a young woman exiting the auditorium.

"Hey," she called in a friendly tone. She trotted down the steps and came to a stop a few above him. "I agreed with what you said in there."

"Thanks," Ryan said with a courteous smile. She was good-looking and around his age. Her glasses added an enlightened impression to her thin face, keen green eyes, and slender shoulders. "It's never easy to take on paid researchers and their prized data with so petty a notion as morality."

She nodded, her wavy hair pulled back and her manner considerate. "Ethics aren't quite concrete enough for most of the scientists I've worked with. They'd rather work with numbers and figures. But morality scares me, too, considering it comes down to one person's opinion."

Ryan laughed in agreement and held out a hand. "Ryan Craig."

"I remember," she said. "Kristen Jordan."

CHAPTER FOUR

Ryan

T he doors to the many nearby halls opened all at once, and the deserted quad filled with students as they departed their early afternoon lectures. A promenade of undergraduates carrying backpacks and hefty textbooks walked across the path below the stairway. Ryan regarded Kristen Jordan amid the bustle.

"I'm getting the impression you've worked with many scientists?"

"You could say that." Kristen smirked wearily and looked over the heads of the Columbia student body. "You hinted in there that researchers aren't concerned about the repercussions of their technologies. What did you mean by that?"

"Well," Ryan said. "The dangers of any new technology are self-evident aren't they?"

Kristen shrugged. "I'm not sure if a technology's potential danger is ever self-evident. Like any knowledge or tool, a technology is only as dangerous as the people that control it."

"Well, sure, but technology is a form of power, and from what I've seen of the world, power is always a dangerous thing—the wrong minds are always drawn to it. By itself a technology might not be hazardous, but inevitably it will be manipulated by people with a hunger for power, whether that takes the form of money or who knows what else."

"And the creators?" Kristen asked, her voice hesitant.

"Useful technologies have a nasty way of slipping from their creator's grasp." Ryan noticed the shadows under her earnest eyes. "I take it you are a researcher of some kind? Are you a research assistant or a graduate student?"

Ryan stepped aside for a group exiting the auditorium. A quiet moment passed between them.

"Sorry." Kristen turned to face him, her expression distracted. "I'm a graduate researcher. Genetics."

"You study genetics? At Columbia?"

Kristen nodded.

"Then," Ryan paused, eyeing her in doubt. "Do you work with the Vatruvian cell?"

"Yep."

"Ah, now I see," Ryan said. Behind this girl's pretty eyes and amiable disposition had to be genuine genius, a truly gifted mind. He had read somewhere recently that thousands and thousands of people apply each semester to the Vatruvian cell doctorate programs. This girl, Kristen Jordan, was one of the two or three that must have made the cut. Ryan pulled out his cell phone and checked to make sure there was time before his Cultural Anthropology class.

"Do you want to grab a coffee?" Ryan asked. "I have class soon, but an opportunity to talk with a Vatruvian cell scientist is too rare to pass up."

Kristen smiled with a touch of grim humor. "Only on the condition that we don't talk about the Vatruvian cell. Sorry, but I spend way too much time stewing over that damn microscopic thing these days."

They descended the stone stairs together and joined the flow of young people heading to the south end of campus. Students in plaid shirts, hooded sweatshirts, sneakers, and blue jeans surrounded Ryan and Kristen. The season was on the cusp of change, and a pleasant bite of chill touched the air. A clean breeze rolled across Manhattan from the west, rustling through the turning leaves overhead and across the meticulously cut lawns.

"So I have to ask," Ryan said as he sidestepped a brunette blathering into her cell. "Where did you go to undergrad?"

"MIT."

"And you graduated . . . ?"

"Two years ago with a degree in biology. I've been in New York working with Professor Vatruvia since. What year are you?"

"Sophomore."

Kristen looked up at him casually. "So you're twenty?"

"Yeah."

"Cool. I've got you by a year."

Ryan slowed his pace momentarily. "Shouldn't you still be in undergrad?"

"Um." Kristen gave a small courteous laugh. "Technically speaking, yeah. I skipped more than my fair share of grades back in the day."

"Right. And you enjoyed being the youngest kid in your high school graduating class?"

"Oh yeah, graduated at sixteen. Nothing like it," Kristen said, her voice laced with sarcasm. "Although I then burned through undergrad in two years, and that was mostly by my own choosing. So I don't know. I guess on some level I'm hurrying to get somewhere in life."

"Where?" Ryan asked, noticing the sharp honesty of her words.

Kristen nodded. "Good point."

"Well, it has clearly worked out for you. Landing a spot researching the Vatruvian cell is a status few can claim."

"*Creating* the Vatruvian cell—I was on the team before it even had a name. But we had an agreement." Kristen held up a finger. "No talking about it."

"Sorry."

"It's okay. Did you spend a lot of time preparing for that debate? I can't imagine going against a lobbyist in front of that crowd was easy on the nerves."

"I practically winged it, actually. You heard my position on the matter—it's not like I needed a lot of data."

"Mmm," Kristen said. "Not much raw data behind naturalistic nostalgia."

Ryan grinned at her as they turned into the walkway leading to one of the campus cafeterias. "The debate team rarely takes up much of my time, unless the subject is something that's data intensive. For the past week I've been writing an essay for the class I'm heading to now. I was up pretty much all night last night putting the finishing touches on it." Ryan patted his bag, where the twelve pages of the assignment were resting inside a spiral notebook.

"What time did you finish?"

"Too late." Ryan said, "Only got a few hours of sleep."

Kristen nodded. "I can certainly relate to that. My whole life is spent working past midnight. Do you think you'll get a good grade on it?"

"Who knows," Ryan said. Though he did know that in all likelihood, he would not be receiving a high mark. His Cultural Anthropology professor, the rather ornery Professor Hilton, had called him into his office after midterms. Professor Hilton expressed his disapproval toward what he, not so tactfully, referred to as Ryan's "overly simplistic" perspectives. *Realism* and *rationality*, he had emphasized, were too often missing from Ryan's main arguments. Ryan guessed the short stack of papers he had in his bag would not prove to be a trend breaker.

"I tend to adhere loosely to the guidelines of an assignment."

"That must do wonders for your GPA," Kristen said with a laugh. "In my little experience with humanities class requirements, I've found writing what the person grading your work wants to read makes both of your lives much easier."

"Yeah, I know," Ryan sighed. "But writing something I don't really believe seems counterproductive to the purpose of a higher education. Besides, if the professor only gives high grades to people who write what he wants them to say, that makes him the stubborn one."

"You're the one that just out debated a lobbyist, I'm certainly not going to challenge you."

Ryan glanced down at her and smiled discretely to himself. He noticed now she had a Vatruvian cell security badge clipped to her slender waist. Her awkwardly smiling photo on the badge looked humorously young. It seemed impossible to Ryan that someone with the obvious intellect and attractiveness of this young woman could be without the slightest hint of pretension. He found himself intrigued, perhaps even mesmerized by her lack of conceit. Stealing an extended look at the teenaged Kristen Jordan smiling clumsily up at him from the laminate, Ryan felt an odd connection to her. This unassuming girl was undeniably one of the most brilliant people in the entire university—in the nation. She was an actual Vatruvian cell researcher.

They strolled into one of Columbia's older dining halls. Long rows of worn cafeteria tables and service counters were packed with students waiting in line or helping themselves to an uninspired salad bar. Ryan and Kristen made their way to the coffee dispensers and poured steaming French roast into styrofoam cups.

"Second cup of the day for me," Kristen said, mixing some skim milk into her cup and reading fall announcements on the nearby bulletin board. "I'm averaging over three cups these days."

Ryan shrugged. "Better than an Adderall addiction."

"Ha," Kristen laughed aloud. "Too true."

"Ryan! Hey, Ryan!"

Ryan turned around to see his friend Tim Richard. Tim was in several of Ryan's freshman-year courses. They shared a European History class on Friday mornings, and swapped notes when either of them missed one of the early morning lectures. Tim played rugby.

"This is the guy I was telling you about," Tim said to his tablemates. They were all thick-shouldered and bruise-covered rugby players. "When are we going to get you to come out to some practices?"

Ryan shook his head, putting a lid on his coffee cup. "Yeah, right. I've seen some of your injuries—no, thanks. How is your lip healing by the way?"

"Please," Tim said. "They sewed it back up fine. Fifteen stitches."

"Yeah, sorry. I'm all set."

Tim's teammates vocalized disapproval, and Tim talked through a mouthful of tuna sandwich. "Are you sure that's the reason, and not that our practices would interfere with your nerd club meetings?"

"It's the debate team, don't disrespect. Broken lips heal quick—a broken ego doesn't."

"Whatever, man." Tim waved a dismissive hand. "I know you'll come around eventually. See you in class tomorrow?"

"For sure," Ryan nodded. "I've got to run though."

Tim's gaze hesitated for a moment on Kristen. He nodded to Ryan with a conspicuous thumbs-up before turning back to his friends. Ryan pretended not to see the gesture, and he perceived that Kristen did the same.

"Sorry," Ryan said. "Tact isn't really his strong suit."

"No worries." Kristen smiled. When they were out of hearing range and leaving the dining hall, she turned to him with a mocking expression as she adjusted the lid on her cup. "So rugby doesn't interest you, huh? You don't want to get out there and show everyone what you're made of? Smack some skulls around and so on?"

Ryan made a sheepish face. "Eh, the whole no helmet idea just seems ill conceived. The last thing anyone would want is for me to somehow harm my facial features."

"Yeah, a broken nose would be far worse than permanent brain damage."

Ryan had an athletic build, and it did not require too much imagination to envision him catching a football or driving a basketball down the lane. It had not been the first time someone encouraged him to join a club team, but Ryan had never been very interested in organized sports. Cerebral pursuits had always struck him as more engaging.

"Did you play any sports before college?" Kristen asked. "I need to know if I'm getting familiar with a jock-type here."

"None worth noting," Ryan shook his head. "Never been much of an athlete."

"Oh, well, me neither," Kristen said, her tone casual. "I'm a train wreck when it comes to athletics. I did winter track my junior year in high school. Hated every minute of it. Asthma and the four-hundred meter aren't a good mix. I ran junior varsity, and it was not a pretty sight."

Ryan envisioned her running laps at a high school track and saw the odd mismatch. "Well, you must be a world-class biologist."

"True, I suppose." Kristen shrugged, a breeze lightly moving her hair. "I guess we all have different skill sets. Where others are good at rugby, you are good at arguing against lobbyists."

"Please don't think of me as a good arguer. Being argumentative is an annoying trait. I just happen to get fired up when people in positions of power twist facts for special interests."

"Fair enough, *argue* was a poor word choice. But you have to admit you can rock a debate. I mean you practically sent that lobbyist running from the podium."

Ryan shrugged. "I suppose if I feel strongly enough about a subject I can defend my stance. But seriously, please don't think of me as someone who is talented at being a dogmatic arguer. Argumentative people frustrate the hell out of me."

"Deal."

"Well, this is me," Ryan said, coming to a halt at the wide marble stairway that led up to the doors of a stone lecture hall. Droves of students, some Ryan recognized from his class, were entering the dignified building.

"Cool," Kristen said with a smile. "I don't think anything's ever brought me in there. I haven't been in most of the undergrad lecture halls, actually."

"Ah, you're missing out," Ryan said. He wanted to see her again and was now being careful not to allow an awkward moment to rear its deflating head. "What's your schedule like tomorrow?"

Kristen raised a slender hand to her chest. "My schedule? I'm not sure. I'll probably be at my lab for most of the morning. Beyond that, I don't really have anything planned. I more or less make my own agenda."

Ryan took a shallow breath and held it, his chest filling with cement.

"You know . . ." He tried to make his voice sound casual, but was fairly certain Kristen could see his heart beating through his shirt. "We should hang out tomorrow. That is, if you have nothing to do during the afternoon—or night, or whatever."

"Hang out?" Kristen looked up at him with a questioning, almost goading expression, taking some amusement in his fumbling. "Hang out as in give you an interview about the Vatruvian cell? Or like a date?"

"Well, now that you mention a willingness to discuss the Vatruvian cell," Ryan pretended to mull it over. "Nah. Let's say a date."

Kristen laughed and nodded offhandedly. "Yeah, sure. I'd like that. But I really should be getting back to my lab; things are kind of crazy today. And you need to get to your class."

They took out their cell phones and exchanged numbers. To his contacts Ryan added the name Kristen Jordan.

"Okay, well, I should be going. Good luck with your essay." Kristen turned with a wave.

"See you," Ryan said, watching her disappear into the crowd. Satisfied, he turned and climbed the stairway. Ryan hurried into a small softly lit classroom on the first floor that smelled faintly of old books and citrus wood polish. A mahogany table, looking nearly as old as the university itself, dominated the room, and around it sat a dozen of his classmates and the imposing Professor Hilton. With his smart herringbone blazer and discerning glower, Professor Hilton was not easily contended with. He led a discussion-based class—a Socratic seminar of the most stressful variety.

"Ryan Craig. You are late," Professor Hilton said without lifting his gaze from his reading.

"Sorry, I got caught up at the student debate."

Professor Hilton, whom Ryan guessed to be in his late fifties, ignored his apology. He cleared his throat and looked up. "You all were to have your essays prepared for today. The topic, globalization: should a native population's cultural independence be protected through governmental law? Why or why not? We will go around the circle, and discuss each of your points. We'll start with you, Jennifer. When you are ready, you may begin."

Jennifer Graham was sitting to Ryan's right. She sat up straight and calmly flattened her hands on the paper-clipped essay in front of her.

"I based my essay on the idea that, if left isolated, indigenous societies will only fall further behind the modern times. As pleasing a fiction as it would be to not interfere with indigenous societies, it's ultimately not a feasible solution. Eventually they will be displaced or disenfranchised. Assimilation, to some extent, with the expanding modern world is unavoidable. This is especially true if children within indigenous populations are to be given a modern education and healthcare. With that said, I think legislation should be in place to protect indigenous and impoverished *individuals'* rights to their own cultural traditions and beliefs."

Although his face elicited none of his internal disdain, Ryan groaned soundlessly. Jennifer Graham's essay was taken virtually word for word from Professor Hilton's lectures over the previous few weeks. Ryan had a sudden feeling he was about to be put through an academic crucible for straying from the table's decidedly well-established ideas.

"Good, Jennifer." Professor Hilton nodded. "Questions anyone?"

He was met with silence. All the other students were clearly preoccupied with the brief presentations they were each going to imminently make. Ryan's peers stared unflinchingly at their essays before them.

"Very well. That sounds well conceived, Jennifer. I look forward to reading it." Professor Hilton said and jotted something down on a pad of paper. "Mr. Craig, you're next."

Ryan shifted in his chair, fairly certain his paper would not escape the scrutiny of the table with the ease Jennifer's had. Sitting up, shoulders tense, he prepared for the worst. "I proposed that it's the inherent responsibility, and even the *duty* of any globalizing power that stakes any claim on morality to allow for the cultural independence of any group of people, indigenous or otherwise. If not, the globalizing power is an imperialistic entity. An encroachment of any form on the belief system of an indigenous society or enclave of people is simply invasion with a more socially acceptable euphemism attached."

"Interesting," Professor Hilton said. He adjusted his glasses. "Would anyone like to comment?"

"I would." Bobby Clark, a student directly across from Ryan, raised his hand. Ryan knew Bobby Clark all too well. They had butted heads all semester over every subject imaginable. Ryan had heard from another classmate that Bobby was the son of Robert Clark III, a prominent banking executive down in the financial district. Ryan despised the certainty and lack of reservations with which Bobby Clark imbued his arguments.

"How can you possibly support that stance?" Bobby stared at Ryan contemptuously, allowing the silence in the room to humiliate him. "Let's say oil is found underneath some random village in an impoverished South American country. The government that *owns* the land over the oil has the right to ask the people living on the land to move out. Is that not true?"

"At this point of time in history, yes, that is true in most countries." Ryan said.

"Please. At any time in history a controlling power would displace a group of people for the greater good of the nation as a whole."

"The greater good is an opinion, and a dangerous one if it's used to force a group to act against its will," Ryan said cautiously. "It's even more dangerous if that group doesn't have a voice in the government."

Bobby rolled his eyes. "Either way, you're arguing that a specific group of people should be given more rights than another group. If we were given enough notice, no one would get in an uproar if, say, the federal government forced my family in Connecticut to relocate against our will to build a highway. Yet if an indigenous family in South America or Africa or Eastern Russia is forced to move, it suddenly becomes an international human rights issue. *That is inequality."*

"Bobby," Ryan said. "Your entire world view doesn't revolve around your local surrounds. Your fundamental metaphysical beliefs—everything you hold true about existence itself—doesn't depend upon your neighborhood in New Canaan. Many groups' entire realities revolve around the localities in which they live. To take away their land, which in some cases has belonged to them for thousands of years, would be to execute their very way of life. You in turn murder more than the people themselves, you murder the perspective they brought to the world."

"Come *on*," Bobby stared at Ryan with condescension. "Like Jennifer said, it's a simple inevitability that indigenous groups will have to join the global world eventually. There's no such thing as geographical barriers anymore. The world can only push on their boundaries for so long before the bubble bursts and the industrialized world crashes through. It might be unfortunate, and sad in a romantic sense, but that's how it is. Why not take the time to foster a viable infrastructure first?"

The words *simple inevitability* rang through Ryan's ears like a hissing gunshot. He opened his mouth in disbelief, staring at his essay on the polished table with anger. "Indigenous groups don't *have* to do anything. They are being *forced* into the global world. And they are being forced by the exact perspective that you are espousing as common sense."

Bobby Clark gave a mocking and sardonic chuckle. "My perspective is based in reality, man."

"And what, amid your pampered upbringing," Ryan said, his tone dropping and his gaze turning on Bobby Clark, "would you know of reality?"

CHAPTER FIVE

The Imperial Council of
the Epsilon

The sharp knife of apocalypse struck without warning, burying itself into the unsuspecting skies of a sun-swept afternoon.

In the northernmost continent of Anthem, the remote city of Municera abruptly reported massive and inexplicable reports of rioting and hysteria. The limited transmissions that came out of the city were fragmented and unclear. Imperial Army regiments were at once dispatched to restore order to the city of Municera, yet all troops lost radio contact within minutes of their arrival. Powerful reverberations shook through the surrounding lands, reaching miles in every direction. It felt as though the gods themselves were hammering the very world with furious impacts. From a distance, billowing black pillars of smoke could be seen reaching high into the sky above the smoldering city. When the smoke and cloud of ash dispersed in the northern winds, the glimmering skyscrapers that had long been an icon of the elegant Municera had vanished from the skyline. Their steel and glass splendor was replaced with a blanket of alarming ruin. By midafternoon, the once prominent city was nothing more than wreckage against the horizon.

Most disturbing were the spreading rumors that a number of Imperial First Class soldiers had flown into the chaos of Municera and had yet to return.

The migration out of the region—an anticipated exodus for which the Imperial Council had quickly prepared—never arrived, and as a disquieting sun set on the remaining cities of the Epsilon empire, the truth became increasingly clear. There were no survivors.

Municera had been home to seven million Primus.

As the long shadows of dusk took hold of the devastation in Municera, countless households listened intently to the Imperial media reports. A primal dread filled their thoughts and plunged them into a global panic. Then similar reports began to rise out of the great Twin Cities to the south of Municera. Whatever caused the annihilation was spreading across the world of Anthem.

Even in that early hour, it was clear the Epsilon empire—and thus the entire Primus race—was under a global attack. From the throne in the capital city of Sejeroreich, Emperor Faris Epsilon summoned a full attendance of the War Council in the early hours of the morning. Every soldier of the Imperial First Class was marshaled to the Sejeroreich barracks. They were ordered to suit up in their armor and prepare for immediate mobilization.

Most of the battle-hardened and ornately decorated councillors and generals of the High War Council had been awaiting the summons. Others made haste to the palace from far-off lands, rubbing bleary eyes as they soared through the inky star-swept skies of Anthem. Once in Sejeroreich, the great leaders and officials apprehensively made their way into the War Hall, each aware that the forthcoming proceedings would be grim.

The strength of the Epsilon empire had long been forged by solitary physical prowess—the power of the individual. Most clashes of wills or issues of contention were reconciled by the strength of the fist. Court through combat. It was commonplace for physical altercations to break out in the midst of a Council session. Sometimes the combatants would have the decency to take their struggle out of the palace, sometimes not. It was said that more people were killed in the War Hall than had constructed feasible battle strategies. Inevitably the final decision agreed upon by the High War Council was to throw tactics aside and meet any challenge head on with the might of Sejero blood. Throughout the history of the Epsilon empire, it had never proven to be a failing resolution. Sejero strength ruled over all, for nothing else could hope to match such infinite power.

Yet everyone entering the hall knew the War Council meeting that predawn would be different. The danger remained a mystery, their aggressors unknown. The Epsilon had faced an attack on their own planet of Anthem. Imperial First Class soldiers—the gods of the Primus race—had flown into the inexplicable madness of Municera and never returned.

The justification for the High War Council's fears was great. Armageddon was a constant truth that weighed heavily upon Primus history. They had faced it before, the near destruction of Anthem and the obliteration of their existence. It had been two thousand years ago, the day the skies turned black and Anthem was nearly lost to the unthinkable technologies of the Zergos. Already it felt eerily similar to the beginnings of the Zergos invasion of old. The mystery, the totality, the abruptness—it rang all too similar to the first days of their race's near extinction so long ago.

But no one was bold enough to turn that apprehension into words just yet.

The Imperial War Hall was a lavishly decorated and expansive pantheon in the center of the great palace of Sejeroreich, the home to the seat of the Epsilon. Vast marble pillars stretched high over the cold stone floor, with ornate paintings barely visible on the cathedral ceiling in the lofty distance. Enormous works of art were carved deep into the walls. Each individual scene portrayed a particular victory in the Epsilon empire's early history. Celebrated legends of courage and glory came to life on the hard stone. Magnificent renditions of ancient men and women, the first Sejero warriors, cast their eternal gaze on the War Council. The stone faces were the visages of ancestors in whose mighty strength waylaid their people's annihilation and reforged Anthem from the ashes. They were the faces of the first Sejero sons and daughters, the gods of their race, who rose amid the fires of extinction and cast off the cold and brutal Zergos with nothing but their fists.

A circle of chairs was assembled in the center of the palatial hall, each seat adorned with intricate carvings on the legs and armrests. Inlaid into the backrests of each chair were the various sigils of the Royal families. The throne of the emperor was twice the size of the other chairs, and inlaid with the sigil of the empire itself, that of house Epsilon.

As the generals and councillors made their way into the hall, their conversation was quiet and troubled. What did they know? Which Imperial First Class warriors had departed to defend Municera and not returned? But most importantly, who or *what* was the enemy?

A number of rumors had begun to circulate, each as unlikely as the next. Many spoke of a biological attack. One described a virus that turned Primus berserk, causing them to kill one another with rabid insanity. Another told of a foreign power that had descended from a distant and unknown planet to destroy them. The only certainty about their enemy was there was no certainty at all.

Once the entire War Council was assembled, Emperor Faris Epsilon entered the hall accompanied by the enormous heights and broad shoulders of his Royal Guard. A son of the purest Sejero family lineage, Emperor Faris was shorter than many of the unnaturally gargantuan generals and soldiers that made up the War Council's ranks. Nevertheless, he commanded their respect. Though lacking in size, the Sejero blood of the few remaining Royal families ran pure—and potent. Such uncouth qualities as height and bulky muscle were no match for the inherent Sejero virility of a Royal child, whose lineage could be traced to the first Sejero warriors.

Emperor Faris had a muscular frame and a thick graying beard hanging from his aging features. Small scars were visible on his face and arms, old wounds from his prime years long healed over. A giant ring gleamed on his left hand. The Blood Ring of the Epsilon. Through generations, the illustrious Blood Ring had been bequeathed from father to son since the very beginning of the Epsilon line, an heirloom from the first Sejero titan that had started the Epsilon lineage. The Blood Ring was worn as a signifying adornment like a crown. It boasted an enormous and exquisitely cut deep-red diamond. The intense red hue of the Blood Ring symbolized the purity of the Epsilon family's Sejero bloodline. Precious few families in modern times could claim such pure heritage, dating back to the same faces staring eternally down at them from the stone walls.

The councillors and generals stood and saluted Emperor Faris with a thundering hail. He returned their salute and proceeded to his throne, making his way across the circle in wide strides. An aura of anxiety exuded from him, and the sound of his boots on the floor echoed in the tense silence that descended upon the hall.

All eyes shifted uneasily to the vacant seat beside Emperor Faris as their leader sat on his throne. To his right, the opulent seat of Emperor Faris's only son was empty. Subtle concerned glances were exchanged between the highest-ranking generals. The absence of the powerful Prince Vengelis Epsilon was worrying. They would need his strength in this hour.

Emperor Faris took a long breath, resting his arms on his throne and regarding the many trusted faces of his councillors and generals.

"This is what we know." The Emperor's voice was deep, and carried easily across the hall. "Municera has fallen. There seem to be no survivors. Whatever happened, it was efficient and deadly. The latest intelligence out of the Twin Cities leads us to believe that the citizens and local Imperial soldiers have all fallen there as well. We have reason to believe the attack did not originate from any nonnative force."

A wave of relief passed across the faces of the hall. Behind their stalwart facades there had been an unmistakable fear of the worst—the unknown. Emperor Faris allowed that heartening knowledge to sink in before continuing. Anything that originated within their world could be stopped by a power from their world.

"None of our satellites or radar systems have detected any recent inorganic or organic entity entering into Anthem's atmosphere." Emperor Faris looked to each intent gaze in turn. "Meaning whatever this attack is, it originated here on Anthem."

"My lord," General Barlow, one of the most decorated generals around the circle interrupted Emperor Faris. The decorum of the moment was evidently lost on him. "Only we have the power to destroy cities in the manner we have witnessed today. The kind of power we have seen only resides in Sejero blood. I have heard talk of some sort of sickness, an insanity of sorts that is turning our people mad. Is there truth to this?"

"Unlikely," said Councillor Harken without looking up, his chin resting on his outstretched fingers and his eyes lost in concentration. Councillor Harken was the head of scientific research, and the intelligence in his voice resonated in stark contrast to the misinformed conjectures of General Barlow. "The speed at which the attacks spread, and the degree of total devastation caused, each rule out biological possibilities. All civilians living in the lands between Municera and the Twin Cities remain unharmed. This means the attack is moving directly from city to city, intentionally bypassing sparsely populated areas. It's impossible for a microorganism to jump locations in this fashion. No. The attacks are directed and intelligent."

"The pattern of the attack leads us to believe the assault we are seeing is consciously controlled. We are being attacked by *someone*, not something," Emperor Faris said.

General Barlow shook his gigantic head and sighed with aggravation. "Doesn't anyone recognize this strategy? The attack resembles the procedure we use when invading new systems. To me the pattern of attack is indicative of a powerful group of soldiers that are limited in numbers."

"I agree with Barlow," said Councillor Maudlan. "Hit a city. Hit it hard and fast. Fly straight to the next city and repeat. It is directly following our invasion protocols. The main goal of our first attack on new systems is always to cause confusion so the enemy doesn't know what is attacking them. If you ask me, that is exactly what's happening here. We have to act immediately and reinforce the Twin Cities with everything we have before this attack is allowed to spread further."

Grunts of agreement filled the hall.

"I'll tell you what I think." General Portid, the largest and most decorated general of the circle stood to his full eight feet. A large scar ran across his face and a scruffy brown moustache hung below his bulbous nose. Being the most powerful man in the room, save for the emperor, the War Council grew quiet out of respect. "There is only one logical source behind this assault or invasion or whatever the hell we want to call it. Emperor Faris said just now that nothing has recently entered Anthem atmosphere. Is that correct?"

Emperor Faris nodded.

"Then to me it is clear," General Portid said. "The attackers *are* Primus. We have all agreed that only beings with the power of the Sejero could inflict this kind of carnage. The attack must be some unusually powerful group of separatists that have slipped under Imperial radar until now. Separatists aiming to rouse panic in the heart of the empire's populace. That is the only possible explanation. Only Primus can cause this kind of destruction!" His expression hardened as he looked to the other councillors, the passion rising in his voice. "And there is no reason to sit idly and talk as these terrorists continue this rampage. I say we mobilize the Imperial First Class and end this today!"

His fervor was met with resounding encouragement from other military personnel around the circle.

Councillor Harken lifted his chin from his hands and stood. "I do believe you are right General Portid. The Imperial First Class should be sent to action. However, we may know more about the nature of this attack than you all are currently aware of. I think it's time to play the recording, my lord."

Everyone straightened and looked to Emperor Faris, their faces incredulous.

"What recording?" General Portid angrily vocalized the consensus of the room.

Beyond the tall, slender windows of the hall, a foreboding violet daybreak ascended silently into the black skies over the rooftops and skyscrapers of Sejeroreich. The low sun, a shadowy and alien effigy of its noon form, lingered behind a veil of motionless dark clouds on the horizon. Emperor Faris's face was grave. "Yes, I believe it is time you are all made aware of what we know. There is something that must be seen. We believe it is directly related to the attacks. A private feed was connected to our network from a research and development facility in Municera. We had been following the progress of scientists working on a long-term multifield project. Much of their work is too complex to delve into, but Pral Nerol was exploring a new technology."

Everyone in the ring of seats shifted anxiously. Pral Nerol was a name known by all. He was a brilliant scientist and inventor. A year never passed without Pral Nerol releasing a breakthrough technology of some kind. What had Pral Nerol created this time?

"From what I understand," Emperor Faris continued. "The research and development has been ongoing for a number of years now. Councillor Harken, perhaps you could enlighten us?"

"Certainly," Councillor Harken said. "The project was called Operation Felix Rises. Pral Nerol proposed that he had the technological means to bestow Sejero anatomical and physiological traits upon entities created in a laboratory. According to what Nerol told us, the end result would be a highly advanced machinelike being fabricated with our very own genes. The important part, as it relates to us now, was that Nerol believed these Felixes could be capable of rivaling even the most powerful Sejero warrior."

A troubled tiding fell upon the War Hall. No technology or inanimate weapon could ever match the natural power of an Imperial First Class warrior. Every substance in existence fell inferior to Sejero flesh and muscle.

"How could blunt materials possibly have the strength to match that of the Primus?" General Portid could be heard calling over the loud rabble of vociferous objections. "Sejero blood makes us impervious. No such element exists!"

"Silence!" Emperor Faris shouted over the ruckus and nodded for Councillor Harken to continue.

Councillor Harken shook his head. "All we can say for sure is that Pral Nerol's goal was to transform inorganic materials into functional tissues using our own hereditary makeup. Meaning, in theory, these Felixes could have the same physical characteristics as a natural Primus and therefore may have inherent Sejero traits. That is my understanding of it."

"Impossible," General Portid insisted, and many nodded in agreement.

"Emperor Faris," Councillor Harken said. "Perhaps it would simplify matters to play the video recording of Nerol's laboratory. I believe the footage speaks for itself."

Emperor Faris's shoulders sunk back into his throne and he raised a resigned hand. "Show it."

An image flickered to life upon a large screen, and some councillors turned in their seats to see it. Not a sound could be heard in the War Hall as the councillors watched with unblinking attention. They saw the older man they recognized as Pral Nerol. The lines and creases in his face had multiplied in recent years, but the withering of his appearance seemed to have done little to slow his ingenuity.

Nerol's cluttered laboratory was visible in the grainy background. A few researchers were with Nerol; men and women clad in white coats moved across the field of vision. Test tubes and gadgets of every description were scattered upon stainless steel tables. The far wall was lined with monitors rapidly cycling through data. Curiously, the palpable tension inundating the War Hall seemed to be equally matched by the blatant trepidation among the research team in the video. Eyes darted nervously, brusque orders were exchanged, and—aside from Pral Nerol—everyone in the laboratory looked on edge.

The ring of councillors focused on a striking sight in the video. A large raised steel platform was built into the center of the laboratory. What they saw on the platform caused a number of the councillors to frown in affronted bewilderment. On top of the platform were four unconscious Primus, two men and two women. Each lay naked and prostrate on the cold steel. All four seemed to be in a profoundly deep sleep, their faces still and lifeless. Yet they did not appear altogether dead. Their unscarred skin held a visible warm touch of life, and they did not have the stiff macabre look of corpses.

Pral Nerol was busy examining the numerous computer screens before he casually turned to the unconscious men and women.

"We watch a video when we should be out fighting!" General Portid shouted suddenly, breaking the confused silence of the War Hall.

"Be quiet, General Portid, or you will be escorted out of this Council," Emperor Faris commanded.

The audio in the video initiated, and the nondescript beeping and whirring sounds of the busy laboratory filled the War Hall. Pral Nerol's voice crackled through the video feed.

"Hello and good morning to all that may be watching. You are witness to the final stage of our research project, Operation Felix Rises. We come to you from the illustrious Imperial research complex in the heart of Municera. With me in the lab are my research assistants, Argos Trace, Cintha Loh, and Vera Gray. Imperial warrior Von Krass has also been gracious enough to join us, as a precautionary measure."

A thick-limbed, enormous man dressed in Imperial armor stepped into the screen. Von Krass's broad shoulders took up a large portion of the background, and he stood many feet over the scientists' heads.

Expressions of confusion were exchanged among the watching councillors and generals. General Portid's eyes narrowed, and even he now gave the video his full attention. Von Krass was an Imperial First Class, one of its most powerful members.

The Epsilon empire had a clearly defined power hierarchy, even within the ranks of the Imperial Classes. In a race unmatched physically by any creation of nature or science, strength was highly glamorized. Somewhat paradoxically, the greatest creation of the Primus civilization was tested in brutally archaic and barbarous combat. Prowess was tested in highly publicized one-on-one physical duels. Deaths during these competitions were common. The enormous soldier standing among the academics in the laboratory was one of the greatest fighters of his era. Only several living individuals were more powerful, two of whom were the man now sitting on the throne and his son Prince Vengelis Epsilon.

The same question now ran through everyone's mind: why would Von Krass himself be at a research laboratory in Municera?

Von Krass nodded to Nerol. He looked like a tremendous sequoia looking down upon a meager oak, his head nearly touching the ceiling; a true Imperial First Class soldier. Pral Nerol examined the readings on a scrolling computer monitor. "The Felixes are ready to be initiated at any moment now."

Pral Nerol wiped sweat from his brow and turned to direct the assistants. He motioned to Von Krass, and the giant warrior visibly readied himself. It was evident to the councillors that behind the guise of Nerol's confidence there was a cause for concern in the laboratory. But what potential danger could possibly have required the likes of Von Krass? Uneasiness grew with each passing moment among Nerol's assistants.

"It is my intention to have these Felixes take the place of the hundreds of thousands of low-ranked warriors who die unnecessarily in combat and training each year," Nerol said as he examined the many computer monitors. He sat down at a keyboard and began to type. "The initiation process for Felix One has begun. We will awaken the Felixes one at a time. Twenty seconds until Felix One attains consciousness."

A thick silence filled the laboratory and the War Hall.

"Fifteen seconds."

"Sir, there's a hormonal anomaly occurring," an assistant murmured.

"Ten seconds," Nerol said as the screens flashed through vital signs.

"Sir, the brain waves aren't matching our projections."

"Five seconds." Nerol remained expressionless.

"Sir?"

Pral Nerol looked up from the keyboard to their creation—the Felix—which lay naked on the lab table. "It should awaken any moment."

Everyone in the laboratory turned to the still body of Felix One. The assistants drew their gaze away from their charts to the peculiar male body.

A long uncertain moment ticked past. Then, just as it seemed the researchers were going to have to retreat back to the drawing boards, a faint spasm traveled through the still body. The pale figure slowly sat up with its upper body, its back as straight as a board, its legs stretched and still against the cold steel. The movement seemed unnatural, as though the man's body were not merely sitting up after a deep sleep, but after death itself.

The Felix then sat completely motionless, its palms resting on its knees. Its eyes remained closed, chest moving in and out with slow shallow breaths.

"Felix One, I am Pral Nerol. Your creator," Nerol said, staring at the Felix's closed eyelids.

One of the assistants swiveled his chair and looked at the Felix in confusion. "The behavioral modifications we installed should have prohibited the first Felix action until it was ordered by us. Something is wrong—very wrong. Pral?"

"I know. Stay calm," Nerol said, staring inquisitively at Felix One. "Felix One, do you hear me?"

After a pause, the Felix's eyelids slowly fluttered open, revealing strangely piercing blue eyes. The retinas were emitting a hint of blue glow, providing the face with a strange and deranged visage. Felix One stared at Nerol expressionlessly for a moment before turning its luminous gaze to the rest of the laboratory. Its attention rested for a moment on the other three Felixes unconscious beside it. Although Felix One's features remained impassive, an unmistakable alertness conveyed from it, as though it was trying to unravel the reality into which it had awoken.

Pral Nerol turned and motioned to one of the assistants, and she tremulously approached the male body to determine initial vital signs. She gently pressed her fingers into the Felix's right arm to take blood pressure readings. Slowly and deliberately, Felix One reached over and took hold of her forearm with its hand.

"Sir? What is happening?" she said and then winced, a sudden panic rising in her voice. "It's *squeezing* me, Pral. It's squeezing me!"

"Felix One, let go of her arm."

The male body, the empty vessel, sustained its grip on her arm as it stared blankly at the far wall. Its face looked inanimate, its eyes like a doll. Felix One turned and stared with its brilliantly cold blue gaze into the assistant's rapidly welling eyes.

Von Krass took a lumbering step forward from the corner.

"It's squeezing me!" the assistant suddenly screamed out as her eyes bulged at the tightening grip on her forearm. A cowed confusion claimed the room, and everyone seemed unsure of how to act. The Felix then turned its wrist slightly. A grotesque popping sound pierced the lab as though a hunk of cement had fractured, and Felix One pulled the assistant's forearm clean away from her body at the elbow.

Felix One held her arm and examined it indifferently as she spun on her feet with a screeching moan and collapsed to the floor in instantaneous shock. Nerol and his assistants lurched backward against the computer monitors in disbelief, sending contraptions clattering to the floor. Felix One slowly moved its legs over the side of the steel pedestal and stood with its bare feet. It looked down upon the assistant convulsing on the laboratory floor. The Felix brought its attention from her—gasping and convulsing in agony—back to her dismembered arm as if trying to understand her behavior. It raised a foot into the air and brought it to a rest on the side of her face, pinning her head against the floor. She let out a momentary shriek of terror as the Felix leaned forward and applied pressure.

The circle of councillors looked away in mingled horror and disgust as the woman's skull audibly collapsed like an eggshell.

The giant Von Krass moved to confront the Felix.

"Get behind me." The Imperial First Class's voice was deep and commanding. The remaining assistants followed his order without hesitation, gathering behind the enormous warrior. One of the men slipped on the dark blood now forming a grisly puddle across the floor. Von Krass easily reached out and caught the man's arm, pulling the trembling assistant out of the way as though he were a child. On the other end of the room Nerol stood in a daze, leaning against a lab table and wheezing heavily.

Von Krass and the Felix stood before each other. Felix One was standing between them and the door, and the assistants could only shrink back and watch.

It was Von Krass that made the first move. He lunged across the laboratory and grabbed at Felix One with his gigantic hands. The Felix remained still, and as Von Krass charged toward him, the Felix lifted its hands and met grips with the giant. Von Krass's momentum halted instantly, and the two were locked hand in hand, grappling like fighting bears. It looked bizarre; the small naked body of the Felix stood its ground with seeming ease as the Imperial First Class goliath bore down on him with gnashing teeth. Then, as fast as lightning, the Felix reversed its strength and pulled the giant's enormous wrists toward its chest. Von Krass's own power now met with no resistance and he stumbled forward from the momentum, doubled by the Felix's sudden pull. At the same instant the Felix lunged forward and head butted Von Krass square in the nose. The mass of the decorated Imperial First Class soldier fell to the laboratory floor with a disturbing thud, dead.

Pral Nerol burrowed his face in his hands and shook his head in an attempt to regain his composure. After a moment of panic he leapt to the side, mashing the security alarm by the door. Instantaneously, flashing lights flooded the laboratory and an alarm boomed. Felix One turned and stepped toward the huddling assistants as the visual and audio feeds cut and the video abruptly turned to static.

The circle of councillors exploded into a storm of questions, and Emperor Faris was forced to shout for silence.

"What the *hell* was that? How did that man do that to Von Krass? No one could defeat him in one hit," General Portid roared. "It's not possible!"

"First and foremost it must be made clear to you all that the Felix One in that video was no man," Councillor Harken called over the other voices. "Second, the video alone proves it is possible, General Portid. The implications of what you all have just seen are staggering. If that Felix could kill Von Krass with such ease, it is logical that it also could have the power to inflict the carnage we have witnessed in Municera and the Twin Cities."

"Good lord . . ." General Barlow muttered.

"We don't have the luxury of time to sit and discuss the plausibility of what we have seen. We believe these . . . " Emperor Faris turned to Councillor Harken. " . . . machines?"

Councillor Harken thought it over, obviously unsure himself. "Felixes. For simplicity's sake, yes, I suppose we can refer to them as machines."

"Very well," Emperor Faris said. "These Felix *machines* are directly related to our assault. Although the video feed ended where you saw, the last security transmissions from the laboratory indicate the other three Felixes had all begun their activation sequences before we lost contact with Municera. It's possible this . . . Felix One . . . initiated them himself, but equally likely that the activation sequences had already begun by the time they hit the alarms. Either way, it must be assumed the other three Felixes malfunctioned in the same manner as Felix One, and are every bit as powerful."

"Why has this attack been allowed to go on so long if we know what our enemy is?" General Portid asked.

"Because," Councillor Harken said, his voice growing heated, "it would be a terrible mistake to act rashly against an entity so powerful. In order to defeat them, we had hoped we could first understand them. If we mobilize the Imperial First Class and fly straight to the Twin Cities like an unorganized horde, it's possible the *entire* Imperial Army could be overrun. Look what happened to Von Krass when he blindly engaged the individual Felix. They are powerful on a scale that we do not yet fully understand. We can't risk underestimating them."

An ominous silence permeated the War Hall as a pale, cheerless dawn passed through the windows and cast the faces of the councillors in pallid gray light. If the Felixes did indeed harbor inborn strength rivaling that of the Royal families, Councillor Harken's words were accurate.

After a long moment, General Portid rose and turned to his second-in-command, who stood at attention behind his chair. "My regiment moves out immediately. Send word to our ranks. They should prepare for battle. This is open war."

"You will hold that command until this Council has decided upon a course of action!" Emperor Faris thundered.

"My lord." General Portid lowered his eyes and bowed. Although older in age, the Epsilon Emperor's physical prowess still commanded subservience. He was a god among gods. "Of course, we will follow whatever path you deem appropriate. Forgive my outburst."

"Forgiven." Emperor Faris turned to Councillor Harken. "What do we know about these Felixes? If indeed we know anything?"

"We can say with certainty that they are as powerful as even the most powerful Primus, as evidenced in the assault upon that poor assistant and Von Krass. The Felixes are as complex as a living system; they are no archaic machines. They are every bit as intricate as living beings."

The implications of Harken's statement were frightening. An enemy that could manhandle Von Krass as though he were no threat at all, and there were four of them. The reality of their situation, the gravity, began to seep in.

Councillor Harken sighed nervously. "We have to act now, and act *appropriately.*"

"I agree." Emperor Faris summoned one of the members of his Royal Guard to his side. "Have we received any update from the Twin Cities?"

The huge man bowed deeply, his voice baritone. "None, sir. We've received no contact for the past few hours."

"What is this madness?" Emperor Faris muttered.

"One thing remains unclear to me. I don't understand the Felix aggression. What reason would the machines have to be so very violent? Why would their first action be to murder and destroy?" General Portid asked.

Councillor Harken shook his head. "That's what we are most confused about. We . . . we don't know."

"If a chance to somehow reason with them arises, we will certainly take it. But in the meantime we must focus on our own defense. It's time for action," Emperor Faris said in a falsely confident tone. Fear was emerging on the faces around him, and he could not allow that to transform into panic—fear among the leadership would trickle down through the ranks.

"I for one have been longing for a good fight for years now," General Portid said with a dry smile.

"Couldn't have put it better myself," Emperor Faris said, embracing his general's courage with admiration. Portid was a true Sejero soldier. "We must mo—
"

A sudden earsplitting eruption emanated outside the palace in the sprawling city of Sejeroreich. The stone floor of the War Hall heaved violently as the palace lurched, and all of the councillors looked up with startled expressions. Sejeroreich was the capital city, the most well fortified place in Anthem. If the Epsilon Palace were to fall, what chance would the empire have at survival? What chance would the Primus have?

A deep alarm began to drone, echoing off the walls and the high ceiling, and a series of thunderous booms resonated from just beyond the palace. The walls shuddered and weighty decorations fell to the floor. Panicked shouts were heard in the corridors surrounding War Hall.

Councillor Harken's face turned pale. "The Felixes."

"Is the army assembled?" Emperor Faris called over the clamor to General Portid.

"The entire Imperial First Class is assembled and ready to fight," there was not a trace of fear in General Portid's worn features. "Permission to lead them, my lord?"

"Go!" Emperor Faris ordered as a dozen mammoth Royal Guards stormed into the hall to protect him.

"My lord," Councillor Harken shouted over the rising calamity and raised a forearm against falling debris from the lofty ceiling. "You *must* call for the Prince! There is too much at stake here to risk the absence of Vengelis!"

"Yes!" General Barlow called. "Prince Vengelis must be summoned at once."

Emperor Faris's mouth moved to speak, but no words came. He rubbed his aged hands together. The calluses of his palms were dry and worn from long years of use. A poignant expression claimed his features, as he suddenly realized his time had passed. His men were looking to another to protect them. He nodded in heart-rending agreement and turned to a member of the Royal Guard. "Send word to my son. Inform Prince Vengelis to return to Sejeroreich immediately. His people need him."

The soldier nodded solemnly and sprinted out of the hall as a closer rumble rattled the ceiling far above. Emperor Faris considered the faces of the War Council. Aside from the stoic members of his Royal Guard, every one looked shaken. The alarms continued to roar as a massive quake shook from beneath the emperor's feet. He craned his head and looked up to the faces of his ancestors. They stared down with their aloof stone gaze, as they had for two thousand years. For two millennia the children of those stone faces had known no fear. Yet now fear rose, unfamiliar and sickly, in the back of the emperor's throat.

"If you aren't a warrior, leave the palace at once! Sejeroreich is to be evacuated," Emperor Faris Epsilon shouted, pulling his gaze from his great forefathers. "If you are a warrior, follow me!"

CHAPTER SIX

Vengelis

In the highest latitudinal reaches of Anthem, not far from the northernmost pole, Prince Vengelis Epsilon stood up to his knees in the snow of Mount Karlsbad. A cold wind was blowing the dusty snow into his dark hair and darker eyes. Vengelis Epsilon was short for a Primus, standing a shade over six feet. Like his father and most children of the Royal bloodlines, Vengelis lacked the unnaturally tall and bulky stature of many Imperial First Class soldiers. His frame was more honed and well proportioned than ungainly.

Heir to the Epsilon throne, Vengelis was undeniably the strongest of his people. From the oldest man to the youngest child, every citizen of the Epsilon empire knew what their prince lacked in size, he made up for in his pure Sejero bloodline and his legendary intensity.

Far from the hubs of Primus society and crowded streets of Sejeroreich, Mount Karlsbad stood in a vastly secluded region of Anthem's northern ice world. Rising out of the endless snows and frigid plains, Mount Karlsbad was the lone frozen citadel in the empty North. The absolute desolation and unobstructed environment proved ideal for training, a harsh and stalwart land suitable for the few mad enough to train there.

It was on the precipitous slopes of Mount Karlsbad that the enigmatic Master Borneo Tolland resided. Vengelis Epsilon had trained with Master Tolland for many years in his teens. Yet still, Vengelis would return to train with his former teacher. In a way Mount Karlsbad was Vengelis's home. He preferred spending time here with Master Tolland, thousands of miles away from the nearest societal distraction.

"Focus," Vengelis whispered into the biting wind, his eyes slowly searching the striking blue sky and the snow desert and winding glaciers far below. There were three out there, but he could not see them. Vengelis had no doubt they were waiting to pounce upon him in unison. Two of the most extraordinary soldiers in Sejeroreich had come north with him to act as his sparring partners. Though strong and stern Imperial First Class soldiers, they would prove little more than practice dummies against Vengelis's skill. His only real concern was Master Tolland, who would certainly wait for Vengelis to make a mistake before he revealed himself.

Vengelis knew they would try to attack from different directions.

A heavy gust off the mountainside churned a snowdrift and blinded him in swirling white. Vengelis closed his eyes at once, freeing himself from the shackles of sight, as Master Tolland had taught him. Vision would be no help to him in this precarious position amid the blinding snow. He would have to feel their approach now.

Vengelis rolled his shoulders and flexed his arms, veins and cords of muscle rising to the surface of his skin. As he centered his mind, the air around him became palpable. The screaming of the polar winds died in his ears. He focused on ridding his lungs of frigid air and his bare fingers of gnawing subzero cold. Vengelis slipped into readiness, no longer relying on any one sense. He concentrated on the approach of his attackers. Like a coiled snake, Vengelis Epsilon stood at perfect attention—ready to lash out in an instant.

A faint ripple moved through the now placid world surrounding him. It was Alegant Hoff lumbering toward him from six o'clock, directly behind. Alegant Hoff was the Lord General of the Imperial First Class, third in command only to the Epsilons themselves, Faris and Vengelis respectively. Lord General Hoff was strong, very strong, but his strength came with a critical loss of quickness and discretion. He was underestimating the powers of his prince; Vengelis could sense it in the recklessness of his heavy footfalls.

Vengelis then felt Krell Darien coming in, head on. If Lord General Hoff was charging at him with a reckless speed, the pace of this young Royal Guard was outright foolish. Darien was a promising member of the Royal Guard, one of the youngest soldiers in history to reach the Royal Guard's renowned ranks. Vengelis had personally selected Darien to join his training after seeing him devastate several of his peers in duels.

Hoff and Darien were two of the most powerful soldiers in the Imperial First Class. Both of their behemoth masses shook the world around Vengelis. He tilted his head into the blustering wind, eyes still closed. Where was Master Tolland?

The monstrous mass of Darien bounded over the ridge just in front of Vengelis, his heavy legs shaking the frozen ground. It was an obvious decoy. Vengelis maintained his focused state, channeling all his concentration on locating the third sparring partner, Master Tolland.

Wait on the attack; let your opponent commit to the first move and then counter. Perfection in execution will always trump brute strength and impulsiveness. Vengelis could practically hear the sagacious voice of Master Tolland in the wind.

Then, like the sharp release of a taut bowstring, his muscles surged into action. With blazing reflexes Vengelis reeled around on the spot. Lord General Hoff's enormous knuckles were mere inches from Vengelis's unscarred and unworn face. Vengelis dodged the thirty-pound fist with searing speed, protecting his still straight and unbroken nose, a testament to his quickness.

Vengelis grabbed the huge thrusting forearm and spun, shooting his hips into the giant's belly and throwing him directly into Darien, who was now mere feet away. The two giants collided with a deafening crack that echoed across the snow-swept plains below like a roll of thunder. Hoff and Darien were momentarily dazed from the impact.

Vengelis smirked in their direction, his eyes still closed.

The two Imperial First Class soldiers each shook their heads to purge discombobulating black stars from their vision, and exploded toward the young leader in unison. Vengelis weaved easily between their full-force attacks, still focusing his attention on detecting Master Tolland's approach. He was toying with Hoff and Darien; their movements were so slow he barely had to concentrate to avoid them.

"Enough of this," Vengelis muttered. He flexed his knees and exploded into the sky with a loud boom as his body ripped a hole through the supersonic barrier. The two lumbering behemoths followed skyward in his wake. And so they took to flight. The three figures soared across the broad sky like great falcons, the very air around their shoulders tearing apart from their speed.

In a split second Vengelis suddenly reversed directions and launched himself directly at Hoff. Before the Lord General could raise one of his hefty arms to block the blow, Vengelis buried a fist into Hoff's enormous barrel chest with vicious force. The blow audibly deflated the wind out of the general, and left him gasping for breath as he plummeted helplessly to the snowdrifts far below.

Vengelis turned and dodged Darien's incoming blow with staggering agility and countered the Royal Guard's strike by sending a knee straight to his stomach.

"Gah!" Vengelis roared. A surprise impact sunk into his back, striking his left kidney with surgical precision. Master Tolland had entered the fray. Like

Vengelis, Master Tolland was of Royal descent, his body lean and hard as steel. Vengelis turned just in time to duck away from a potentially crushing blow to his chin.

"You're getting sloppy, Vengelis!" Master Tolland roared over the wind and burst forward. "Too many nights in Sejeroreich!"

Vengelis smiled and engaged him. The flurry of attacks that ensued between them was without restraint. The two warriors battled brutally, the speed of the strikes accelerating with each passing moment. From below, the two beaten giants Hoff and Darien heaved for breath as around their thick legs snow melted.

"Mother of god," Darien muttered, his hands resting on his knees, strikes echoing across the barren lands from overhead.

Hoff blinked as he tried futilely to track the movement of the two Royal warriors—old and young— across the sky.

"Vengelis . . . crazy." The Lord General panted.

Darien nodded. "Master Tolland, too."

There would be no draw. Even in a training session such as this, it would not stop until blood was drawn or someone submitted. That was the way of the Sejero warriors of old, and that was the way of Prince Vengelis Epsilon. Every spar he entered ended in blood, and every duel he fought would end in his death before his submission. To Sejero warriors, fighting was not a sport. It was life. Or it was death. In a world where the very cohesion of society depended upon the raw power of the greatest few, those few regarded that power with the utmost solemnity.

Vengelis had been able to best the aging Master Tolland for many years now, but he still believed the man had more to teach him. For Vengelis, unlike many of the Sejero soldiers of the day, there was no laid-back, contented post-training stage in life—no juncture at which a warrior could proclaim aptitude and rely upon the tutelage of a former education. Refinements could always be made. New techniques could always be discovered. The day a warrior stopped bettering himself through ferocious and disciplined training was the day he witnessed his own defeat. There was no room for the soft among the strong. As a young teenager, Vengelis and his compassionless fists had proved this to many former champions before their swaggering challenges stopped coming.

Now in the prime of his fighting life at twenty-one years old, Vengelis had not been challenged in years.

Despite his celebrity and prestige, Vengelis liked returning to the harshness of Mount Karlsbad for days or weeks at a time to spar with the only worthy partner on Anthem: the eccentric and mysterious Master Tolland. Vengelis had traveled north with Lord General Hoff and Darien three days previous. As always, he had issued strict orders to the Imperial Army not to interrupt their stay. Vengelis Epsilon's orders were always followed.

"I think you're losing your touch, old man," Vengelis said as he locked arms with Master Tolland.

"Oh, I don't know about that," Master Tolland murmured. Now over sixty years old, Master Tolland was only a shadow of his former physical self. Nevertheless, he could always provide a challenge for Vengelis—an accomplishment few could claim. Even as Vengelis taunted, Master Tolland nearly caught him in a leg lock. Vengelis rolled out of it, defending the ligaments of his knee with practiced grace.

"You leave your legs open for submission too oft—" Master Tolland sunk below a furious high kick. "Good!"

Vengelis smirked. "And to think, you would have me *hide* my power."

"Of course I would not have you hide it. I would have you appreciate the nature of your Sejero gifts."

"You think I don't appreciate my power?" Vengelis shouted, burying a fist into Master Tolland's raised forearms. The deafening sound of knuckle against arm echoed for miles in every direction.

"I would have you appreciate the"—Master Tolland dodged another blow—"*Effects* and ramifications of your actions."

"When will you ever give up on lecturing me? You and your conservative perspectives on Sejero strength. I'll never understand your stale theories on leadership and morality. You know, some of my generals in Sejeroreich say you lack the courage to embrace Sejero power. They say you're frail, though never in my hearing range."

"And tell me, have any one of these ruthless and sedentary generals ever left the warmth of their palace to issue me a formal challenge?"

Vengelis smirked. "They may be sedentary, but they're not stupid."

"A sense of relativism is not weakness, Vengelis. It is strength. It takes courage to consider all ends, and not simply believe in what you choose or what you're taught."

"I'm a realist," Vengelis grunted, trying to catch Master Tolland in an arm bar. "I place my convictions in power, and power alone. All other beliefs are conditional upon the might to see them through. Those without the strength of fist have no right to word of voice."

"You're not cruel, Vengelis," Master Tolland panted. "In no way overtly sadistic or tyrannical like many of your forefathers. But one day I hope you are able to rise above the politicians and sycophants of Sejeroreich. You could be so much more."

In the midst of their titanic spar across the sky, both master and former student suddenly pulled away from one another and looked into the distant horizon. Still far away, someone was approaching from the south.

"Were you supposed to be somewhere today?" Master Tolland asked through heaving breaths, his hands on his hips in exhaustion.

"No," Vengelis said, squinting into the horizon and breathing steadily. "Are you expecting anyone?"

"What do you think?" Master Tolland asked.

Vengelis laughed. In all his time spent on Mount Karlsbad, he had never seen Master Tolland host a guest aside from himself.

"Whoever it is, they're certainly an Imperial First Class, and moving at top speed."

Vengelis nodded. "If it's someone looking to become a student of yours, I'll certainly provide them with a lesson."

"I don't think it is." Master Tolland glared uncertainly at the tiny figure in the horizon.

Hoff and Darien, seeing the spar had stopped, ascended to them as Vengelis and Master Tolland hovered freely a few thousand feet over the desolate glaciers and snow plains.

"This is something new. A draw?" Hoff called. He was hunched over slightly, still shaken from the punch he took from Vengelis.

"Someone is coming from the south." As the words left Master Tolland, the tiny black dot grew larger in the cloudless sky.

They all simultaneously began to move in the direction of the dot. As the four great warriors drew closer, they saw the visitor was indeed an Imperial First Class soldier. Like Darien, he was armored in the raiment of a Royal Guard. The messenger came to a stop before them and wheezed violently, appearing on the verge of losing consciousness from his maximum speed flight.

"Here is someone who has made a large mistake in judgment," Vengelis said. "I gave explicit orders not to be disturbed."

"M-my lord Vengelis." The man gasped for breath. "Your father Emperor Faris calls for your immediate return to Sejeroreich! The capital is under attack. Anthem is under attack!"

Vengelis's face constricted, his lips thinning. "Explain yourself."

The messenger coughed repeatedly and threw up his arms in exasperation. "We aren't entirely sure. From what I understand, powerful machines have demolished Municera and the Twin Cities. My lord, *millions* have been killed. The machines are in Sejeroreich now. It is open war."

Vengelis's eyes narrowed. "Machines?"

"Yes, my lord. Machines."

"What the hell has the army been doing?"

"The Imperial First Class has risen in Sejeroreich's defense. The battle is underway as we speak, my lord."

"We must go at once," Master Tolland spoke calmly and looked to the south. "Our path will take us past Municera and the Twin Cities. Perhaps we will be able to learn something about this attack on the—"

Vengelis exploded southward, splintering through the frigid sky and accelerating out of sight into the blue almost instantly. Master Tolland was immediately after him. Hoff and Darien looked speechlessly from the southern horizon to the winded messenger.

"If this is some sort of trick, it will cost you your life," Hoff said.

"I wish it were, Lord General Hoff. I wish it were."

Both giants hurried in the trail of the two great warriors, leaving the exhausted messenger alone.

Vengelis roared southward, countless miles falling away beneath the deafening sound of his speed. The featureless plains of northern snow soon gave way to vast frozen tundra and thick boreal forest as he flew ever south. Here and there, broad striations and wide craters dug deep into the very curvature of the planet: enduring scars from the uncivilized weapons of the ancient struggle against the Zergos that led to the rise of the Sejero. Confusion claimed him as he exploded across his pocked and marred land.

Vengelis tried to make sense of what he had been told. Millions have been killed. There was no logic in the messenger's words. How could this be true? Municera was home to dozens of Imperial First Class soldiers. Surely they would have risen to defend the city?

As he neared Municera airspace, the sky before him was brushed with an undulating ocean of clouds that separated the radiant blue of the upper atmosphere from the concealed lands far below. Vengelis lingered in the serenity above the clouds for a moment before plunging toward the ground and directly into the top of a brilliantly white towering cumulus.

The dazzling sunlight instantly dissipated into obscure gray shadow as Vengelis descended through the mist. Water from the cloud's precipitation beaded on his armor and face, gathering and rolling off him in plump drops. Briefly he was blind within the veil. Then, through the bits of parting cloud below, he caught fleeting glimpses of the land beneath.

"W-what?" Vengelis murmured aloud in disbelief.

The distinct smell of pungent sulfur and smoke filled his nose as he attempted to see through the shifting cloud. A faint heat emanated from the land far below. The obfuscating clouds that engulfed him transitioned in color to a dense and unnatural gray-brown. Through the cloud curtain, jet-black streaks and cindery red flames flashed from the lands below. The sight aroused in Vengelis a sensation of descending from a shining heaven into a surreal hell.

Vengelis penetrated the bottom of the cloud cover head first, and at once he beheld Municera. The sight shook Vengelis, and he lost focus, falling momentarily into the noxious air, but he quickly steadied himself. He rotated from horizon to horizon in horror. The city—if it could still be called as such—was completely devastated. Blocks and avenues were unrecognizably scorched, raging fires burning in every direction. Flames leapt from collapsed buildings and severed gas lines, vehicles sat overturned and charred, ruined skyscrapers and street corners were pulsing with heat like glowing embers. Acrid smoke and ash hung thick and blocked the daylight. The only illumination came from smoldering fires far below. It was as though a nightmarish underworld had risen in the city's stead.

"*How?*" Vengelis mouthed in disbelief.

He floated alone far above the city, taking shallow breaths, attempting to rationalize what he was seeing. He had lived in Municera during his early teenage years, and in a sense considered the city a home. All of the landmarks of the great Municera were barely identifiable in the carnage. The Grand Arena, a triumphant marvel of his empire's engineering, was torn down to its skeletal frame; bits of the stadium seating and tall walls reached out of a sweltering bed of sheer dark flames.

After what felt like a very long time, Master Tolland descended silently alongside Vengelis and placed a hand on the young man's shoulder.

"We have no time to contemplate this, Vengelis. We must make for the capital." Master Tolland paused, clearly also shaken. The fires from far below reflected in his troubled eyes. "A battle may still be underway in Sejeroreich. If there is, they'll need you desperately."

"Yes," Vengelis said numbly, his arms shaking with fury and shock.

"Your people need you with a clear head, Vengelis. Rage will dull your senses. You *must* keep your composure, now more than ever before!"

Without another word, a deafening boom echoed across the hellscape as Vengelis burst toward the south once more. Master Tolland hurried after him, but Vengelis pulled away within moments. Vengelis seethed as he accelerated southward across the skies. He knew he was the greatest warrior of Anthem—

the purest of Sejero blood and the strongest of mind. All knew Vengelis Epsilon was the most powerful warrior of the modern age, perhaps the most powerful warrior of any age. The supreme sentinel of Anthem had been in the middle of nowhere training and arguing philosophies as a holocaust tore into his world. He had not been there when his people needed him most, and that truth was poison.

Vengelis clung to the hope that it was not too late.

Without even a glance downward, Vengelis soared over the rising carnage of the ruined Twin Cities. What if he was too late? What if there was nothing left to protect?

As he moved south Vengelis could see the imposing towers of Sejeroreich rise on the horizon. Above them, the sun loomed at high noon, and the sky was clear save for several pillars of black smoke that hung over the capital. From his distance Sejeroreich looked to be nearly in the same condition as the other burning cities he had bypassed. But in Sejeroreich many towers still stood, a testament to the hardened defenses of the city. He passed over columns of spires, the sound of screams and wails mixing with the indiscernible destruction. Many skyscrapers were gone, vanished into piles of rubble in the streets.

The sounds of war raged, and bedlam had taken hold of the city, but Sejeroreich was not completely lost.

Through the smoke he saw the Epsilon Palace still standing in the high ground of the city's center. The Royal Tower was leaning dangerously to one side, and looked as though it may collapse any moment. It was horrible to behold; Vengelis thought of the sacred heirlooms that lay within. He could not imagine them lost. Vengelis turned to look in his wake; Master Tolland was too far behind to be visible, and Lord General Hoff and Darien were probably just passing Municera. Vengelis descended through the darkening sky and flew directly into the leaning Royal Tower, shattering through the stained-glass windows outside the War Hall.

A group of middle ranked soldiers standing guard in the hallway fell back in surprise as Vengelis crashed through the hundredth-story windows.

"Where is my family?" Vengelis asked at once.

They all breathed a sigh of relief upon seeing the son of the emperor. One of the guards with a callow face gave him a trembling salute. "L-Lord Vengelis! The Imperial First Class has fallen!"

"Steady yourself." Vengelis regarded the man's fear with distaste. "Where is my family?"

"We're not certain, my lord. The communication lines have been down for hours. The final transmission we heard was that the Epsilon family had been moved to the bunker underneath the palace barracks. Your father joined the battle alongside the Royal Guard and the Imperial First Class. We've received no word on their status. The machines . . . people are calling them Felixes . . . they are indestructible, my lord."

"Indestructible?" Vengelis said.

"Y-Yes. People are saying it is the second coming of the . . . of the apocalypse, my lord."

Vengelis lunged forward and struck the guard in his chest. The man launched backward into the opposite window and crashed through the decorated pane, falling with a scream into the daylight outside the tower. Vengelis turned to the rest of the guards, each of them looking meek and scared.

"Get to the front! You are Imperial soldiers. Is your Sejero blood so diluted that you have no strength or will left?"

Vengelis glared as they bowed and sprinted to the nearby stairs. He lifted off from the polished floor and flew out the shattered window. Rising high over the city, Vengelis examined the devastation occurring in the palace and surrounding blocks. Where were these machines? He had been expecting to see massive steel juggernauts or eclipsing ships overhead. All he could see were Primus—his people—running in every direction. He descended into the open air and landed outside the palace barracks. A regiment of imposing Imperial First Class guards stood at the tall gates.

The moment Vengelis landed, all of the guards snapped to attention and saluted, thundering in deep unison, "Hail, Emperor Vengelis Epsilon!"

Vengelis hesitated for a moment in his approach to the gate, which cranked open to greet him. A pit formed in his stomach as he distractedly returned a salute. They had addressed him as emperor, not prince. He shook the notion from his mind as the barracks chief officer hurried out of the gate to greet him. Grime and dirt covered the older man's face and sullied his armor. Despair bled from him like an open wound, but he saluted Vengelis robustly.

"Where is my family?" Vengelis said, falling into step with the officer. His voice sounded hollow in his own ears.

"My lord, your sister and mother are in the bunker far below. They are safe for the time being. Though safe has quickly become a relative term. We need to evacuate the Royal families from the planet as soon as possible. Your father has fallen."

The exhausted officer placed a hand on Vengelis's shoulder and directed him toward the bunker. The man was not wearing the armor of a general, or even an upper ranked Imperial First Class soldier. Vengelis did not need to ask to realize the entire power hierarchy had already fallen—the superiors of this middle ranked soldier were dead. The officer was talking hurriedly, providing an overview of the morning's events and Sejeroreich's remaining defenses. Vengelis stopped suddenly, and the man came to a halt before him.

"My father has fallen?"

The downtrodden officer dropped his gaze to his own boots. "Yes, my lord. Emperor Faris died defending the palace early this morning during the beginning of the attack. He fought with the full might of the Royal Guard. They . . . they all died. I heard from a soldier near the battle that Emperor Faris died an honorable death. A Felix claimed his life."

Vengelis could barely register the words. His father was gone. The chaos of the capital suddenly became faded, dreamlike. The frenzied world fell out of focus, and Vengelis felt overwhelmed. For the first time in two thousand years, the Epsilon dynasty was in mortal jeopardy. Vengelis steadied his breathing and attempted to regain his composure. He turned and looked out over the gardens of the palace courtyard. It seemed as though the entire Imperial First Class lay wounded or dead, medics frantically moving the few survivors into the barracks.

What miniscule fraction of the Imperial Army remained for him to lead? Vengelis felt fear strip away his confidence. Icy panic slowly seeped into his mind, but he quickly replaced it with resolve.

"Take me to my family," Vengelis said with a steady authority.

"At once, my lord. Follow me."

The officer turned and led Vengelis at a brisk pace through the bowels of the palace barracks, their footfalls echoing off the deserted stone hallways and the armor of the stoic guards standing sentry along the way. They entered an elevator and wordlessly descended dozens of floors far into the underground bunker of the palace. Vengelis tried to grasp confidence. So be it if the entire Imperial Army and the Royal Guard fell. His power alone was on a magnitude beyond these men. A hundred lesser warriors standing by his side would not increase his odds. It made no difference that the Imperial First Class had fallen, for even when the entirety of the ranks stood together, the final defense of Anthem inexorably came down to him alone: the last Epsilon.

The elevator doors slid open, and a sterile and militarily outfitted bunker came into view. A cavernous room, the bunker was filled to capacity with parents and children of the Royal families and various high-ranking officials. The faces ranged the gamut of his people, the shrill cry of infants rising alongside the pained moans of wounded soldiers. Vengelis was repulsed by the sight. It was as though he was looking at a refugee camp, and yet these were the strongest of his race—these were living deities bleeding out on the floor like wounded animals.

The moment Vengelis stepped from the elevator into the teeming room, a hush descended. All eyes fell on the young Epsilon. Vengelis could feel the gazes searing into him, their eyes piercing him with pleas for protection. He alone was their last tenuous hope of salvation. Everyone knew it.

"Hail, Emperor Vengelis Epsilon!" a number of wounded Imperial First Class warriors shouted from one corner. Their voices rose and fell, a quiet trepidation taking hold of the bunker immediately after their determined salutes.

"Where is my family?" Vengelis asked the officer impatiently, his gaze surveying the grim surrounds. The man raised a hand to the rear of the room and nodded Vengelis forward. His mother was standing in solitude against a corner, her head resting against the wall. Beside her, Vengelis's little sister Eve was sitting on the floor, her hands around her knees. Surrounding them were the last hulking members of the Royal Guard. He thought his mother and sister looked fragile and out of place, like revered statues tucked away in sudden shame. They hurried to him and collided into his armored chest, embracing him tightly.

"Vengelis, your father has fallen." His mother was sobbing, her hands wrapped tightly around something. Vengelis looked down numbly and saw she was holding the Blood Ring. He had never seen it off of his father's hand. His father would have died before he gave up the ring, and so it had been.

"Eve . . ." Vengelis said, wrapping an arm around the slender, elegant shoulder of his younger sister. Though her formal name was Evengeline, she had gone by Eve for as long as he could remember.

"I'm so glad you're safe," Eve spoke into his chest. "Our fear was that you had been lost too. The attack hit Sejeroreich in the early hours this morning. People are calling them Felixes, some sort of Primus machines. We don't know anything for certain. The whole Imperial First Class is scattered and broken. Father fought with the Royal Guard, but they all fell."

Vengelis could not bring himself to speak, for no words seemed appropriate. Not one hour previous, he had been training on Mount Karlsbad without a care in the world. How was any of this possible? They must be mistaken. No power could destroy the entire assembled Royal Guard. His head felt empty, his mind incapable of forming thoughts.

"A transport is being prepared to take us from Anthem," Eve said. "We are going to escape until this attack dies down, until we know more about these machines."

"Escape?" he found his voice and looked down upon their anguished faces.

"Vengelis, you two are the lone surviving Epsilons," his mother said. She placed a hand on his arm, her many rings and ornately jeweled bracelets brushing against his skin. "You both have to flee. There is no choice in the matter. If you were to fall, it would be to the ruin of the Primus race. The Epsilon line has *never* been broken. It cannot be risked."

Vengelis pulled back from her grasp and inclined his head with an adamant conviction. "I stay."

Eve shook her head, her pretty chin quivering with grief and fear. "You can't, Vengelis. I know it's hard for you to flee, but you must. You are emperor now. You have to do what is right for your people, not yourself. You are the last Epsilon—"

"I need no reminding of my heritage. You are right. I am the last surviving Epsilon. I will not leave Anthem. I will defend it to my death, as my fathers before me."

"But there can be no victory!" Eve said. "The Felixes have decimated all of our defenses. The *entire* Imperial First Class was scattered. And Father . . ."

"These . . . Felix machines . . . have not yet bested me," Vengelis said in a cold fury. "I will not run while Sejeroreich and all of Anthem is laid to waste. I will not run and hide while an execution is carried out upon people who look to me for deliverance." His voice had inadvertently risen to a shout, and he realized every soul in the bunker was listening.

"We are facing obliteration. You will serve no use to your people dead, son," his mother whispered.

"There will *be* no more people if I don't put a stop to this madness." Vengelis raised an infuriated hand with finality and turned to Eve. "I will face the machines. They may have defeated lesser warriors, but they will find a challenge in me. That much I promise. When I engage them, you must make your escape as quickly as you can. You and I equally share the Epsilon bloodline."

Eve shook her head. "Don't do this."

"One of us must escape, and it cannot be me. It *cannot* be me. I couldn't live with the knowledge that I fled while so many others fought and died. If the last Epsilon were to flee when Anthem needs him most, then the strength of the Sejero is already lost."

"I don't want you to die, Vengelis."

Vengelis stepped forward and placed his hands on her shoulders. "I won't. When I make my stand, all of you must escape. Do you understand?"

Eve wiped a trailing tear from her face and embraced her brother. This was not the first time she had said goodbye to him before he risked his life. He could see the growing faith in her eyes, the sudden hope in the face of his strength.

She was looking up at her fearless and invincible older brother. Eve had never seen him lose. No one had ever seen Vengelis Epsilon defeated. She sighed deeply and nodded. "I understand."

Vengelis looked to his mother, but she merely shook her head in futile desperation. She was incapacitated with grief. Without another word Vengelis turned to leave them, but Eve reached out and took him by the wrist. She had taken the Blood Ring from their mother's grasp. Slowly, and with a grave earnestness, she placed the gigantic family heirloom on his left hand. The Blood Ring and Vengelis's hand looked as though they had been crafted as one.

"The Blood Ring belongs to our emperor, long may he live," Eve said. She rose up to her toes and kissed Vengelis on the cheek, then turned to the frightened crowd and shouted as loud as she could across the subdued quiet of the bunker, "Hail, Vengelis Epsilon! Our champion rises to the call of war!"

For the slightest moment, her shout was met with dead silence. Then, at once, applause and cheering erupted from the huddled groups of families and wounded soldiers. It was surely fate. The greatest Epsilon in recent memory was crowned emperor at the very moment when his world needed him most. It was the making of a new Sejero legend. This was the prodigy who had challenged the most brutal warrior in the world to a fight to the death on his fourteenth birthday. This was the only living warrior who had never tasted defeat. Vengelis, the pride of his race, the greatest Sejero warrior in the world, a living god, was joining their fight.

Not hesitating for a moment, Vengelis pushed through the roars of encouragement toward the elevator. The Blood Ring pulsated a fiery red, and all in the room recognized that Vengelis Epsilon had been destined for this day. When he was a teenager, many had thought him arrogant and brash. Now a man grown, the valor of the old Sejero heroes stood reincarnated before their very eyes. This was no dawn upon a day of reckoning; to a lesser race perhaps, but the Primus wielded the power of the Sejero.

There would be only victory. Their strongest son, their emperor, would return their victor.

CHAPTER SEVEN

Vengelis

A heavyset Royal Guard tried to step into the elevator to fight alongside him, but Vengelis shook his head sternly and motioned the soldier back into the cheering bunker. "Protect them," Vengelis said to the brave Royal Guard as the doors shut between them with finality.

The lone journey to the surface seemed to last ages as Vengelis blinked at the closed doors. It was hard to conceive the yoke that now rested on his shoulders. As the elevator rose, so too did the rate of his heart. He could feel it pumping furiously, spilling oxygen and rushing adrenaline into his muscles. Vengelis clenched his fists and cleared his mind. His palms were sweating, and his ears rang.

His face was stoic.

The elevator opened with a hiss. Vengelis sprinted through the barracks and into the terrible massacre that greeted him in what once was a florid courtyard. He looked around him, unclear on how he was going to find the machines. Overhead, black smoke was gathering like a storm above Sejeroreich. Vengelis lifted off the ground and ascended into the caustic cloud cover. The midday sun barely held authority over the sky, it was merely a shadowy dot tethered in the billowing blackness. In the unseen distance of the city beyond the palace walls, sounds of unspeakable destruction and torment were swept up in the wind and carried to Vengelis's uncomprehending ears. Dozens of dark skyscrapers appeared in the veiled sky around him, though many more had fallen.

"Where are the machines?" Vengelis screamed as he scanned the city below. It was impossible to discern anything, least of all these so-called machines. He shouted again and again, not knowing what else to do.

An oil line caught flame and exploded suddenly outside the palace, causing a spire of bright red flames to leap high into the air below him, the blaze in sharp contrast with the shadowy streets. He bore down at once, descending toward the whooshing flames. As he approached the inferno, Vengelis saw that a melee was underway. He slowed, hoping to catch a glimpse of a Felix.

The first thing Vengelis saw amid the fire was a man. Initially, he thought it was a member of the Imperial First Class that had shed aside his armor, but he changed his mind at once. This man looked like a demon born of fire. He moved amid the roaring flames that leapt from the spewing oil line. Sheets of burning fluid covered his body, his face and arms engulfed by dark crackling flames. Yet he was unaffected. The burning man was moving with faultless coordination, and a speed such that Vengelis had never before witnessed.

A soldier in Imperial First Class Armor with huge limbs and monstrous hands lumbered toward the burning man. Without even seeing the soldier's approach, the burning man jumped over soldier's broad shoulders and landed directly behind him. A burning arm wrapped around the Imperial First Class's head and twisted his neck, easily snapping the giant's spine. Another Imperial First Class started charging, fist cocked. The burning man covered the distance to the soldier in an instant, flames leaping around him, and launched his elbow squarely into the soldier's solar plexus. The soldier gasped as a smoldering leg slammed into his chest, launching his body across the street. The Imperial First Class's dead form crashed into a building, which collapsed inward from the impact. The burning man then turned, sending a smoldering fist straight through the chest of another Imperial First Class. Dark blood spurted from the soldier's punctured armor and sizzled in the blistering heat.

Vengelis exploded down toward the flames, stopping just above their reach. He was livid with this burning man. Why would Primus be fighting Primus at this hour? He tracked his gaze across his surroundings, all around the flames and street beyond, but he lost the position of the strange burning man. He cursed and descended to the street level, touching down outside the flames.

Vengelis was reaching down to inspect a fallen Imperial First Class captain's corpse when a young boy ran by, dragging an enormous wounded soldier across the street. The boy was covered in dirt, his face streaked with dried tears. Vengelis swallowed hard, immediately recognizing the boy as the son of Councillor Harken: a child of Royalty. The nearby blaze screeched and crackled, the wind spreading eager flames.

"My lord! You must escape, they are all around us!"

"Steady yourself, child." Vengelis's voice came out strong, confident.

The boy stood as straight as he could and saluted. He was younger than eleven. "Forgive my weakness, Lord Vengelis."

Vengelis nodded with admiration. The child's bravery filled him with a swelling pride. "Where are the machines?"

"They're all around us, Lord Vengelis. They look just like us. The army has been fighting them since dawn, and I will die before I surrender."

The boy was valiant, his Royal lineage obvious in his grit.

"Good boy," Vengelis nodded. "But get yourself to the palace barracks and join the Royal families in the bunker. This is not your fight."

"Yes, Lord Vengelis!" the boy called, but suddenly froze with fear. The boy began trembling, his chest convulsing in terror. Vengelis slowly turned and looked in all directions. Hysteria was rampant; men, women, and children were running every direction, many horribly wounded. None of them were soldiers. The fire was blazing out of control, and the entire block was immersed in raging flames.

A woman standing nearby, just below a broad tilted awning, remained unscathed. Her appearance contrasted strangely with the mayhem around them. She was thin and average sized, of Royal appearance, with blonde hair and bright blue eyes. Tattered ribbons of the awning and bits of orange cinders and ash blew all about her. She was smiling at Vengelis, her teeth white and perfect. Vengelis was taken aback.

Her eyes.

Vengelis squinted through the billowing ash and felt an eerie sense of disquiet surface within him. Her eyes were not quite right. There was a glowing property to her stare, as though her eyes were emitting a strange blue radiance. She was beautiful, but the serene way she was smiling in the midst of the madness was peculiarly horrifying.

"State your name and rank!" Vengelis called out.

The boy stifled a small cry as the woman's smile broadened. Vengelis glared and turned his attention from her to the boy. In a corner of his mind he already knew he was speaking to one of the Felixes. She moved her unsettling gaze from Vengelis to the boy. The boy let out a terrible sob and released the soldier he had been dragging. The woman took a step closer to the child.

There was no longer any doubt in Vengelis's mind.

The woman whirled into motion, dashing toward the boy and reaching for his throat. The boy flinched and locked his eyes shut, expecting instant death. But it did not come. He peered through his trembling eyelids after a moment passed. The woman was still reaching for his throat, though now just in front of him. Vengelis had closed the distance and grabbed her wrist with his left hand, stopping the strike in its tracks. Her fingernails were reaching out longingly, inches from the boy's neck. The woman turned to Vengelis, her expression vacant.

"Huge . . . mistake," Vengelis growled through gritted teeth, his knuckles white from the vice grip on her wrist. "Get out of here, kid."

The boy looked up at the famous Vengelis Epsilon as he stood over him, protecting his life with such raw passion. A hero had come to save him from this nightmare. For a moment the boy froze in awe of his emperor. Then he followed the order. He grabbed the dying warrior on the ground, arched his back, and pulled with all his capacity, carrying the unconscious soldier by his enormous leg toward the barracks.

The woman's glowing eyes looked from the retreating child to Vengelis with an emotionless gaze. Close now, Vengelis looked into her eyes. Her retinas were a shifting and shimmering blue. He was looking into the eyes of a machine. The Felix's mechanic gaze looked to Vengelis's hand on her—its— wrist. The Blood Ring clung with a conflicting opulence to Vengelis's clenched fingers.

Vengelis wound up with his right hand and punched the Felix with all his might on the side of the head, a perfect temple shot with the strength of an earthquake. The Felix's head rolled back, and she stumbled a few feet in a daze, her hair flying about. Vengelis could not believe the machine remained standing. The punch had been strong enough to level a mountain. The ringing sound of the impact of his fist with her head resonated like a deep gong, as though her skull was made of iron. Pain radiated up Vengelis's forearm. He immediately shook it off, clenching his fist without showing the slightest grimace. Nothing was broken. If machines did not feel pain, neither did he.

Once more the woman looked at him with her sapphire stare, her eyes luminous against the shadows of ash and dark flames around them.

Vengelis charged her with another fist, but this time she sidestepped with ease. His fist whistled through empty air. He turned around, furious, and launched several more blows as hard as he could. The muscles in his chest, back, and legs expelled all of their strength to no avail. His fists and legs met only the swirling smoky air as he swung and kicked at the machine. The Felix was impossibly fast, weaving across the street with a velocity he had never before encountered.

In the midst of her elusive turns and sidesteps, the blonde Felix unexpectedly lashed out with an open hand at Vengelis's face. He ducked, but not fast enough. A long sharp fingernail cut deep into his cheek. Vengelis could feel hot blood trickle down his neck and patter onto his gilded chest armor. Without a second thought, Vengelis erupted into the sky, hoping for an advantage in the air. The Felix was after him immediately, soaring easily in his wake. A few hundred feet in the air, Vengelis turned directions abruptly and attempted the same blow he had delivered to Lord General Hoff earlier that day.

The punch landed with devastating force, pummeling straight into the machine's face. He watched as the Felix's body reeled backward through space, spinning round and round with limbs askew. And at that moment, as the Felix fell through the smoky air, Vengelis knew he could win. He could destroy this machine.

But suddenly, an arm wrapped around his neck, and the back of his head was pulled into someone's unseen chest. The chest was burning, and Vengelis felt the tingle of flames sift through his hair. He knew at once it was the male Felix he had seen in the flames. Struggling, Vengelis could not break the unyielding grip. The sizzling flames of the Felix's forearms and chest were nothing but a tickle against Vengelis's impervious flesh, but the snakelike chokehold was suffocating him by the second. Dizzying blood began to pool in his head. Vengelis flailed his body as the caustic stench of his smoldering armor filled his nostrils. A dark hole began to spread from the center of his vision, and soon he could see only black. Vengelis thrashed his limbs into the mysterious body in frenzy, though the Felix easily sustained every hit. All he could feel beyond the strangulation was deep and infuriating confusion. In the midst of his despair, Vengelis felt a rocking blow in the darkness. The arm wrapped around his windpipe released at once.

He was free.

Vengelis fell into space, descending into a dim oblivion in a barely conscious haze. As his body rotated and spun in freefall, the pressure in his head steadily subsided. His vision began to return. Within the same instant he was upright and regaining his composure floating far over the rooftops of Sejeroreich. He looked up to see Master Tolland engaged in combat with the burning Felix.

His teacher had saved his life.

Vengelis burst upward toward their struggle. No words needed to be spoken between the two Sejero warriors. Together Vengelis and Master Tolland assailed the lone burning Felix. As they did so, the blonde Felix returned. Vengelis gladly focused his attack on her. She evaded several of his advances until he leveled a strike into her gut that sent her reeling across the rooftops of the city and nearly out of sight.

"Vengelis, this is not a winning fight. There are more of these machines down in the streets. That first punch broke my wrist." Master Tolland was winded already, breathing heavily with forceful wheezes and cradling his malformed right hand in his left. He looked older and wearier than Vengelis had ever seen him. "Trust me and do as I say, Vengelis. You have to escape. We . . . together . . . can't beat these demons."

"I can't." Vengelis screamed to him. "You of all people know I can't!"

"You must go! I know it will be difficult, but in order to defend your people, you have to leave—and leave right now. I wish I were younger and could be of greater help to you, but my time has passed. Go to Filgaia"—as Master Tolland spoke, the west portion of the palace collapsed beneath them with a roar that drained out his voice. When it subsided Vengelis only heard—"only if you work *together!*"

Panicked and shocked by the volume of the historic palace's collapse, Vengelis ignored Master Tolland's plea. He saw the blonde Felix coming, and he charged full speed toward her with everything he had. Either he or the machine would be dead before this fight was through. They met with a blur of speed. Vengelis launched every ounce of power within the well of his being at the strange machine. One after another his hits began to hit their marks. Vengelis was faster than her, he was certain of it. He caught the side of the machine's face with a brutal fist, sending it stumbling, and he broke away for a split second, out of breath and exhausted. Nausea rose in his core and his muscles burned from fatigue. Vengelis looked down to the barracks far below, and saw something that turned his blood to ice. The enormous Royal Transport was lifting off from the barracks, ascending into the shifting ruinous skies over Sejeroreich. Eve and his mother were on board, along with all of the Royal families and the hopes of his people. This was the moment. They were following his last order to escape while he distracted the machines.

As the prodigious transport rose from the barracks, Vengelis discerned something flying after it. With sudden dread, Vengelis exploded toward the lone pursuer. In his heart he knew it was another one of the Felixes. As he did so, the blonde Felix charged after him as he bore down on the huge transport. Without the slightest difficulty, she caught up to him. He was flying as fast as he could when from his blindside a burning elbow careened into the center of his face. Vengelis felt his nose break and his face burst with a crunching of bones and cartilage.

The Felixes had surrounded him.

Vengelis squinted through watering eyes and unspeakable pain as the distant Felix caught up to the Royal Transport and tore into the side of the giant craft like a missile, disappearing entirely into the steel hull. The transport split down the middle, and for a moment Vengelis caught a glimpse of its riven innards: steel supports, command decks, hallways. Then the fuel cells sparked, and the craft erupted into white-hot flames. Two smoldering halves of the gigantic ship plummeted to the ground far below, marring the sky with a broad streak of smoke.

Desperate, Vengelis now turned to see the blonde Felix brutally beating Master Tolland. His teacher was going to die, and Vengelis had not followed his last order. But Vengelis could not bring himself to flee. He turned his back to Master Tolland and began to fly toward the falling wreckage. Yet another Felix was already on him. His last vision was the pieces of the transport crashing through the roof of the maimed palace far below.

There were too many of them. His family was dead, and he knew he would soon follow. Vengelis reached out to the distant calamity as the blonde Felix—having defeated Master Tolland—mounted her legs around his midsection and began to unleash a flood of eager punches at his undefended face. Vengelis vaguely felt his head rock back and forth from each blow. His jaw cracked and each of his cheekbones shattered from the consecutive knocks. Soon the strikes felt like nothing at all, he was so loosely clinging to consciousness.

Vengelis descended limply through space, free falling toward the ground, his face unrecognizable and his armor cracked and shredded to ribbons. Closer he fell toward the ruined and burning intersections of his once beloved Sejeroreich.

...

Throbbing pain pumped relentlessly in the vast emptiness. Excruciating blackness. From his head through his body to his feet, he was only aware of the blinding, pulsing pain. His thoughts were a torturous mixture of inadequacy and dread.

Death. The savior gods, the Epsilons, had fallen at last.

An incoherent whispery voice came through his stupor, perhaps his own. It was cracked and parched, foreign to his ears. Vengelis tried to force his eyelids open, but all he could see was a slit of light through the swelling of his eye sockets. The pulsing blood pumping through his ears drowned out all sound. His consciousness slipped away, and Vengelis sank into the abyss.

CHAPTER EIGHT

Kristen

The two cups of coffee on her desk were both empty, and computer print-outs from the previous year were piled around her. Kristen was deeply concerned in the wake of her conversation with Cara Williams. Her entire afternoon had been spent sifting through past Vatruvian cell research for any clue—even the most miniscule or trivial figure—that might explain this crisis. Genetic codes for the Vatruvian cell's unusual protein structures scrolled across Kristen's monitor as Cara Williams's confession churned through her thoughts. With a frustrated sigh, Kristen let her shoulders sink into her chair and took a sip of water from her Nalgene bottle. She knew Cara Williams had told the truth.

The Vatruvian cell was anatomically superior to the very cells in which it replicated.

According to Cara's data, the Vatruvian cells were flourishing in habitats that killed their natural counterparts. Their synthesized cells were flourishing in one-hundred-eighty-degree environments. That was up in the temperature realm of rare extremophiles, not run of the mill research bacteria. It was not right. Kristen was scouring her old research in hopes of finding some over-looked detail that might explain this strange phenomenon.

Professor Vatruvia clearly did not share Kristen and Cara's reservations. He was accelerating headfirst into a technology so immensely groundbreaking that no regulations existed to control it. On the contrary, from what Kristen could gather from the Department of Defense representative at their meeting, gov-ernmental powers seemed keen on keeping apprised of the technology and promoting its progress. And now it was becoming clear that the basic properties of this technology were not fully understood by the very people who created it. Kristen cursed man's lack of respect for the awesome forces of science and nature. How many times in history had an overzealous scientist endangered or even taken human lives in the name of progress? How many victim stories would have to be relived in each generation?

During the early days of X-ray technology, the first pioneers of radiology had no knowledge of the inherent ionizing radiation within their new marvel. The unobservable exposure, a byproduct of their own creation, eventually killed them all. Scientists demonstrated their new wonder to audiences and colleagues by sticking their own hands, even their heads, under the hazardous X-rays. The captivating images of their underlying skeletal structure were breathtaking, and in the process they all developed terminal cancer from the obscene levels of exposure. It was not until years later that scientists realized it was in fact their own technology causing the radiation poisoning.

Regulation came after it was too late.

Kristen also thought of the early days of nuclear bomb testing in Nevada. US government scientists tested their new toys of destruction in an area that came to be proudly named the Nevada Proving Ground. Twenty years later, people that had the misfortune of living downwind from the test site had developed fatal nuclear fallout poisoning. The government provided sincere condolences and monetary compensation, but it was no comfort to the people who had lost their loved ones to science's brash enthusiasm.

Regulation came after it was too late.

The list went on and on, through every epoch of history. Collateral damage was an undeniable byproduct of any revolution, social or scientific. Now Kristen Jordan found herself, a scientist of the technologically and ethically *mature* modern age, jumping right onto the same bandwagon: blindly pushing a technology forward with little regard for the consequences and inherent dangers.

Kristen's head ached from frustration and too much caffeine as she tried to figure out the root of the Vatruvian cell's anomalous physical traits. She placed her bottle down and was about to delve back into her old notes, when a voice nearly startled her.

"Hi there, kiddo."

Kristen swiveled to see Professor Vatruvia standing beside the door. He invited himself into her workspace and sat down in the seat beside her, crossing his legs and casting her a calm smile.

Pulling herself out of her internal ravine of morose thoughts, Kristen nodded. "Hey, professor."

"How goes your workload?"

"Same as always." Kristen minimized her genetic notes from the year previous and pulled up an application with her current work. "Monotonous mostly."

"Well, we've all certainly spent long hours doing less spectacular laboratory chores in our day." Professor Vatruvia's eyes shifted from the computer screen back to her. "Monotony is, unfortunately, a necessary part of the research game."

"The presentation seemed to go over well," Kristen said, her tone measured.

"About that," Professor Vatruvia leaned forward, the bottoms of his slacks lifting from his loafers and revealing patterned socks. "Kristen, I'd like to have a conversation with you about the Vatruvian cell research. I've been doing some serious thinking, and I believe you deserve some answers."

Kristen allowed him to continue. "Deserve some answers" was the understatement of the century. Her knowledge of genetics had been used like a prize racehorse at first, and then cast away like nothing. She knew that in Professor Vatruvia's mind, Kristen Jordan's reservations were her fatal flaw as a scientist.

"It seems your sentiment toward the Vatruvian cell is spreading among the research team. Recently, Cara Williams has started asking me the same questions you've been asking for months now. It seems as though both of you are concerned about the practical applications for this technology."

"Really?" Kristen said, barely bothering to feign surprise.

"Well, it certainly doesn't surprise me. She is directly involved with the stress testing of the cells, and you are the most inquisitive of the team. Cara told me you two had a discussion about the physical traits of the Vatruvian cell this afternoon?"

Kristen lifted her gaze from her notebook, unsure how to react. Cara told Professor Vatruvia about their conversation? He had threatened to fire her if she told anyone about her findings. Cara must have been willing to accept the threat of forced resignation over falsification of data.

"We spoke briefly," Kristen said. "She told me the Vatruvian cells are exhibiting higher anatomical thresholds than the original cells they replicated. It's not a total surprise. After all, that wouldn't be the first peculiarity we've seen. The original Vatruvian cell from last year is still functioning in its petri dish. It's still surviving despite the fact that it hasn't received any nourishment in over a year. So, to some degree I had already considered what Cara told me."

"Indeed," Professor Vatruvia said, and fell into silent thought as he rubbed his chin. "From what I've found, the cells copy most of the physiology and anatomy of the template cells but share little of their biological limitations."

"So it would seem," Kristen said.

"Look . . . Kristen. I believe you only have the best intentions at heart in your concerns over our work. Is that correct?"

Kristen tilted her head tentatively and leaned back in her chair, uncertain what he was after. "Well, yes."

"That's good. That's very good. It is, after all, a favorable trait for a scientist to be skeptical."

"I'm skeptical, but of course I only have the best intentions in mind. That is to say, the best intentions for what the Vatruvian cell can provide for society and the furthering of applied science."

"Yes," Professor Vatruvia said. "For society, of course."

"Look, professor." Kristen sighed wearily. "The only thing I want to know is what the applied use of all this bioengineering is going to be. That's it. The fact is we have one of the most unique technologies ever created at our disposal. Yet there hasn't been the slightest word as to what the Vatruvian technology will *provide*. What it will *actually* do. We are forging an incomprehensibly elaborate and complex tool with no notion of its implementation."

"I understand what you mean." Professor Vatruvia nodded slowly. He removed his glasses and bit one of the stems, surveying her expression as if there was something to exhume in its subtleties.

Kristen was not in the mood to deal with his interrogative stare, and she shook her head in exasperation. "What is it?"

Professor Vatruvia leaned down to his messenger bag. He took out a black leather-bound planner and removed a piece of paper, handing it to Kristen. "You were—are—essential to the development of Vatruvian cell technology. I would like to give you the answers you seek, but you have to understand that I must protect myself and our fragile technology from any unforeseen obstructions that could hinder my vision for the Vatruvian cell."

"What is—" Kristen began to ask, but her voice fell short as she recognized the paper was a nondisclosure contract. Covered in threatening legal argot and the names of various stern-sounding law firms, there was a line at the bottom for her signature. She held the paper at arm's length, as if it was something sordid. And indeed she thought it was.

"You're going to make me sign a nondisclosure agreement?" Kristen asked with revulsion. "Are you *serious*?"

"Quite serious, yes. You must understand how important this delicate period of our research is. One slip up and the entirety of the future of Vatruvian cell technology could be altered permanently. Before you sign, I would draw to your attention the signature of the Secretary of Defense on that paper. If you breach the agreement of the contract, you will be in jeopardy with the various contracted law firms listed, but you will also be accountable to the Department of Defense."

Kristen looked up from the paper and blinked at Professor Vatruvia. "I don't understand. Are you threatening me?"

"Goodness gracious, no. I want to impress upon you how seriously you should take that signature should you choose to sign your name. But if you do sign it, I will show it to you. I will show you what the Vatruvian cell will provide. Well, one of its more grandiose implementations at the very least."

Kristen found herself staring at him, both dubious and apprehensive. What was he talking about? There was a tangible *it* that could to be shown to her? After hearing those words there was no way she would not sign the paper. This was too big not to be a part of. Kristen reached across her desk, picked up a black pen, and on the dotted line signed her name. She stood from her chair, holding out the signed contract to him. "Okay, my mouth is sealed. Show me."

Professor Vatruvia took the contract and placed it in his planner. "You made the right choice."

They exited her lab, and he led her straight up the stairs to the off-limits laboratories on the third floor. The building was empty and quiet, most of the research staff having gone home for the day. Walking through the empty hallway, Kristen felt breathless and fearful at the notion of seeing something beyond the Vatruvian cell itself. Professor Vatruvia stopped before the keypad entry adjacent to one of the heavily locked doors.

"I don't understand," Kristen said as she waited beside him, arms folded across her chest, looking uneasily at the steel door. "What is *it?*"

"You'll see," Professor Vatruvia said, his voice distant as he entered a complex combination into the keypad. The lock beeped and the indicator turned from red to green. He pushed the heavy door open and a rush of air lightly pulled at Kristen's hair. She turned her head in astonishment as her hair fell against her shoulders; the room was an air lock. Professor Vatruvia politely stepped aside and allowed Kristen to enter the laboratory. She stared into the pitch-black darkness beyond the threshold and felt uneasy. The air coming from the laboratory smelled recycled and clean. After brief indecision, Kristen's curiosity claimed her and she stepped in. She stood in the sliver of light coming from the doorway, a high-pitched squeaking sound filling her ears. Professor Vatruvia turned a switch in the darkness, and fluorescent lights flickered on. They stood in a windowless room, similar in size to the downstairs laboratories. But this was the only likeness. No laboratory tables, no recognizable equipment, the lab was foreign to Kristen. The cold steel and recycled air provided the empty room with an unnatural and oddly alienating feel. The door shut behind them, and the whir of the airlock reengaged.

Kristen was alone in the closed atmosphere with Professor Vatruvia, who was standing silently and awaiting her reaction. Her shoulder's slumped as she looked around the room, not sure what to find but expectant of anything. The room was entirely empty: tile floors and vacant walls. Kristen's attention was drawn to the far wall where she heard many small squeaks in the otherwise silent surrounds.

"Uh . . ." Kristen vocalized unconsciously as she realized the source of the squeaking. The far wall was lined floor to ceiling with organized rows of enclosed glass cages, each housing a research mouse. There were dozens of mice, every one secluded in an individual cell.

"We don't use animal testing." Kristen said as she regarded the test mice with a growing unease. "What is this?"

"This is what you wanted to see," Professor Vatruvia's voice was cautious. "The applied technology resulting from all of our efforts."

Kristen scanned up and down the row of cages, and then turned to make sure there was nothing else in the room she had missed. She had been expecting a table with an assembled microscope and a Vatruvian cell slide. "I don't understand. Am I missing something here?"

Professor Vatruvia raised an arm and pointed to the mice. "Right there."

"The test mice?" Kristen stared blankly at the scurrying mice.

"Yes, the mice," Professor Vatruvia said. "Or, to be more specific, the Vatruvian mice."

Kristen felt gooseflesh rise on her arms.

"No," she blurted out, shrinking away from the cages and shaking her head with severity. "No. No. No. That's not possible, absolutely not possible. Even it if were possible, that would be . . . years . . . decades . . . ahead of our progress. We're still at the *cellular* level."

"The team is still at the cellular level. I have been doing my own independent work, allowing the team to provide the appropriate progression for consistent funding." Professor Vatruvia's voice was steady, rehearsed.

Kristen was no longer apprehensive, but outright frightened. She interlocked her fingers on top of her head and shut her eyes. This was grossly unethical—even illegal? Or was it? The mice really represented no greater evil than cloning, and that was legal, though regulated intensely. Hell, cloning was an antiquated technology compared to the Vatruvian cell. But this was different—in some obvious yet elusive way it was inconceivably more disturbing to Kristen.

"These . . ." Kristen motioned to the glass cages in disbelief, her face pale, " . . . aren't real mice?"

"They're Vatruvian mice."

"These are *artificial* mice?" Kristen raised her voice.

"You know the technology," Professor Vatruvia said. He moved to the cages and looked in on the mice with an excited expression. "They are Vatruvian mice, no fundamentally or morally different than the Vatruvian cell."

Kristen knew he was telling the truth. It would not have been a stretch for her to create the mice herself with her knowledge of the Vatruvian cell and genetics. The mice were Vatruvian organisms. She also recognized that on some perversely theoretical level he had a point—artificial life was artificial life, what did it matter the size or complexity? Yet it felt instinctively wrong as she stared at the frantic movements of the mice behind their glass cages.

"I know what you're thinking. That this is unethical. But it isn't. These mice are no more alive than the glass surrounding them or the steel on which you stand."

"They seem pretty goddamn alive to me." Kristen turned to him and spoke over the high-pitched squeaking of the mice.

Professor Vatruvia's gaze moved from mouse to mouse. "All it took was the first cellular replication. Once I established that, the various tissue structures fell into place easily given the knowledge of the mouse genome. After I showed you the Vatruvian cell replication images earlier, I realized it was useless to hide this work from you; you would figure it out anyway. You're just as capable a scientist as I."

"Of course I *could* have figured it out . . . *could* have conceived of it." Kristen felt herself getting angry, disgusted. "But I would never have gone ahead and *done* it!"

"To be perfectly honest, part of me was concerned you would consider moonlighting and creating a Vatruvian animal for a private research company."

Kristen took a deep breath and tried to think clearly.

"This is *bigger* than me, professor. This is bigger than you. Artificial life is way, way too large a discovery to be sitting in an air-locked room like this. If Columbia finds out that you've been creating these mice without their approval, they will almost certainly let you go. If the government and international watchdog agencies get wind of this, I don't even know what will happen. This is super, super immoral!"

"Now hold on one minute, Kristen!" Professor Vatruvia held out a stern finger. "First of all, no one is going to find out about this in the near future. You signed the contract. Secondly, nothing will happen when people find out about this development. These Vatruvian mice might be something we're not accustomed to, but for all intents and purposes they're blunt instruments with biological construction. They're no different than the first Vatruvian cell—and that was celebrated by the public and academia both."

Kristen shook her head in frustration. "No one is going to consider these *mice* blunt instruments."

"All new technologies are feared at first. But that fear can't be allowed to hinder the search for potential in the unknown. Think about electricity, or the airplane o-o-or one of the first vaccines ever administered. Of course, they were a bit . . . scary at first. But think of how far they have brought civilization. There is *nothing* unethical going on here, just unadulterated pioneering. A synthetic organism is the only logical progression in synthetic biology. You said so yourself in your own undergraduate thesis. This is what we've been working toward."

Kristen's mouth moved to speak, but she stopped herself, in disbelief of his one-dimensionality.

"Professor," she said with strained earnestness as she pointed to one of the mice. "*This* isn't electricity, or transportation, or some medicine. We're talking about the creation of a new form of life. A form of life that, according to our data, is more efficient than biological life. You really don't think there is some inherent danger behind creating a synthetic mouse that is physically superior to a natural mouse?"

"No. I don't," Professor Vatruvia said with a rising anger in his own voice. "Not at all. And don't you dare go down that road, implying Vatruvian organisms are fundamentally dangerous. There is not one single solitary aspect of their construction that would substantiate that standpoint."

"You mean beyond their very existence? Beyond being alive?"

"Being alive makes something dangerous now?

"Yes, it absolutely does."

"How?"

"By ways so self-evident that they require no explanation."

Professor Vatruvia took a step away from her, his expression hurt. "You yourself helped me create the genetic code for the Vatruvian cell, and thus for these mice. I assure you they are not dangerous in any way. Our computer scientists designed a computer chip that's embedded in their brains; it controls their entire endocrine systems and brainwave functioning. They can only act through controlled response. I made that a fundamental part of their design."

Kristen's mind raced as she considered his argument. "Prove it."

Professor Vatruvia walked to the side of the cages and picked up a remote control labeled *twenty-two* from a tray. "Look at the mouse in cage twenty-two," he said as he examined the remote.

Kristen scanned the glass enclosures for twenty-two. The cage was at her eye level. On the other side of the glass, a little brown mouse with white mottled spots was moving about frantically. Kristen frowned. The mouse's movements seemed unusually agitated. It was charging the walls of glass over and over again. The impacts of the mouse's head against the hard surface did not sound as though they came from a light mouse, but from a much heavier object. Kristen was glad it was enclosed in its cage; she would have been standing on a table if the mouse were loose in the room. The physical appearance of the mouse seemed to match a natural mouse flawlessly. Its fine whiskers and ungainly tail looked much like any other. Kristen watched the mouse pause for a moment and scratch the front of its button nose with tiny paws before running headlong into the glass once more. One would never consider that this little breathing animal before her was a synthetic organism.

Then Kristen noticed the mouse's eyes.

She took her glasses out of her shirt pocket and pushed them against her nose, leaning closer to the glass and peering at the little mouse. The retinas did not look right. Kristen studied the mouse's strange eyes for a long moment. They were an odd bluish color, strikingly inconsistent with the rest of its shabby pigmentation. The color was not a dull milky paleness from cataracts. The mouse's eyes were almost . . . bright. Kristen could not be sure if it was due to the odd lighting of the room, but the eyes seemed to be emitting a bluish glow.

"Watch this," Professor Vatruvia said. He pressed one of the buttons on the remote, and instantly the mouse fell on its side, completely unconscious, its pink underbelly rising and falling with rapid breaths.

"How?" Kristen asked, slowly taking her attention away from the sleeping mouse back to Professor Vatruvia.

He smiled proudly. "Like I said, a microchip in the brain provides us complete control."

The few dozen other mice were scattering about their holding cells. Kristen sidestepped slowly across the wall of cages, her eyes lingering on each mouse in turn. The mice all appeared perfectly normal in every aspect, except for the overexcited behavior and the blue eyes. Kristen noticed every one of them had the same strange blue retinas. For a long time Kristen watched the mice, feeling only shame. Their research was no longer standing on the precipice of a slippery slope—it was careening and plummeting downward. Professor Vatruvia was playing god, a life giver to the concrete sentience of a new kingdom of life. And if Professor Vatruvia was to be Zeus, then Kristen undoubtedly also sat on a throne among the pantheon of Olympians.

"Now there is no longer any concealment. No more secrets to hide," Professor Vatruvia said at last, turning the controller in his hands. "I hope you will understand the prudence of my keeping the knowledge of these mice private. But it was time for you to see them."

"Who else knows about the mice?" Kristen asked.

"Very few, and no one on the research team. That is a testament to my trust in you, Kristen. But you see," he placed the remote back into the bin by the squealing cages, "on Friday we are scheduled to give a presentation at a hotel down in Midtown. Are you familiar with the ICST?"

"The International Committee on Science and Technology?" Kristen asked, perplexed. "Yes."

"Well, their yearly convention is coming up. They've asked me to give a presentation on our research progression. The scientific world is begging for an update, and I think its only fair that I deliver."

"You're going to reveal the mice?"

"No, not the mice. But I will show the public our advancement of Vatruvian cell cellular replication. The same development you and the team saw today. The mice will have to be revealed after a series of slow steps."

"Many minds will jump to the same conclusion I did," Kristen said. "Your peers will realize the significance of the cellular replication, even if the majority of the research team at the meeting didn't."

"You overestimate the minds of the scientific community, I think."

Kristen found nothing to say as she stared at the cages.

"Well," Professor Vatruvia sighed. "The convention is at the Marriot Marquis hotel next week. The ICST event planners asked me to come with one of my top graduate students to help present our work. The scientific world wants to know more about the young minds I choose to work with. I thought you might enjoy the networking opportunity."

Kristen was familiar with the convention. The ICST was a huge foundation that published a number of prominent peer-reviewed journals. It was a big deal. There would be top scientists in attendance from all around the world. Professor Vatruvia's presentation would almost certainly be the main event. It would be a huge opportunity for her, though at the moment Kristen was unable to focus on anything but the Vatruvian mice squealing beside her.

"What do you think?" Professor Vatruvia asked. "Want to do me a favor now that there are no secrets between us?"

Kristen stared at the mouse in cage twenty-two. It was still out cold, its tiny chest moving with breaths. "Yeah, I'll go to the hotel convention. But I'm not finished with questions about these mice. And I'm *absolutely* not through with questions on the applications of this technology."

"Well. Security closes the building down at six." Professor Vatruvia said, checking his watch. "It's five of."

Kristen slowly drew her attention away from the unconscious mouse. All the other mice were moving excitedly, hysterically. The nature of their movements seemed strange, not timid like one would expect from a mouse. But Kristen thought she may have perceived it that way because she knew what they really were. "I will come along with you and explain what I have done for the project. But if I'm asked what I think about the ethical issues around Vatruvian technology I *will* give my honest opinion, which is that they are in desperate need of regulation."

"Look," Professor Vatruvia said. "We'll have plenty of time to discuss all your issues. I wouldn't expect you to answer any question at the convention untruthfully. I'm only going to announce the Vatruvian cell's replication for now. I don't think the public is ready for the knowledge of the Vatruvian mice. I showed you them so you understand we are on the same page. No secrets."

Professor Vatruvia opened the stainless steel door to a gust of the airlock and they left the mice in darkness. As they walked through the lobby and out of the building, Kristen found herself unable to hold a thought. The enormity of what she had just witnessed was hard to comprehend, his nonchalant attitude staggering. When they reached the cool autumn air and bustling crowd of the street, Kristen turned south toward her apartment, and Professor Vatruvia began to walk north. She paused, her gaze lingering on the rooftops of Columbia's buildings. She knew what she had to do. If she did not do what was right, who would?

With mustered resolve she turned and jogged down the sidewalk after him. "Professor!"

Professor Vatruvia turned to her and stepped aside to avoid the crowding sidewalk. "Yes?"

Kristen shook her head, fully aware of the significance of her decision. "I'm sorry, professor, but maybe you've made a mistake in telling me the truth. If you don't want to tell the scientific community at the convention about what I just saw, fine. But I want proof that you've privately informed regulatory agencies about these mice in the next few weeks. If you don't, I'm going to resign from my doctorate program and go public with what I just saw. I know how much it means to you, I really do, but this is too immense to be held secret between a few people."

Professor Vatruvia looked physically stunned, his expression crestfallen. He shook his head with deflation and leaned against the glass of a storefront. "You would jeopardize everything we've done? All the things we can still achieve? And for what? So some opportunistic journalist can vilify what we are doing and twist the nature of our work until the self-righteous voice of the naive masses demand us to stop?"

"I—"

"We have a chance to achieve *greatness* here, Kristen, a chance to introduce the world to a future brilliant with innovation."

Kristen shook her head. "I'm sorry, professor. But this is too big. The world needs to know."

CHAPTER NINE

Vengelis

Dreams, nightmares mostly, emerged and receded like the ebb and flow of a shadowy tide in Vengelis Epsilon's unconscious mind. Familiar faces cried out in pain, and venerated buildings fell to ruin with excruciating vividness. All the while perilous blue eyes stared unblinking at him through the void, filling his heart with hopelessness and exhaustion. Memories came to life in his tumultuous visions. Vengelis looked through a window into his own distant past.

In his mind he was sixteen again.

Vengelis recalled the day. Frost in his lungs, cold air against his skin, the wind swirled around him and whistled in his ears. It was his first journey to the bitter North, his first glimpse of Mount Karlsbad and Master Tolland. He was up to his knees in snow, a thick coat wrapped him in his own heat and a bag of spare clothes slung over his back. He stood in front of a rundown wooden cabin that was little more than a shed, its walls barely standing upright against the blistering gusts in the late afternoon dimness. Gathering clouds brooded around him, impenetrable against the side of the mountain. A smell of coming snowfall filled his nostrils. Vengelis called out to the cabin, knowing he would soon be enveloped in what the clouds had to offer him.

"Tolland! Master Borneo Tolland!"

After a moment the door to the hovel opened. Vengelis caught a passing glimpse of a fireplace burning within. From inside the cabin, an average-sized man emerged. The hermit looked to be in his early sixties, his features more seasoned than old. He was holding a wide ceramic pot against his chest. Taking no notice of the heir to the Epsilon throne, the graying man turned and trudged through the deep snow toward a lofty snowdrift left by the relentless wind. As Vengelis watched him, flakes of snow began falling silently from the gloom of clouds. They eddied around him, weightless and beautiful. Vengelis pulled his fur hood over his head and took a step toward the man, who seemed entirely unaware of the impending storm or the bone-freezing cold as he brushed loose snow into the pot with an outstretched arm.

Master Tolland then spoke.

"This is perhaps the most crucial chore to living here, because it is the only real necessity. The snow must be boiled down of course—even this northern isolation provides little reprieve from the pollution of Anthem. But among the many other unnecessary chores, creating water is a must." Master Tolland peered up into the dark drear overhead. He said nothing for some time and seemed to savor the imminence of the blizzard before he lowered his eyes and looked at Vengelis. "But that is ultimately the purpose of living here. Only necessities."

Vengelis remained silent, taking note of the man's unkempt condition with disapproval. Behind this man's disheveled appearance was unmistakable Royal blood. His brow was sharp, cheekbones high, and his hands looked strong and enduring, but it was hard for Vengelis to look past his threadbare impression. He was not impressed.

"Though over time," Master Tolland smirked, as if he could read Vengelis's thoughts. "Over time I can't deny that I have developed an appreciation for the mundane. There is some cathartic value to the structure daily chores provide. It is, after all, our routines that root us in our reality. I take it you are Prince Vengelis Epsilon?"

Vengelis nodded, in disbelief his father had ordered him to this place—to this unsophisticated man.

"Even here, rumors have reached my ears of your deeds," Master Tolland said. "Very impressive to be declared the greatest warrior of Anthem at your age. Especially considering your lack of formal training."

"I have received formal training."

"Is that so?"

"I worked with the most prestigious coaches of the Imperial First Class for many years. They awarded me their highest rank when I was thirteen. Their lessons were marginal at best." Vengelis's tone was indifferent. "Now I teach them."

"Hmm." Master Tolland raised his eyebrows. "Tell me, Vengelis, how old are you?"

"Sixteen."

"Do you think you'll be able to disregard my tutelage as easily?"

"Yes," Vengelis said at once.

"Perhaps you will."

"I read about you before I left Sejeroreich," Vengelis said. "You used to be quite a warrior. Used to be. I have to say, you're older than I was expecting."

Master Tolland chuckled in a genial, confident manner. "It seems as though we are experiencing similar disappointment in our first impressions. You are shorter than I had envisioned."

"Bold of you to insult an Epsilon. I'll give you that at the very least," Vengelis said. "You are the last of the Tolland family line as I understand it?"

"I am."

"And you have no heir?"

"My Sejero bloodline will die with me, if that is what you are getting at."

"Waste," Vengelis said with genuine anger. "It's against the law for a Royal son to have no heir. Though I'm sure you already know that."

"I do not consider myself a member of your father's empire, in case you couldn't tell." Master Tolland raised a hand, indicating their thousand-mile harsh isolation on all sides. "As such, I am not obliged to follow anything but my own will."

Vengelis nodded skeptically.

"You are here by the mandate of your father?" Master Tolland said after a prolonged silence.

"Yes."

"Welcome to Mount Karlsbad. Here you are a guest. Here you are the student, and I the teacher. Such superficial notions as lineage and heredity are irrelevant here."

Vengelis smiled smugly as he looked at the veritable beggar standing before him. He tossed the bag of spare clothes his servants had packed for him into the snow, and he began to limber up. "All right, I've had enough. I'd like to get back to Sejeroreich by sundown, and it's cold as hell out here. I came here to appease my father, but this is becoming ridiculous. I really don't want to inadvertently kill you, old man. If you submit and walk back into your . . ." Vengelis eyed Master Tolland's shack. "*House.* I won't tell anyone. I can lie and say you put up a surprising fight for a guy your age."

"I suppose this is one way to do it." Master Tolland placed his pot in the snow beside his front door. He also began to limber himself, stretching with a flexibility that surprised Vengelis for a man his age. "If you can defeat me, I will allow you to leave for home immediately. I will write a personal letter to your father, Emperor Faris, stating that I have nothing of worth to teach you. Does that sound fair?"

Without the slightest word or nod of agreement, Vengelis erupted forward, throwing his right fist at the man's nose. Master Tolland easily sidestepped, and Vengelis's arm crashed through the door of his cabin. Warmth and the fragrance of simmering stew wafted through the doorframe.

"Your first task will be to build me a new door."

Vengelis laughed and launched another wild swing. Then something happened he did not entirely understand. He registered Master Tolland moving very quickly, and then within an instant, his back was buried in the snow. The old man had tripped him. Vengelis tried to jump to his feet, but Master Tolland had a strange hold on his right arm. He was pushed shoulder first into the snow once more, and Vengelis realized with a shock of pain in his elbow that he was caught in a submission lock.

He seethed. He screamed. He threatened.

"What are your thoughts on discipline, young Prince?" Master Tolland asked from behind his shoulder, his voice as calm as it had been a minute previous.

Vengelis was covered in snow. It melted on his fuming and trembling cheeks.

"I . . . don't . . . have . . . thoughts . . . on . . . discipline!" Vengelis screamed, his eyes nearly bursting out of his sockets with rage. The pain in his arm was beyond anything he had ever felt, beyond anything he could have imagined.

"*How?*" Vengelis gasped.

Master Tolland released him and Vengelis rolled over and sprawled his limbs through the snow as he gasped for breath, steam pouring off his body from the exertion.

"Then that is your first lesson on the subject," Master Tolland said. "The subject of discipline, that is. I suspect it will be the first of many."

"I don't . . ." Vengelis coughed as newly falling snow landed on his face. "I don't understand."

Master Tolland looked at the young man through the veil of snowfall. "I take on one student at a time. My last pupil recently completed his training. I would not normally take on someone your age as a student. However with him gone, and your unusual circumstances—being heir to the throne—I will accept you. If you wish to possess the kind of abilities I have just showcased, then I encourage you to stay with me here in this northern desolation. I will teach you how to unlock the true potential of the Sejero blood that resides within you. Your training will be complete the day you are able to best me. You will learn technique and theory of the physical arts, as well as the philosophies of power." Master Tolland crouched down to him and placed a hand on his shoulder.

"There is more to Sejero power, in all of its infinite glory and peril, than the blunt strength and foolish arm wrestling contests of the Imperial First Class and the Grand Arena. I hope one day you will come to see that."

Pitch-blackness descended over Vengelis's memory. His dream began to shift and dissipate: thin rays of light penetrating into his chasm of darkness. Even in the diminishing oblivion, hopelessness dominated. Real vision began to come into focus, and with it came excruciating pain.

Vengelis jolted upright with a rattling gasp for air. His eyes burst open in panic and darted across his surrounds. He was in a bed in the middle of a small room. Pure white walls stared back at him on all sides. Beside him a number of monitors and meters beeped and blinked mechanically. Vengelis's lips quivered wordlessly as he looked down at his body. Hospital garments were draped across his shoulders. He shook the heavy snow of his dreamy recollection from his mind and strained to recall his memory, but he found himself unable to hold a thought. Everything was blurry, and a horrible fatigue weighed down his mind.

Throwing his legs over the bed, he attempted to stand but was forced to lean heavily against the wall. His knees wobbled, his arms felt depleted. Dizziness and nausea struck as a rush of blood hit his head from standing so quickly. He hastily pulled off the many life support wires that clung to his body and made his way with slow unsteady steps toward the door. He rubbed cold sweat from his fevered forehead with clammy palms. Where was he? What happened?

A mirror was mounted against the door. As Vengelis approached the narrow reflection and looked upon himself, his chest deflated in shock. His face was barely recognizable. His nose was grotesquely inflamed. A black bruise rounded with deep purple edges extended from the bridge of his nose outward across both cheekbones. Each eye socket was bloated and distended, deep blue black and swollen nearly shut. He painstakingly moved his chin from side to side and attempted to open his mouth. A spasm of pain shot through his jaw past his ears, traveling to the back of his head. One prominent laceration extended deeply across his cheek. It was held together with heavy sutures.

Vengelis averted his eyes from his beaten face. The knuckles and fingers on his right hand were black and scraped. His left hand—

Every nerve in his body went ice cold.

The Blood Ring, his father's ring, was still on his hand. The gleaming crimson diamond shined brilliantly, and at once a tidal wave of agonizing recollections flooded his mind. His battered face contorted, and his fists clenched with blind rage. Vengelis raised his head and let out an agonized scream as he thrashed at his reflection in the mirror. It shattered loudly. The door behind it splintered in two, sundering backward and revealing a white hallway beyond.

He was alive.

Vengelis squeezed his eyelids shut and prayed desperately to be dead. He could not take living—even for a moment—with the torturous memories that now stormed his mind.

The sentiments taking hold of him felt equally foreign to him as the pain in his body. Vengelis had not lost a fight since he was a child, not since Master Tolland bested him on that snowy eve. His first true loss had been to the ruin of all. He reached up to his bruised and tender neck, now remembering all too clearly what had happened to him.

Vengelis's entire body shuddered as he recalled his last moment of consciousness.

The Royal Transport carrying Eve and his mother distinct against the smoke scattered skies beyond. The man-machine that followed in the ship's wake. The schism that tore the craft in two and the plume of bright flames as the ship crashed into the palace. His family was dead and Sejeroreich had been razed to the ground under his watch. Everything massacred by the machines that looked so much like Primus. Vengelis thought for a moment, unable to remember their name. For a long time he stood with his eyes closed, trying to remember.

"Felix," he spoke aloud at last, his voice shaky. Vengelis opened his eyes and pushed through the pieces of the broken door, stepping into the narrow hallway. He recognized the surrounds. A feint and steady vibration beneath his feet registered in his senses.

He was on a ship.

A few indistinguishable doors trailed off in each direction. The hallway was silent except for the barely audible thrusting of the muffled engines. Affixed to the wall a few paces from the room he had just exited was a plaque displaying a blue-and-white diagram of a small spacecraft, surely the one he was now aboard. His perplexity grew. Vengelis did not recognize the simplistic floor plan. It was miniscule compared to the Epsilon Royal Transports. There was a command bridge, two medical rooms, and enough space in the living quarters to provide for a few people at most. Below the diagram a plaque read: *Harbinger I, sister ship to the Traverser I. Both ships created under the specifications of Pral Nerol.*

Vengelis stared at the plaque. *The Harbinger I.* It was by far the smallest ship he had ever boarded. The Epsilons normally traveled in the extravagance of vastly larger ships that held hundreds of passengers and servants. He turned from the diagram and walked toward the command deck. Someone had some explaining to do, and they would be punished for robbing him of a death in battle. The metal door hissed open as he reached the command bridge.

A lone man was sitting in the deck examining several monitors as Vengelis stepped in. The man jumped to attention, startled by Vengelis's abrupt entry. "Hail, Emperor Vengelis Epsilon!"

Vengelis was familiar with the generously proportioned mass of his sparring partner, the Royal Guard Krell Darien.

"It's good to see you on your feet again, my lord," Darien stammered, his deep intonation breaking the strained silence. "For a while we weren't sure if you would make it."

Vengelis simply stared at his Royal Guard at a loss for words. His infuriation was transforming into dangerous volatility, ready to ignite with the slightest spark.

"With much luck and through great adversary, my lord, we've escaped Anthem. Lord General Hoff is on board with us as well. It's the middle of the night—though there's really no difference between night and day on this ship. He is sleeping in his quarters. We've been taking shifts and awaiting your arousal for several days. The Lord General and I were able to find you and flee Sejeroreich. All has been lost to the power of the Felix, but—"

"Escaped," Vengelis said, his voice weak. "Escaped. What does that mean, *we escaped?*"

"My lord, the palace was completely destroyed when Hoff and I arrived at the capital. Sejeroreich was . . . unrecognizable. You and Master Tolland were much faster than us; we didn't make it to the city until long after you. We tried to establish what was happening, but . . ." Darien trailed off, his expression bleak.

"Yes?"

"But there were no soldiers *left* still standing, my lord. We encircled the city and searched for you and Master Tolland." Darien paused, unable to look Vengelis in the eye and instead staring at his boots, affecting a childlike demeanor. "We eventually found Master Tolland in the midst of the massacre. He . . . he had fallen, and lost a lot of blood by the time we found—"

"What happened to him?"

"He was . . ." Darien shook his head. "He was killed by a Felix, my lord."

"A Felix . . ." Vengelis murmured, his mind unable to function.

"Master Tolland was at his last breath when Lord General Hoff and I came upon him. But, my lord, he was conscious. Master Tolland told us you were buried in the rubble of the building beside him. He ordered us to find you and take you to his ship, this ship, the *Harbinger I*. It was docked outside Sejeroreich. He ordered us to leave Anthem with you on board and head to some unchartered planet called . . ." Darien glanced down at the monitor in front of him. "Filgaia."

Vengelis stared at Darien icily.

"Master Tolland gave us the coordinates to the planet and then, then he . . . he passed on."

"Are you lying to me?" Vengelis said.

"What?" Darien immediately bowed and lowered his gaze to the floor. "I would never lie to you, my lord. I swear upon my family's honor that I tell the truth. Lord General Hoff can confirm my story if you wish to wake him."

Vengelis frowned. It was clear Darien was not lying. What had Master Tolland been talking about? He had surely been delirious and these fools followed his order without question. "Turn the ship around immediately."

Darien tensed, as though he had been saving the worst news for last.

"Direct the ship back to Anthem. We return to Sejeroreich right now," Vengelis repeated, emotion rising in his voice. "The last Epsilon is not going to flee from the destruction of Anthem."

"My lord, that is something we can not do."

"Excuse me?"

"Th-the ship was ordered to be placed under irreversible autopilot until we reach Filgaia."

A silence fell between them, the whir of the engines and the soft beeps of the control station making Vengelis dizzy. "Who issued that order?" Vengelis asked, his expression turning more deadly by the moment.

"Master Tolland," Darien said quietly. "It was his dying breath. Hoff and I obeyed."

Vengelis placed his hands on his face, moving his fingers across the sutured gash that ran across his cheek. The laceration penetrated through to the inside of his mouth, and he tongued the sutures. He recalled the fingernail of the woman that had so easily inflicted the wound, the fingernail of the Felix. His logic began to flounder, unable to find a foothold. Vengelis stared down at the Blood Ring. All the generations of the immensely powerful Epsilon forebearers that came before him had worn this ring. For two thousand years the Epsilon family dynasty had survived, only to collapse due to his first failing act as emperor.

"What is Filgaia?" he asked at last, still looking at the illustrious ring and his scabbed knuckles.

Darien looked up in astonishment. "It's a planet that's really far away, from what we gathered from Master Tolland's coordinates. It doesn't seem to be in the Imperial database." There was concern in his Royal Guard's voice. "Hoff and I assumed you would know what it was. We thought you would understand why Master Tolland directed us there."

"I have absolutely no idea. I've never heard of it." Vengelis shook his head. "And what are we supposed to do about Anthem and the remainder of my people while we are out in the middle of nowhere?"

Darien gave a great sorrowful sigh. "All is lost."

"It is not lost." Vengelis looked at Darien threateningly. "It cannot be lost. And if it is lost, then it will be remade. We—I—can't *leave* while the Primus race falls." Vengelis realized he was screaming hoarsely, his temper overtaking him. "I am the most powerful Primus alive, the strongest Sejero warrior to ever live, the last living Epsilon. I can't be absent while Anthem falls to ashes. The purest Sejero blood flows through my veins. I am a living god, and gods do not bow to machines!" Vengelis stopped short in an attempt to check his fury. "This is the last time I will tell you to turn the ship around."

"I really am sorry, my lord, but there is no possible way I can disengage the autopilot until we reach Filgaia. That's the way the computer systems are wired—we are merely passengers now. The ship won't arrive at Filgaia for a number of days. Once we get there and the lock on the autopilot disengages, I will be able to take us back to Anthem as quickly as possible." Darien sat down in the pilot seat and attempted to show him the autopilot lock.

Vengelis stood behind the Royal Guard. "Stand up."

"Sir, we were only following Master Tolland's direct command to us," Darien said.

"Master Tolland is dead! For all of his humility and caution in the face of our power, an even more malicious force has now devoured us. Did the Felixes give a damn about morals? Master Tolland's pacifism, his unwillingness to see the truth for what it really is, forced him to an early grave. Every hour spent listening to his endlessly reproving lectures should have been spent brutally training, training harder than we could have imagined. Now it is lost." Vengelis looked down at Darien. "I said get up."

"Yes, my lord." Darien stood, towering eight feet tall.

"I was robbed of an honorable death in defense of Anthem. My legacy has now been forever tarnished. You will take me back to my planet so I can die alongside my forefathers."

Darien shook his head sadly. "My lord, if I could, of course I would. You are the emperor and I would not fail you were it within my power."

"Your power?" Vengelis repeated. "You have no power. You are weak. You live off the scraps of those who are strong. The Sejero blood is so dwindled in your veins that you should be ashamed to even call yourself a Primus."

Vengelis almost reached out to strangle Darien by his substantial throat, but instead he turned away from the giant Royal Guard. "How far is this Filgaia planet?"

"Far, sir. Filgaia is well beyond the range of most Imperial ships. The autopilot won't disengage for many days."

"And there is absolutely no way to turn it off?"

"No, sir. Pral Nerol himself constructed this ship for Master Tolland. There's no way we'll be able to get around his programming."

Vengelis closed his eyes in a futile attempt to calm himself. The Emperor of the Epsilon would be traveling through space on the spontaneous whim of a dying man while Anthem fell to devastation and his people were slaughtered. What would future stories say of his actions if indeed a future were certain?

"I'll be in the captain's quarters," Vengelis said, and without another word turned and exited the command deck, pacing the narrow hallway. He stopped briefly to check each of the other living quarters. Alegant Hoff was sleeping in one of the rooms. Vengelis paused for a moment and watched his Lord General's enormous chest move up and down with breath. Hoff should have known better than to listen to Master Tolland. Vengelis gingerly flexed the muscles in his right forearm. Shooting pain, surely a broken wrist. He would need more time in one of the medical rooms, but not right now. Vengelis entered the captain's quarters and locked the door behind him.

There was work to do.

CHAPTER TEN

Gravitas

A brisk wind rose from the high country in the cloud darkened north and roughly blew his brown hair across his face. His solemn expression was cold and hard like the landscape far below. Gravitas Nerol opened his eyes, bringing into focus the shimmering frozen vastness of nearby mountains and the lonely hills scattered about their slopes.

His looks were winsome and Royal like his father's once had been, though Gravitas's young face was etched in maturity beyond his years. Gravitas broke from his meditation with a long deep breath. The frigid air felt sharply rejuvenating, its icy touch reaching the depths of his lungs. His nose was runny from the cold, and he sniffed as he pulled the hood of his tarnished crimson cloak over his head. The worn fabric of the cloak was thick and ragged. Old burn marks had left holes in the faded red stitching and along the blackened lower hem.

Gravitas turned in the mountain air and flew northward against the wind, traveling through towering craggy peaks that rose in daring enmity between earth and sky. The heavy crimson cloak billowed wildly in the wind beyond his feet. Though he was as accustomed to the cold as the sparse scattering of high-elevation wildlife below, he tucked the cloak's scorched fabric across his chin and nose to insulate his face from the biting wind. Only his eyes were then visible through the masklike visage, providing him with the dangerous appearance of a bandana-clad rogue.

Snow-capped peaks and dirt-encrusted glaciers passed by far below, and a wispy trail of moisture shifted between the precipitous mountainsides. Aside from the vigorous wind, the entire landscape sat in absolute stillness. The silence was his sanctum. Gravitas flew with little haste across the sky, appearing as a tiny speck from the towering mountains far below, before he disappeared into a gathering of gloomy snow clouds.

Gravitas enjoyed his time spent here in the blustery high altitudes. He was somewhere in the northern reaches of the Canadian Rockies, though precisely where he could not venture a guess. It was here, far away from the sounds and worries of the world, that Gravitas felt most at peace. The touch of wind against his face and the frigid air in his nostrils brought him back to a childhood on Mount Karlsbad. Grueling days spent training with Master Tolland, and nights spent shivering by the drafty fireplace immersed in passionate discussions on the great responsibilities inherent in bearing Sejero blood. Did his old teacher still live on Mount Karlsbad? Did his parents still think about him? Gravitas wondered if anyone still thought about him: the last heir of the Nerol line who one day vanished and never returned.

But this ultimately was his fate—his immense punishment—to never know.

It may as well have been a death sentence, his banishment. The exile had been the death of Gravitas Nerol. Yet he had come to terms with his forlorn desolation many years ago. Over time the intensity of his piping hot emotions had dulled into bitter acceptance. One had to accept his lot in life or succumb to the great weight of doubt and self-pity.

A realization snuck up on him and shook him from his silent meditation. It was the fourth anniversary of his exile—the banishment from his home.

His home.

"Anthem," Gravitas Nerol whispered to the stoic mountaintops, perhaps to remind his heart that his memories were real. Yet Anthem was a perilous world, a perilous word, and he dared not speak it too loud—not even to the vastness of the mountains. Gravitas did not want so awful a phrase to ever be uttered upon this place. His expression betrayed a hint of sadness after his whisper faded in the wind. The people of his past felt more distant and obscure to his own recollection than ever before. Familiar faces, comforting idiosyncrasies, and soothingly recognizable voices of those whom he had loved were veiled by the cruel curtain of time. The good memories, the ones worth keeping, always seemed to fade.

It was the pitiless memories that lingered on with persistent and vivid clarity even after these long four years had passed.

Gravitas remembered so clearly the mask of disdain that had branded itself into Emperor Faris Epsilon's dignified features as the leader brought the side of his fist down hard against his throne three times; three portentous booms initiated the trial and echoed across Gravitas Nerol's life. The Imperial War Council had been thrown into a state of upheaval, and it was because of Gravitas. An unscheduled and unrecorded trial had been called behind securely locked doors. Oaths of secrecy under threat of death had been demanded of all councillors in attendance.

Holding a scorched crimson cloak in his arms, Gravitas Nerol had stood alone before the entire assembled War Council. His magnificent armor and adolescent face were caked in dust and grit, just having returned from the frontline. His feet had tracked a trail of dirt into the War Hall. He was a lone David within a ring of enraged Goliaths. The hardened gazes of the gargantuan generals and shrewd councillors burned with hate—and a touch of envy—for the teenager standing before them. This boy was the soldier who had caused all the mayhem. This was the young man behind the hushed whisperings and murmured stories.

Gravitas Nerol was sixteen.

Like the others, Emperor Faris Epsilon's gaze bore into the young man, his words steeped in antipathy. "You have brought embarrassment to the entire Imperial First Class."

A roar of agreement resonated around the circle of councillors. Jeers and insults blended into an indiscernibly malicious uproar around Gravitas Nerol.

"I did what was right, with full knowledge of repercussions." The solitary young Gravitas spoke to the stone beneath his sullied boots, unable to conceal the resentment in his articulate voice. "And I will accept any punishment this Council deems appropriate."

"Useless coward—you're no Imperial First Class! I should spill this hall in your blood!" The taunt came from behind Gravitas, and once again he was enveloped in condemnation from all sides. It was a rare occurrence—the War Council had found a communal scapegoat.

But Gravitas was a warrior, and this unprovoked threat stirred anger in his chest. He turned his head to the side, so as to address the insult. "I will accept any challenge without hesitation—it need only be given."

The threat in his voice was not lost to the room, and most of the enormous generals and military councillors had risen to their feet in outrage. They were pointing and barking like a pack of dogs closing in on wounded prey. This degree of disrespect and lack of decorum toward a superior was unheard of in the lowest dregs of the Imperial Army, least of all in the presence of the War Council and the emperor himself.

Yet despite the affronted furor, no challenge came forth.

They had all heard the rumors, and no one was going to face this peculiar young man. Many doubted the details of the report. It was, after all, illogical.

Gravitas was Royalty—of the Nerol family line—but still, the account of what happened on Orion could not be accurate.

"Quiet!" Emperor Faris shouted, staring at the besieged young man as he cleared his throat. "You are officially charged with the highest degree of crime against the Epsilon empire and your people. Grand treason on planet Orion, the murder of the Lord General of the Imperial Army." Murmurs followed his assertion, but Emperor Faris's voice carried over the hushed doubt. "The attack of a superior officer is a treason punishable by death. Now, it is normal military procedure for a superior officer to carry out the execution of the perpetrator at the time of the infraction. This case is obviously unusual in that none of your superiors will volunteer to carry out the execution."

Gravitas took a step forward and looked imploringly at Emperor Faris. "With respect, the Lord General broke our military procedure first, my lord. He issued a genocide order on a vastly inferior civilization that posed no threat to our troops or our extraction efforts on Orion. The Yabu race had no physical capabilities whatsoever, and their technology consisted of spears and arrows. The Yabu saw us as gods, not as a force to fight against. There was no cause to attack them, least of all to order a holocaust against them."

Emperor Faris sighed in distaste, his face darkening. "We are assembled to issue a punishment for the killing of Lord General Bronson Vikkor, not to discuss the petty woes of some insignificant race."

Gravitas tightened his grip on the crimson fabric, his fingers stained with dried mud. "They were called the Yabu, my lord, and they posed no hindrance to our invasion."

"Extraction, not invasion." A woman spoke from the ring of councillors.

"I challenge anyone who was there on Orion to refer to our presence there as anything but an invasion. But call our intentions on Orion what you will, the genocide order issued by the Lord General was more sadistic than strategic." Gravitas turned to face the many councillors, his tone measured. "Bronson Vikkor ordered the genocide of a people that lived in huts and brandished sticks and stones. I tried to reason with him, to explain to him that the Yabu were incapable of stopping our extraction rigs. I could not let the Lord General issue the genocide order unchallenged, and if you were there, you would not have wanted the Yabu blood on your hands either. If the leader of the entire Imperial First Class can't be held accountable for—"

"*Enough!*" Emperor Faris roared. "Have you completely lost touch with reality, boy? Do you need a history lesson?"

"I certainly do not, my lord."

"It is not our responsibility to show courtesy to our enemies. We received none when it was our turn to face the merciless firepower of the Zergos."

"The Yabu weren't our enemy," Gravitas urged. "That is exactly what I am trying to impress upon you."

Emperor Faris shifted against his throne, his agitation appearing as though it might spill out of him. He brought the side of his fist down savagely on his throne's armrest, splintering it to pieces that scattered across the stone floor. "You are too sensitive, boy." He pointed to the great stone faces of their Sejero ancestors over the War Council, the Blood Ring glinting on his finger. "Where would we be if house Nerol's forefathers had been as weak as you? It sickens my heart that someone as shortsighted as yourself bears Sejero blood. You lack the fortitude necessary to call yourself a warrior. You are feeble—if not in body, then in mind."

To this the War Council applauded in agreement.

"I am strong enough to best your Lord General," Gravitas said, his voice cold and his eyes brimming with passion.

Every councillor and general jumped to his or her feet, and Gravitas Nerol gladly centered himself into a fighting stance. He was prepared to take on every one of them without hesitation. Behind their facades of superficial prowess, most of these men and women were sycophants and bureaucrats. They were no fighters.

Gravitas was a fighter down to his very marrow.

"Enough! Enough! Sit back down all of you!" Emperor Faris shouted and considered the teenager, his expression filled with aversion. "You have dishonored us all, young Nerol. If you think our ways so horrid, our strategies of war so uncivilized, then your punishment is obvious." He rose from his throne with finality. "You have brought shame to this Council. You have desecrated the pride of the entire Imperial First Class, and caused the death of one of our people's most beloved leaders. You have permanently tarnished the Nerol family line, and brought disgrace upon the nobility of your forefathers. Were it not for the history of your lineage, I would call for your death—and I would have it. You have lost touch with the conviction that the strong must overcome the weak, lest they become weak in turn. You are lost, young man, and it is out of the respect I hold for your house that I give you this . . . mercy. By nightfall today, you are to leave Anthem. Gravitas Nerol, I banish you from our world."

A subdued silence fell upon the War Hall. Gravitas allowed his mouth to fall open in astonishment for an instant before he averted his eyes from the emperor and stared silently at the crimson fabric in his hands. It was the highest punishment the emperor could give. Exile was worse than death.

"If I may, my lord." Alegant Hoff, the largest and most ambitious of the generals in attendance, stood from his seat. "How will we explain the death of the Lord General—or for that matter the disappearance of a Royal son?"

Emperor Faris traced the forefinger bearing the Blood Ring across the fractured armrest of his throne in contemplation. "The official report of the incident that occurred on planet Orion is to be altered before it gets released to the public. The death of Lord General Bronson Vikkor will be attributed to the engine failure of his transport. The Lord General's transport broke down in space during the return passage from Orion to Anthem. He met a tragic and regrettable demise in transit." The emperor regarded Gravitas for a long moment. "Gravitas Nerol was on board the same transport as the Lord General. They died together when the ship fell out of contact somewhere in the wastes of space. We will hold a day of mourning across Anthem, both for the loss of our Lord General and the loss of one of our most powerful sons. That should bring this regrettable situation to an end, I believe?"

"Undoubtedly so, my lord." Alegant Hoff nodded and sat back down.

"Send word to Pral Nerol. The Nerol family will be charged with providing this traitor with a means of exportation from the planet. He has cost my empire enough as it is. Open the doors. This Council is adjourned. General Hoff, get Gravitas Nerol out of our sight, and see to it he finds his way off Anthem at once," Emperor Faris Epsilon said, not lifting his hard gaze from Gravitas as the doors to War Hall scraped open and a group of Royal Guards marched in to escort Gravitas away. "Seek atonement from our ancestors as you reflect upon your crimes, young Nerol. For you'll receive none from your people, or from me. Now leave us."

Gravitas had been too numbed by the verdict to hear the applause that claimed the Council as General Hoff and the Royal Guards took him by the shoulder and escorted him out. The polished dark marble hallway beyond the War Hall was empty and silent—temporarily off limits due to the secrecy of his trial. Gravitas allowed the Royal Guards to direct him down the hallway and past a row of tall windows. Beyond the glass, a waning summer sun hung low over Sejeroreich. The city stretched far into the horizon. Range upon range of magnificent skyscrapers gleamed in the solemn light of the setting sun. Looking sidelong past the glass, Gravitas thought it paradoxical that a city so beautiful could house such callousness. He realized, staring out over the great city, how little one man's beliefs mattered against the glory of a thriving people.

Emperor Faris was right. He was lost.

General Hoff suddenly halted their procession. Ahead of them, Master Tolland was sitting silently on a bench that stood in their way, his expression pensive and tired.

"Lord Tolland, you know you shouldn't be here. The top floors of the palace have been vacated for the evening," General Hoff said with more than a trace of concern in his voice. He raised a huge hand and placed it against an alarm on the wall. "Emperor Faris has passed his judgment, and the boy is to be exiled. If I press this alarm, hundreds of soldiers will be here in moments."

"And who would come that could add any clout to this group?" Master Tolland motioned to the dozen Royal Guards—the strongest ranks of the Imperial Army—that stood imposing and silent behind General Hoff. "But there will be no need for that. I wish only to speak with my student."

General Hoff shook his head. "I can't allow that."

"You can." Master Tolland unhurriedly stood from the bench. "And you will. I have no intention of thwarting your charge as my student's warden, general. If I did, you would not still be conscious. I only wish to speak to Gravitas. Now please, allow us a quiet word together."

General Hoff moved the hand reaching toward the alarm to touch a communicator in his ear. "Yes. Very well." He spoke to the communicator and turned to Gravitas. "Your father has departed Municera and is bringing a ship to the palace's roof hangar. We will wait with you here until he arrives. If you agree to carry on without incident, you may speak with Tolland."

"I agree," Gravitas murmured and stepped away from the Royal Guards to approach Master Tolland. Together they walked a short way down the hallway to get out of earshot from the general's company.

"It's all over." Gravitas Nerol's voice was hollow. "Unless I choose to face off against them, against the entire Imperial First Class, there is nothing that can be done."

Master Tolland placed a hand on his shoulder, knowing any words would be lost on the youth. Gravitas leaned forward and rested his forehead against the glass of a window. Far below, the courtyard was brimming with tourists to the palace, all of them looking upward and embracing its soaring height with reverent wonder. Celebrations were underway across Sejeroreich: the Epsilon empire had secured the boundless resources of another world, of Orion. The years of plenty would endure for another age, and another inferior race had fallen to the power of the Sejero. Looming over the jubilation of the crowds, the gigantic banners of each Royal family shifted in the breeze against the palace walls.

"I failed them," Gravitas said, his throat constricting as he stared down at the Nerol banner.

"Failed who?" Master Tolland asked as he surveyed the burnt crimson cloak.

"Everyone." Gravitas could not bring himself to speak of Orion or the Yabu people. "You should have been there. You should have seen what we're capable of. I watched as the Imperial First Class killed them all. We murdered every last one of them, to the smallest child. We descended from our transports in the high atmosphere and they tried to defend themselves with wooden spears."

"I am familiar with the barbarities of the Imperial Army. You are not the first to witness the horror of the Epsilon empire. Nor will you be the last."

"I'm sorry, Master Tolland, but I cannot endure a lecture. Not now." Staring down out the window, Gravitas sighed in despair. "I don't understand it. Aside from the Epsilons and some of the generals, the rest of the War Council isn't even powerful. I could have taken on all of them. Are the other Royal families really so intimidated by the Epsilons that they would rather cower than stand their ground? Emperor Faris doesn't intimidate me—I do not fear his Blood Ring or his armies."

"You do not know what you're saying," Master Tolland said. "It is through the lineage of the Blood Ring and by exercising the fear of his legions that Emperor Faris derives his true power. Do not believe his power lies purely in his prowess. You alone could not defeat the authority that adorns him. It is a truth I came to terms with long ago."

Gravitas turned from the window and pointed to the crowds at the base of the palace. "These people are celebrating a holocaust!"

"They have been taught no better, Gravitas. A man is only as aware as his upbringing allows him to be. You cannot blame them for their lack of view, or their ignorance."

Gravitas nodded. "I know that. But I wanted to show them a different way— a better path. Now I can't do anything but flee from them in defeat."

"I must say, Gravitas, I am somewhat surprised that this banishment upsets you so."

"What do you possibly mean?" Gravitas said, his voice growing hoarse with frustration. "*You* made me how I am. Flawed. And now you don't care in the slightest bit that I can never step foot on Anthem again. You think you can throw me away and forget I exist. Everyone thinks they can. Well, that's not going to happen. I'm not going to let it happen. They've built a structure that values only strength, and now they fear me because I'm as strong as they are, and I don't agree. I'm going to fly to the center of the city and make my stand. Let the challenges come. They have ordered me to leave, now let's see them try to force me out. I need to know these murderers had to face a power equal to themselves for once in their lives."

"Calm yourself," Master Tolland said.

"NO!"

"Calm yourself," Master Tolland repeated, his tone not negotiating. He pointed to the celebration far below. "You answer your own dilemma, Gravitas. Those people are not ready to see their emperor fall. They value him above all else. They see a polarization between those who have the right to take, and those who—by their own limitations—allow themselves to be taken from. In their eyes, planet Orion was theirs for the winning. And it was the power of Emperor Faris that won it for them. Should you rise against him, you will be seen as the villain, Gravitas. They will fear you, they will rally against you, and your family will be made to suffer for it."

Gravitas trudged to the nearby bench and sat down angrily. His dirt-encrusted armor and mud-stained face looked strikingly out of place among the clean surfaces and pristine windows of the hallway.

"I've known you since you were a young boy." Master Tolland's aging face lifted in a furrowed smile as he sat down beside the teenager. "I consider you a son. You are the child of one of my oldest friends, and the greatest student I have ever had the pleasure of teaching. I remember the first night you spent on Mount Karlsbad vividly. You were so . . . confused . . . to be away from your home, to be living with a stranger in the cold North. But even then you were so strong, Gravitas, so immensely strong, both in body and—infinitely more important—in mind. You learned to make the best of it."

"So you think I am going to *make the best of it* again?" Gravitas glared at him. "You think I'll simply move into a further isolation than I've already wasted my childhood mired in?"

Master Tolland ignored the interruption. "Even in the beginning, I understood why your father wanted a different life for you, a life outside our contentious world. You were a remarkably inquisitive child. As a boy—without any exposure to such ideas—you questioned the authoritarian rule of the Epsilon. You took nothing for granted, assumed no truths, and perceived of morality before it was taught to you. You were born with a truly unusual degree of independent thought. My goal in training you was to preserve and cultivate that natural independence. It was my lofty aspiration to prevent your deep sense of morality from dying out through the acceptance of what is considered normal among those people celebrating down there."

"Well, it has all been for nothing," Gravitas said.

"It has not been for nothing. I have succeeded in training you to become a powerful fighter, perhaps even the most powerful of our day. Your Sejero blood is as pure as any can claim, and your mind is hardened to the life of a warrior." Master Tolland paused and leaned closer to Gravitas. "But far more importantly, immeasurably more significantly, I provided you an upbringing where you were allowed your own perspectives. You will never be anyone's slave, whether it be literal slavery or the unseen shackles of socialization."

Gravitas stared quietly out over the spires of Sejeroreich.

"And so we arrive at today," Master Tolland said. "A day that I, and deep down I believe you as well, always knew was coming. You are too powerful to be suppressed by the strength of any hand, and filled with too much integrity to allow indifference to shrivel your willpower. This is the day when my brilliant and powerful student—the pride of my life—has committed himself to his first self-determining action. And yet, having acted upon these convictions I have instilled in his core since he was a child, my student now seems to feel regret, regret of an independent choice made out of free thought. And this, you see, confuses me."

"My regret is that I did not cast my Imperial armor to the dirt of Orion and die defending those slaughtered Yabu against my brothers in arms," Gravitas murmured. "It is not a mistake I will make again. I am flying to the center of Sejeroreich and challenging the emperor to a duel to the death."

"And tell me," Master Tolland said. "Once he is dead, will you take the Blood Ring for yourself and proclaim your own beliefs as right and true? Will you appoint yourself judge, jury and executioner—or perhaps simply emperor?"

"You know that's not what I want," Gravitas said.

"Of course it isn't. What you want is for the people's values to change, but that cannot happen through the will of one man."

Gravitas stared down at the cheering masses and knew Master Tolland was right. "Fire cannot stop fire."

Master Tolland nodded. "One of the first lessons I taught you."

Running his fingers across the coarse fabric of the crimson cloak, Gravitas smirked sadly.

"Time's up, Nerol!" the deep voice of General Hoff called out. Gravitas lifted his gaze from the window and saw the general along with the ranks of Royal Guards walking down the hallway toward him and Master Tolland. "Your father arrived to the roof hangar with a ship. Time for you to go."

"And who will force me to the roof?" Gravitas asked, insulted by the general's tone. He folded the crimson cloak loosely around his left arm. "You are ordering me around, general, yet I could kill you where you stand—all of you."

"Shall I call for reinforcements? We can do it that way too, if a scene is what you want. It's all up to you, Nerol."

"Do not do this, Gravitas." Master Tolland placed a pleading hand against his chest. "You have followed my advice all your life. I beg you to follow it for just a little longer. There is still a path for you, though you cannot yet see it."

"Well? What will it be?" General Hoff said, his hand poised over the alarm. "Which will you embrace, exile or death?"

Gravitas looked to Master Tolland, and seeing the hopeful sureness in his teacher's expression, he allowed his tense shoulders to relax. "Show me to the roof, general."

"Very good. We'll take the stairs so no one sees you." General Hoff and the Royal Guards sauntered forward and guided Gravitas beyond a doorway and into a narrow stairway leading up to the roof. Up and up they trudged through the many floors of the upper palace. Gravitas did not know what to think. He felt numb and hopeless, a pawn of his teacher and a titan rendered useless through philosophy and reflection.

"I think you should return to Orion, Nerol," General Hoff spoke as they rounded the steps. There was a smear of mockery to his tone. "I heard our soldiers saw to it that Lord General Bronson Vikkor's final orders were followed through with such determination that not a single one of those Yabu escaped our fires. Every last one of them burned. You should go back to see their corpses and the resource extraction rigs at work."

Gravitas said nothing. They reached the top of the stairway and stood before the closed door. General Hoff turned and looked down at him. "Where did you get that cloak?"

"It belonged to a child." Gravitas said. "If you try to take it from me, if you even touch it, it will cost you your life."

General Hoff seemed to think his words were amusing. "Put it on. I don't want your face to be seen."

The general and a few Royal Guards chuckled in amusement at the cloak and pushed open the heavy door to the hangar as Gravitas draped the fabric over his head. A warm summer wind blew against them as they stepped out onto the roof of the palace. Dwarfing all of the surrounding skyscrapers, the palace roof severed the very clouds that were cast in the violet light of the setting sun. Waiting at the docking bay in the center of the roof, Pral Nerol was standing alongside his ship, the *Traverser I*.

Gravitas walked to his father, his long cloak flapping and his profile casting a mysterious silhouette against the vanishing sun. "I thought you weren't com-

ing," Gravitas said, crashing into his father's shoulder. "I thought you were going to believe the lies they're spreading."

Pral Nerol squeezed Gravitas against his chest as the Royal Guards circled
around the *Traverser I.* "Of course not."

Master Tolland followed behind Gravitas, his gaze held eastward to the
darkening horizon. "He is to be exiled by sundown, Pral. We must be succinct
in our discussion. What's done is done, for we do not have the time to discuss
it. You have chosen a path, Gravitas, and now we need to make a plan for that
path's future. Is the *Traverser I* prepared to depart?"

"Yes, the ship's in fine order," Pral said, still holding his son.

"Good. Then the most important decision now must be made. Where
should the boy go?"

"I will return to Orion and destroy the extraction teams there," Gravitas
said, his voice grim and assured.

"It's true that you could return to Orion and combat the Epsilon presence
there until you die of exhaustion. But it would not bring back the locals who
perished, or restore the resources that have already been withdrawn from the
planet. And once you are out of the way, the Epsilon will begin their extractions
once more." Master Tolland sighed apprehensively. "Ultimately, you would
never bring redemption to Orion or its people."

"It's what I want to do."

"A wasted sacrifice is the brash desire of a young man," Pral Nerol said. "You
are far more valuable alive than dead, Gravitas. Tolland, there is a place better
suited for him than Orion."

Master Tolland and Pral exchanged a long uneasy look, as if each in turn
was ruminating over a great internal conflict. Gravitas noticed the severity of
their expressions and turned from one to the other. "I don't understand.
Where?"

"I think it is a fairly clear choice. I did the calculations on my way here—the
Traverser I can make the journey," Pral said, his voice solemn and imploring.
"He could flourish there."

Gravitas shook his head, the hood of the cloak billowing against his cheek.
"Where?"

"I'm not sure." Master Tolland looked out over Sejeroreich for some time.
He ran a hand across his gray beard in contemplation. After a long moment, he
turned to look at Gravitas, though he spoke to Pral. "I thought we had decided
on immaculate preservation."

"Has this very specific dilemma not proven his convictions?" Pral asked.
"The atrocities Gravitas witnessed on Orion, and the choices he made in the

face of them demonstrate his awareness of the fragilities we each swore to protect. The actions he made on Orion speak louder than any promise he could possibly give to us now."

"Yes. Yes, I agree." Master Tolland nodded at last. "Gravitas has proven himself. He will go."

"Filgaia," Pral said with a measure of reverence Gravitas had never heard in his father's voice.

"Filgaia?" Gravitas asked with bewilderment.

"I will provide you with no preconception of the planet, and I will leave it up to you to form your own perspectives of the place." Pral Nerol placed an encouraging hand on Gravitas's shoulder. "You have decided your course, and now you must embrace its consequences. I am proud of you beyond words. We are placing great trust in you, Gravitas. Do not let us down."

"Some things are more important than race or faction, Gravitas," Master Tolland said as they led him to the *Traverser I*, its engines roaring. "Principles are one of them. Principles transcend both time and place, and they will keep us united despite our distance."

"It's all over," Gravitas murmured, stepping torpidly into the threshold of the *Traverser I*. He looked the part of the refugee, the crimson cloak concealing the glint of his stained Imperial Armor underneath. He turned back and looked at Master Tolland and his father. General Alegant Hoff and the dozen Royal Guards stood around the ship like statues, and beyond, the lights of Sejeroreich twinkled against the approaching dusk.

"Your past is over," Pral Nerol said sadly. "But your future remains to be seen. I know you'll make me proud, Gravitas."

The steel door of the craft hissed shut. It was done.

The first lonely nights aboard his father's craft in the cold emptiness of space were the worst of his life. No person to console him or listen to his voice, and only his dark thoughts to dwell upon. Gravitas knew that the Yabu people would be driven to extinction, their innocence and boundless potential erased from the pages of history. A fragile chance for the glory of civilization dashed by the brutality of life. Millions of years of delicate and miraculous growth snuffed out by the fleeting order of the Lord General: an obtuse and uneducated man bestowed at birth with perverse and unnatural power.

Gravitas realized his people had become the technologically cold-blooded Zergos they had once struggled so desperately against. Where once they were victim, in time the Primus had become the very evil that had sought their ruin.

Was that the inevitability of all intelligent life, of all societies, to strangle out all less capable than themselves?

All of his beliefs and hopes were swallowed up by depression and despair. Gravitas desired with all his heart to turn the *Traverser I* back to Anthem and assault the Imperial Palace and all of Sejeroreich with his torturous hate. All of it, all of the grandeur of his people had been built with blood and misery. He envisioned toppling the columns of the palace and striking down the members of the War Council and Emperor Faris himself, all the while screaming that he was punishing them for the Yabu. For the Primus. The Primus race that could have been. The Primus race as it existed before the taint of Sejero blood and the profound scar of their near apocalypse so long ago. But Gravitas knew there would be no returning to Anthem. He was marked now as the bloodthirsty one, the enemy.

A reality where cruelty and indifference flourished, and the innocent shriveled away did not seem a reality worth living. Then, it was as though the very cosmos reached out and placed a reassuring hand on the tormented young man's shoulder. Gravitas's salvation came in the form of the first transmission from the planet Filgaia.

The humans.

When the list of received transmissions from Filgaia began to pile up, the language matrix started identifying and assembling languages. Gravitas put on the headphones and began learning all of the foreign tongues.

Gravitas spent the remaining days and nights fanatically learning everything about the human race. He read about the civilization's history, cultures, sciences, arts, religions, and anything he was able to translate. The humans seemed like such a multifaceted and conflicted people. One thing was clear to him. The human race was still striving. They were still motivated to learn more, still determined to be more.

That was something the Primus had given up on a long time ago.

Gravitas was immersed in researching the humans when the *Traverser I* began to decelerate as it neared its destination.

Filgaia appeared no larger than a glowing dot, barely discernible among the stars in the encompassing blackness. But the celestial wonder grew larger and larger beyond the glass of the command bridge. Soon Gravitas was forced to squint from the brilliance as the gleaming and enormous globe filled the entire command bridge window. He gazed out at sprawling emerald continents, vast yellow deserts, snaking mountain ranges, oceans and seas glimmering in hues of brilliant blue beneath clouds of impregnable white. Against the expanse of endless nothingness, Filgaia danced in the radiance of its sun and the verdant dignity of its life. Gravitas embraced the majesty of being as Filgaia struggled stalwart and undimmed against the infinite cold of space. Both the sanctity and the resilience of this persistency shook him, and the splendor of the planet and its vitality left him speechless.

In that moment he understood why Master Tolland and his father had never spoken of Filgaia to a living soul. It was far too precious to endanger, and too beautiful to jeopardize. Here was a developed planet that had never been tainted at the hands of an overly voracious power. The flourishing lands he now looked upon had never been forced to host an all-encompassing war. The human race had never awoken to the screams of a cindering dawn and a reckoning cataclysm.

It was a new chance.

Gravitas could not help but feel a deep sense of hope and inspiration while taking in the young planet, and at the same time a pang of sadness at the fate of his own. He reached across his seat and picked up the crimson cloak, quietly holding it as he looked upon Filgaia.

Orion—a planet even younger than this place—was being sucked dry of its resources. The caustic runoff and pollution caused by the extraction process would be left to fester like clutter cast aside by a misbehaved child, the dead Yabu left to rot in the spots where they had fallen, carrion to time alone.

Gravitas came to a decision while holding the cloak and beholding the shimmering glory of the world before him. He would be no invader, for good or ill. His presence would go entirely unnoticed by the inhabitants of Filgaia. His life would be one of solitude. A lifetime spent ready to rise in defense of that which deserved it beyond all else. Until his last breath, Gravitas Nerol would be Filgaia's sentinel—its unseen god and champion.

Years later, Gravitas now thundered across the lofty mountain range, the world below shaking under his inconceivable power. He exploded through the sound barrier between the narrow rows of peaks. His heart soared in the morning air.

With blinding speed Gravitas roared high over the land as peaks gave way to rolling foothills, the frozen ground falling farther away beneath his increasing altitude. He turned upward and ascended elegantly through the clouds and into the upper atmosphere, the crimson cloak whipping against his legs in the wind.

He looked around and carefully examined the surrounding sky. A few days previous, he had seen an airplane plummeting in the distance. It was over such a secluded area that Gravitas had made the decision to risk rescuing it. He had easily caught it on his back, placing it to rest in a field to the south.

Today, however, the open sky belonged to him alone. Gravitas took a few deep controlled breaths as he focused his mind and senses. The frigid air seemed to ebb and crackle from his power. He snapped into action, throwing a shadow punch that echoed across the barren landscape.

His daily training had begun.

CHAPTER ELEVEN

Ryan

Ryan pushed open the door to Kristen Jordan's apartment building and paused before pressing the doorbell to her third-floor studio. The entrance hallway was warm from the sunlight beaming through the glass doorway. Ryan stopped to check his appearance in the dusty mirror nestled between the rows of narrow mailboxes and grid of doorbells. He was wearing a dark gray button-down shirt and jeans. Turning slightly from side to side, he decided the attire looked appropriate—neither dressy nor unkempt. After an encouraging nod to his reflection, he pressed the buzzer to her apartment.

"Ryan?" Kristen's tinny voice sounded from the ancient speaker.

He pressed the button. "Yeah."

"Hi, I'll come right down."

Ryan turned his attention to some stacks of catalogs that were too big to fit in the mail slots. Kneeling down, he saw one of the stacks—addressed to Kristen Jordan—was comprised mostly of scientific journals, the majority old editions, some dating back to the previous winter. There was a sound of feet descending the stairwell, and the locked door opened.

"Hey there," Kristen said.

"Hi." Ryan rose from his haunches. "Just looking at some of your old mail here. I take it these journals don't interest you?"

"Um, no. Not particularly." Kristen's lips turned in a smile. Her hair fell below her narrow shoulders and rested weightlessly against the curves of her chest. "They keep sending them though. Columbia must subscribe their graduate students or something. I certainly never signed up for them."

"Cool," Ryan said, returning her smile. During their recent text correspondence, he had been caught up in Kristen's intellect and forgotten how attractive she was. In a simple faded chambray shirt and shorts, she was remarkably attractive. Kristen pushed her shoulder against the heavy door and let the cool outside air into the balmy atrium as she held it open for him. Ryan buried his hands into his pockets as he walked out to the sidewalk. He noticed a fruity scent, probably her shampoo—her hair was still damp.

"How did your essay go over?" Kristen asked.

"Eh, mostly how I thought it might."

"So . . . not well?"

"The class pretty much shot down my ideas," Ryan said. "They're critical of any perspective that hasn't been hashed out to them in detail during Professor Hilton's lectures. You have to love it when people laugh off your views as naive just because it differs from the ones they've been taught."

"I know it." Kristen reached out a hand and languorously dragged the tips of her fingers across the coarse bricks of an old walk-up. "I've found people often disregard views that differ from their own, especially at the highest echelons of education. The more you think you know about something, the more stubborn you tend to be."

Ryan nodded. "Totally. But what really bothered me was that they relegated my stance as not only unrealistic, but outright *impossible*. I mean what kind of one-dimensional thinking is that?"

"It can be scary, that's for sure," Kristen said, casting him a sidelong expression of admiration. "I think the most rational outlook is the one that isn't convinced of its rationality."

"Yes. True intellect is doubt."

"I couldn't agree more. But I wouldn't sweat your classmates. They're just trying to get A's, not break any philosophical ground or earn a Nobel Prize with a midterm paper. You shouldn't let them get to you." Kristen took in a long breath and let it out slowly, her arms folded against her chest. The autumn trees lining the sidewalk were roused to life, their branches swaying at the caress of a breeze rolling off the Hudson. "Beautiful day, huh?"

"Yeah, it's incredible." They strolled southward across the Upper West Side sidewalks, the leaves of the maples and birches overhead painted in rich russet and gold. Their exquisite rustic quality, even in the heart of New York City, was a herald of the season's change—of things grander than urban concerns. Under their feet, the brittle and curled fallen leaves crinkled pleasantly against the drab concrete. A chill lingered in the autumnal air, yet the sun still held warmth.

"Want to go for a walk in the park?" Ryan asked as he looked up into the clearness of the pale blue sky. They had not yet hammered out any plan for their afternoon.

"Yeah, I'd like that. I haven't been outdoors much recently. Work with the Vatruvian cell has been . . . well . . . it's really picked up steam. I've lost count how many hours a week I spend in my lab." Kristen walked closely beside him, her head barely reaching Ryan's shoulder. Their strides in harmony, they passed several blocks of brick walk-ups and stately awnings, all the buildings looking especially striking in the sleepy fall afternoon. They crossed into the broad expanse of Central Park and found they were far from the only ones to have considered a stroll. The bench-lined paths and open fields were busy with people walking side by side, clutching leashes of eager retrievers, or sitting in the grass with a book and enjoying what was likely to be one of the last basking days of the year.

"How is your research going?" Ryan ventured. "If you want to talk about it, that is."

"No, no. It's okay. It's going great, really great. I just . . . " Kristen faltered and fell silent, staring at her shoes as they trod over leaves.

Ryan looked down and saw she was holding back emotion, her expression filled with conflict. He could tell her thoughts were somewhere else. "What's wrong?"

"Oh, it's nothing. I'm sorry—it doesn't have anything to do with you." Kristen gave him an apologetic smile. "The research work has just been stressful this week."

"Is everything all right?"

They were walking across an old stone footbridge that rose over a perpendicular path below. Kristen stopped and leaned her elbows against the railing under the shade of an elm's golden foliage. A sweet smell of cut grass and fresh soil lingered in the breeze, and a faint buzz of a lawnmower could be heard. Aware that his gaze might make her feel uncomfortable, Ryan shifted his attention to some teenagers tossing a Frisbee.

After some time, Kristen let out a sigh. "To answer your question, I don't know if everything's all right."

"Do you want to talk about it?"

"I'm just worried about the Vatruvian cell, and frustrated with the negligent bureaucrats in charge of regulation agencies. They should be vigilantly watching our research, but instead they're sitting on their hands while this technology grows in the hands of—in my honest opinion—reckless minds working behind closed doors. And the notion of the media acting as a watchdog is laughable; all journalists seem to have is praise for the Vatruvian cell. I feel waves of hopelessness sometimes, like nobody has the slightest touch of integrity or common sense." Kristen brushed away a few strands of hair the breeze had blown across her cheek. "Something as groundbreaking as the Vatruvian cell shouldn't be under the authority of one mind, and no one seems to feel that way but me."

"Well, I wasn't aware people beyond myself consider the Vatruvian cell to be potentially dangerous. My impression is that the scientific community is in agreement that it's a harmless technology."

"It was." Kristen said.

"*Was?*"

Kristen did not seem like the type to be easily flustered, and she suddenly looked sick with anxiety. Behind her reserved quirkiness was undeniable sophistication, and Ryan knew there must be a just cause behind her obvious trepidation. "I came out to get my mind off of all this heavy stuff." Kristen turned from the railing. "The weather's too nice to spend wallowing in dark thoughts."

Ryan smiled, but regarded her with concern. "Yeah . . ." He looked to the lightly swaying trees and sky beyond. "This is pretty tough to beat."

"So, Ryan Craig."

"So, Kristen Jordan."

"*So.* What made you decide to come to Columbia? I'm sure there were plenty of other good schools you could have attended."

"You mean beyond the obvious?" Ryan said, indicating their surrounds.

"Yes, apart from it being in New York City—though I'm partial to Boston myself. Where are you from?"

"Chicago."

"Oh," Kristen said. "I'm surprised you didn't want to go to college there. I've heard it's an awesome city—lots of top notch schools, too."

"Yeah, that's true." Ryan paused in contemplation. "But I needed a change of scenery. Plus I figured I would have the best odds of finding a situation I was happy with in New York." He absentmindedly kicked a pebble on the path, sending it forward a few feet. "Also, I'm not from a lot of money, and Columbia offered me a serious scholarship."

"Well, it sounds like you made the right decision," Kristen said. The afternoon was waning as they reached the bank of a pond. The colors of nearby trees reflected off the still water like an Impressionist painting. A faint breeze rippled over the water's surface. People were scattered around the water's edge, sitting on the soft grass or benches. The moving shadows of Ryan and Kristen fell elongated beside them in the late afternoon sunlight. For awhile they stood quietly admiring the harmony, Kristen with hand on hip and Ryan with arms crossed.

A man's shout abruptly broke the near silence of the pond. Ryan and Kristen shot each other a confused look. The shout came again, ringing with a howling tone.

"What *is* that?" Kristen turned her head after several more shouts.

"I don't know," Ryan said with a bemused expression. He was unsure whether to laugh or be concerned at the strange shouting. After a moment, a gaunt man with a poster board slung across his chest rounded a turn in the path and stumbled into view. The derelict man, his face weathered and leathery, had the volatile look of a schizophrenic or one prone to unstable episodes. He wore a filthy flannel shirt, torn jeans, and tattered shoes, the soles hanging off and dragging on the pavement. Waving his arms, he brandished a bunch of hand-written pamphlets and a poster that bounced against his chest painted sloppily with the words THE END IS NEER, THE WORLD WILL BERN. The dark red paint of the lettering had dripped in spots before it had dried and—whether intended or not—resembled blood.

"The end! The end is coming! All of you will burn! Repent! Run!"

The man was shouting at the top of his lungs, his voice haggard and raspy. He came quite near to them, and Kristen took a nervous step closer to Ryan as the man looked directly at her, his eyes jaundiced and askew as he screamed through missing teeth, "You'll burn!"

The man lurched forward, waving one of his pamphlets in the air as though it were aflame.

"Move along. We're not interested." Ryan's voice was forceful, and his face serious. Yet the man seemed to take no notice of the command and continued stumbling on, screaming and mumbling irrationally. Ryan realized the sick man was entirely unaware of his surroundings, least of all their presence. His shouts faded as he turned a corner in the path and continued his warning elsewhere.

"*Ugh*! I can't stand the creepy people who do that. It's so unsettling. Now I remember why I avoid the park near sundown." Kristen exhaled and folded her hands together nervously.

"Please—that was nothing. You should see some of the end-of-the-world spokespeople in Chicago."

"Hah." Kristen smiled uncomfortably. "But I don't know if it's comforting or disturbing to know those people are a global presence."

Ryan laughed. "Either way, I think it's safe to say their apocalyptic premonitions are a direct result of their mental disorders and not prophetic powers."

"Yes, thankfully."

They sat down on an oak bench overlooking the pond. The day was dwindling, and the divergent line of the setting sun's coppery rays passed over the treetops and came to rest on the broad facades of nearby skyscrapers—a radiant amber above and nightfall below. There was a nip in the air, and they sat close.

"Do you have any plans for after you finish your doctorate?" Ryan asked in an attempt to change the mood from the eerie encounter.

Kristen shook her head. "I'm not sure. There's talk of the Vatruvian cell moving into the private sector, so maybe I'll stay on the roller coaster and see the project through to its end—whatever that may be. But I don't know, it's strange to think about. I've always simply graduated to the next level of education. It's all I know. Now that I have reached the pinnacle, I can't really envision what I'll end up doing. How about you?"

"I have absolutely no idea, to be honest." Ryan leaned back against the hard wood of the bench. "I wouldn't mind going to graduate school myself, but it's way too early to say. I guess my plan—if I could even say that I have one—is to wait for something to come along that really catches my interest."

"I like that. No predetermined agenda," Kristen said. "There's no telling where you'll end up, anyway, when you really think about it. If you asked me two years ago, I never would have imagined I'd be working on something like the Vatruvian cell."

Ryan nodded. "Ambition and direction can only get you so far, anyway. The rest comes down to uncontrollable variables. Fate, I suppose."

They stared across the lengthening shadows of the pond as the wrought iron lamps lining the park flickered to life, casting soft rings of yellow light across the pathway.

"So you believe in fate?" Kristen asked, her lips drawn in a sardonic smirk.

Ryan laughed. "Eh, I don't know about fate, per se." He looked out over the darkening water. "I like to think I'm in control, whatever the hell that means. But when I look back at the past, it doesn't really feel like I've always been in the driver's seat."

"You mean you've had no say in the cut-and-dry path we're all on? Going straight from high school to college and straight from college to graduate school . . . so on and so forth?"

"Something like that."

"Well, do you feel in control of your life right now?"

"I can't honestly say."

Kristen thought over his words intently, her tone turning serious. "Yeah, me either."

Her hands were in her lap and she was biting the side of her lower lip in contemplation. Ryan regarded her silently as she surveyed the lights of the skyline shining against the twilight. "How about you? Do you believe in *fate*, if we're willing to devolve to such ideas?"

Kristen shrugged. "I believe we were each intended to do something with our lives, whatever that may be."

"So it's a matter of seeking that out?"

"Well, take your passion in the social sciences for instance." Kristen brought her gaze down to meet his. "Although it may still be obscured to you, maybe one day—all philosophical relativisms and moralistic nonsense put aside—you will *truly* help people somewhere."

"I like that."

She smiled. "Me too."

"And you?" Ryan asked. "Do you see the Vatruvian cell helping people somewhere down the road?"

Kristen's smile faded, and she shook her head with slow uncertainty. "I thought so once."

For a long while they sat in silence with only the breeze in the trees and the familiar city sounds breaking the stillness: distant police sirens, the high-pitched note of brakes and the faded honking of taxis. Ryan felt an uncharacteristic sense of contentment, being so close to Kristen. He felt frozen in time, removed from the world that existed beyond the two of them.

"What's your family like?" Kristen asked after a bit. "What do your parents do for work; how old are your siblings? Give me the rundown."

Ryan scratched his chin and hesitated to gather his thoughts. "Well, what can I tell you? I grew up in Chicago. My father worked as a research scientist and my mother was a stay-at-home mom. No siblings."

"Your father was a scientist? What did he research?"

"It varied," Ryan said. "His research was always changing from year to year. He never talked much about it, truth be told."

"Hmm," Kristen said. "And he worked in Chicago I take it?"

"Yep." Ryan said, running a hand through his hair. "Do you think we should find somewhere to eat dinner?"

"Sure, I'd like that," Kristen said with a mix of confusion and empathy. She had surely registered he was discussing his parents in the past tense. "What was your mother like?"

"She was smart, like my father." Ryan said.

"I'm sure she was very bright to have raised you," Kristen said with a warming smile as she placed her hand on Ryan's, where she left it resting.

Ryan was stunned by the well of emotion that moved through him from her touch. He knew he had to say something. "They died when I was a teenager," he forced out. "Car crash."

"Ugh, I'm so sorry—" Kristen stopped, overtly unsure what to say. "My mother passed away when I was fifteen. Lymphoma. It's awful losing a parent. I can't imagine losing both. But I'm sure they would want us to live to our fullest and pursue what we want to. Right?"

"Definitely," Ryan said.

"I guess we have a lot in common," Kristen said, breaking their eye contact and looking up into the skinny arms of the shadowed trees.

"I'm sure we have plenty more in common than our sorrows, but it's nice to know someone who understands how pain can feel," Ryan said.

CHAPTER TWELVE

Vengelis

The hours monotonously and claustrophobically passed as the *Harbinger I* traveled onward through the vastness of space toward the distant Filgaia. As the initial shock of their plight waned, a fog of bleak misery descended upon the living quarters and narrow hallways of Master Tolland's ship.

Darien was sitting in the command deck fruitlessly attempting to disengage the autopilot of the *Harbinger I.* The Royal Guard found the computer system of the craft to be remarkably complex, and far beyond his limited comprehension of programming. Pral Nerol himself had designed the *Harbinger I*, and Darien knew he had no hope of prevailing over the brilliant scientist's mind. Any attempt to divert their course back toward Anthem seemed to be utterly futile. There would be no impressing Vengelis with his technical abilities. Darien gave up and slumped back into his chair, irritably pushing the control console away from him with a mammoth palm.

"Take it easy there. I wouldn't risk breaking any of those controls if I were you," Lord General Hoff said as he walked into the command deck. Hoff had to lower his huge stature through the doorframe, his head taking up half the width of the threshold.

Darien regarded Hoff quietly. "I was trying to turn off this damn autopilot."

"Ah yes," Hoff yawned, and winced from a broken rib he had received during their spar with Vengelis on the side of Mount Karlsbad. "Did Vengelis wake up yet?"

Darien nodded. "He woke late last night."

"I take it he didn't appreciate that we initiated the locked autopilot?"

"That would be an understatement," Darien said. "I thought he was going to kill me when I told him it wouldn't disengage until we reached Filgaia."

"I expected as much. Don't worry, once he cools down he'll forgive us. Vengelis would have been angrier had we not followed Tolland's orders." Hoff sat down in one of the command seats, which yielded considerably under his bulk. The two warriors looked incongruously out of place as they sat in the command bridge. The *Harbinger I* had clearly been constructed for the transport of Royal sons, and the two giants looked like adults sitting in a child's playhouse, their broad hips extending beyond the seats and their hands larger than the keypads themselves.

The abnormal height and robust musculature of many contemporary Imperial Army soldiers lacking Royal descent, especially those holding positions in the Imperial First Class, were the consequence of a merciless custom. Although a number of Royal and well-bred lineages—including house Epsilon, Bregarion, Tolland, Grahman, Nerol, Prill and many others—meticulously recorded and maintained their inherited Sejero purity, countless lesser families did not. The ancient Sejero, their sanctified ancestors who had risen amid the mushroom clouds of the Primus race's darkest hour to stand against the brutal technological firepower of the Zergos, had been few in number. Separated by long wilting years of time, a vast majority of the modern Primus population only had trace amounts of the transcendent and unnatural Sejero traits remaining in their blood. Every year more sons and daughters were born weak, ineffectual—some even lacking the gift of flight and others susceptible to bleeding from simple wounds.

The resolution to their concerns surfaced in the form of eugenics. Only the largest and most powerful of the warrior classes were allowed children, and spousal selection fell under the strict jurisdiction of the Imperial War Council. Though the draconian efforts ultimately did little to preserve or revive dwindling Sejero purity, the venture did give rise to the unnatural size and muscle mass of many lesser bloodlines. Both Hoff and Darien, along with most of the Imperial First Class ranks were the children of equally gigantic parents, and their parents before them, going back generations.

Though in the end, the hulking size and strength of the colossally bred warriors proved to be inferior to the inherent vigor of Royal blood.

"Vengelis will be angry when he realizes we didn't join the fight against the Felixes," Darien said, failing to hide the unease in his voice. He recalled all too clearly the look of rage on Vengelis's beaten face before he had stormed out of the command deck.

Hoff cast him a cautious look. "We didn't join the battle because we were *ordered* not to by Master Tolland. I am the Lord General. Do you think I would rather be here in this ship instead of leading the Imperial Army?"

"No, of course not. But we *didn't* come to the defense of Sejeroreich."

Hoff dismissed the idea with a confident shake of his head. "We were following orders. It wasn't our privilege to question Master Tolland."

Darien was not accustomed to the intensity of Vengelis Epsilon. His whole life Darien had dreamed of being recruited into the Royal Guard—the highest attainable honor for a warrior of his birth. Yet it had taken nearly all of his willpower not to give up his post after his savage first training session with the young Epsilon prince. Darien had never experienced anything like it. Vengelis had nearly beaten him to death in cold blood during what was scheduled to be a half-speed spar—and to Vengelis Epsilon that is what it had been. That was the way of the Sejero of old, and that was the way of Vengelis. After the initial thrashing, Darien knew that he would have to adapt or die, and so he resigned himself to stoicism. In the process he had transformed himself into a warrior he never would have thought possible.

"We haven't received a single transmission from Anthem." Hoff groaned and leaned back, his seat creaking under him. "What did Vengelis say about Filgaia?"

"Nothing," Darien said. "He had never heard of it."

"*What?* I thought he would understand the significance."

"Vengelis was just as confused as we were. I for one have never heard of a planet Filgaia. What if it doesn't exist, Hoff? What if Master Tolland was delirious when he gave us his orders?"

"He wasn't," the Lord General said flatly, but he did not look entirely convinced.

"There's no way of knowing," Darien said. "What are we going to do if we reach the coordinates of this 'Filgaia' and find nothing there?"

"I don't think that will happen. Master Tolland gave us the explicit coordinates of the place. He told us exactly where Vengelis fell within the entirety of the chaos in Sejeroreich. He told us where the *Harbinger I* was docked outside the city. Hell, he was lucid enough to specifically order us to engage and lock the autopilot before Vengelis awoke, knowing Vengelis would demand to reverse directions back to Anthem. Tolland ordered all that despite his condition. Delirious men don't speak with that kind of precision."

"I guess that's true."

"But it doesn't matter anyways."

Darien looked up with surprise at the unusually bleak and caustic tone of the Lord General.

"There's no goddamn empire left to save," Hoff said. "If Vengelis was defeated, that's it. The might of the Sejero has fallen. We're at the mercy of the Felixes. If they choose to destroy Anthem and kill every last one of our people, then it will happen—and to me it seems as though the Felixes made their intentions quite clear."

"You really believe no fight can be made?"

Hoff stared out the command bridge window into the eerie blackness beyond. "I will say this. If there is a way to defeat these Felixes, Vengelis will find it. Vengelis isn't like his father Faris—may he rest in peace. Vengelis is an Epsilon of old. He wasn't born to be a politician or a thinker. Vengelis Epsilon was born a fighter. It can't be chance that his rise to power coincided with this catastrophe. I've known him since he was a little kid, and I've never seen him back down from anything. On board with us is the greatest warrior in many ages, and that notion gives me hope."

As the door to his quarters shut hours earlier, Vengelis had sunk to the floor on his hands and knees in despair. After nearly two thousand years of consecutive reign, house Epsilon had fallen. All the people he knew and loved had been ruthlessly massacred and left to ruin. His hands trembled and his body convulsed as emotion poured out of him. Vengelis raised his gaze and stared at the banner of the Epsilon empire hanging before him. It hung from wall to wall, the sigil of house Epsilon woven in black fibers. He rose, unsteady and drunk with rage, and ripped it from the wall. Tears of fury slid down his face as he tore the thick fabric into shreds with his beaten hands. How could it have come to this?

It was a holocaust.

The Primus had been powerless. The limitless might of the Sejero had been merely brushed aside like nothing at all, and the magnificence of his people erased. He wanted more than anything to embrace death and accept the same fate as his family. Vengelis thought of Master Tolland, how he had wheezed hoarsely alongside him during the struggle with the Felixes. He remembered the hundreds of Imperial First Class bodies littering the streets of Sejeroreich and the millions more who had been swept away in the indiscriminate killing. He remembered the hope in the eyes of the young boy he had saved from the blonde Felix. Surely the boy was lost now, as was Master Tolland and all the others who had risen to face their peril.

Each and every one had died with the hope that where they failed, Vengelis Epsilon would triumph.

But Vengelis had let them all down. He blinked at the bare wall, his breathing heavy and pained. With great effort, he exhaled his rising rage and tried to expel with it his tempestuous passion. Mustering every ounce of discipline in his body, he straightened himself and stood. Vengelis shut his swollen eyes and relaxed his sore muscles, allowing his constricted forearms to release their clenched fists. There was only one choice, only one course of action, and it was up to him to do it.

Redemption.

Hours later, with bruises spanning his body and wounds still weeping blood, Vengelis meticulously scanned through the Imperial database for information on the inexplicable Felixes. Only the glow of his monitor illuminated him against the pale stars and blackness beyond the narrow porthole.

Vengelis started from the beginning. The Imperial messenger that had reached them on Mount Karlsbad and interrupted his spar with Master Tolland had specifically called the attackers *machines*. Why? The Felixes looked like Primus. Eve and his mother had also called the attackers machines. Having known nothing about the attackers, Vengelis would have thought the Felixes were fellow Primus; anyone would have—they were identical to the Primus in almost every respect except their eyes. There must have been some sort of broadcast or rumor that described the Felixes as machines. Somewhere tucked away in the Imperial database there had to be information on these Felixes, and he would not rest until it was uncovered.

Vengelis scanned through his father's itinerary from the days preceding Sejeroreich's destruction. If information did exist on the Felixes, however minimal, his father would have been made aware of it. The attack had been underway for nearly an entire day before the onslaught reached Sejeroreich. He recalled all too vividly the fires of Municera and the Twin Cities. A meeting of the War Council would have been assembled after their fall.

Sure enough, in his father's automated itinerary Vengelis found that the War Council had been convened in the early morning. It had been held just before the alarms of Sejeroreich sounded. Vengelis hastily opened the file. Two notes and a video file were in the content of the meeting. One note read: *Meeting of War Council. Open war declared. Imperial First Class dispatched under the direction of General Portid.* Vengelis shook his head and sighed scornfully. General Portid was a fool. With effort he quelled the sudden rise of frustration and continued. The second note read: *Sejeroreich under assault.* Vengelis drooped and forcefully rubbed the bleariness from his vision. After a moment he moved the cursor over the video file thumbnail expecting it to be a recording of the proceedings.

It was titled: *Pral Nerol research laboratory. Municera. Morning of attack.*

Vengelis jolted upright and shook away fatigue. He touched the play button and watched as a video of a laboratory sprung to life. At once, he knew he had found exactly what he had been looking for, and simultaneously felt the blood drain from his face. On a steel pedestal among three other bodies and interspersed with laboratory workers moving back and forth, was unmistakably the blonde Felix that had nearly killed him.

"What the hell is this?" Vengelis muttered in disbelief.

Pral Nerol began to give his introductions. Vengelis stared at the talking image of Nerol and listened attentively. He was only vaguely familiar with house Nerol. They were a prestigious but reclusive Royal family, mostly academics and scholars in recent generations. Vengelis also recalled headlines of Pral Nerol's son being one of the soldiers that perished in the famous Orion transport disaster several years back. The death of any Royal son or daughter was a grievous loss.

"With me here in the lab are my research assistants: Argos Trace, Cintha Loh, and Vera Gray. Imperial warrior Von Krass has also been gracious enough to join us, as a precautionary measure," said the image of Pral Nerol.

Vengelis's eyes narrowed. Von Krass was powerful, almost as powerful as Darien and Hoff. He was absurdly high ranked to be required as a mere "precautionary measure" in a laboratory in Municera. The researchers must have known there was some danger involved with the Felixes. Clearly, they had vastly underestimated it.

Knowing what he already did about the Felixes, the gruesome remainder of the video feed came as no surprise to him. When it cut, Vengelis sat silently for a long time tapping the tips of his fingers on the monitor, his face alight with a hope renewed. The origin of the machines was known, and it provided Vengelis a glimmer of optimism. The Felixes had been conceived by a Primus mind and created by a Primus hand, and therefore a Primus could unmake them accordingly.

At once Vengelis's fingers burst back into action, typing feverishly on the keyboard. He needed to find Pral Nerol's research notes. The scientist's information might have contained some details on a weakness or exploitable attribute of the Felixes. The Royal Epsilon username could override any password protection, so Vengelis had all the information that existed at his disposal. It was simply a matter of finding it in the entire Imperial network. If Von Krass was present at Pral Nerol's laboratory, it meant the Epsilon empire had been aware of the project beforehand. Someone high up must have received a copy of the research proposal in order to approve it for testing. Though they were likely dead in the rubble of Sejeroreich, the information would still be sitting in their account.

But who would have evaluated it?

Vengelis quickly scanned his father's inbox. Nothing. One by one he arduously scanned through every councillor's personal account. Finally, while sifting through Councillor Harken's inbox many draining hours later, Vengelis found Pral Nerol's research notes.

Councillor Harken had been the one to approve it. Vengelis frowned in disappointment. He had always considered Harken to be an exceedingly intelligent and capable advisor—one of the few. All things considered, Vengelis had also always admired the ingenuity of Pral Nerol. How was it possible the risks of this Felix project had been so fatally miscalculated by such brilliant minds? He shook his head in disapproval of their irresponsibility as he clicked on the file.

Operation Felix Rises
Nerol, Pral; Trace, Argos; Loh, Cintha; et al.

Our research aims to investigate the complex tissue structuring potential of the recently discovered Felix cell. The Felix cell is a highly anomalous artificial form that mirrors the physiology and structure of a biological cell. Recombinant Felix cells were imbued with Primus genetic sequences with the intention of producing a synthetically derived Primus entity. Potential alterations of complex muscular-skeletal system physical traits resulting from the aberrant and anatomically enhanced Felix cells are unknown, but likely to match the Primus genetic sequences used as templates. It is predicted that the Felixes will exhibit Sejero traits, though to what degree is currently unknown.

Vengelis read through the abstract warily. *Potential muscular-skeletal alterations unknown.* At least they had that part right. He scrolled through the rest of the report. It was well over two hundred pages, and he did not even recognize, least of all comprehend, half of the dense scientific terminology. A small light flashed next to his monitor. It was the ship communication speaker. Darien had been good about not disrupting him, and he must have relayed the command to Hoff, who had also yet to butt in.

Vengelis pushed the button. "What?"

"My lord, we've reached transmission distance from Filgaia. Master Tolland was correct in his coordinates. It is very far, but a planet does appear to exist exactly where he guided us. We're a little over two days out," Darien's baritone voice spoke through the speaker.

"I'll be right there," Vengelis said. He looked back to the text of the Felix report. It was going to take a while to get through the pages, and he had two days to study it with little else to occupy his time. He stood and limped down the narrow hallway toward the command deck, keeping as little weight as possible on his tender right leg.

Both giants stood at attention when he entered the command deck and roared, "Hail, Emperor Vengelis Epsilon!"

Vengelis's face flickered irritably. "Spare me. You need an empire in order to call yourself an emperor."

Darien and Hoff exchanged an uncertain look.

"Forgive us for interrupting you, my lord, but we have found a trove of . . . strange . . . archival information on planet Filgaia. We thought you would want to see it right away," Darien said.

"What does it say?" Vengelis asked with little interest.

"Well . . . quite a bit, my lord," Hoff said. "We're very confused."

"What?" Vengelis looked to his Lord General. "I thought Darien told me there was no information on Filgaia in the Imperial database."

"Well, there isn't." The light of a nearby monitor cast a greenish light on Hoff's baffled expression. "You had better come look at this. It's from this ship's own private archive."

Vengelis approached the monitor and stared at it. There was a scanned copy of a handwritten note.

Pral,

Greetings. I have thoroughly investigated the unchartered planet Filgaia. You were correct in your prediction. The planet's ecosystems closely resemble accounts of a pre-Zergos Anthem. The planet is inhabited by, among countless other species, a sister-species to the Primus: human. Human chromosomes are identical with pre-Sejero Primus. Inherent inferences arising in the discovery of a sister-species are nearly beyond my comprehension. The humans are vastly inferior to Sejero power and must be preserved at all costs. I shudder at the thought of the empire invading the young world. Though I believe its remoteness will insulate Filgaia from colonization and extraction, as a precaution I would advise you to immediately fabricate evidence that will discourage long distance exploration into the region. Perhaps a lecture to the Science Council on the evidence of a black hole in the region will suffice? I will leave the creative end up to you.

Best regards. See you at the next Council.
Tolland

Vengelis slowly read the personalized note. After a long puzzled moment he asked, still staring at the correspondence. "What exactly is this?"

"We have no idea," Lord General Hoff said with equal confusion.

"It would appear as though the *Harbinger I* and this other ship that's referenced, the *Traverser I*, have an independent database separate from the Imperial network," Vengelis mumbled as he began to scan through each of the ship's logs. "You said this ship, the *Harbinger I*, belonged to Master Tolland, right?"

"Yes. He told us to get on board his ship, this ship, and leave Anthem," Darien said.

"The other ship mentioned, the *Traverser I*, must have belonged to Pral Nerol," Vengelis said. He had seen that Pral Nerol had constructed each spacecraft on the plaque outside his medical room. It was unheard of for a private individual to own a deep space craft, even among the tremendously rich Royal families. Vengelis cursed Pral Nerol's resourcefulness; the man truly was a genius.

"Did Master Tolland ever mention Pral Nerol?" Lord General Hoff asked. "I wasn't aware they even knew each other."

"Tolland only mentioned Nerol in passing, if at all," Vengelis said as he looked through the ship log at previous journeys of the *Harbinger I*. "Though based on the familiarity of the message between the two, it appears as though Master Tolland and Pral Nerol were friends."

"They clearly knew each other well enough for Pral Nerol to give Master Tolland the *Harbinger I*," Darien said.

"The date on this correspondence about Filgaia is from twenty years ago," Vengelis said with a frown as he pictured a young Master Tolland sitting in the same command bridge around the time of his own birth.

"Yeah," Darien said. "Back when they both held a seat in the War Council."

"Now I'm even more confused," Vengelis said. "Why after twenty years of working with Pral Nerol to conceal the knowledge of this Filgaia place would Master Tolland send me there in his last breath? It doesn't make any sense. There are several hospitable planets he could have directed us toward, and all of them closer than this Filgaia."

Lord General Hoff shrugged. "I can't imagine."

"There must be a reason specific to Filgaia," Vengelis murmured. "And I need to find out what it is."

Reading the note once more, Vengelis decided he did not like its contents. Could Master Tolland have sent him to Filgaia in order to start anew with this so-called sister-species? Vengelis shook the notion from his mind. He knew Master Tolland too well; his teacher would have chosen the extinction of the

Primus race before he would send Vengelis along with two recognized war-mongers to inevitably subjugate an inferior people.

And yet there must have been something unique about the planet that had brought it to Master Tolland's dying thoughts.

"Wait a minute, wait a minute." Vengelis suddenly sat upright, placed his hands on his head, and closed his eyes in concentration. He vaguely remembered the last thing Master Tolland had shouted to him far over Sejeroreich as they together had fought the Felixes. The memory was hazy, but he was certain of it. Master Tolland had shouted something about a place called Filgaia. Vengelis's pulse quickened as he tried to conjure up what Master Tolland had yelled. The deafening sounds of the chaos in Sejeroreich and the collapsing of the Imperial palace had filtered out his voice. Vengelis let his hands fall to the armrests, and he opened his eyes to see Hoff and Darien staring expectantly at him, not daring to break his concentration. "Program the ship to record all broadcasts coming out of Filgaia. I want a language matrix to begin immediately. We're going to have to resign ourselves to patience."

"And what's our plan, exactly?" Darien asked.

"Master Tolland clearly thought there was something of use to us against the Felixes on Filgaia," Vengelis said. "He held hope in something, though its identity is obscured. He must have been absolutely certain of it, or he wouldn't have risked our trespass on the planet. We will land on Filgaia and entrust ourselves to Master Tolland's bearing."

"But I don't understand." Darien shook his head. "What could possibly be there? It says in the note that the planet needed protection from us. If it needs protection from us, what use could it be against a foe greater than us?"

"For one thing, there may be scientists," Vengelis said. "The complexity of the Felix research is beyond me. I'm going to have Nerol's report translated into their languages. I want to get the report into the hands of their most capable scientists. It's possible there are elementary aspects to the report that I don't understand but are basic to even an obsolete scientist. It's likely Felix technology is hundreds if not thousands of years ahead of them, but it's the only reason I can think of for Master Tolland sending us there. I will use their networks to find a congregation of their scientists, and I will put them to work helping our cause."

"My lord." Hoff looked up suddenly.

"What?"

"I've found something else of interest. I'm going through the old records of the *Harbinger I* log to find any other correspondences between Master Tolland's *Harbinger I* and Pral Nerol's *Traverser I*."

"I've already looked through the rest of the *Harbinger I* log," Darien said. "There's nothing of note."

"Well, no, there's nothing in the *Harbinger I* log. But I just opened up the *Traverser I* ship records."

Vengelis and Darien both rose from their seats to look at Hoff's monitor. The *Traverser I* ship log was opened to the last entry.

Traverser I Ship Log
120/1K13/3AB09
Record: Anthem to Filgaia
Passengers: 1
Current Docking Location: (183.27, 243.45) Filgaia

"I don't understand," Darien said, staring at the *Traverser I* log. He scratched his head. "What's the big deal?"

"The ship made no return journey." Vengelis stared at the screen curiously. "*The Traverser I*—and its lone passenger—stayed on Filgaia."

"Pral Nerol's ship," Lord General Hoff whispered to himself incredulously, his expression tightening. "Four years ago . . ."

Darien shook his head. "That doesn't make any sense. I thought Master Tolland and Pral Nerol wanted to hide the planet? Why would Nerol have sent someone to Filgaia aboard his ship?"

"A researcher maybe," Vengelis muttered, his gaze held on *Passengers: 1.* "Some academic sent to observe and report on the planet and its people. That's the only possibility that seems logical."

"Maybe," Hoff grunted, his tone distant.

"Well, this must be it! This person must be why Master Tolland sent us to Filgaia. Maybe he or she is a scientist that's familiar with Felix technology. They can help us defeat the machines."

"That seems very unlikely," Vengelis said. "Whoever it is has been secluded on the planet and out of transmission range for four years. Pral Nerol didn't come up with the Felix technology until recently. I'd venture to bet that he or she has no idea about the Felixes."

"So they'll know nothing. We're going to have to tell them Anthem has been destroyed?" Darien asked.

Neither Vengelis nor the Lord General answered him, and the command deck fell to silence, save for the continuous thrumming of the engines.

"This changes nothing," Vengelis said after some time passed, his momentary interest vanished as he settled himself back at his own monitor. "I'm sure it's just a researcher of Pral Nerol's who is making an analysis of ecosystems or something of that nature. Whoever it is will be grieved to learn that while he was busy studying Filgaia, his own world was lost."

"It sickens me that Anthem lays in ruin while this planet is allowed to carry on." Lord General Hoff pushed his keyboard away from him angrily. "Haven't we been through enough trials as a race? First the Zergos and now the Felix . . . how many times must we be forced to face destruction? It isn't fair."

"It's not unfair," Vengelis said as he scanned through the rest of the old *Traverser I* ship log.

"I beg your pardon, my lord?"

"There is no fair or unfair, just or unjust, and so on. All of that is nonsense. Morality, justice, religion—they're all just conceptions people conjure up to add a sense of stability to the chaos of their lives. Against the inexorability of ruin, all beliefs unveil themselves as delusion, Hoff. Life is neither fair nor unfair—it is deadened and disinterested."

Hoff and Darien exchanged a perturbed glance.

"Are you saying your only belief is the certainty of destruction?" Darien asked.

"I don't believe in anything," Vengelis said flatly. "And based on the things I have seen, I don't see why anyone would."

Lord General Hoff nodded. "Does that mean we are going to bring ruin to Filgaia?"

"No. No, we don't need to conquer the place to get what we require. All we need is to gain submission. That's assuming these people have intelligence that can be of use to us. Unfortunately, the time needed for diplomatic requests is a luxury I do not have. People resist against invaders, but in the presence of a god they merely kneel. We will show them a fleeting glimpse of their own destruction against our omnipotence, and then I will grant them the option to avert it by helping us."

Lord General Hoff nodded. "And what of the Primus who traveled to Filgaia on the *Traverser I*?"

Vengelis considered the *Traverser I* log entry, *Passengers: 1.* "I have no doubt that when I prod their scientists, our presence will stir him or her to greet us."

CHAPTER THIRTEEN

Ryan

Ryan walked through the softly lit hallways of the Columbia Anthropology department, a faint smell of preservative chemicals and floor cleaner lingering in the air. He paused here and there to look into the glass displays of ancient artifacts and recent excavation finds from around the world: ragged woven fabrics, gnarled and knotted wooden devices, inlaid shards of worn ceramics, and brittle bones of slaves and lords equally forgotten.

Pausing before the closed door to Professor Hilton's office, Ryan leaned against a wide display case and examined an odd-looking stone figurine, its angles and curves softened with time. He felt reverent as he considered the time and place in which this peculiar stone idol had been carved. The chipped sockets stared blankly at him, and in their deadened gaze Ryan could feel the enormity of all the tales its withered face would tell if given the chance.

These hallways and the fantastically exotic historical artifacts on display always inspired him in some warmly quixotic way. Ryan yawned heavily as he looked at the stone carving. It had been a long day, and there had not been a moment to rest since he had awoken at sunrise for his shift at the library.

Professor Hilton's door opened, and a girl stepped out looking rather perturbed as she pushed a pile of papers into her backpack. Ryan caught the closing door and entered the office behind her.

"Mr. Craig, good to see you." Professor Hilton was at his desk, and he seemed more amicable than usual. His windowless office was cramped, the walls covered with shelves of thick textbooks and faded maps. "Come sit."

"You wanted to see me?" Ryan let his backpack fall to the carpet and took a seat in a chair opposite the professor.

"Yes, I did." Professor Hilton leaned back and folded his hands across his stomach. "I was surprised by your essay's thesis this week."

Ryan held back his knee-jerk response of frustration, and instead asked, fully knowing the answer, "What surprised you about it?"

"Well, you seem to have completely disregarded the suggestions we had discussed after your previous essay. I thought we had made a plan to improve the quality of your work."

"Quality?"

"Well, perhaps not the quality. But as of this assignment, every paper you have handed in contains a thesis that's too impractical to be considered academic. We talked about the importance of some degree of applicability in your positions; they must be anchored in the real world. I told you to reevaluate your techniques and create a *moderate* stance for the essay that was due today."

"You told me to write your stance." Ryan swallowed his rising infuriation and brought his attention to a frayed map on the nearby wall of racial demographics in South Africa.

"Ryan. You need to discuss in your essays what we cover in lecture."

"Professor," Ryan said. "I'm not going to take a specific position just because it's the easiest to defend or because it's what you taught in class. I believe what I wrote, and I defended my points adequately."

"I flipped through it." Professor Hilton tapped the stack of stapled essays. "I will say you made a valid argument. But you need to understand that these essays are assessments of what you have learned. If you don't relate your stances to ideas we have discussed in class, then you might as well not be a student. It is my hope that you will *learn* in this class. The bottom line is that throughout this semester you have strayed from the directions of your assignments, you cite preposterous sources, and you take stances that aren't discussed in lecture. This is not an open discussion class, Ryan. The standard of grading in my classroom is not to be decided upon by my students. Either write about what I teach you, or you'll receive a poor grade."

Ryan rose from his seat. "We should write what you want to read—your own words regurgitated—or you'll fail us. I think I get your message." He picked up his backpack and exited the room, pausing as the office door shut behind him. For a moment he considered turning around and berating Professor Hilton for his unjust grading system. But he quickly thought better of it. Best not to further anger a man who held complete qualitative sway over his entire grade. Instead, Ryan turned down the hall and made his way past the rows of spotless glass displays and out of the building. He walked along the sidewalk toward his dorm, the grassy tree-lined quad on one side, and the busy street on the other. Overhead, the late afternoon was punctuated with broad clouds rimmed with the warm light of sunset. Here and there the high-rises of Midtown peeked between the roofs of nearby buildings.

Ryan kicked through a scattering of leaves as he sent Kristen a text: *Meeting with professor went exactly as expected.* His thoughts were exhausted and bleak as he swiped his keycard to enter the dorm. Flagging sunlight streamed through the windows of his room as Ryan tossed his belongings onto the floor and switched on his laptop. He allowed his shoulders to sink into his chair, and he glanced around the concrete dorm room he called home. The limited floor space not taken up by the desk and narrow bed was scattered with a hodgepodge of clutter. Ryan slouched over and picked up some library books, stacking them into a pile by his desk. A few were overdue. He gathered all of the dirty clothes and slid open the closet door, dropping them into an already overflowing hamper.

The closet was its own calamity of disorganization. Ryan had only been living here since August, and he wondered how it was possible that so much stuff had already accumulated. He folded his arms and leaned against the doorframe, scanning the heaps for anything that could be thrown away. Most of the contents were winter clothes that had not yet come into season and pairs of rarely worn shoes. A few clean shirts still hung on hangers. He would hold off on laundry until the weekend.

Ryan turned wearily from the closet and flopped down on his bed, bouncing lightly on the squeaking springs. Professor Hilton had pitched him over the edge of frustration, so for the time being Ryan allowed himself a break from thinking about grades. He strained his arm out to the stack of books on his desk and ran his finger over the spines, pulling out a weathered copy of Mary Shelley's *Frankenstein.* The library cellophane wrapped around its cover was crinkled and worn with age.

Propping pillows behind his head and resting the book against his chest, Ryan slowly surrendered to the narrative as dusk took hold of the world outside his window. He turned page after page, and his mind ambled out of time and place as he engrossed himself in the strange tale. Although Ryan may have been in the warmth of his dorm room, his imagination was in a disconsolate and gloomy nineteenth-century Europe. With each passing page, Ryan's eyelids grew heavier, and he began to doze. With half-opened eyes, Victor Frankenstein's voice echoed in his mind.

It was on a dreary night of November that I beheld the accomplishment of my toils. With an anxiety that almost amounted to agony, I collected the instruments of life around me, that I might infuse a spark of being in the lifeless thing that lay at my feet. . .

Ryan started, his head nodding briefly. The sleepiness felt euphoric in its serenity, and his eyes grew heavy once again as he continued.

. . . It was already one in the morning; the rain pattered dismally against the panes, and my candle was nearly burnt out, when, by the glimmer of the half-extinguished light, I saw the dull yellow eye of the creature open; it breathed hard, and a convulsive motion agitated its limbs . . .

Ryan's eyes drew back, and his head sunk into the pillow, his mouth open and his chest drawing slow steady breaths.

. . . But now that I had finished, the beauty of the dream vanished, and breathless horror and disgust filled my heart . . .

Ryan floated into an elusive realm of his own dream. A darkening veil of nighttime had fallen across him, and he stood in a lost forest. Heavy snow fell silently through still trees rising above him. Snowflakes landed weightlessly against his shoulders and brow. He held out his hand, and the snowflakes came to rest on his palm and melted to nothing. Overhead, a curtain of snow clung to the dark fingerlike branches of the trees. Beyond the shadowy branches, midnight clouds hung low and tranquil over the woodland, quietly expelling their wondrous endowment. He turned and looked around him, then began trudging slowly through the silent forest. The snow was accumulating quickly, and his feet were already buried to his shins.

Ryan peered into the hush of the night.

As his awareness mounted, a disquieting dread began to surface, a terrible fear like sludge in his chest. Suddenly, he did not like the trees, or what might be hiding behind them. The gathering snowfall began to worry him. And he felt cold, a cold somehow unrelated to temperature. It was some other type of cold—an iciness of anxiety. With the onset of his chilled heart came a distinct awareness of another presence in the woods. Something was with him, and it was watching his movements from the shadows. When he moved through the snow, he thought he could hear it move with him, and when he became still to listen, so too did it. What it was Ryan could not be certain, but it was near, and it was hiding—perhaps behind one of the thick trunks or a step out of sight in the enveloping snowfall. Ryan could feel its gaze upon him. He stopped to listen more carefully, and squinted into the rows of thick dark trunks. A twig snapped somewhere to his right, and he turned to face the source of the noise.

At first he saw only skeletal bushes, weighed down by the heft of the storm. But then he saw it. Through the obscuring snowfall and darkness, something was hiding behind a tree. It was peering out at him, its body close against the other end of the trunk to conceal itself. Ryan's anxiousness disappeared as he realized the creature was not a threat.

It was a child. The child was shaking, and Ryan realized that it was scared of him.

"Hey," Ryan called out in a soft tone, but the child flinched at his voice.

"It's okay. Are you lost?" Ryan lifted a leg from the snow and took a step toward the tree. The strange child pulled its head back from the sight of his approach and let out a piercing melancholy sob that resonated in the winter beauty of the night.

"It's okay, I'm not going to hurt you," Ryan said, and slowly approached the tree. "I can help you."

But he stepped too near, and the child fled with an upturn of snow. Ryan watched in bewilderment as it ran into the shadows of the forest.

A long crimson cloak flowed in the child's wake.

Ryan began to trot after it, the sound of his footfalls squeaking as his feet pressed into the deepening snow. His heavy breath rose and fogged his vision as his pace quickened. Something was wrong—the child needed help. It would die on its own in these cold woods. In a sudden panic, Ryan lifted his forearms to cover his face and lurched onward through the underbrush, twigs snapping and breaking against his body.

"Wait!" he called out. "Wait!"

As he followed the tracks left in the snow by the child, a familiar smell began to gather around him. It was the pleasing smoky redolence of a crackling wood fire. Ryan took some comfort in the rustic scent, but he needed to make sure the child found its way home—that it returned to the fire. And yet as he gained on the child's small tracks, the smell of wood fire intensified to a dense smoke that Ryan could now see lingering amid the falling snow. The fog of smoke gathered around him, as if the forest itself was burning. Just as he began to question the source of the smoke, Ryan crashed out of the last stand of trees and staggered into an open field. There was a great bonfire in the middle. It shone like a great flickering candle in the distance, its warmth glinting through the shifting smoke and snowfall. Ryan made for the bonfire, trudging forward through the knee-deep snow, much deeper here in the field.

He could hear only the swish of his legs as they slashed through snowdrifts, but as he came closer to the fire, he began to discern other sounds. Carried faintly through the snowfall came screams of anguish. Shrieks were rising and falling against the storm. And as Ryan came closer still, the screams multiplied, and he saw the bonfire was far larger than he had first thought.

Ryan halted in disbelief of a sight that turned his heart black.

What he had thought was a bonfire was an entire village caught ablaze. A dozen burning huts, made with little more than straw and sticks on walls of stones, were raging furiously against the snow. Flames roared and sticks crackled and broke with piercing snaps. Ryan saw the inhabitants of the village. They looked ancient and out of place and time, like a primitive people. Their numbers were uncountable as they fled the ring of huts. He realized now that the child had been running away from this village. The child had not been lost; it had been fleeing for its life.

An evil presence had descended upon this ring of huts.

A person who looked different than the others walked past the shadows cast by the fires. The man looked bizarre and foreign. He wore strange armor that glinted in the red firelight and he carried a gun-like weapon. This man looked so unlike the rest of the people with their furs and sticks. The villagers were running from the man with the gun and into the cover of forest. Ryan watched as a number of stragglers snuck into one of the huts that had not yet caught aflame to hide from the stranger. The armor-clad man calmly approached the hut and leveled his gun.

"No!" Ryan screamed as fire belched from the gun's barrel. The hut erupted into searing flames. Now much more visible in the luster of the blaze, the man wiped his brow with his forearm and moved to the next hut.

"Stop! Stop!" Ryan called out, sprinting toward the man. "Why?"

As the man turned around and aimed at another hut filled with wailing villagers, Ryan ran in front of him. The gun screamed, but its fire sizzled and went out against his chest. Ryan somehow knew that while in this dream, neither fire nor injury could harm him; he was invincible. Stunned by his sudden intrusion, the armored man fell back into the snow.

"What the *hell* are you doing?" the man shouted, his voice so familiar to Ryan. The man rose to his feet, spitting snow out of his mouth and brushing it off his shoulders in indignation.

"What are you doing?" Ryan screamed, unable to hold back his emotions at the burning horror raging around them. "Why are you doing this?"

The armored man laughed. It was a great jovial laugh full of personality and humor. "What do you mean? You got the last order—kill the intelligent ones."

Ryan swallowed hard. "Why?"

"How the hell should I know why?"

The fires in the village were spreading quickly now, leaping eagerly between the huts. Snow sizzled and evaporated with a high-pitched whine against the flames. The village people were scattering, their screams of despair horrendous. An infant stumbled out from one of the burning huts and fell to the ground with flesh blackened and smoking. Ryan looked in disbelief from the carnage to the man with the gun. "How could you possibly do this?"

"If you want to be court-martialed, that's fine with me." The soldier moved to push past Ryan, but Ryan grabbed him by the shoulder. He had never felt such fury, such certainty of hate.

"Are you serious, kid?" the man looked down at Ryan's hand. "It's almost over anyway, who cares?"

"These people are wielding *sticks* and *stones!*" Ryan screamed over the unspeakable massacre.

The man wiped his forearm against the sweat of his brow and shrugged, pulling the gun back up to this shoulder. "Just following orders."

Ryan peered through the gathering smoke as the villagers tried to beat down the fires and usher their young away from the village and into the forest. Smaller children were foundering in the tall snow, unable to push through its weight. Ryan's heart was pounding like a sledgehammer, his breathing constricted.

"Well, what's it going to be?" the soldier said with the vacant certainty of one relying on authority. He held the gun out to Ryan. "Your turn."

In a daze Ryan stumbled from the armored man and into the chaos of the burning huts. He realized the villagers were fleeing him just as they were running from the man with the gun. Something rough hit his back, and Ryan turned around to face one of the bigger villagers who was staring at him with rage. A wooden spear with a chipped stone head lay splintered and broken on the ground from the blow to Ryan's back. The villager wound up and threw another spear. The spear sliced a path through the smoky air and fractured in two as it bounced off Ryan's chest. Ryan looked down at the shattered spear, and for the first time realized he was wearing the same armor as the horrible man with the gun.

They were together.

"I—I'm sorry," Ryan muttered, feeling nauseated by the hatred in the large villager's eyes. A family was sobbing beside a burning hut. Some ran into the fiery entrance, but were driven out by the roaring heat. One after another, Ryan watched them leap over the flames but then fall backward, unable to stand the torrid heat. They were obviously trying to rescue someone trapped inside. He ran to them and slipped past the blazing doorway. Ryan felt nothing—he was utterly impervious to the heat—as he stood amid the crackling inferno and surveyed the pulsing cinders and roaring flames. Prostrate on the scorched dirt floor, amid a bed of fire, was a young child. With a horrible gasp Ryan realized it was the child he had encountered in the woods.

The child was dead.

Blistering burn marks covered its pitiable body and an expression of dread and agony was etched on its face. It had endured a death by fire, not smoke. Ryan stepped through the flames, picked up the pathetic form and carried it out as the hut collapsed in embers. He placed the child in the snow and for a long moment stared into the young terrified eyes. The terror upon the child's expression ripped a gaping hole through Ryan's soul as ashen snow fell softly on its face. The long crimson cloak was still hung around the poor child's body. A few spots were still smoldering, and Ryan patted the embers into the snow and pulled the burned cloak off the child's slender shoulders. A few of the villagers, perhaps the young one's family, watched from the distance as he looked down at their child.

Another spear hit Ryan's back.

"I'm sorry. I—I'm sorry," Ryan murmured. He turned to the armored man with the gun, who was busy setting fire to the last remaining hut. A sweltering wrath like he had never known surfaced within him, and Ryan sprinted at the man in an absolute rage. His velocity felt unreal, the strength in his legs and arms incomprehensible as the snow in his path exploded from his speed. He felt the power of a god within him, and his fury. . . .

Ryan let out a broken shriek, his body suddenly sitting upright in his dark dorm room.

The copy of *Frankenstein* had fallen from his chest and lay open on the tile floor. An inky evening claimed the sky beyond his window, and the dorm room was cast in shadows. Ryan was covered in a cold sweat, and he wiped his forehead on the sleeve of his sweatshirt with a long quivering sigh in the still darkness. Steadying his feet on the floor, he stood shakily and flicked on his lamp. He leaned his palms against his desk and stared quietly out the window. Under the streetlights students were walking to dining halls for dinner.

It had been a year since the last time he saw that child's burned face in his dreams, and Ryan had even begun to think—to hope—that he had at last made peace with his recurring nightmare.

Ryan turned, his socks sliding against the tile floor, and walked to his closet. He sat before it, his gaze resting on a locked trunk pushed to the back. A plaid shirt lay draped over the top, the wrinkled arm falling over the front of the trunk and concealing a heavy padlock. His attention lingered on the heavy trunk for a long time, his expression pained. With a heavy heart he reached out and pulled the trunk to him, the metal scraping against the tile. Slowly and despondently he turned the dial of the padlock and removed it from the latch. Ryan carefully opened the trunk and stared in suffering silence at what lay within.

With a delicate touch, Ryan reached into the trunk and slowly pulled out the child's burnt and tattered crimson cloak. He held it up silently and looked with anguish at the armor that rested underneath it. On the breast of the armor, a grave and familiar symbol reminded Ryan that it was not a dream, but a memory. He stared silently at his Imperial First Class armor and the embossment upon the chest: the crest of house Nerol.

CHAPTER FOURTEEN

Kristen

Kristen Jordan sat quietly on her couch, untouched takeout sushi for two on the coffee table and a television program murmuring on her dated flat screen. She could not bring herself to look at the containers of food or the show, so instead Kristen stared contemplatively out the window into the fall night. Beyond the rusty fire escape and the building across the street, her studio had a surprisingly impressive view of the city considering her monthly rent. The lit skyscrapers of Midtown shone through a dreariness of fog that had taken hold of Manhattan. High above the lofty rooftops, she could trace a dome of light as it illuminated the moisture hanging over the city. With a tired gaze she looked out at the skyline as the rooftops disappeared into the foggy mists of the heavens.

Ryan was coming over, and Kristen was thankful for it. There was something about him that calmed her. By all accounts he should have made her nervous, as she was usually shy around guys she liked. And yet every time they were together she felt at peace with everything. At first glance he was so attractive, painfully so. It was sometimes hard to hold his eye contact and keep herself from blushing. But his looks were of an athletic type that she did not usually go for. Her affection for him was not based on his attractiveness; it was something about the way he carried himself that drew her in.

Looking out over Manhattan, Kristen realized that she would have been utterly alone in this city—in her little social sphere of scientists and laboratory small talk—were it not for him. Her research had come to alienate her from everyone. She would not let it stand between her and others any more, especially Ryan.

The thought of the next morning's scientific convention at the hotel amid all those tall buildings made her ill with angst. The day would prove to be a great networking opportunity, but Kristen's discovery of Professor Vatruvia's private research had left a vile taste in her mouth. Any thought of the Vatruvian mice in their secluded cages made her feel sick. Kristen could not stop thinking about Cara's revelation: the Vatruvian cells were stronger than the natural cells they replicated. Would the same phenomenon hold true for larger systems? Were those mottled mice with their bluish eyes *superior* to natural mice?

Kristen's apartment doorbell rang and snapped her out of her thoughts. She roused herself from the couch and pressed the intercom button. "The buzzer's broken, I'll come let you up."

She slid her feet into her slippers, pulled on an old MIT sweatshirt, and walked out to the stairwell, leaving the door ajar behind her. Beyond the lobby, the October night was chilly and wet. Ryan was waiting outside, the hood of his rain jacket pulled down over his forehead. He smiled at her through the drizzle. She folded her arms with a shiver as she pushed open the door. The damp autumn air was cold and laden with the smell of cigarettes from people smoking outside the bar next door.

"Hi," Kristen said.

"Hey. I brought some booze." Ryan held a bottle of wine wrapped in a brown paper bag. "You like red wine?"

"If it has alcohol in it, I'm happy. I need a drink." Kristen laughed mirthlessly and held his gaze.

"Yeah," Ryan sighed. "Me too."

Kristen looked to the congregation of smokers standing under the nearby awning. Someone must have said something funny, as there was a great roar of laughter. "I'm okay with going out for a round or two if you want. Don't feel as though we have to stay in—I can totally throw on a change of clothes and go out for a while."

"Eh," Ryan shrugged and regarded her thoughtfully as he passed into the doorway. "I'd rather stay in, to be honest."

"Okay. I ordered some sushi."

"Perfect."

They walked up the several stories of aged stairs to her apartment. Kristen took the wine from him as he looked around her tiny studio, the bed by the window and the living area set up around narrow walls of exposed brick.

"I like your place," Ryan said.

"Thanks. The rent is actually pretty reasonable, considering." Kristen flipped on the kitchenette light and rummaged through a drawer for the wine opener. "Tell me about the meeting with your professor."

Ryan let out a halfhearted groan as he took off his shoes and sat down on the couch. "More of the same. I think I'm going to have to turn my mind off and play the game."

"And whose advice was that?"

"Yours," Ryan admitted. "I guess I'll have to start following your advice more often. How are things going with your research?"

Kristen twisted the wine opener into the cork and smirked grimly down at the bottle. "That's a loaded question."

"Oh yeah?"

Kristen nodded. She picked up two glasses from the cupboard and sat down with him, curling her legs beside him. "Professor Vatruvia has really let me down, to be honest. It's strange. He's so brilliant in some regards, and so woefully lacking in others. I don't think he's thinking clearly about what we're doing with the Vatruvian cell. It's as though he has no notion of the fact that we're working on something that could have a huge impact on the world—whether it be for good or bad. He's pushing forward just for the sake of pushing forward."

" 'Now, I am become death, the destroyer of worlds,' " Ryan said quietly, his voice matter-of-fact as he leaned forward and poured some of the silken burgundy wine into each glass.

"I beg your pardon?"

" 'Now, I am become death, the destroyer of worlds,' " Ryan repeated with a dark smirk. "It's what Robert Oppenheimer said when he watched the detonation of the first atomic bomb. The bomb he created."

"Right," Kristen said with a slow nod. There was a sadness to Ryan that she just noticed, not maudlin or readily apparent, but nonetheless there behind his sharp gaze. It was easy to overlook amid his good looks and easy smile, but she saw it clearly for a moment. He was trying to hide how much he truly cared about a world that had little interest in hearing about its flaws. People wrote him off as uncompromising, but Kristen could see that it was not based in stubbornness—it was based in sorrow. He carried a curious grief within himself, as if it were a memento to something in his past. Kristen decided to let him divulge that grief in his own time, and simply said, "I thought I recognized the saying."

"He was a genius and an artist, the visionary of an age, and his gift to the world was a weapon. I wonder if it was at that moment—only right then—as

Oppenheimer watched the mushroom cloud rise into the skies over the desert," Ryan shook his head, "that he realized the true nature of what he created."

"I think it's sad," Kristen said, "I'm sure he never really thought anyone would drop one. He invented the technology and then lost all say in its use to lesser men."

Ryan took a sip of his wine. "More motivated men."

Kristen nodded.

"It's not with the calculations in front of them, but in the man beside them that most brilliant minds make their blunders. The science is the easy part, from a certain point of view."

"I assure you, what we have done with the Vatruvian cell has been anything but easy." Kristen tilted her gaze at him. "If that's what you're implying."

"No, no. That's not what I meant." Ryan shrugged his shoulders uncertainly. "I have my own past to bias my opinion on the matter, so don't think this is directed at you. It's just that, my father was a pretty serious scientist, and I always resented his blind faith to the notion of progress."

Kristen sipped her glass of wine coolly. It was the first time he had mentioned his parents since he told her they died when he was a teenager. "What do you mean?"

"Well, you'll have to take my word for it, my father was no fool. In fact, he was far from it. But you don't need to be a historian to know that throughout history technology has been used for evil just as much as it has been used for good."

"Of course," Kristen said.

"So despite his intelligence, he chose not to acknowledge that one simple truth. Ultimately, I think the world becomes a better place only through the willful actions of living men, not from the furthering of scientific knowledge." Ryan brought his palm to rest on Kristen's leg. His hand felt warm on her thigh. She liked it. "Take my father for instance. He devoted his unbelievably brilliant mind to the search for answers in technology, when—in my opinion—no true answers have ever, or will ever, be found there. What answers could he have discovered had his brilliant mind been devoted to solving one of the countless everyday problems facing society instead of trying to expand academia's rote knowledge of physics and chemistry?"

"And by *answers*, you mean what exactly?"

"I couldn't even venture a guess. You know, the grayer social issues. Human rights, politics, poverty and so on. I don't know—but I also could never claim to be genius." Ryan laughed silently and met her gaze with a serious expression. "Just an observer of it."

Kristen sighed heavily and took a generous gulp of wine. She rose and walked to the window and looked out over the foggy skyline. A cool draft rippled off the glass. Down on the sidewalk a growing line of stumbling young professionals were waiting to get into the bar. She could faintly hear their pent up rowdiness through the windowpane. Kristen leaned against the window in silence, holding her wine numbly. She felt powerless, like she was a little girl once more, with an infantile voice that could be easily disregarded. Next to the world renowned Nicoli Vatruvia, her opinion meant nothing to anyone. Kristen could not stop thinking of the strange bluish eyes of the Vatruvian mice.

With all her heart she wanted to tell Ryan everything she knew, all the things she had seen. Ryan seemed so grounded, so trustworthy. He was unlike all of the men she worked with every day in her labs: each of them so academically gifted and yet so unsophisticated. She could see Ryan in the room's reflection against the dark window. He was humble—a trait she rarely saw among university crowds. Ryan regarded his intellect and his handsomeness without the slightest hint of conceit or self-absorption. She desperately wanted to trust him.

"What is it?" Ryan asked, a genuine concern in his voice.

Kristen turned from the window with a sigh. The notion that Professor Vatruvia had made her sign a nondisclosure contract was too much to bear. It was selfish and ignoble of him. The reason he lacked trust in her was because he knew she would have the wherewithal to tell people about the mice. It was her common sense he mistrusted. Kristen recalled the wavy signature of the Secretary of Defense on the contract, and the tacit threat in Professor Vatruvia's voice as he had pointed it out to her. Artificial life, one of the greatest discoveries in the history of science, was being propelled by a handful of like minds behind locked doors.

Kristen was glad Ryan was with her, that she did not have to be alone for the night with nothing but her own disillusioned thoughts to keep her company.

"I agree with you, in part," she said with a swig from her glass. "The ambition of science can be scary. It's the awareness of that ambition that makes me fear the future of the Vatruvian cell."

"How do you mean?" Ryan asked.

"I've seen something that has challenged every conviction I have, as a scientist and a person. And now I don't know what to do."

After she fell silent for a time, Ryan leaned forward on the couch. "Are you going to tell me what you saw, or leave me guessing here?"

"I can't tell you," Kristen said quietly, feeling suddenly overwhelmed. "Professor Vatruvia made me sign a nondisclosure contract backed by the Department of Defense. When I signed the contract, I agreed not to tell anyone what I saw."

"Department of Defense?" Ryan said, bewildered. "What do they have to do with your research? I thought the Vatruvian cell was an amoeba sitting on a microscope slide?"

"It was."

"Was . . ." Ryan repeated with a hint of misgiving. "And what is it now?"

Kristen finished her wine and sunk back down next to him. She poured herself another more liberal portion. "It's something gargantuan enough to force a mere witness of it into signing a nondisclosure contract drafted by the Secretary of Defense."

"Man," Ryan said. "You must be in a tough position. Secrets aren't easy to live with."

"Yeah." Kristen rested the side of her head on his shoulder. "The burden of what I saw is weighing on me like nothing I could have ever imagined. And the position I'm in now is atrocious. I'm stuck between keeping my word to a zealous man I barely recognize anymore and the despotic nondisclosure agreement he made me sign, or risking my entire future by breaking my word and going public with what I saw."

"So I take it there's now something more to the Vatruvian cell than what was applauded in the *60 Minutes* special I watched the other month."

Kristen nodded, her cheek still against his shoulder.

"Well, if what you saw really is overtly dangerous, then I think the public will approve of you coming forward with what you know. Even the Department of Defense can't compete with the will of the people."

"But I'm sure there will be some people who don't think it's dangerous at all," Kristen scoffed angrily. "They'll think it's novel and fascinating. Harmless. Innovative. *Cool.*"

"Kristen, you're smart on a scale most people can't even imagine. If you of all people deem what you saw as dangerous, then it must be. They will listen." Ryan placed a reassuring hand on hers. "Sometimes the hardest thing to do is to have faith in what you believe. Having faith in others is easy—it requires only surrender. All of your studies, all of your trials and struggles have existed for you to exercise the intellect you now possess. It would be a disservice to the very institutions and people who provided the road to your genius to not stand your ground and speak—no, shout—your opinion, even if it's not what Professor Vatruvia and the Department of Defense want to hear. You have to find the courage to hold confidence in your own convict—"

Kristen's lips silenced his words. She met his mouth with her own, and Ryan's body stiffened as she pushed herself against him. He was right, and she knew it. It was clear to Kristen now. Her whole life spent in the pursuit of a prestigious education and career had been missing one crucial component. She had been blind to it for all these hectic years, but Ryan had just convinced her.

No one had ever taught her to be brave.

Ryan raised his hand from hers in surprise, but he then wrapped his arm around her midsection and pulled her closer to him.

"All this talk of courage," Kristen murmured, her lips against his. "And I had to make the first move."

PART TWO

APOTHEOSIS

CHAPTER FIFTEEN

Huntington, Vermont

Not unlike a small meteor, a metal object soared unseen through the cloudless morning skies of New England, traveling silently over expansive miles of vibrantly colored fields and woodlands before colliding into the broad side of a mountain with a faint thud. A barely perceptible concussion reverberated outward from the wilderness and through the small village below. From the far side of the mountain, a flock of white birds took to the sky, the only inhabitants to take notice of the disturbance in the otherwise pristine day.

A rather unimpressive white-and-green police cruiser—the only one on duty—drove across a long-neglected country road. Faded lettering on the side of the vehicle read, *Huntington Police Department.* The fenders were beginning to show peeling rust spots, and the tires needed replacing. In a large sense the outdated cruiser matched the pastoral outlandishness of the town. Situated a comfortable distance from the lone state highway that ran across Vermont, the only visitors to pass through Huntington, aside from the one or two thousand locals, were passing tourists from southern New England—most often sightseers looking to experience authentic Vermont foliage or hike Camel's Hump, one of the region's larger mountains. The Huntington village center consisted of little more than a gas station variety store and a family-owned hardware shop at the foot of the mountain.

To some Huntington would most aptly be described as comfortably quaint, to others, unsettlingly secluded.

Officer George Henderson, a twenty-year veteran of the force, drove the cruiser with his rookie partner Mike Fuller sitting next to him. The season's foliage was in full bloom, and the maple trees that loomed over the wood fences on either side of the road shown brilliant red, yellow, and orange in the morning sun. Dryness unique to autumn hung pleasantly in the air, accentuated by the drifting note of a wood fireplace or burning pile of leaves smoking somewhere in the nearby hills.

"Dispatch to cruiser, dispatch to cruiser." The radio on the dash awoke the two officers from their gentle reveries.

"What's up, Beth?" George said, taking his attention away from the fields outside his open window as he leaned forward to the dashboard and spoke into the transceiver.

"We just got a trespassing call up on Baron Road," said Beth, the third and only other officer on duty. Beth was back at the station, which consisted of an office, a few desks, and a holding cell. Her voice sounded uncharacteristically apprehensive.

George and Mike exchanged a confused glance and Mike doubtfully shook his head.

"You've got to be kidding me," George said into the transceiver. "Trespassing on Baron Road? That's practically halfway up the mountain."

"Yeah, I know," Beth's voice crackled from the outdated radio. "The call was really weird. Mrs. Janson was shouting something about men from the woods trying to get into her house."

George brushed it off with a wave of his hand. "I'm sure it's just some hunters or a group of hikers that wandered off the trail and need to use a phone."

"I would think the Jansons are used to that kind of trespassing by now, George," Beth's voice paused with concern, and the static worsened as their cruiser passed between two hills. "I could barely make out what Mrs. Janson was saying. She was hysterical. They live on fifty-eight Baron Road. Get there quick, you guys. I'm sure it's no big deal, but the call gave me the creeps. I'm pretty sure I heard her use the word *giant*."

"I know where the Jansons live," Mike said. He leaned forward and flipped on the sirens. "I used to deliver firewood up there every fall."

"All right. We'll head right over. Thanks Beth." George turned the cruiser down an empty road leading to the mountain.

"Beth's right you know," Mike said. "I don't think I've ever heard of someone on Baron Road calling the police over a trespasser. Think about it. None of the trails are on that side of the mountain, and the woods are too thick to pass. Last hunting season I tried to make it up there with some buddies, and we couldn't get through the underbrush for the life of us."

"Eh, who knows. It's probably just some doped up kids who got too fried to follow the trail or some hunter who drank too much whiskey."

Both officers laughed. Siren sounding, the cruiser sped along as it traversed wide fields and wooded hills, fallen leaves whirling in their wake. They drove by unmanned farm stands, shelves filled with squashes, pumpkins, and apples sitting on beds of hay; the cash registers nothing more than wicker baskets sitting by the produce. Their siren echoed across the land and traveled far in the dry air, joined only by a light breeze from the west. Outside their windshield, the lone mountain rose into the sky. It was blanketed with trees, a carpet of deep red and orange leading to a summit of bare granite a few thousand feet overhead.

"You hear Kalinoski's youngest is getting recruited to play hockey at university?" George asked.

"Nah. Last I knew he was just making the high school team." Mike was looking past the spots of old white sap streaked across the windshield to the fast approaching mountain. "Man time flies."

"You got that right."

They took a sharp left onto Baron Road and pulled off the smooth pavement onto a dirt path that vanished into the shelter of trees. The tree cover was so thick that the road could have passed for a hiking trail as it ascended in a narrow sinuous course up the eastern side of the mountain.

"Can't imagine living out here," Mike murmured as he rolled down his window, vacantly staring into the dense wilderness to each side.

"Different strokes for different folks, I guess. I just hope the suspension makes it through here." George was squinting and gripping the steering wheel, white-knuckled, as he carefully avoided the boulders and roots that lined their way. "You might as well turn off the sirens. It's not like we're going to run into any traffic."

"Good point." Mike leaned forward and shut off the blaring horns.

The moment the sirens subdued, a pall of absolute silence fell. The deep forest surrounding the cruiser seemed to swallow them whole. It felt as though their siren had been the last trace of their pleasant town and cloudless morning. Now they traversed through a narrow path of bright orange and yellow leaves that oddly contrasted with the near darkness caused by the tree cover. Dark tree trunks stood a mere foot away from both side mirrors, evoking an unsettling sentiment, which was left unmentioned by either officer, though each ran a hand across his holstered .38 revolver.

"Is that a house?" George asked, peering around a turn in the road as the car jostled.

Skeletal rays of sunlight filtered through a break in the trees and shone down onto a long overgrown lawn and a dingy log house. George slowly pulled the cruiser past the shack. Years of accumulated leaves lay wet and rotting on the roof, which in places was missing shingles and dilapidated. It was unimaginable that someone could or would live in this degree of squalor, yet there was a thin tendril of smoke rising from the mold-covered chimney, and on the overgrown grass a large stack of logs waited to be chopped.

"What number is that?" George moved his gaze uneasily across the neglected yard.

"I'm not sure on the numbers, but if I remember correctly, the Janson's house is next."

They rolled past a larger clearing of trees and another set back house. With a nod from Mike, George pulled into the Janson's gravel driveway, coming to a stop behind a faded pickup truck. From the driveway nothing appeared out of the ordinary about the Janson's property. The house had some wholesome character compared to the last. The front and back yards were fifty feet on either side, scattered with sun-worn plastic lawn furniture. On the front porch a rocking chair was unmoving in the still air. A partly rusted bicycle lay on the driveway, its front tire rotating slowly.

George and Mike stepped out of the cruiser and made their way to the front door. The air was stiff with silence, as though even the chirping of the birds and the rustling of squirrels in the underbrush had retreated farther into the surrounding woodlands. The crunch of their boots on the gravel was loud against the stillness.

George crossed the front porch with heavy steps, the wood sighing under his weight. He gave the door a firm knock. "Mrs. Janson! This is officer George Henderson of the Huntington police department. We are here in response to a nine-one-one call made from this address. Please open the door!"

There was no response.

"Mrs. Janson?" George called again. He turned to Mike and lowered his voice. "What do you think?"

"Let's go around back," Mike said.

George stepped off the porch and they rounded the house. As he walked past one of the windows, George heard a barely audible thump from inside the house. He hesitated and peered through a dusty window, but could not see anything. The curtains had been drawn. He shifted uneasily and turned away from the sill.

"Mike," George hissed in a whisper, unable to justify the urgency of his tone to even himself. "I heard something inside."

Mike did not respond, and instead turned the rear corner of the house into the backyard. George watched as Mike instantly recoiled, stumbling backward and tripping over a log in the grass. He landed hard, his butt crashing into the patchy grass. George instinctively unclipped his holster and ran to him. Mike remained on the ground, his back sinking into the wet grass as he stared at something in the backyard. As George hurried to help the rookie, he saw a horror in his partner's eyes like he had never seen upon any man's face. Almost reluctantly—knowing his reaction would surely be no different—George turned and looked.

A lightheaded fluttery sensation traveled through his extremities. "W-what the hell?" George sputtered, and stepped backward.

Standing in the backyard, beside an old charcoal grill and in front of a weathered picnic table, were two gargantuan beings. *Beings.* George felt his ability to rationalize blur; his mind could not process what his eyes were seeing. Were they human? The two things must have been well over eight feet tall and easily six hundred pounds each, if not closer to half a ton. Their heads practically reached the windows of the second floor, and standing side by side they were almost as wide as the entirety of the house. The exposed muscle of their legs and arms did not look real. It was as though they were made solely of muscle, like body builders, though less human and more distended and grotesque. They were wearing bizarre and intricate attire that looked supple and reinforced. In some animalistic and primal sense from within, George felt certain something was very wrong.

One of the behemoths turned and saw the two police partners: one standing and gawking, the other on the grass, both of their faces frozen in terror. One giant pointed at them, and the other turned to look. The officers and the giants stared at each other in equal disbelief for a moment. Then the enormous monsters did something that was altogether human, and all the more terrifying to George.

The two hulking masses began to laugh.

One of the giants suddenly spoke, its voice shockingly deep. *"Shingaz rakevis atool ha."*

George's chin began to shake, and his body trembled. The voice could not have been a human. It sounded deranged and malicious.

"George, let's go." Mike's voice sounded cold and detached from behind him. "George, I want to go right now."

One of the giants leaned a head the size of a car engine forward and examined them closely. After a moment the giant shouted, its voice rumbling. It shook the ground as though his vocal cords were a subwoofer. *"Ashkalez beeshtas forgasis vengeliskah."*

George's hand was still resting on his holster. He attempted to bring his mind back to his training at the academy in Montpelier twenty years previous as he pulled out his gun and clicked off the safety. The voice of his old grizzly

Army vet instructor rang through his ears. *Keep your composure! Always be ready to call for backup!*

But there was no such luxury as backup in Huntington, aside from the neighborhood watch and the prostrate young man beside him. George would have to take control of the situation by himself until the State Police could arrive.

"W-what is going on here?" George was barely able to enunciate the question, but felt somewhat empowered with the gun now in his hand.

The giant closer to the house turned and laughed with unmistakable amusement.

"*Porskis farzalork veesh sa.*" The giant moved his monstrous leg a step toward George and laughed when George retreated backward a step. The giant dwarfed over the six-foot-tall officer as though George were an elementary school boy holding a toy gun.

"George, I want to go. I want to go right now. This isn't right," Mike said from the grass.

George Henderson held his ground.

"What have you done with the Jansons?" George mounted up the courage and demanded, though his voice still sounded weak and lacked conviction. He cocked his gun, pointing it at the approaching behemoth. "Don't think I won't use this!"

The other giant turned to the house and yelled with a voice as deep as the first. "*Yariles vengeliskah!*"

A young man suddenly strode out of the house through the sliding patio doors. He looked to be in his late teens or early twenties, and was wearing the same strange attire as the giants. Although he looked like an athlete, his appearance was much less monstrous than the other two. Where the vacuous faces of the giants could have passed for wild animals, this smaller man's face was lined with sophistication. Although the young man certainly did not look like he came from Vermont—George likened him to a professional athlete or some sort of celebrity type—he did appear to be *human*, which was encouraging.

Judging by the body language of the two giants, it was obvious even to George that this new arrival was the one in command. The young man looked at the gun aimed in his direction and shook his head with unmistakable disdain.

"Please tell me you speak this language. Yes?" the mysterious young man asked. His voice was calm, articulate, and carried no accent whatsoever.

"W-what is going on here? Where are the Jansons?" George shouted and stepped forward, keeping the gun aimed at the smaller man. The young man's face remained unwavering, almost tiresome, as the gun pointed directly at him.

"I have no intent on harming you. Put the weapon away," the young man said. "All I need is for you to tell me where we are. My men and I have no quarrel with you gentlemen or the family in the house."

"Where are the Jansons?" George shouted.

The young man frowned. "Are you slow? I just said they're in the house. Again, I need to know where we are on Filg—Earth. I found a map in the house but I don't know where we are located on it. That is all. Then we are out of your way." The young man ran a hand across his chin, and George noticed a gigantic red ring on his finger. "This region seems isolated. You'll be safe here."

"Now excuse me, son! You are talking to a police officer! I need to see the family bef—"

"Enough!" the young man snapped. "You are a soldier of your people, not a group of children and an old woman like that family. I won't hesitate to rip your arms off to get what I want. Or you can simply give me what I want, and we can go our separate ways."

George was frozen, his mind lost in shock. He could sense Mike trembling beside him. Mike had also drawn his gun, but his back was still on the grass.

"Get against the house and put your hands behind your head!" George yelled, pushing his gun toward the young man.

"Decide," the young man said with a cold finality.

A deafening bang pierced the tense silence as Mike fired his handgun from his ground position. Simultaneously, the young man stretched out his hand. A moment of silence passed, then the young man looked down at Mike as though he were a petulant child. A smoking and deformed bullet was resting in between the young man's thumb and forefinger. He let the bullet go and it fell dramatically into the grass.

The young man turned and looked to one of the giants and spoke a phrase in the unusual language. One of the monsters lurched forward with surprising speed. He raised his foot and brought it down on Mike's chest. The enormous foot was nearly the size of the rookie's entire midsection. Popping sounds filled the yard as Mike's ribcage split. Mike frantically aimed the gun at the giant and emptied half the clip. Five shots. The giant looked down at him and shook his head as he stomped his foot on his chest, killing him instantly.

George frantically pointed his gun at the giant, his body convulsing.

"What do you want from us?" he sputtered, terrified.

"Are you serious?" the young man demanded with a dubious look. "I *just* told you. I want to know our location. If your friend here had just given me what I wanted, he would still be alive and well."

"O-o-o-okay. Okay. We are in Huntington."

"Huntington. Good. See? Now we are making progress," the young man said. "What is Huntington?"

The circuitry of George's mind was quickly fraying, and he was losing touch with reality. He felt a mordant nausea rise from his stomach to the back of his throat. "What the hell is going on?" he gasped through quick breaths.

The young man snapped his fingers impatiently, as one would to a dog. "Stay with me here. Your life is on the line."

"Huntington. Huntington, V-Vermont."

The stranger sighed and shook his head impatiently. "Okay, this isn't getting us anywhere. Look, I need to find New York City. I placed it on this map, but I don't know where we are."

"New Y-York? Why do you want to go there?"

"Where are we?" the young man ignored his question and walked up to George holding a map of the United States.

"We're here," George said, pointing a trembling finger to northern New England.

The young man nodded with a contented expression. "Wasn't that easy?" he looked at George as he shook violently.

"Y-y-yes," George said as he watched the giant who had stepped on Mike wipe the gore off his boot on the patchy grass. George leaned over, hands falling to his knees, and vomited on the grass.

The English-speaking man stepped closer to him and kneeled down beside him, looking disgusted. "You two were the first ones to fire your weapons—intending to kill us. I acted no more uncouth or boorish than you did."

The young man then turned on the spot and exploded upward into the sky, becoming a rippling dark dot in the glaring blue between the trees almost instantly. The two giants followed in his wake, flying over the mountaintop and out of sight behind a thin white cloud. George looked back and forth from the sky to the corpse of Mike Fuller.

George Henderson attempted to walk to his cruiser, but the blood rushed out of his head and he fainted in the yard.

CHAPTER SIXTEEN

Vengelis

The lack of answers was gnawing at Vengelis as he looked down on the sprawling lands of Filgaia. In Master Tolland's last moment of life, amid the indescribable carnage of Sejeroreich, this peculiar place had come to his mind. Master Tolland had thought of this place *and* of a salvation from the Felixes.

The two were somehow connected.

Far below, rolling hills dotted with town centers and fields passed by. A thin ribbon of highway snaked north to south, and Vengelis followed the faint reflections of tiny windshields that glinted in the sun. Having spent many healing hours in the medical rooms before the *Harbinger I* touched down, his features were back to normal. He looked every bit the Royal son once again, but Vengelis regarded his healed face with bitter embarrassment. It was the face of a failed sentinel. Though his expression was free of bruises and lacerations, there were shadows of sleeplessness under his tired eyes.

The Felixes haunted his every waking thought. The memory of the rampant death in Sejeroreich had rendered sleep impossible for many nights. Even now, under the brilliant sun, Vengelis saw only the eyes of the machines. The startling blue gaze filled him with an enervate dread. Vengelis had never felt so powerless. The Felixes had beaten him, and so too had the complexity of Pral Nerol's research. He could not handle either. From what he could piece together, Pral Nerol and his researchers had used Primus blood to create the machines that nearly took his life. The Felixes used Primus cells to architect their own form. This made intuitive sense to Vengelis, as the machines *were* Primus. Yet Vengelis recalled striking the blonde Felix in the temple. The side of her head had felt like a block of heavy iron against his knuckles. He remembered the profound ringing sound of the impact—it was as though he had struck a giant gong. There was nothing natural about that skull, or that woman.

"What is the plan?" Hoff called over the rushing air as the three unwelcome visitors soared southward across the expansive sky.

"While I was researching on the ship, I found a planned meeting of scientists that's going on today in a city to our south," Vengelis yelled into the wind, which pushed back his hair and roared in his ears. "I've had Pral Nerol's research translated into their languages. My plan is to arrive at this meeting, present the scientists with Nerol's work on the Felixes, and demand that they help me unravel its cryptic nature. If I can learn anything, it will be worth the effort. From there, I do not yet know what our long-term plan will be."

"And what if they don't give in to your requests?" Darien asked.

"They will," Vengelis said, and brought his attention to the blurred collision of navy skies and rolling hills against the southern horizon. "Based off the reaction of those people in the woods, I'd say it's clear we aren't going to blend in here—or at least not you two. I got the impression that family in the house thought I was a human and you both were . . . something else. They were begging me to help them get away from the two of you. Also those men with the firearms were terrified before they even realized their weapons were useless. Judging by that behavior, I think there's something unnatural about both of your appearances. I'll venture a guess it is your sizes."

"They're so small with their little guns," Hoff called. Vengelis turned to him with an expression of cool disdain, and Hoff quickly clarified his meaning. "Small as in weak, not in a Royal sense."

"Not everyone was *bred*, Lord General. But small or large, I want to attract as little attention as possible until the time is right. It would be advantageous to catch the scientists off guard. The last thing I want is for an alarm to sound and cities to evacuate before I have a chance to corral them."

"So what will you have us do?" Darien asked.

"I'm going to visit the city alone and attempt to immerse myself among them, at least for a short while. But that's not my intention for the two of you. We will have to separate. I think it's safe to assume you both will cause a panic if you step foot in a populated area. Or at the very least, you'll inadvertently do something that will result in panic. It doesn't require a stretch of the imagination to envision a scenario escalating." Vengelis shook his head. "I'm not going to take any chances. I will go to this city alone. There's too much on the line here to take an unnecessary gamble."

"Then should we head back to the ship and wait?" Hoff asked, failing to conceal the disappointment in his tone as he scanned the boundless landscape far below.

"No, no. There's only a small chance that the scientists will be able to help me to begin with. But I will need them to realize there is nothing they can do to stop our will."

Darien turned to him and called out, "How?"

"They need to be shown there will be no negotiating with us," Vengelis shouted over a loud gust of wind. "We don't have the time to make requests or respectfully ask for their help. I will present the scientists with a straightforward choice. Either help me in my understanding of the Felixes, or face total annihilation."

The Lord General veered in close to Vengelis, this development piquing his interest. "And where do Darien and I come into this?"

"You two will show them a vision of their obliteration at our hands."

"How?"

"Simple." Vengelis's face was stone. "Devastate them until they unequivocally surrender to our command. I can think of no better way to expedite our errand. My hope is to return to Anthem while there are still people left to save. As such, you two will demonstrate a succinct and irrefutable display of our power, and I will gain absolute submission."

"What will be the nature of our display?"

"You will maim one of their cities in the most brazen manner you can muster. At the same time I, after gaining their compliance, will force the greatest of their minds to figure out Pral Nerol's research. Regardless of whether they can prove helpful or not, we will be back en route to Anthem as soon as we possibly can—so don't go overboard."

Hoff looked over at him. "What do you mean?"

"You know exactly what I mean, Lord General. Hit surgically and hit hard, but nothing excessive. I want to show them a glimpse of our power, not break their civilization's backbone. We're here to save a race, not to destroy one. If time permitted, I wouldn't make our presence known to their greater population at all. But this is an unfortunate situation, as time is a luxury we do not have. I've weighed the cost of their lives against my own people. Our cause is more dire, and so we must harden our hearts until we determine why Master Tolland sent us here. At the very least, your display hopefully will rouse the passenger of the *Traverser I* to come meet us. Whoever it is has been here for four years. Pral Nerol's researcher will know much about the people down there. He or she might be able to provide some insight into Master Tolland's intentions."

The three fell silent as they soared southward across the broad sky, undetected bullets moving among the fair clouds. Vengelis was struck by the richness and clarity of the world around him. The vibrancy of the lands, trees, and skies seemed to be clearer than any he had known on Anthem. The recollection of his own world felt drab and colorless by comparison, the lands of Anthem less splendorous, and the skies uninspired and insipid. The world below him had never been disfigured by the thrashing mania of man standing alone against the ruin of his existence.

Yet it was Vengelis's ancestors who had stood alone in that final hour, and their strength still lived in him.

They passed into an immense tower of white cloud that rose from the ground far below to the very roof of the atmosphere. Vengelis closed his eyes in a moment of repose as cool perspiration beaded and rolled off his face and shoulders. The moisture felt soft in his lungs and against his skin. Part of him wished he could die in this extraordinary white world, as if somehow the cold cloud vapor could heal his soul and shelter him from the role he was being forced to play. But as quickly as they had entered the great cloud, the three Sejero warriors pulled out the other end.

As the dry air greeted him, so too did trouble. The rounded rear of a massive jetliner soared before them as they shook water from their armor. They swiftly approached the roaring plane's wake, flying easily above the profuse exhaust fumes spilling from the wings' turbines.

The two giants looked from the jetliner to Vengelis, waiting for his command.

A long moment passed as they were forced to decelerate drastically and fly a short distance behind the hulking steel wings. Vengelis looked down; the land was barely visible, but he could make out a slender river and clusters of towns stretched across the landscape. They were far out of discernible sight from the lands below, and the plane was in their way. It was flying directly south—they would have to pass it in order to continue toward New York City. If they passed the plane, the passengers would see them fly past the windows. Even though it was likely that no one else would believe them after they landed, that kind of exposure could not be risked. Not yet at least.

The hour of mercilessness had struck.

"Do what you will," Vengelis called with an empty voice.

"Finally!" Hoff shouted and smiled broadly. Darien nodded wordlessly. They simultaneously accelerated forward and came up alongside the plane. Vengelis rose over the elongated jet and peered to the far south in hopes of seeing the tall buildings of his destination, but still saw nothing but gently sloping lands.

The Lord General accelerated toward the front of the plane and moved directly past the cabin windows. A number of passengers were staring absent-mindedly out into sky. As they looked at the distant cloud formations and blue heavens, they watched a giant man move easily alongside the plane. As Darien moved along the other side, the giants saw the people behind the small circular windows pointing, panicking. Their mouths opened in what were obviously screams and shouts.

The two Imperial First Class soldiers moved to each wing and effortlessly tore the roaring engines from the holdings. The massive metal turbines fell, screaming hunks of scrap metal plummeting into the hills tens of thousands of feet below.

"They can still send transmissions!" Vengelis yelled.

The now engineless jetliner began to drastically lose speed, and with it altitude. With each passing moment the plane began to descend faster and faster through the sky. Soon it was plummeting straight downward. Vengelis watched in stunned disbelief as the Lord General and Royal Guard made no move to perform a coupe d'état on the aircraft. With an irritated grunt, he shot downward in the wake of the falling plane. He reached the nose, wind pushing and pulling at his shoulders, and peered into the front of the cockpit. Through the large windshield he saw two men sitting side by side and strapped to their seats. They were staring straight at him in utter dismay. Vengelis watched as one of the pilots distinctly mouthed over and over into his mouthpiece, "Flying men! Flying men! Flying men!"

Vengelis shouted in exasperated fury and descended past the plane with a deafening boom, accelerating far below the plummeting jetliner. Farther and farther he descended toward the ground far below, easily gaining distance from the falling plane as the sound barrier tore at his shoulders. He pulled to a stop and turned his gaze into the sky. The gigantic form of the jetliner was rotating wildly, falling rapidly at the mercy of gravity. With a thundering rumble, Vengelis erupted upward toward the jet.

He collided with it like a missile.

Vengelis's head and shoulders penetrated straight through the steel of the plane's nose and tore through the entire length of the fuselage. There was a momentary sound of shrieking and sundering steel, and then his body shot out of the tail. As he tunneled through the length of the jet, his body tore the fuel cells open. They ignited at the same moment he pulled out, and the entire jet burst into an incendiary fireball in his immediate wake.

Without a moment's hesitation, Vengelis flew straight from the exploding jetliner toward Darien and Hoff. They were both wide-eyed, their faces frozen in a mingling of awe and apprehension.

"That was . . . unbelievable!" Hoff shouted. He brought his hands together and began clapping.

Vengelis closed in on the Lord General and cracked him in the face with a ruthless backhand. Hoff launched backward into open air. Vengelis then turned and charged Darien, directing a brutal knee straight into his gut. Hoff clutched his nose as it started dripping a snotty blood, and Darien lurched over in woozy agony. They both floated unsteadily in the air.

"Do you have no sense of the gravity of our situation? You just gave those pilots all the time in the world to get a transmission off. What do you *think* was the content of their transmission? They were shouting back to their base about people *flying* outside their windows and tearing the plane apart with bare hands! What part did you not understand when I said I wanted our presence to go unnoticed?"

"I'm sorry," Hoff's voice was nasally, his hand held over his dripping nose.

Darien simply shook his head, doubled over in pain.

Vengelis looked past his feet and watched as the distant fiery wreckage fell through the open sky far below. A vision of Eve and his mother's Royal Transport, smoldering and bursting in half against the backdrop of a burning Sejeroreich, flashed through his mind. He shook the image from his head and cursed before turning his attention to the two soldiers.

"It's time we go our separate ways." Vengelis reached into his armor and took out his remote control to the *Harbinger I.* All three of them had each taken one of the remotes before they left the ship concealed on the side of the mountain to the north. Each remote functioned as everything from a long-distance radio transmitter to a direct controller of the *Harbinger I.* "You two will wait until my command to make our presence known. My guess is they will panic and order the larger populations to evacuate their cities once they find out about our presence. Before that happens I want to have the scientists gathered." Vengelis looked to the south. "I am going to head to the city to meet these scientists. While I'm doing that, find another city worthy of our spectacle. I will use your assault as leverage against their resistance to my demands."

"Which way should we go?" Darien asked, turning around and looking from horizon to horizon uncertainly.

"I don't care where you go, just seek out the most condensed population you can find. Let me know when you find such a place. And be ready to display our power. But before that, you do nothing—*nothing*—without my order."

"Very well. We'll go that way," Hoff said, looking up from his own *Harbinger I* remote and pointing across the lands to the west.

"Keep your heads on your shoulders," Vengelis said. With a last look downward at the diminishing fireball and growing tower of black smoke far below their feet, Vengelis accelerated southward and away from his two subordinates without another word.

CHAPTER SEVENTEEN

Kristen

The side of her face resting against a bunched up pillow, Kristen watched the bedside clock approach eight o'clock. She reached out and turned off the alarm just before the apartment filled with its noise. Kristen rolled onto her back and stared quietly at the ceiling. Ryan was snoring faintly beside her, and cool morning light peered through the window. Whether it had been trepidation about what lay ahead for her that day or the sharing of her bed with another, Kristen had tossed and turned all night.

Yet it was amid the throes of her restlessness that she came to her decision, and now in the pale light of morning she was all the more certain of her choice. The Vatruvian mice could not be kept a secret among a few people. She would tell the convention of the breakthrough, and willfully accept the fallout of her treason.

For a few minutes Kristen lay quietly and listened to Ryan's rhythmic breath. She decided to let him sleep. With a protracted sigh she rolled out of bed and walked over to the window, the old hardwood floor cold underfoot. She placed her palm against the chilly window, and the glass around her fingers fogged from the touch. The street below was busy with people scrambling to the nearby subway station. Something about the morning rush comforted her as she watched. She walked to the bathroom and twisted the knob to the shower. The reflection that looked back at her was tired and overworked, her hair disheveled. It was not the face of someone prepared to present a lecture to a crowded convention. She allowed herself an extra long and relaxing shower, took her time running a brush through her hair, and pulled on some clothes from her dresser.

Hair still damp, Kristen sat down next to Ryan on the bed and placed a hand lightly on his chest. He placidly stirred awake. "Hey." His voice was raspy with sleep. "What time is it?"

"Early. Before nine." Kristen smiled down at him.

"Oh." Ryan groggily rose to his elbows, the sheet pulling across his chest. "I guess I should probably get going."

"No rush. I don't have to be in Midtown for a couple hours. I was thinking about getting some breakfast if you wanted to join me."

"Sure," Ryan said. Kristen held his gaze for a time, and he inclined his head. "What is it?"

"I decided that I'm going to breach the nondisclosure contract," Kristen said with a composed defiance. "I don't want to be an accomplice to something I don't agree with."

"Good. I think it's the right thing to do."

"Mice."

Ryan sat up and stared at her in bewilderment. "What?"

Kristen nodded grimly.

"I don't understand, what does that mean?"

"Professor Vatruvia has created mice using the Vatruvian cell." Kristen almost brought herself to laugh at the hopelessness of her circumstances. "He made artificial mammals using the technology I helped create."

Ryan stared at her, unable to speak. Kristen ran her fingers through her hair and nodded significantly.

"Mice?"

"Yep. Little mottled mice that are currently scurrying around in cages at the labs," Kristen said. "Each one of them one hundred percent synthetic. And if I were willing to place a bet on the idiocy of people, I would gamble that an equal percentage of the public will applaud it as amazing—as opposed to thinking it's potentially the most dangerous thing ever created."

Ryan reached to the floor and picked up his tee shirt. He pulled it over his head, his expression adrift. "Mice . . . how is that possible?"

"It was easy, in a way," Kristen said regretfully. "Once the first Vatruvian cell functioned, I knew it was a possibility. Professor Vatruvia compounded the same replication techniques to a larger scale. So yes, I knew it was feasible. But I never thought anyone would do it so soon. And there's more . . ."

"By all means," Ryan said, beginning to look nervous himself. "I almost don't want to believe it."

"Believe it. But beyond the mice, one of my coworkers found a disturbing trait of Vatruvian cells. It's a trait that I'm beginning to think Professor Vatruvia knew about since the beginning of our research. Evidently Vatruvian cells are stronger than the original cells they replicate."

"So these mice we're talking about," Ryan said. "These mice are . . . *stronger . . .* than normal mice?"

Kristen shrugged her shoulders and lay beside him. "I don't know. Professor Vatruvia got really guarded about the whole thing when he saw my reaction to the mice. I can't imagine he'll tell me anything more about them now that he's seen my reservations. But there it is, I guess. I've officially broken my nondisclosure agreement, starting with you."

"I'm glad you did," Ryan said in disbelief. "You need to pass this on. The knowledge of something like this is way too big for one person. If I were you I'd tell every media outlet and regulatory agency that's willing to listen. Professor Vatruvia has clearly lost touch."

"That's the plan. Will you come to the convention today?" Kristen asked. "I'm going to need support when this whole goddamn thing comes crashing down around me."

"Of course," Ryan said.

Kristen smiled with reassurance despite the weariness behind her eyes. He was the only ally she needed. "Come on. I'll buy you breakfast."

A stunning fall day greeted them as they stepped out of her apartment building. The air was crisp, with a hint of breeze, and only a few wandering clouds scattered the brilliant blue sky. Deciding against one of the campus cafeterias, they walked at a gentle pace up the avenue toward a bagel shop. Her spirits lifted by the finality of her decision, Kristen told him every last detail she could recall. She described the mice and their bluish eyes. She told him of Cara Williams and her stress tests of the cells—the Vatruvian cells surviving in temperatures that killed their biological counterparts.

The morning rush appeared to have already petered out as they walked into the bagel shop. There were only a spattering of customers in the booths and a small line at the register. Kristen bought coffee and bagels, and they took a seat at an empty table in the back.

"It's strange," Ryan said as he sat down and stirred milk into his coffee. "I've never heard of a technology like this Vatruvian cell. Synthetic cells and so on."

Kristen stared at him with a penetrating dubiousness. "No kidding, we're just past the cusp of creating it."

"Yeah, true. It's scaring the hell out of me. I really think you're doing the right thing. How do you plan on getting the word out at the convention?"

"I suppose at the end of my presentation I'll include an announcement that we've surpassed single-celled organisms and launched into creating mammals in one single year of research."

Ryan smirked. "I can't wait to see how that goes over."

"It won't be pretty," Kristen said. She was midway through a gulp of coffee when she saw one of the workers behind the register waving for her attention.

"Would you mind turning up the volume on that TV beside you?" the worker called over to them.

There was an old chunky television mounted on the wall above their booth. Looking up at the screen, she at once understood his request. Kristen stood and turned the volume all the way up. The headline on the local tri-state news broadcast read: *JETLINER CRASHES IN ALBANY MINUTES AGO.*

An anchorwoman in a purple blouse was talking frantically from a street corner as indistinguishable charred wreckage smoked and burned several hundred yards behind her. Emergency crews and first responders were running around by the dozens in the background.

"We are just getting word that the plane came down in three parts," the anchorwoman said. "Three *separate* sections. The fuselage appears to have crashed in one piece here in this neighborhood in Albany. There are reports that the turbines landed in surrounding towns. I am being told the jetliner caught fire during its descent. A number of buildings behind me were crushed by the impact. We have yet to receive any information on whether people were inside the destroyed houses. We can only hope they were empty. An onlooker here in Albany managed to capture the crash on video."

As she spoke, the video feed of the news broadcast cut to a low pixel recording someone captured on a camera phone. Against the clear sky, a burning mass plummeted through the open air. Three of four people in the video were screaming in dismay as they watched it unfold before their eyes. The falling jetliner in the grainy image looked more like a fuming and blazing meteor than a passenger plane. As it fell against the clear blue backdrop, it belched a trail of black smoke that billowed wide in its wake. Just before it hit the ground, the falling inferno vanished behind the shingled rooftop of a house. The camera shook as a feint boom could be heard from the plane meeting with the ground somewhere out of the recorder's vantage point.

The newswoman continued, "We have reports that one of the turbines crashed down in the town of Latham and the other turbine landed in Menands. Both towns are north of Albany. The US Air flight eight-thirty-two had taken off without incident from Montreal. It was bound for New York City."

"Cindy, has any information yet surfaced on what could have caused this accident?" a man with a Windsor-knotted tie asked from the studio desk.

The anchorwoman held a hand over her ear and nodded, listening to his question over the calamity around her. She vehemently shook her head. "Not currently. All we know is that the plane apparently came apart and caught fire. The airline and the FAA have yet to make any official statement, except to recognize that the plane was indeed US Air flight eight-thirty-two—"

"Sorry to interrupt you Cindy, but we have just received a statement from the Department of Homeland Security. Their press secretary has stated it is *unlikely* that the accident is connected to terrorism. I will repeat: at this point it is unlikely this tragedy was the result of terrorist action."

"Mother of god." A worker in a white apron had come over under the pretense of refilling Kristen's coffee. He took his time to watch the report as he tilted the pot into her mug.

"Yeah." Kristen nodded. "Awful."

"Sounds like it got shot down if you ask me."

Ryan looked up at him with a questioning expression. "I think it's a little early to suggest that."

"Think about it. A plane loses radio contact en route to New York? Do you really think they're going to let a plane that's gone black come anywhere near the city?"

"True," Kristen said. "But they didn't say the plane lost contact."

"And why would they?" the man swilled the coffee in the pot and watched the television skeptically.

Kristen shrugged and took another bite of the bagel, though her mouth had gone dry and her appetite had vanished from the image of the plane's fiery descent.

"What would you do if you were the government?" the worker said with a thick Long Island accent. "Even if they did shoot it down, it's not like they would ever admit it. And if terrorists had actually done it, they probably wouldn't admit that either. It would cause a panic, you know?"

"That's a scary line of thought. I don't think shooting down commercial jetliners is outlined in the homeland security handbook," Ryan said. "Or covering up terrorist attacks."

"Maybe." The worker wiped his hands on his apron. "Can you imagine if it was goddamn terrorists again? I mean, Jesus *Christ.* I'm glad the government took action if it was. The plane was coming here. I can't imagine another attack." He seemed visibly shaken by the idea as the television replayed the descent of the plane again.

Kristen watched the inferno silently and pushed her bagel away. "I can't imagine it either." She paused for a moment, considering if the question on her mind was inappropriate. "Were you in the city on nine-eleven?"

"Yeah." The worker's response was cold, his tone exact and his eyes still on the broadcast. "I used to be a bike messenger downtown. I was in the crowd watching the smoke of the north tower when the second plane hit. Nightmare."

Kristen nodded slowly. "That must have been a truly traumatic experience. I'm very sorry."

"Don't be. I'm not. I'm glad I saw it firsthand. I'll never forget the way all those innocent people died in the name of who knows goddamn what? Thousands dead because of some convoluted brainwashed bullshit. It'll stay with me, you know? It won't just become an old news headline—some dutiful moment of silence. I lived through it. I've seen the height of the world's insanity."

"I think it'll stay with everyone," Kristen said, remembering vividly where she was on that September day so many years ago. She had been in a chemistry class with much older kids when the principal had made the first announcement of an attack on the World Trade Center. Neither she, nor any of her classmates grasped the magnitude of it at first. The teacher had wheeled in an old television on a cart, and they watched the news silently from their desks. He had told them to be quiet, because they were watching history. A soft-spoken girl in her lab group had a parent in the twin towers on business. It was a sobering moment when she was quietly ushered out of the classroom. Her expression was numb, vacant, as the principal had walked in and told her to come with him.

The day had been sunny and warm, as fair as any.

It was strange, the little details one recalls. What Kristen remembered of the darkest hours of recent humanity: blue skies and cancelled after-school sports. She was thankful she did not have to witness the carnage firsthand. "It'll certainly stay with me," she said quietly.

"That's good to hear." The worker lifted his shirtsleeve and showed them a tattoo on his forearm of an American flag set over the words: *Never Forget September 11, 2001.* He left the sleeve rolled up and looked at Ryan. "You want a refill?"

"I'm all set, thanks," Ryan said.

"All right, well, take it easy you two."

"The engines came off in the middle of the flight?" Ryan glared at the burning wreckage of the broadcast as the worker walked back to the counter. "I'll admit he has a point. That certainly doesn't sound right."

Kristen shrugged. "I wish they'd stop replaying the video. Do they realize there are people out there who had family members on that plane? I wish the media would show some respect for once."

"Yeah," Ryan said. "What could cause a plane to come apart at thirty thousand feet?"

"Who knows?"

They watched the broadcast as little more information came in. It seemed as though no one could yet postulate as to what happened to the jetliner. Kristen reluctantly checked the time on her cell phone and sighed. "I should probably be on my way to Midtown."

"Okay." Ryan turned from the television. "When should I head down there?"

"In a couple hours. I'll text you when I know what time the Vatruvian cell presentation is scheduled. The convention is at the Marriot Marquis in Times Square."

Ryan nodded.

Kristen looked back to the television. It was clear there were going to be no new developments for the time being. The worker had brought up a good point. Planes did not blow up out of the blue. As the broadcast now depicted a mile-wide tower of smoke rising from the neighborhood in Albany, a missile or bomb did seem plausible.

"Okay, I should probably be going." Kristen reluctantly drew her attention away from the news and drummed her fingers against her thigh. "I really appreciate that you're coming."

"Absolutely," Ryan said. He rose from the table and Kristen followed his lead out of the shop, giving the worker a friendly wave as she walked past him.

They slowed to a stop on the sidewalk as they neared an intersection.

"I, uh . . ." Kristen said with more than a trace of awkwardness. She tried to act cool, but was quite certain the attempt failed. "I'm pretty sure I'm starting to like you."

Ryan smiled and laughed. "Yeah. I'm pretty sure I'm starting to like you too."

"Good," Kristen said and shrugged her shoulders inelegantly. "Good."

"Look," Ryan smiled down at her after she could not find any words. "You need to focus on the convention. Get that out of the way, and don't think about anything else until it's done. I'll be there to watch the firestorm unfold."

Kristen nodded. "Okay."

Ryan leaned down and kissed her on the cheek. "Good luck."

"Thanks. I'll see you there, then," Kristen said. They locked eyes for a moment, and she turned to walk toward the subway with a wave. Her mind was decided as she descended the steps into the subway station: it was time for a major career change. She did not care if she was having an early-life crisis or an overworked breakdown. The days spent pent up in dreary windowless labs and staring at endless computer screens of genetic sequences had to stop. She had lost her youth in the name of a head start, and that trail was now at an end.

The Vatruvian mice were the last straw.

As Kristen pushed into a stuffy train, she wondered if her actions at the convention might in some way provide the world with some *respect* for the incalculable power and elegance of science. But more likely, she knew, the infallible influence of ambition would act to silence her voice. For the moment, however, she decided not to care.

CHAPTER EIGHTEEN

Vengelis

The unmistakable silhouette of towering buildings rose against the sharp contour of the horizon to the south. Even from his distance Vengelis could see that New York City was vast, its edifices tall. He squinted at the distant city's profile before cautiously decelerating and soaring in an elegant arc toward its skyscrapers, his altitude shrouding his approach from any unsuspecting skyward eyes below. A surreptitious hand would be the one of choice for the time being.

Vengelis could not help but feel a small pang of conflict over allowing Hoff and Darien to venture out on their mission of inevitable annihilation. They, and he, would shortly become heralds of torment and death to these unwary people. The men and women far below were about to be swept up in a conflict based far away, a conflict in which they were in every way faultless.

But there was no other choice.

The danger of innocence is that it is eventually lost. In the end innocence is not enduring; rather it is a transient state that has yet to be exposed to all the aspects of reality. Vengelis would provide the people down in the city with the same level of mercy the Primus race had received at the hands of a more advanced species: none. Despite the invasion the Primus race encountered—a traumatic and scarring holocaust that tore through the fiber of their worldview—still the Primus stood. Stood more powerfully and proudly than ever before. In a way the forthcoming tribulation would be an enlightening experience for the adolescent civilization below, a chance for it to evolve and grow. Vengelis would alter their conception of their world much as a parent teaches a child to look before crossing the street. The child may not be aware of a speeding bus coming, but that does not change the fact that the bus *is* coming. No warning came for the young Primus race before the Zergos invasion of old ripped through Anthem. No hand of mercy was extended to his people as the Felixes slaughtered them in the present. Vengelis knew he could not allow himself the indulgence of compassion. Reality may be heartless, but it was better than false beliefs based solely on one's tiny world.

And for the naive people far below, reality was banging at their door.

The strong command the weak. When pushed close enough to the brink, compassion, empathy, and morality were all just words. Power was the only balance—the only truth behind society's falsehoods. If Vengelis had been stronger, at that moment he would be sitting on his throne. If the humans were stronger, they would have no reason to fear his wanton intrusion. But such as it was neither he nor the humans were strong enough in their own respective plights.

Pulling to a stop high over the enormousness of New York City, Vengelis lingered silently above the countless array of skyscrapers for several minutes, examining the teeming streets and rooftops. He had to admit the enormous glimmering city was attractive. But so too had been the noontime splendor of Sejeroreich. The meeting of their scientists, his single source of hope, was in one of these tall buildings below. The scientists would be tasked with finding a cure to the scourge of the Felix. Vengelis had no other option, and thus neither did they.

Vengelis reached into his armor and pulled out the *Harbinger I* remote. A three-dimensional image of the peculiar Felix cell rotated slowly on the display. All of his suffering, peril, and fears resulted from this one technology—this one trivial-looking cell. With great effort he consolidated his array of emotions into wrath. Someone far below would provide him with some insight, or his frustration would be forced to spread like a pandemic across this world. He placed the remote back into his armor and descended toward the city with a faint popping sound. Far below, the sound of his descent went entirely unnoticed, lost in the raucous streets.

Vengelis landed with a cracking thud onto the roof of one of the taller buildings in the northern stretch of the city. A depression yielded into the concrete of the roof below his feet. The rooftop was situated among a cluster of skyscrapers, and many steel pinnacles rose to his lofty height on all sides. Beyond their glass and steel, the horizon extended to the radiating ocean to the east and open lands to the west. Vengelis strode to an iron door adjacent to a number of droning ventilation fans. He easily threw aside the thick padlock securing the handle, stepped into the darkness, and jogged down a dingy stairwell. Floor after floor passed as he sped down the stories, his footfalls echoing back and forth off the tight walls. He reached a landing where the steps abruptly ended, and a sign beside a door read: *Rooftop Access Stair.* Vengelis pulled apart another padlock and burst out of the dim stairwell straight into a packed office.

A man sitting by a desk that flanked the access door looked up in alarm. "Excuse me," the man said. "Custodians don't use that door. Who is your manager?"

The man picked up the phone on his desk, his flabby chin wobbling and his tie strangling his pig neck. Thick glasses sat on his flat nose, and sweat stained his armpits. Vengelis stared at the man with blatant derision. He was insulted to have been addressed by such a pathetic person. After glaring at him for a pointed moment, Vengelis walked wordlessly past him and down a row of cubicles. Men and women were sitting at orderly desks separated by bland beige partitions. All of them were talking into phones or headsets. Each of the office workers glanced at him for a questioning moment before quickly bringing their attention back to their work.

Across from the elevators, a young woman sat at the reception desk and spoke politely into a telephone. As Vengelis stepped in front of the elevator doors, she looked up at him. "Can I help you?" she asked.

Vengelis turned to her as he pressed the glowing down button. "No."

"Do you have a visitor pass?"

"No."

"Then you'll need to sign in with the security personnel in the main lobby." Her lips turned in a pleasant smile. "I wouldn't get caught without a visitor pass in that costume if I were you."

Vengelis looked at the young woman, his expression mirthless as granite. "Where is the Marriot Marquis?"

"Seventh Avenue," she said, her tone matter-of-fact. The phone on her desk rang for half a ring, and she picked it up immediately. "Grayson Fletcher Feinstein, New York office. This is Alexandra speaking, how may I direct your call?"

The elevator door opened and Vengelis stepped in, pressing the button for the main lobby. The young woman cast him an uncertain look as she spoke distractedly into her phone, "Yes, I will pencil you in with Mr. Cooper at two o'clock." They met eyes, and she blushed as the doors closed.

The elevator opened to a lobby crowded with people, all looking somewhat glazed over in their dull gray and black business apparel. Every person Vengelis walked by cast him either a contemptuous or amused glance, as though his attire was a joke, something to be mocked. Vengelis was certain that his highly wrought Royal Armor probably looked eccentric and outlandish. A passing woman smiled at him and said something about his fantastic costume. Vengelis ignored her, though his face darkened in a wave of distaste. His raiment was likely worth more than this entire city, not counting the value of the Blood Ring.

He would allow them their judgments for now.

On the sidewalk his surrounds became almost too much to bear. Men and women walked this way and that, gladly going about their daily routines. The sun shone brightly on them all, the air cool and clear. It felt like a dream, the passing faces were familiar and yet so foreign to Vengelis. These men and women, these cows, were oblivious to every truth in which he lived. That these ignorant cattle could live so contentedly in their world of wasted prosperity while his war-hardened and disciplined people lay in devastation was nearly too much to shoulder. The illogical and arbitrary nature of it all made him feel deadened inside. Vengelis leaned against a newspaper stand and closed his eyes, desperately combating his bitterness. People elbowed by, grunting irritably at the young man standing obtrusively in their path. These men and women, these craven domesticated swine, were living in a remote Eden with no appreciation for the greater order of things, no appreciation of things that would swallow their existence whole in a fleeting instant.

Vengelis focused his mind on disregarding them. His fight was not with them, and resentment was an emotion of weaker men. He brought his thoughts back to the Felix—to Anthem. He was not doomed to failure. Not yet, at least. Master Tolland did not send him to Filgaia to outlet his anger. If these men and women were to be cattle, then Vengelis had to milk any information he could get out of them. He focused on the dire blue eyes of the Felixes and allowed his resentment to turn to resolution. With a long deep breath, Vengelis pacified his emotions and continued to walk down the sidewalk. The convention was at a hotel called the Marriot Marquis. He looked up at the dozens of skyscrapers around him. How would he find the correct building? Monoliths of concrete, steel, and mirrored glass jutted into the bright sky dotted with full clouds and the fading contrails of airplanes.

A television propped against a storefront caught his eye. Playing on the screen was a video of the jetliner he had obliterated not an hour previous. A ball of fire and ruinous smoke plummeted through a blue sky on the television. Vengelis cursed Hoff and Darien for forcing his hand, though there did not seem to be any mention of the cause of the crash, which was advantageous. But Vengelis remembered all too clearly the look in the pilots' faces just before he had ended their lives. They had unquestionably sent a transmission about the attack, Vengelis was certain of it. Somewhere out there, at that very moment, a team of authorities was meticulously evaluating the bizarre mayday call: two panicked pilots screaming about flying men tearing the plane apart.

Vengelis watched the soundless broadcast through the window as the din of the city travelled past him: people in conversation, taxis honking in traffic, police sirens, planes overhead, street vendors shouting. They were sounds not entirely unfamiliar to him, mostly similar to his own cities. But an unusual sound filtered through the racket around him. Excited, almost feverish shouting was rising from somewhere nearby. Again and again a motley roar rose and fell. Vengelis inclined his head as he tried to trace the cause of the incongruous racket. He turned to face the source and saw an old grungy building crammed tightly between two taller ones.

A sign above the only door read, *Giovanni's Gentlemens Club*. Below the garish blinking letters, a pink neon outline of a woman's body cycled back and forth in a dancing motion. Vengelis glared at the revolving neon figure, wondering vaguely what could be the cause of the shouting, though he ventured a guess as he heard another roar of men.

Vengelis checked the *Harbinger I* remote. There was still some time until the scientific convention began, and he had specifically told Hoff and Darien to lay low until he gave them word. It had occurred to him that it would be prudent to recruit the support of a local person in order to direct him to the convention and deal with any unforeseeable problems that might arise in translation. Now was the time to find such an individual, and it was possible that someone on the fringe of society would be more pliant to his will. He smirked; the situation was rather amusing. Emperor Vengelis Epsilon, son of Faris Epsilon, bearer of the Blood Ring, direct descendent of the first Sejero and rightful heir to the throne of Anthem, was walking into what he guessed was a brothel.

A large man dressed all in black stood by the entrance to the club. He had an unsavory and brutish look to him, not entirely unlike Hoff and Darien—though far smaller. With thick limbs and a broad neck, he stood a head taller than Vengelis.

The large man gave Vengelis a contemptuous smile and laughed aloud. "Buddy, Halloween isn't for a few weeks."

Vengelis shifted his weight on his hips, his arms crossed and his body language calm. "Excuse me?"

"Halloween. You're a couple weeks early. Freakin' weirdo."

"What is Halloween?" Vengelis asked, his expression vacant.

The man rolled his eyes. "Man, this place always brings in the nuts."

"I would like to enter this establishment," Vengelis said.

"Well, there's no cover at this time of day, so go ahead." The man lifted a satin rope that blocked the entry to a dark entrance hall. "But buddy . . ."

Vengelis looked up at him. "Yes?"

The bouncer lowered his attention to Vengelis's strange attire. "Be careful in there. It's the unemployed and alcoholic crowd at this hour . . . if you follow me. Most of them have been in there since last night. They don't have much to lose, that group. They're a little rough around the edges, and you look a little fruity, no offense."

Vengelis blinked at the man, coolly considering killing him with a flick of his wrist. "Am I to take that as an insult?"

"Uh . . . I guess not," the man said. "But we don't use metal detectors, so just watch your back. If something goes down, we bouncers sure as hell aren't going to get involved. Ten bucks an hour isn't worth getting stabbed by some wino."

"I'll be careful." Vengelis turned and made his way into the hallway, rubbing his eyes as they adjusted from the bright day to the shabby darkness. The floor beneath him shook from a heavy bass that moved through the walls. Beyond the entrance hall and a few more bouncers was a spacious, dimly lit club. Vengelis took in the entire place, his sharp gaze moving slowly from face to face. A long wood bar lined one wall, softly illuminated by recessed blue lights, and a few dozen tables littered with disheveled men stood between the bar and a raised stage in the far corner. Tall mirrors were set along the rear of the stage, and flashing strobe lights hung from the ceiling, blinking and rotating in a range of colors.

Some unsavory types were piled in the chairs along the stage with drinks in hand. They looked riled up with intoxication and quite rowdy. Many were shouting out orders to a number of scantily clad women who walked about the tables and brought them their drinks. Most of the women's outfits consisted of high heels with low-cut shirts, their expressions a mix of flirtation and misery.

Vengelis took it all in expressionlessly. He acknowledged that all societies had undesirable facets, but this was pushing the limits. Vengelis walked past some empty tables and approached the bar where an overwhelmed bartender was making drinks. She looked as though she could have been pretty a few years ago, but too many long nights had left a waxen look to her features. He took a seat across from her.

"Hello," Vengelis said to the bartender.

"The waitresses take drink orders, talk to one of them. I'm busy." She did not look up from her pouring.

"And who might the waitresses be?"

The woman said nothing, rolling her eyes at a bottle of whiskey as she poured it into a row of shot glasses.

"Well?"

"Come on, buddy, give me a break. We're undermanned today." The bartender looked up angrily, but stopped short upon seeing him. Vengelis stood out glaringly, comically. She drew back her hair from her face and wiped sweat from her brow. "Sorry. I'm really overworked here. I thought you were just another old pervert. Can I get you something?"

"No." Vengelis noticed she had a slight underbite, of which he did not approve.

"You know the basic idea is for the customer to spend money on drinks, right?" she asked as she simultaneously poured him a glass of ice water. When he ignored it she cast him a strange look. "Where the hell do you work that makes you wear that weird costume?"

Vengelis was moving his attention across the ragged furniture and peeling walls. The place stunk like dregs of booze and society. He stared disapprovingly at the men by the stage; they were shouting obnoxiously and pushing one another around, roaring in drunken camaraderie. Men had died for lesser displays of rudeness in the presence of an Epsilon, but Vengelis found that he was so depressed he could not bring himself to care.

"Is it customary for men to get drunk in the middle of the day here?" Vengelis asked, gazing lethargically as the group by the stage began to bicker.

"No," the bartender said. "But these slobs aren't really customary types. Or men. Not a morning drinker?"

"Busy day."

The bartender looked at him skeptically as she picked up another drink order and poured a round of beers from a tap. "Well, that's too bad. Especially with my shift ending so soon."

Vengelis smirked, more bemused than intrigued by her lack of subtlety. The music cut short and a magnified voice bellowed through the tall speakers in the back. The crowd around the stage had grown, and the men underneath it looked like a pack of overfed beasts gathering round a kill.

"Gentlemen!" a man shouted into a microphone from the side of the stage. His announcement was met with slurred cheers and a smattering of applause from the faces in the crowd. "It is my pleasure to introduce you all to our newest girl. Let me tell you, she is really something. I mean, *really* something. It's your lucky day, folks. I know you'll give her a warm welcome. Without further ado, I present to you, Madison!"

The lights dropped and strobes rose, covering the stage in hypnotic flashing. Thumping music tore through the club, and the crowd erupted into muffled sputtering cheers. Vengelis sipped the water he had been given, his gaze traveling across the room with little interest. He checked the time on the remote once more.

Then Madison took the stage. Every person in the room was immediately captivated. Cheers rose, glasses of beer fell to the floor, and weak scraggly jaws dropped with infatuated, confused leers.

To his astonishment, Vengelis was not an exception.

CHAPTER NINETEEN

Kristen

Kristen stepped out of the subway station and into the bustle of Midtown. The crowded streets and busy intersections reminded her of moving through the bottom of a man-made canyon, with rows of coruscating skyscrapers rising high overhead on each side of the avenue. In the morning sun, Times Square shined in storied brilliance. Lurid advertisements of every description blinked and glowed. All Kristen could do was gawk at the flashing lights, smiling celebrities, and fall's new lineup.

The Marriot Marquis turned out to be a towering and opulent architectural marvel directly in the center of Times Square. Kristen trudged wearily past a golden atrium and into the marble of the main lobby, her hands grasping the straps of her backpack. She was stunned by the lofty height of the room that ascended above her. The pristine white lobby rose all the way to the barely visible roof of the hollowed out skyscraper. Turning her gaze upward, Kristen felt the sensation of being outdoors. It was as though some enormous hand had reached down and carefully gutted out the entire center of the towering building, leaving only open air in its space. The tiers of individual floors visibly encircled a series of extravagant open-glass elevators that gracefully raised and lowered the guests within.

The convention was being held in the Lutvak ballroom on the second floor, and Kristen ascended the main stairs as her sneakers squeaked faintly against the rich carpet. The ballroom was an expansive space with a few hundred chairs aligned into rows around a raised stage sporting a broad projection screen and a ring of tables assembled around the perimeter walls. A large banner hung across one of the walls with the words: *Welcome to The Twenty-First Century of Science.*

Several grand chandeliers shimmered above the heads of the crowd, and elaborately designed moldings added a chic touch to the ballroom. The folding tables along the walls were set up with poster boards and laptop monitors depicting the progression of various research groups from around the globe. There looked to be easily two or three hundred people crammed among the rows of chairs. Most of the researchers and university professors were engrossed in eager discussion or quietly watching small research pitches.

Kristen rolled her eyes at the predictable demographic and scanned the tables for the Vatruvian cell. She found Professor Vatruvia standing by a display along the nearest wall. A conspicuous assemblage of men in stern military uniforms was congregated around him. Kristen shifted her backpack against her shoulders and eyed the buzzed haircuts and square jaws distrustfully. What possible new development would this prove to be? She felt confident that whatever their purpose, it would no doubt displease her. Kristen reluctantly stepped forward and passed through a group of quietly mingling geologists.

"Hi, professor." Kristen forced her best smile as she met him and the many military men.

A Vatruvian cell research display had been haphazardly set up on the table, consisting of little more than an open laptop with a rotating image of a unicellular Vatruvian cell. Several copied stacks of stapled research overviews were there for the taking. The display was humorously simple compared to some of the others she saw around the Lutvak ballroom. Kristen had no doubt Professor Vatruvia was planning to impress the convention with their lecture, not their display.

"Glad you could join us, Kristen. I wanted to introduce you to General Peter Redford." Professor Vatruvia raised an arm to the most decorated of the military men. "General Redford, this is one of my most gifted students, Kristen Jordan."

Kristen held out her hand, and the tall broad man met it with a firm shake. General Redford was in his fifties, and had a pleasant though authoritative impression. There were four polished silver stars on each of his shoulders and various insignias Kristen did not recognize on his chest. He had a kindly paternal look to him, perhaps akin to a high school sports coach. In her miserable mood, Kristen did not take a liking to him. General Redford weighed Kristen up and down, noticing her sneakers and jeans with an amused smirk.

"Ms. Jordan, how are you?" General Redford smiled warmly. "Very impressive to be involved in such prestigious and avant-garde work at your age."

"Will you be able to stay for our presentation?" Professor Vatruvia asked the general. "Kristen will be presenting most of it."

"Unfortunately, no. I'm just stopping by," General Redford said. "I'm on my way to make an address at the UN, then back to Washington by this evening. I find this Vatruvian cell technology terribly interesting though . . . a shame I'll miss it. It really is truly incredible. You should be very proud, Ms. Jordan."

Kristen nodded and broke his courteous gaze, drawing her attention to his chest and wondering what all the insignias could possibly stand for. She turned to Professor Vatruvia and measured his broad smile suspiciously. Why did he seem to be so keen on speaking to the military about Vatruvian cell technology? Kristen tried to maintain an unreadable expression despite her rising frustration.

"Well, I do what I can," Kristen said. "We're a large team, I do my part."

"Kristen, don't be modest." Professor Vatruvia leaned against the table. "She has been with me from the very beginning of our work. Kristen's been integral to our progress."

"It's always a pleasure to meet bright young Americans. I'm sure you have a very auspicious future ahead of you. Are you nearing the end of your PhD program?" General Redford asked.

"Yeah." Kristen nodded. "I'm hoping to finish my doctorate over this next year."

"Any plans for after graduation?"

"Eh." Kristen shied away from his eye contact again. "None at the moment. I'm putting off any job decisions until I complete my PhD."

General Redford nodded. "Well, I'm sure you'll be successful finding work with such a glowing recommendation from Dr. Vatruvia on your resume. I'm certain there are plenty of military contractors that would jump at the chance to snatch you up. If you would like, I can pass your name along to some of my contacts."

The thought of working for a military contractor nauseated her, but Kristen merely shrugged. "Maybe."

"If you'll excuse me," Professor Vatruvia interjected and turned away from them to greet several other eminent synthetic biologists who had gathered to shake his hand and talk shop. The conversation among them at once reached a level of technicality that would likely come off as gibberish to most.

Kristen sighed in their direction as General Redford leaned down and stared at the image of the Vatruvian cell on the open laptop. He shook his head in wonder. "The sky is the limit as far as I can see with this technology of yours, Ms. Jordan. Who could have predicted it ten years ago? Or even one year ago for that matter?"

"Yeah, it's a scary new world."

"Scary?" General Redford looked up. "Interesting word choice. But I can't say that I disagree. It makes me feel old as my knowledge of science becomes so glaringly obsolete. I can't help but wonder what the world will be like when I'm tucked away in retirement somewhere."

"If the world is still here," Kristen said.

General Redford burst into a laugh that took Kristen aback. "Well put. But that's what all this is for in the end, right? Technology, advancements, and so on—self-preservation is the name of the game."

"If self-preservation is indeed the actual driving force."

General Redford stood to his full height and dwarfed over Kristen. His presence was powerful, and even if he had not been in his distinguished uniform, he would have commanded respect. He waved a hand to the entourage of reticent soldiers beside him, and they walked out of earshot and stood by the doors to the ballroom.

"I suddenly get the distinct impression you were being polite when I suggested a career in defense research," General Redford said.

"No, not really." Kristen shrugged. "I pass no judgment on military research. Or at least I make a conscious effort not to. I mean, to each her own. But I don't think that nature of research is cut out for me. That is to say, the kind of research that holds the end goal of killing people. I like to cling to the idealistic belief that science should be used to help humanity."

"There's certainly nothing wrong with that perspective, Ms. Jordan. I guess it takes a specific type of person to step outside the rigidity of pacifism. Someone who accepts that hard decisions have to be made, that evil flourishes if given the opportunity, and that conflict is simply an aspect of our very existence. The rational minds have to secure their power. And in this world we live in, the technological advantage is everything."

Kristen said nothing as she mulled over his words.

General Redford leaned down and again examined the laptop monitor that depicted a rotating Vatruvian cell. Kristen watched his face intently. Surely this military mind had no idea of the significance of what he was watching.

"Are you familiar with our work?" Kristen asked.

"Oh, yes. I've been following it closely since the first Vatruvian cell. To think that the technology is still in its infant stages is almost too difficult to grasp."

Kristen felt herself taking a liking to General Redford. He was undeniably thoughtful, not at all what she would have imagined a high-ranking military officer to embody. He seemed clearheaded, poised, and coherent.

"I'd say there are some fairly substantial questions that arise about the future of the technology," General Redford said. "If you don't mind my asking, Ms. Jordan, how *does* the Vatruvian cell operate—in simple terms? Dr. Vatruvia tried to explain it to me and it went right over my head."

Kristen stirred uncertainly. "Um, okay. Well, to put all the convoluted synthetic biology aside, Vatruvian cell technology has always revolved around the idea of allowing a given biological design to integrate specific artificial proteins we created in the lab using computer programs. What we do is not just an injection of foreign DNA into a pre-existing cell, but the ground up creation of a new cell by using novel genetic coding. The Vatruvian cell still follows the basic genetic architecture of a template cell, though. It uses the altered genetics we created using lab techniques and a ton of advanced software to mimic the form of a template organism. So the Vatruvian cell is similar, but also very different than the given species it copies."

General Redford shook his head in awe.

"If it's any consolation, I *know* how it works and it still scares the hell out of me," Kristen said.

"I'm sorry if my basic knowledge of the technology is so insufficient that this question is ludicrous. But, let's say purely theoretically, would it be possible for things larger and more complex than cells to be replicated by this technology?"

Kristen hesitated and stepped out of the way as a woman took one of the pamphlets from the display table. She thought the question interesting. If he already knew about the mice, he never would have asked it. Kristen turned to look at Professor Vatruvia. If high-ranking generals did not yet know about the mice, who did? What would General Redford think if he knew how advanced the technology had really become behind locked doors—if he knew Professor Vatruvia was years, decades, ahead of what she just described.

"It would be possible to create more complex systems, yes," Kristen said.

"Good lord, I miss the days when technological advancements took place in fields like production and aviation. Tangible, logical things." General Redford gazed at the Vatruvian cell. "I remember being amazed the first time I saw a laptop. Now we tamper with *life*. I agree with you, it is a scary new world."

"Indeed it is," Kristen said. "But I'm confident international regulations will soon oversee the technology. Between you and me, I would venture a bet that in ten year's time Vatruvian technology, along with all synthetic biology, will be supervised strictly."

Kristen's thoughts wandered to what Cara Williams had told her. The Vatruvian bacterium cells had greater resilience, strength, and efficiency than their natural versions. Did the frantic little Vatruvian mice have the same traits?

Would larger mammals? The skin on her arms broke into goose bumps at the notion.

"Are you okay, Ms. Jordan? You look pale all of a sudden," General Redford asked.

"I'm fine. Just tired. Been working around the clock recently."

General Redford was about to say something, but his cell phone rang. He held up a hand to Kristen in apology. "Redford here . . . Flight eight-thirty-two? Yes . . . The plane crash . . . right . . . only what I've heard in the news." His eyebrows narrowed, his lips tightened. "Repeat that last sentence . . . I beg your pardon? What are you talking about? Flying p—"

General Redford looked up at Kristen then turned away, pushing the speaker against his ear and lowering his voice. "Explain yourself!" he demanded. "How certain is the airline? And the FAA? The possibility that lines were crossed has been ruled out of the question? That was the actual mayday call? Not some mistaken transmission? They are absolutely certain? Okay. Yes, I'll teleconference in right away."

General Redford snapped the phone shut and turned to Kristen with a twitching smile. "Well, Ms. Jordan, it was very nice meeting such an accomplished young woman as yourself, but I have to leave."

"Okay, it was very nice meeting you too, general," Kristen said with a questioning tone. "But wait. Was that phone call about the plane crash in Albany? Flight eight-thirty-two?"

"Goodbye, Kristen." The general's tone was final. He turned on the spot and exited the room with a swift stern gait, pointing to the group of military personnel. The soldiers immediately followed in his wake. Kristen watched them until they turned a corner and moved out of sight down the stairs toward the lobby. She felt suddenly nervous. Kristen sat down at a folding chair and placed her forehead into her hands, resting her elbows on the table. The beginnings of a stress headache were forming in her temples. She folded her legs under her and wished she was anywhere but this stupid convention.

Professor Vatruvia, who had been beckoned over to one of the other nearby displays, walked back to their table and shook hands with nearly every person that passed him. Everyone wanted to meet the visionary, to ask his opinion on so-and-so, to fawn over him.

"Did General Redford leave?" Professor Vatruvia asked disappointedly, scanning the room.

"Yeah, he left in a hurry," Kristen said, her face still held in her palms.

"Did you explain to him the basics of the Vatruvian replication? He seemed a bit lost when I tried to draw it out for him earlier."

"Yep. I think he had to leave because of something involving the plane crash in Albany, but he didn't say."

"That's strange," Professor Vatruvia said with a frown. "Who knows what a general's daily schedule is, right?"

Kristen shrugged.

"I just talked to the organizers. We're going to present our research second on the itinerary. I'll have you go up to the stage first and introduce the Vatruvian cell and so on. Then I'll take the reins for the close out. We'll keep the lecture short and sweet."

"Okay," Kristen nodded, knowing that before she finished her portion of the lecture she would tell everyone in the hall of the Vatruvian mice. Her gaze shifted to a nearby table where the international winners of a youth synthetic biology competition were discussing their work. These children were surely being taught that the only limit to their tampering with life itself was their own imagination. Look at what Nicoli Vatruvia did, kids. Look at what Kristen Jordan did. The high schoolers' faces were beaming, exuberant as they discussed their work. Kristen thought for a moment she was going to throw up.

She was glad Ryan was going to be there for support. Her words would set off a firestorm of questions about the Vatruvian cell, but Kristen also felt certain that everyone who had a hand in synthetic biology would be after her blood for slamming the brakes on the locomotive. Ryan would be her ally, her protection against the zealotry.

"Excuse me, if I can please have everyone's attention for one moment." A blaring voice rose over the crowd, magnified through the Lutvak ballroom's speaker system. Kristen lifted her head and looked to the podium. One of the hotel workers stood at the pedestal on the main stage. "Once again, may I please have everyone's attention? This will only take a moment."

The man cleared his throat and loosened his necktie as the room reluctantly grew silent.

"It has come to our attention that the Department for Homeland Security has issued a national security alert." Immediately, whispers and hushed voices extended through the room. The hotel worker spoke over the rabble. "At this point no specific city or form of public transit or anything like that has been threatened. The president has issued assurances that the alert is strictly precautionary, and not cause for panic or alarm. To those of you visiting from foreign countries, we want to stress upon you that this is not an altogether uncommon occurrence here in the United States. Again I must emphasize that there is no cause for panic. We at the Marriot Marquis will do our best to keep you updated on any developments issued by the media." He smiled professionally and held an arm to the nearby tables. "The lectures will begin momentarily. Until then, the buffet tables are still well stocked if anyone desires a snack. Thank you for your attention, and I hope everyone enjoys the presentations."

The momentary concern of the room evaporated as quickly as it had arisen. A knot turned in Kristen's stomach, and an unsettling sensation ran up her spine. General Redford did not seem like the type of man who was easily shaken, and his face had looked severely disturbed by whatever was said on the other end of that phone conversation. At the same moment the government had issued a national security alert. It could not have been a coincidence.

Something was happening.

Kristen's first thought unwillingly went straight to terrorism. Unwelcome imagery of explosions, airplanes, and skyscrapers formed in the depths of her mind. She felt a strong desire to be tucked away in the middle of suburbia and far from the masses of a city. Instead, she was in Times Square, the epicenter of New York City and the entire western world.

CHAPTER TWENTY

Vengelis

Madison was, in a word, devastating.

The young woman who stepped onto the stage to the deafening music could not have been real. Vengelis stared up at a rendition of feminine Royalty: flawless looks and a commanding grace. Her movements were masterful. In a place filled with wretched and corpulent excuses for men and women, Vengelis found himself looking upon perfection. Through the flashing lights, Madison's dark hair flowed past her slender shoulders in waves, her green eyes emotionless with focus. A black leather top and bottom scarcely contained her implausible shapeliness. Every individual aspect of her was so arresting that he found it difficult to admire any specific attribute by itself, and all together it was nearly overwhelming.

Vengelis could not pull his gaze away from this extraordinary woman; she was a Sejero daughter personified, the epitome of elegance. A part of him was sickened that a woman so transcendent could be objectified by this rabble of depraved men. Yet that seemed to be the case, as it became clear at once that Vengelis was not alone in his sentiments toward Madison. The majority of men had risen from their tables and crowded against the stage. They were howling and screeching at Madison, leaning onto the floor of the stage and reaching up longingly at her as she moved past them.

The song progressed, guitar riffs and choruses echoing across the walls. Fistfuls of dollar bills were thrown at her feet from all sides. The leaning grabs of drunkards' yearning hands came closer to the young woman as she moved, but Madison nimbly avoided the groping with obvious athleticism. Vengelis watched the scene unfold with growing fascination, though part of him was mortified that she was going to strip for these undeserving scrubs.

After a minute or so, the shouts and cheers of the rabble audibly transitioned from excitement to frustration. The audience was growing angry. Even the man in charge of the music beside the stage seemed irritated, holding his hands in the air in exasperation. Vengelis did not understand it at first, but then it dawned on him. Madison was not going to strip for them.

Vengelis smirked as this realization moved through the mob by the stage.

The atmosphere of the club began to transform dramatically as the drunken audience realized this woman had no intentions of bearing all. Whistles and howls turned to shouts and jeers. One of the fat men in the front row reached out to take back the dollar bills he had thrown in front of her on the stage. But Madison was too quick for him, and pulled the bills away from his reach. He stood up, furious, and screamed at her through the deafening music and flashing lights.

Madison laughed in his direction and began to move to the other end of the stage. The man lunged up and grabbed her leg. He pulled violently at her ankle. The crowd cheered and applauded. Madison looked down at the man and waved a finger at him, telling him no.

The crowd booed her, cheered the man on.

As she turned to get away from him, the fat man reached up and tried to pull at her boots. The grab almost knocked her over, but Madison did not fall. Instead, she rounded on him with a look of absolute ferocity. She raised her knee and buried a stomp straight into the fat man's face. The heel of her boot pierced his cheek, and a number of his molars scattered onto the stage.

Vengelis sipped his water as the crowd erupted into fury around the lone young woman. Madison urgently turned from the man at the speakers and then to the smug bouncers by the entrance, but they only shrugged at her through the bedlam.

The fat man was with a group of friends, and a half-dozen men were now standing and shouting at Madison. They were spitting and slurring any curse that came to mind. One of them clumsily crawled up onto the stage in between her and the back exit. When she turned to run off the stage only to see him, he leered through booze-soaked eyes, his beard dripping with beer. Without the slightest hesitation, Madison walked up to him through the flashing lights and slugged him square in the face. He fell to the stage as though he had been punched by a prizefighter.

Vengelis's eyes widened with astonishment. Her grit was admirable.

Madison then tried to step over the man she had punched and exit out past the back of the stage, but he grabbed her. She tried to deliver a heel at him, but he held her long legs together at the knees. The group of men all began clambering onto the stage. Madison looked with confusion toward the bouncers, who averted their eyes and walked out to the front entrance, pulling packs of cigarettes from their pockets and leaving her to deal with her own mess.

The men surrounded Madison, and two of them took hold of her arms. Another lunged at her, but Madison swung out with a freed foot and caught him in the crotch. The men shouted and swore. She screamed and spat at them—matching their insults with ones of her own. All of the shouting was nearly impossible to hear over the music. The man that she had heeled in the face was back on his feet now. He swayed, blood trickling down his chin. He pulled his arm back and hit her savagely. Madison's head recoiled back, and when it came forward again she spit in his face.

Vengelis placed his glass down on the bar.

The fat man moved his face inches from Madison's, laughing at her through the hole in his cheek and pulling out a thin knife that glinted in the flashing lights. Madison screamed in rage, her arms held behind her, as the man began to slash at the leather straps of her top. Madison thrashed dreadfully, her eyes filled with fury and fear.

"Hey!" Vengelis called, unexpectedly filled with a genuine fury. His voice carried over the music. Heads turned as he leapt through the flashing lights and onto the crowding stage.

"Get lost ki—" The fat man with the knife turned just in time to catch a fist to the face. There was a sickening crack as his head rocked backward from the blow and his spine snapped like a board of plywood. The man's body launched backward, crashing into a mirror and collapsing into a heap among lights and speakers.

The group of drunkards all fell back in fleeting shock, but held their ground when they realized their overwhelming numbers. Madison had fallen to the side. She stared up at Vengelis in disbelief from the black stage floor.

The sound of the punch had been chilling, even over the deafening music.

"Walk away," Vengelis said. His eyes flashed around the group of men, his voice commanding. In that passing moment he looked the part of an emperor as he stood his ground against the pitiful drunkards. One of the men stepped forward in the flashing lights, lifting his jean jacket and showing a handgun tucked into his belt.

"You really want to get involved with this?" he shouted at Vengelis.

Without hesitation Vengelis reached out and grabbed the gun from the man's waist before the fool could even flinch. Vengelis turned the pistol in his hand and cracked the butt of the gun against the bridge of the man's nose. The man fell to the stage at once, his face mangled.

An amateur and incalculably inferior punch was swung at the back of Vengelis's head. As the mere muscles in the man's shoulder flexed into action, Vengelis turned and brought his right fist upward into the attacker's gut. The man reeled upward, smacking into the ceiling and then falling to the floor. Debris fell from the pulverized ceiling tiles, filling the stage with a dust that changed color in the flashing strobes.

The club began to empty in a frenzy, everyone evacuating out through the entryway to the front of the building. Something horrible, something unnatural, was loose in the midst of the flashing lights and music.

As they ran away, Vengelis turned his attention to Madison. She was on all fours on the stage, thrown down in midst of the mayhem, holding together the top of her outfit. She stared up at Vengelis uncertainly, unsure if she should join the flight out of the room. They looked at each other, each equally unsure how to act. With a nod to her as if his actions had been nothing but a respectful favor, Vengelis turned and made to hop off the stage and leave the club through the entrance hallway.

"Wait," Madison called as she stumbled to stand. The music had died out, and the disarrayed room was now quiet. "The bouncers will have called the cops by now. Don't go out the front. They'll arrest you for starting that fight. Trust me."

Vengelis looked back to her for a moment, but turned once more to walk off the stage.

"Well, enjoy the handcuffs, I guess," Madison said with a puzzled frown and staggered through the door in the rear of the stage.

The door swung shut behind her, leaving Vengelis alone and wondering if he had made a mistake in his brashness. He was beginning to realize that manipulating people would prove to be a more challenging task than commanding them. Crumbled bits of ceiling tiles fell here and there in the stillness. Shattered and overturned liquor bottles behind the bar trickled their heady contents into puddles. Vengelis knew he had to follow her: he had found his guide. He needed an interpreter to take him to the scientists at the convention. With a sigh he hastened after her through the back door and into the dressing room.

Madison was alone by a cracked vanity mirror, throwing belongings into a bag. She had changed into civilized clothing, but jeans and a tee shirt did little to detract from her allure.

"I uh . . ." Vengelis said, and she spun around to face him.

Madison relaxed when she saw that it was him, though she regarded him with a wary glare. "Still here?"

"I . . . need. . . your help," Vengelis said, unsure whether his tone should be coaxing or demanding.

Madison narrowed her eyes. "I suppose I owe you one. But it'll depend on what you mean by help."

"Do you know where the Marrio—"

"Shut up for a second," Madison said, holding up a finger and turning her head.

The sound of shouts rose from back in the club.

"Yep." Madison nodded and slipped on a pair of shoes. "That'll be the cops. Come on, let's go."

Vengelis stood his ground, but when she took him by the arm he allowed her to lead him through a back hallway stacked with old rusty kegs. Madison pushed past a creaking steel door and they were engulfed by gusty autumn air and midday sunlight. They hurried past a dumpster and a tremendous pile of stagnant trash bags in the alleyway.

"So what's your story?" Madison said, looking even more stunning now that the sunlight shone on her face. Her eyes were emerald green, luminous against her dark skin. "Who are you?"

"It's Madison, right?" Vengelis said, halting their walking.

"Yes."

Vengelis suddenly felt a surprising degree of angst. He found himself not wanting to involve her. Beyond that, the mortification that would claim the faces of his departed family and high councillors if they knew he asked for the aid of a woman such as this was beyond words. Eve would likely slap him in the face.

"I have to go. Good luck," he said flatly and began to walk away from her.

"Hey!" Madison looked affronted, as if this was the first time in her life a man had walked away from her. She stormed after him. "Why did you risk your life for me?"

"I risked nothing," Vengelis said, still walking away from her. Though he knew it was a lie. He had risked too much, for a gain of nothing.

"At least tell me who you are. Call it a courtesy to ease my mind. I don't like being indebted to someone I don't know."

"You're not indebted to me. Forget about it."

As Vengelis turned out of the alley, he saw two police officers standing watch over the rear of the building. He recognized their uniforms; they were similar to the ones worn by the two men on the mountain far to the north. One of the officers held a hand up as Vengelis approached and eyed his armor uncertainly. "The building's been locked down. Crime scene—no one can leave until we sort it out."

Vengelis opened his mouth with the intention of giving the man a singular verbal warning, but Madison was too quick.

"Officer!" Madison grabbed Vengelis's arm and leaned against it as though she had an injury. "Some sicko just groped me in the dressing room. Ugh, he was so creepy! I barely got away from him. He's still in there—with the other girls. He said he has a gun."

"Uh, okay. Okay. We will take it from here, miss," the police officer stuttered. Both of the uniformed men gawked at her gorgeousness.

"Well, hurry then!"

Holding their gazes sidelong at her, they ran into the building by the side entrance, shouting into their radios and clutching their holsters with heavy steps.

Madison pulled her weight off Vengelis at once.

"Well, I would say it was nice meeting you, but I guess we didn't really meet," she said. "So, uh, thanks, I guess. I'll see you around, hotshot."

Madison gave him a bewildered expression and turned without another word, taking off down the street. Vengelis watched her walk away without the slightest lingering hesitation in her step. He tried to decipher what he was thinking. She was a human, a pitiful shadow of his own people. Though he had to admit that, provided with Royal attire, she could easily have passed for a daughter of even the most prestigious of Royal lines. Madison did not let that rabble of men get the better of her for the slightest instant. Vengelis's face unconsciously broke into a smirk as he considered the look of burning intensity that had taken hold of her as she fought them off. Even now as she walked away, Madison had a dignified kind of swagger. Vengelis sighed with uncertainty, knowing she was soon going to be caught up in the obliteration that was about to claim her world. His very own hand could unknowingly kill her.

"Wait," he called out.

CHAPTER TWENTY-ONE

The Lord General and Royal Guard

The two stoic Imperial First Class soldiers soundlessly traversed the skies over an expansive countryside. They were making their way steadily westward. A pair of massive birds of prey, Hoff held position a few body lengths ahead of Darien. They moved high over broad stretches of forest and narrow lakes nestled between humble hills. Here and there a highway or gathering of shingled rooftops would gleam up at them.

They were unwelcome strangers in a land blind to their malevolent presence, and they had no minds for leisurely sightseeing as they embraced the wooded country below. On the contrary, the lush carpet of vibrant foliage that fell away beneath them only stirred up feelings of anger and resentment. If the two soldiers possessed a greater ability to express their tangled emotions, they would have identified their shared sentiments as envy. Envy of the lands the people below called home. In their terse exchanges, Hoff and Darien agreed that an untested and unproven race did not deserve such a flourishing sanctuary.

The pale blue skies of the coastal east gradually gave way to cold blustering clouds that brooded tumultuously around them as they moved west. A cold drizzle touched their armor and the skin of their arms as they examined the lands. After some time soaring through the cold rain, Hoff held up his hand and came to a stop. The Lord General floated still in the dark sky, and Darien came to a stop at his side. The ground beneath them had noticeably shifted topographically; the hills had smoothed into level flatlands, and the broad gray mass of an immense lake extended across the vista to the north and commanded the horizon. The gigantic lake's dreary surface was that of an ocean, flecked with white caps and shadowy menacing swells. A number of rather unimpressive towns were scattered across the bank, and the infinitesimal movement of cars could be seen on the wet highways. Here and there a few buildings reached into the sky from the most prominent hub, perhaps a city. Aside from the several tall steel structures, the coast was cluttered with low rises and parking lots between stands of woods.

"What do you think?" Darien asked as he looked at the sodden roads and rooftops.

Hoff wiped cold precipitation from his brow. "I'm looking down at this world and these people and seeing nothing. I see a civilization that can barely hold back the wilderness that presses in around it. I see people that don't deserve even a shadow of our likeness. This mission is not going to get us anywhere. There's nothing of help to us here. Why Vengelis wants us to hold back at all is lost on me. It's shameful, staying out of sight of these people in this reverent manner. We're hiding from sheep."

"We're not hiding out of respect, Hoff. We're laying low so Vengelis can reach the scientists," Darien called over the growing wind as he squinted below. "But we only need to stay concealed for a little while longer. For now we just have to play our part."

"These...towns...won't serve for a spectacle. There aren't enough buildings down there to draw attention even if they were to fall." Hoff called and spat into the air. He watched his spittle fall far into the swirling rain. "We need to find a more populated city before we make contact with Vengelis."

"Yes," Darien said.

Hoff turned and eyed each horizon. In the north, the slate gray lake stretched beyond sight. To their south, rows of orderly neighborhoods and wet treetops encompassed everywhere the eye could see, which was not very far through the obscuring downpour.

"Do you think such a city exists?" Darien asked.

The Lord General shook his head uncertainly and took out his *Harbinger I* remote. He brought up a simple map of the North American continent. The screen of the remote glowed in the dreariness, and the Lord General held a forearm up to shield if from the pelting rain.

"According to this map, there's a population of about three million to the west of us. Only a few hundred miles."

"Are they densely concentrated?" Darien called over the growing vehemence of wind.

Hoff raised his gaze, heavy eyebrows dripping as he nodded dispassionately and turned to the west. The two giants continued their expedition, flying underneath the cathedral of churning storm clouds that loomed overhead. It was frigid at their altitude, but the two seemed unaware of the temperature or the worsening rain. Below, the rainstorm was falling heavily on grids of flat fields and endless acres of crops. A thick fog enclosed the region in a drab gloom. Looking down upon the pastoral lands passing them by, Darien felt a sharp despairing sentiment toward their situation. The glory of his race was being forced to seek salvation among farmers. He drew his gaze away from the lands and pulled in close to the Lord General. "Do you think they have any defenses?"

"Doesn't matter."

"I suppose not."

"Their most advanced defenses should at the very least shed some light on their advancement of technology. We'll see the pinnacle of their power. In that sense I really hope we're not left underwhelmed," Hoff said, squinting through the rain.

"I've never been on a planet other than Anthem," Darien said. "This place feels so surreal. I feel like we've traveled in time, not place."

"You've never been off Anthem?"

Darien shook his head.

"I'm surprised you weren't recruited for the Orion campaign. Most of the top soldiers were sent there."

"I was too young." Darien's face darkened, the memories still souring him. "Missed the Imperial Army cut off by three months."

"Well, at least you went on the make the Royal Guard. If it's any consolation, the Orion campaign was tedium."

"Wasn't there intelligent life there?" Darien asked with surprise.

Hoff weighed out the question uncertainly. "Technically, yes, I suppose. You're thinking of the Yarbu, or Yabu or something like that. They were little more than docile animals. It was . . . *excessive* . . . to call in the top ranks of the Imperial First Class on that one. A couple blundering low-ranks armed with a gun or two could have secured Orion."

"Either way, I wish I had been there." Darien shook his head wistfully. "It's always been a goal of mine to fight on foreign soil."

"Well you're getting that chance now, aren't you?"

Darien shrugged. "I suppose."

"Trust me kid, Orion was grunt work. They were a bunch of cave people and savages. You didn't miss much."

"You were there?"

"Well . . . not for the initial expeditions. I was general of the Royal Guard at the time. They sent for us when one of the soldiers broke rank. The whole thing was hushed up big-time." Hoff paused and considered something for a moment. "But what do classified secrets matter now?"

"There was dissention on Orion?" Darien asked. "This is the first I've heard of it."

"To call it dissention would be to put it lightly."

"What happened?"

Hoff hesitated. "Let me preface this by asking you not to tell Vengelis what I'm about to tell you. Okay?"

Darien gave him a questioning look. "Why?"

"Because he'll be mad that he was never made aware of it. But the truth of the ordeal was kept from everyone—generals and Royalty included. Everybody involved was forced to swear under penalty of execution that they would never speak of it. Emperor Faris himself ordered the cover up."

Darien stared at Hoff with a look of fierce anticipation. "By all means continue."

"Do you promise not to tell Vengelis? He won't see the excuse that I took an oath on my life directly to his father as justifiable. He'll only see it as me having withheld the truth from him. You know how he can get with things like this."

"Yes, yes. I won't tell Vengelis. Please just go on," Darien said.

"Okay. Do you remember the media coverage of the space transport accident that happened on the return journey to Anthem after the Orion campaign?"

Darien had to think back for a moment. He remembered it vividly, mainly because he was thankful not to have been involved. Had he not been too young during the recruitment trials, Darien easily could have been on board himself. The story had stayed in the news for weeks in the aftermath. A number of high-ranking military officials in the Imperial Army had been killed in a transport accident. Several famous soldiers had been lost.

"The accident with the generals, right?" Darien asked.

"Correct."

"Sure I remember." Darien nodded. "One of the transports lost contact in space. Worst accident in modern Imperial First Class history."

"But it wasn't any bunch of generals." Hoff pointed out. "The Lord General Bronson Vikkor himself was killed."

"Vikkor, yes." Darien said. "We lost the commander of the Imperial First Class because of some defective engine. I remember watching his fights in the Grand Arena when I was a kid. He was fierce."

"Yes, he was," Hoff said. "I was appointed to the open position of Lord General after his death. Bronson Vikkor was an old friend. I guess you could say I was a protégé of his."

Darien nodded slowly, rivulets of rain spilling off his broad chin. "I'm sorry to hear that. But what does any of this have to do with soldiers breaking rank?"

"Well, in short it has everything to do with it. The entire story of the space transport lost in space, from start to finish, was a fabrication."

"What do you mean?"

"I mean the whole transport accident was a cover story." Hoff veered closer to Darien and took a long dramatic breath. "Lord General Vikkor didn't perish because of some engine failure on the return journey. He was slain on Orion."

Darien immediately stopped his forward flight and halted in place, his head inclined skeptically. Hoff came to a stop as well, basking in his younger partner's reaction to this groundbreaking revelation. They floated separate from their surroundings as the unmentioned downpour gusted in sheets around them.

"*What?*" Darien demanded, his tone skeptical.

"It's true. Bronson Vikkor was assassinated in the command bridge of the transport," Hoff said with an expression of significance. "And three Royal Guards were hospitalized with wounds when they came to his aid. It was all done by one person."

Darien shook his head. "That's not possible. No one in the Imperial Army could have bested Vikkor and three Royal Guards. Maybe an Epsilon, but even then I would have to see it to believe it."

"I thought the same thing at first." Hoff nodded. "Until I saw the security footage myself."

Head still shaking, Darien's lips moved inarticulately, unable to forge a question. Then he blurted out, "Who was it?"

"Lets keep moving," Hoff turned and accelerated nearly out of sight into the storm.

Darien quickly soared alongside him. "Who?"

"Some Royal nobody," Hoff said. "Pral Nerol's son."

Darien's expression almost looked insulted as he pictured the old Pral Nerol and his research building in Municera. The Nerol's were a disgraced Royal house—scholars and academics for many generations. They were no warriors. "*Who?*"

"Pral Nerol's son."

Darien shook his head. "I don't believe you."

"You don't have to," Hoff shrugged. "But it's true."

"The Nerol's have amounted to nothing but useless thinkers. They're a stunted and fallen Royal line. I mean for god's sake, look at Pral Nerol: the son of one of the most immaculate Sejero bloodlines in history became a *scientist*. It sickens me. They're no soldiers!"

"Evidently this one was."

Darien scoffed in disbelief. "If this Nerol was so powerful, how come I've never heard of him?"

"Emperor Faris and the War Council exiled him from Anthem immediately after his dissension on Orion."

"Exiled? Shouldn't he have been executed? He assassinated the Lord General . . . that isn't exactly a minor offense."

"Are you really forgetting Imperial military protocol so soon? In no way should the kid have been exiled, or even punished for that matter. The young Nerol should have been awarded Vikkor's position as Lord General. The security footage of the command deck was combed over for days after the incident. The kid did issue an open challenge to Vikkor before attacking him. Technically speaking, the Epsilon war treatise states that young Nerol was within his rights. But Emperor Faris intervened and issued a Royal mandate for the kid to be exiled. His word superseded military law. Vikkor had a lot of friends in high places—he was not someone the kid should have messed with."

"The kid? What do you mean, the kid?"

"Nerol's son. He was a teenager at the time."

Darien glared through the rain. "A teenager?" he blurted out with rising contempt. "I will not believe a teenager bested the Lord General of the Imperial First Class."

"I swear on the Blood Ring that I'm telling the truth. I saw firsthand the security footage of the Nerol kid taking down an entire command deck of some of the most highly decorated soldiers in the military. Three former Grand Arena champions were on that deck. He took them all on at once. To this day I've never seen anything like it, beyond sparring with Vengelis. Supposedly the young Nerol spent his childhood training with Master Tolland, which is why nobody knew about him. Even discussing the boy was a crime punishable by death, so no one did. But between you and me, the Nerol kid is what prompted Emperor Faris to have Vengelis trained by Master Tolland."

Darien was in complete disbelief that a truth this substantial had been hidden so successfully. He—along with the rest of Anthem—had been under the impression that the venerated Lord General Vikkor died in the middle of space during the ship's return journey. Darien remembered all sorts of theories on how the ship's navigation system failed, and a call to increase the frequency of inspections. It had been treated as a terrible tragedy. If Hoff's story was true, it was obvious why the War Council would keep it from public attention. If a teenager could defeat the Lord General and three other soldiers in single combat, how powerful really was the Imperial First Class?

"After the command deck fell, they called in the Royal Guard to take the Nerol boy down," Hoff said. "You wouldn't believe the mayday transmission that was sent out from Orion. Imagine receiving a transmission stating that the Lord General was dead." Hoff shook his head, his gaze lost in memory. "We didn't know *what* the hell we were in for, but expected the worst. Maybe the local civilization had some advanced weaponry we had been unaware of. Maybe some higher race had intervened and come to Orion's defense. Maybe we had finally pushed too far and brought the hammer of the gods down on our heads. We had no goddamn idea. I'll tell you this though, the last thing we were expecting was that a teenager had thrown a tantrum."

"Unbelievable . . . " Darien said. He tried to envision how strong this lone Nerol must have been. "How did you get him into custody? Did you fight him?"

Hoff shook his head. "We didn't have to. Nerol's son had locked himself in his quarters before we even arrived. I'd be damned if I was going to be the one to open the door and talk to him. We said to hell with it, and directed the ship back to Anthem with the kid on board."

"Where they proceeded to exile him?"

Hoff nodded. "Where Emperor Faris exiled him, yes."

"And he just . . . left? It sounds like he could have put up one hell of a struggle in the palace."

"I have no doubt that he could have. It probably would have been a fight for the history books. But think about it. We would have simply threatened to kill his family to settle him down. Old man Nerol used as leverage." Hoff chuckled at the thought.

"So this young Nerol just left Anthem?"

"He left that same day. The same day everyone involved took their blood oaths of secrecy."

"How did the kid leave?"

"Darien, the kid was a pure blooded Nerol, not the son of some ragtag middle class family. I'm sure he was given some plush one-way transport somewhere."

"Does anyone know where he went?"

"My guess would be Orion, since that's where he lost his marbles. But no, as far as I'm aware no one knows where he went."

A splitting crack of thunder boomed from just over their heads, deafening at their proximity. It startled Darien and he lost his concentration, falling for a brief moment into space before quickly steadying himself. Right above them, fierce dark swirls of storm clouds expelled ever thickening rain that pelted angrily against their upturned faces. To Darien it felt as though the very planet itself now sensed their unnatural presence and was roaring at them to leave, to go back to the war-pocked and ravaged Anthem and take their troubles with them. Yet the storm cloud's command went unheeded by the two soldiers. Hoff merely let out a rumbling laugh at Darien's brief loss of control.

"Don't tell me you're afraid of a little thunder? It's the lightning you have to watch out for. It can singe your hair if you get hit by a big strike."

Darien clenched his fists. "It just startled me. I'm obviously not afraid of thunder."

"Oh, I don't know. You should have seen the look on your face. You better not flinch like that when the humans bring the height of their firepower against us. I assure you it will be louder than that."

"Enough!" Darien shouted, his tone dangerous. He wiped the torrential rain from his face and continued westward.

"I'm just giving you a hard time, don't sweat it." Hoff clapped a palm against his back, soaring alongside him.

"Why did the Nerol kid attack Lord General Vikkor? Was it a power grab?" Darien asked in an attempt to take the attention away from his display of weakness. Thunder continued to emanate from above them, and long purple-white forks of lightning began to illuminate them against the churning gray sky in sudden flashes of brightness.

"Eh, I guess that's possible, but from what I heard it wasn't a power grab. The soldiers on the command deck said the quarrel had started with a dispute over orders. I think it was the genocide order of the local aboriginals. The Nerol kid thought it was unwarranted."

"Was it unwarranted?"

"Who cares? Bronson Vikkor wasn't—how should I put it—*considerate* to inferior races. I have no doubt that Vikkor would disapprove of Vengelis's caution at the moment with these humans. He would have descended on these people with fist and fire. So yes, it would not surprise me to find out it had been an unnecessary order. But it was followed by the Imperial Army regardless."

"And the aboriginals? The Yabu?"

"They are as equal a part of history as Lord General Vikkor—and us, for that matter." Hoff said.

"We're not history yet. I still think Vengelis can defeat the Felixes and re-claim the Epsilon throne. Even now, in the midst of all the carnage back home, it seems to me like he has a clear head."

"Maybe," Hoff muttered.

"Master Tolland believed Vengelis could defeat the Felixes too," Darien said. "Don't forget that."

"I'll stick with maybe. Master Tolland also sent us here to find a weapon against the Felixes. What weapons do you see? I see nothing but pathetic indi-gents. I'm beginning to wonder if Master Tolland was not entirely coherent when we found him in that pile of rubble. He *was* at death's door after all. At the time it made sense; it was an order to cling to, anything that could give us hope. But now that I'm here, I can't understand why he sent us to this place."

"No," Darien said. "Master Tolland may have been dying, but he was alert. Even you thought so. His orders were so specific. There must have been a rea-son. Maybe Vengelis is right to think that the human scientists can deduce a way to defeat the Felixes. What if the answer is right in front of us and we can't see it? I think—"

"Darien," Hoff interrupted suddenly, "Look."

The Lord General's eyes were wide. He raised an arm and pointed into the discernible expanse before them. They had pulled through the storm and out of the rain. Situated along the bank of another huge body of water beneath them, a gargantuan city ascended into the clouds through a thick cover of fog. Countless dark structures rose through the dreary mists and into the tempestuous sky. The shrouded metropolis extended for miles and miles up the coastline. In the center of the cluster of larger structures, a colossal black building ascended like a citadel above all the others; it was nearly as large as the very Imperial Palace or the Sejero Tower. The city sprawling out of the fog before them looked nothing short of Sejeroreich itself.

"I . . . I can't believe it," Darien stammered.

Hoff shook his head in disbelief, his mouth open. "I had no idea these people were capable of feats like this."

Darien was staring down at the tiered roofs of the immense towers rising out of the mist. "Do you think we should make contact with Vengelis?"

"Yes. This is the place." Hoff pulled out his ship remote and on the screen carefully examined the map he had previously consulted. In a moment the re-mote connected with Vengelis's, so far east of them.

"We have found an appropriate city, my lord," Hoff said at once.

The voice of Vengelis responded somewhat grainy and distorted. "How many people are congregated there, and what is it called?"

"The remote says three million, my lord. We're looking down at it now. It will definitely suffice for a spectacle. The map says the city is called . . . Chicago."

CHAPTER TWENTY-TWO

Vengelis

The sunlight danced on Madison's flawless complexion and the dark waves of her hair as she turned at the street corner and watched him jog after her. Vengelis shouldered past a few passersby and halted before her, meeting her gaze with an expression bent in conflict.

"Look." Vengelis gazed wearily into the busy intersection as cars and taxis veered by. "This city . . . this city isn't a safe place to be today. You need to get as far away from here as you can."

"And why would that be?" Madison reached into her bag and pulled out a pack of cigarettes.

He dismissed her curiosity with an agitated shake of his head. "It's really too much to get into. But you need to get out of this city. Go anywhere but here."

"Like Jersey? I'm all set."

"I don't know what Jersey is, but if it's far away from New York City, then, yes, go there."

"Hmm." Madison tilted her head as she lifted a cigarette out of the pack with elongated fingers. She put it to her lips, lit it thoughtfully and took a long drag. "Nope. That doesn't feel right. No offense, but I think I'll stay."

"You really need to listen to me. This entire city is in imminent danger. Your *world*, collectively, isn't safe. I'm formally asking you to leave."

Amusement surfaced on her lips as Madison regarded him, her judgment of his character obviously vacillating. He watched her eyes move to his body and take in his uncanny, though unmistakably valuable attire. The obscenely massive Blood Ring on his hand surely looked elaborate and genuine, even to her untrained eye. Perplexity passed across Madison's face as her attention paused on the Blood Ring. A seed of uncertainty surrounding the man before her had taken root in her mind.

"Where are you from?" she asked, her tone abruptly intrigued.

"Far."

Madison cast him a doubtful look. "Like Europe? You sort of have a European look to you I suppose. Your . . . clothing . . . and that ring definitely scream un-American."

"No, much farther than Europe."

"So, like . . . where?"

Vengelis took in an extended breath and let it out slowly, both his frustration and his nerves growing. Time was running out, and he knew he was past due to check in with Hoff and Darien. "Are you going to leave the city or not?"

Madison shrugged. "I don't see why I would."

The traffic light across from their intersection signaled walk, and Madison stepped out onto the crosswalk along with a few other pedestrians. As she turned away from him, Vengelis reached out and held her shoulder. Madison turned back to face him, insulted by the gesture. Vengelis regarded her coldly; he was about to tell her more forcefully to evacuate when a beep sounded from within his armor. With his left hand he pulled out the *Harbinger I* remote.

"What the hell is that?" Madison asked, staring at the extraordinary contraption.

"A remote control to my ship," Vengelis said simply.

Madison visibly thought over his nonchalant statement. Then once more she tried to casually pull her shoulder away from him, but found his grip to be implausibly strong. A concern began to surface across her face, as if it suddenly became clear to her that the man before her was not entirely stable.

"I mean you no harm, stop squirming," Vengelis said, his attention on the remote.

"Then let me *go*." Madison pressed her cigarette down against his arm and it fizzled out against his impervious skin. She brought her free arm down against his grasp and beat against his forearm several times. "Let me go!"

"No."

"Let me go!" With mounting anger Madison tried to free herself, but his grip was inconceivably strong. She reached around to dig her fingernails into the taut cords of muscle in his forearm and her mouth fell immediately agape. The ends of two of her nails cracked. "Your skin . . . it feels like rock."

"I'm still in the process of helping you," Vengelis said. "You're not aware of the danger you are in."

Another beep sounded from the remote, and Vengelis raised the remote and answered.

"*Cinga avar zitutha*," were the words Madison heard from the remote. Vengelis recognized the voice as belonging to his Lord General Hoff.

Vengelis looked into Madison's eyes, his face distant. "*Marza e'kuff vashkara nompanta.*"

Madison's expression twisted in bewilderment as she stared at him; the incoherent words belonged to no language she had ever heard. Her lips moved inarticulately and she stopped squirming. A cautious trepidation claimed her as she listened to the sharp transformation of Vengelis's tone and intonation.

"*Lorvesh ritak levkaraska e'ta Shikago,*" the voice spoke again.

Several more exchanges were passed in the language that Madison surely only recognized as a strange and foreign tongue. Vengelis then paused and considered something, before switching back to English. "Are you familiar with a city known as Chicago?"

Madison futilely tried to yank herself away from his grip. "What the hell are you talking about?"

"Are you, or are you not, familiar with the city of Chicago?"

"Yes, obviously."

"*Keez arakla.*" Vengelis looked at her with complete stoicism and repeated the command in English for her benefit, perhaps to enlighten her of her plight. "Show them our power."

Vengelis slipped the *Harbinger I* remote back into his armor and released the grip on her shoulder. He calmly wiped off the ash her cigarette had left on his forearm. Madison saw the unharmed skin underneath and recoiled away from him suspiciously.

"Now you realize the nature of danger you're in by staying in this city against my guidance," Vengelis said.

Madison rotated her arm and massaged her shoulder where he had held her. His fingers had left marks on her skin. "You . . . are some sort of terrorist?"

"No. Well . . ." Vengelis considered the question. "At least not a terrorist in the sense you're probably envisioning. Though I have no doubt my presence here will inspire terror."

"Who are you?" Madison said as the fear in her eyes began to turn to dread. She was surely now remembering all too vividly the inhumanness of his attack on the men in the club. What had happened in there was not normal—not natural. She sighed, stepped closer to him so no passersby could overhear, and begrudgingly rephrased her question. "*What* are you?"

"My name is Vengelis Epsilon."

"What kind of name is that?"

"A foreign one."

"And you are from where exactly? I can recognize a lot of languages and I've never heard anything remotely like what you were just speaking. I don't—"

"I'm from Anthem."

Madison blinked. "And that is . . . some city in the Middle East or a town in Eastern Europe or something?"

Vengelis shook his head and she took a shrinking step away from him. Madison turned to leave him for good, but again he reached out and took her arm.

"Let me go!" she said quietly, leaning into him, her eyes furious. A number of passersby turned their heads, but no attempt was made to intervene. Instead they drew their attention to the restaurant fronts across the street or the dried gum on the pavement; all walked by without a word, making the choice not to involve themselves.

"Please let me speak. After I have said my part, if you still wish to disregard my warning, I'll let you go without argument. I already told you that I mean you no harm." Vengelis slowly released his grip on her arm, and when she did not run, he took a step back.

Madison massaged her knuckles over her shoulder. "Okay. Tell me."

"My name is Vengelis Epsilon, and I am here for a very specific purpose. That purpose will include the maiming of the city my men have now reached. I do not relish in its torment, it is a necessary means toward the end I require."

Madison stared at him.

"Hopefully it ends there," Vengelis said, and decided some exaggeration might help his cause. "If after witnessing our power in Chicago, your people are still not convinced of our superiority, if they still refuse to aid me in my purpose, it is likely I will be forced to hurt New York as well, along with as many other cities as will be necessary in order to gain submission."

Madison continued to stare blankly for a long moment before her mouth turned upward and she laughed aloud. "Why would you want to do that?"

"That is . . . rather complex. But where my personal errand affects you is in the potential harming of New York." Vengelis looked up past the hanging traffic lights to the tall glass windows that loomed far overhead.

"This is either a very bizarre prank or you're a complete lunatic," Madison said with a nervous laugh.

"Far from it, I assure you I am quite lucid. You need only ask me to prove my words."

"Prove what? That you aren't insane?"

"No," Vengelis said. "That I'm not human."

Madison's laughter died. "Okay, man," she said, her tone sober. "You did help me back there, and I appreciate it. And you are intriguing in a weird sort of way. But I don't have the time to deal with someone who is mentally unstable. If you are sane, and this is some weird joke, then you really need to find something better to do with your time. Please just walk away and leave me alone."

Vengelis sighed regretfully.

"Sorry, *Vengelis*, although I'm sure it's really Eric or Dan or something. I'm leaving."

"You'll regret this choice. That is a promise. Within the hour, your civilization will never be the same. This society will collapse around you. You will be stuck here, unable to get out, with the remembrance that you were warned and did not listen."

"For god's sake!" Madison shrugged in exasperation. Once more she looked down and embraced his armor. He guessed that his appearance added some credibility to his strange story. A simple action would add quite a bit more, but he awaited her.

"Fine," she said at last. "I'll play along a little while longer. Do it. Whatever you can prove, prove it right now."

"Okay, but I'm unfamiliar with the limitations of the human form. Ask me to do something a human couldn't do."

Madison cast him a skeptical and anxious smirk, then turned to look around the intersection. Cars and taxis beeped and brakes squealed through the busy street. Congested groups of people moved past them along the pavement, entering and exiting the nearby restaurants and stores.

"Okay, *Vengelis Epsilon*," Madison said. "Go and stop one of those cars with your bare hands. Weirdo."

Vengelis wondered how fast the authorities or governmental powers would react to the assault of this city of Chicago. He did not want to provide any window of time by which the scientists could evacuate his vicinity. "I'll need a promise from you first. Well, two promises actually."

"Oh yeah?" Madison said. "Name them."

"First, you must promise you won't panic when I do what you've asked of me," Vengelis said.

Madison let out a melodious laugh. The humor of the situation was evidently coming back to her. She looked past him, perhaps looking for a hidden camera crew. Vengelis gave her a grim look. He knew there would be no way she could be capable of holding back her forthcoming panic.

"Deal," Madison said.

"Good. Second promise. After I have proven myself to you, you will lead me immediately, without a moment's delay, to the Marriot Marquis. Do you know where that is?"

Madison narrowed her brow at the specificity of the request. "Yes, I know where it is. If you can stop a car without any stupid tricks or games or whatever, I will bring you straight to the Marriot Marquis. You have my word."

"Believe me, there will be no tricks," Vengelis said. He looked at her with a stern severity. "Are you absolutely certain you know where the Marriot Marquis is?"

"Obviously. It's right in Times Square," Madison said and nodded toward the street. "I'm waiting here."

Vengelis brought his attention to the intersection. The deal would be off and he would leave her if she did not follow through with her promise. He was running out of time and needed to get to the convention soon. If Hoff and Darien had started their assault, New York City would likely be in chaos within minutes.

"Very well. How about that vehicle coming down the street? Will that suffice?" Vengelis asked her. An enormous eighteen-wheeler was hauling toward the intersection, flagged onward by a green light. The broad wheels and bulky steel frame hogged nearly two lanes. The driver must have been in a rush, as the truck was travelling well over the speed limit.

"Yeah." Madison rolled her eyes. "That will work."

"Okay. Remember your promises."

Madison nodded doubtfully.

Without another word, Vengelis turned and stepped off the sidewalk into the roaring traffic. A red Don't Walk sign blinked from across the intersection. The cars waiting behind the red lights adjacent to him beeped and windows rolled down. People shouted at him to get out of the road, most thinking this young man was going commit suicide right in front of their eyes.

The oncoming truck powered with enormous momentum toward the intersection. The thick steel grate and grinning fender rattled and bore down upon the Lord of Anthem. Behind the windshield, the driver was busy adjusting the radio, his eyes off the road. The look on Madison's face suddenly filled with horror as she realized Vengelis was actually going to go through with the challenge. The young man before her was psychotic; she had inadvertently sent some mental patient to his death. She took a step off the sidewalk and reached out to him in panic.

"Holy shit! I was kidding, come *back*!" Madison screamed out to him.

Vengelis looked back to her as if to convey a reminder of the promise she had made. He then turned and broke into a dead sprint up the avenue toward the incoming truck. Jaws dropped in disbelief as the young man launched himself directly at the massive semi. The driver lifted his head only to catch a fleeting glimpse of someone in his path; he did not even get to slam his boot into the brake pedal. Vengelis pumped his legs forward and lowered his head, driving his shoulder and upper body straight into the hulking bare steel grill of the truck.

An ear-splitting and hideous crunching sound resounded across the block as the front of the semi crumpled from the overwhelming impact. In an instant the truck was barely recognizable as a vehicle at all, and became a pile of indiscernible steel carnage. The concussion of the impact caused all of the bystanders, Madison included, to launch backward onto the pavement. The thick panes of glass restaurant fronts and car windows shattered from the shockwave of the impact, sending shards to the pavement. The truck's gigantic rubber wheels along with various pieces of the vehicle launched in every direction.

In the very center of the stopped intersection, in the heap of scrap parts, Vengelis pushed aside pieces of the surrounding white-hot wreckage. He stepped out from the twisted steel nest, which had been the fender of the truck, completely unscathed, casually brushing off debris as he crossed the street and approached Madison. Behind him, the truck driver—miraculously still alive—stumbled out of the driver's side door and crawled across the pavement to get away from Vengelis. The bystanders were divided between those who had seen the event unfold, and those who had been surprised by the sudden calamity. Those who witnessed his eerie rush into the truck fell back in revulsion as he approached the sidewalk.

Madison had crashed painfully onto her back on the concrete. In a stunned state she numbly ran her fingers over her body to check for any injury. Her eyes were wide with disbelief and her body was shaking with shock. The fall to the ground must have been painful. Sirens sounded from nearby as Vengelis stood over Madison. She was turning and writhing on the glass-strewn pavement. Madison looked at him and sputtered for words, the terror rampant in her eyes.

"Now," Vengelis said to her. "Take me to the Marriot Marquis."

CHAPTER TWENTY-THREE

The Lord General and Royal Guard

The wind whipped and roared in Darien's ears as he barreled in Lord General Hoff's wake through the heavy clouds lingering high in the atmosphere over Chicago. Needles of rain pelted against his face, and he strained to keep Hoff in sight as he nearly disappeared in the mists below. It required all of Darien's focus to keep the eagerly accelerating Lord General from pulling ahead.

As he descended through the lashing precipitation, the grand city seemed to increase in magnitude as the height and breadth of the skyscrapers appeared. The tall dark spires, beautiful and solemn against the rainstorm, pierced the very heavens. Their sharp lines and dark forms jutted through the pallid fog that hung among the concealed streets below.

A city doomed to fall, like so many before. This city's grandeur would descend to tragedy against the might of Sejero power. He, *he*, was going to destroy this place. It was brutal, but it was an order. Orders were followed. Darien would destroy this city for the cause of the Felix and the salvation of the Primus race—his race. Darien was the last surviving Royal Guard of the Epsilon, a quintessential vision of Sejero prowess and loyalty. If he did not have the stomach to do what must be done, who did? He shook away the slight compassion rising in his heart as he descended from the sky. Now was not the time for half measures, now was the time to prove his tremendous worth. Focusing all his power into his speed, he accelerated his meteoric plummet and pulled alongside the fellow giant. The Lord General Hoff turned and gave an impressed nod as they simultaneously erupted downward.

...

"Yes, ma'am, I completely understand, and we are doing all we can to make your switch over to our service as pleasant as possible."

Alyssa Ware sat at her office desk—though it was little more than a booth—and spoke into the mouthpiece of a headset while she drew doodles on the back of a weekly memo. She was an entry-level customer service rep for a cell phone provider with a bachelor's degree in Sociology. Alyssa graduated last spring from the University of Illinois, Chicago, with honors. But times were tough, and this position was the only employment she could find. It was her second week on the job, and Alyssa already hated it.

"No! The salesman at the store told me my monthly bill would be seventy dollars. Now I'm sitting here looking at a bill for . . ." the shrill woman on the other line scoffed, "ninety dollars! I knew y'all would pull some sort of trick like this!"

Alyssa closed her eyes. "Yes, ma'am, the first month's bill includes a sign up fee. It's a one time payment that—"

"No! This is unacceptable, missy. I want to talk to your supervisor right now!"

Alyssa wearily opened her eyes and looked out the window with a sigh. Her company leased the fortieth floor of the building, and despite the innumerable negatives of her job, she did have a desk facing the window. The lofty view of the other skyscrapers in the financial district of Chicago provided a nice distraction during monotonous afternoons.

The weather outside the rain-streaked glass that hour was unusually bleak and dismal, even by Chicago standards. A misty fog draped among the tall skyscrapers outside, and the street level far below was lost in the gloom. Alyssa's desk, often saturated in bright sunlight, was today only illuminated by the faintly humming fluorescent bulbs overhead. Her workspace was cast in a greenish artificial hue.

"Ma'am," Alyssa said as brightly as she could. "The sign up fee isn't negotiable. But again, it's only a one-time payment. Your next bill will be for the amount you had signed up for. I can put you through to my manager, but he will tell you the same thing."

"*Pfft*! Put me through to someone that can do something! I'm getting nowhere with you. Y'all are useless."

"Certainly," Alyssa said. She took her time finishing the final touch on a drawing she had been working on: a surprisingly good cartoon of a girl playing an electric guitar in front of a microphone. One hand of the cartoon rocker was raised above her head making a fist. With a satisfied nod, Alyssa hit the button to talk to her section manager Stan Reed.

"What's up, Alyssa?" she heard his voice through the speaker in her ear, and from his desk a few seats over.

"I have a present for you." Alyssa chuckled humorlessly. "Another sign up fee complaint that wants to talk to a supervisor."

Stan groaned. "Put it through."

Alyssa allowed her shoulders to droop back into her chair and gazed pensively out into the lofty gray mists, moving her hand to hit the transfer call button.

Her hand halted abruptly.

Something caught her eye outside the window. Alyssa narrowed her eyebrows in disbelief. Impossible. *Impossible.* She rubbed her eyes forcefully and rose from her seat; she had to be hallucinating. Taking a few dazed steps toward the window, Alyssa moved her face to within mere inches from the pane of glass. The cord connecting her headset with the telephone on her desk pulled taut and disconnected. Rivulets of rain ran down the other side of the thick window. Her breath fogged the glass. She squinted into the distance, her face locked in an expression of disbelief.

"Alyssa? Put the call through." Stan's voice came from a thousand miles away.

"W-wh . . ." Alyssa could not seem to find her voice. She had to be dreaming. For the first time in her life, Alyssa Ware began to shake uncontrollably. It started in her jaw, her chin quivering and her teeth chattering audibly. Then her entire body succumbed to the trembling. What she saw outside the window filled her with a shock she had never known.

She was staring at a man.

Above a high-rise a man was floating. *Floating.* She could see him as clearly as she could see a coworker at the other end of her office. The man was suspended in space about fifty feet over the rooftop, his head turning from building to building. She could not quite tell from the distance, but he looked impossibly enormous. Alyssa stared in bewilderment. Someone was flying outside her office. In an absolutely certain yet indescribable sense, she could tell it was not some sort of optical illusion. It was real. His—its—movements were otherworldly.

"Alyssa?" Stan leaned his chair back and saw she had left her desk. Alyssa was standing against the window with her back to him, her yellow blouse contrasting against the darkly threatening panoramic view of the skyline. He shook his head in annoyance. "Alyssa you forgot to put the call through. And if you want to go on break, you have to wait until—"

The rumbling began.

The office began to shake from the tremors. A fluttery feeling rose in Alyssa's stomach as she stood by the window; she now was acutely aware that her office was hundreds of feet off of the ground. Along with everyone in the office, the realization of their lofty height seeped into their minds. The floor began to shake. They were on the fortieth floor of a sixty-story building.

Unlike the rest of the office, Alyssa was too preoccupied staring at the floating man to worry about the earthquake. As her coworkers grabbed solid objects for support, she simply stood by the window. The man was now moving through the air above all the buildings. Was he a man? The proportions of the body looked somehow inhuman, far too tall and wide. He was so huge. Alyssa tried to speak but found herself still unable to find words.

Stan was holding onto his desk as if it would provide him with protection against the shaking of the building. "Alyssa!" he called to her. "Get away from the goddamn window, are you nuts?"

At last Alyssa's voice returned to her and she gasped loudly. The floating man had suddenly flown straight toward the top of their own building. She caught a clear glimpse of him as he flew skyward past the window. He *was* a giant, and he *was* flying.

"It isn't a man . . ." Alyssa stammered weakly, almost whining. Her eyes were wide with fear. Alyssa, a fervent agnostic, suddenly conjured up images of soaring gods and angels, devils and demons. The blood rushed from her head, and she swayed woozily on her feet.

"What the hell are you talking about?" Stan shouted. "It's an earthquake! Get away from the window!"

A sharp bang from a floor far above caused everyone to jerk up their heads in concern, all eyes staring intensely at the ceiling tiles and now flickering lights. A twanging sound emanated from behind the elevator doors by the receptionist's desk, followed by a deep whooshing from behind the closed steel doors.

The elevators had fallen loose.

A cacophony of terrified voices broke out among the call center desks. There was panicked talk of evacuating through the stairwells. The building was in structural danger—everyone had to get out right away. Another harsh bang sounded from above the ceiling. The optimistic and courageous part of Alyssa's core tried hopelessly to pull her mind out of the well of dread into which it now sunk. She tried to blink back tears, but they rolled uncontrollably down her face and dripped off her quaking chin.

A jolt came from above, and the entire office swayed as though it was a carnival ride. People ran to the emergency stairwell doors, bottlenecking at the narrow frame. The stairway visible beyond the doors was at a standstill, already clogged with hundreds of hysterical office workers from the other floors. Alyssa felt the rising of a dreamlike helplessness. She unconsciously let out a guttural moaning scream. Perhaps simply out of reflex she pulled her cell phone from her pocket, opened the contact list, and called Home.

The lights flickered and went out, and a ceiling tile dislodged and broke against her desk. The phone rang twice.

"Hello?" it was her Mom, and her voice was tender and familiar. She was probably folding laundry in the family room with Barkley, the family's youngest member, a particularly rambunctious Corgi.

Alyssa shut her eyes as plump teardrops rolled down her already streaked face. "M-m-mom."

"*Alyssa?*" her mother nearly screamed, immediately recognizing the genuine panic in her daughter's voice.

The building jerked and roared above her. Alyssa sobbed, for a moment thinking it was collapsing. She moved away from the window and sat down heavily next to her desk, folding her arms around her numb, shaking legs and burying her face into the knees of her new khakis.

"Alyssa what is going on? Are you at work?"

"Mom, I d-d-don't—" Alyssa sobbed like her mother had not heard since her daughter was three years old. "I don't know what's happening."

"Alyssa are you all right?" her mother screamed.

BOOM-BOOM-BOO-BOO-BOO-BO-BO-BO-B-B-B.

Although she had no idea how it had come to this, Alyssa knew what the sounds were. It was the thundering of the floors above her collapsing on each other. By the stairwell people clawed and screamed to get through the doors, but they were on the fortieth floor. There would be no escape.

"Alyssa! Talk to me!" her mother shrieked.

Alyssa sniffed noisily. "I—"

For a split second, Alyssa peered over her knees as a wide section of the ceiling in the center of the office imploded. The carpeted floor at her feet disintegrated. For a brief moment her nervous system recognized the unmistakable sensation of free falling. None of her senses registered anything individually, just the distinct feeling in her stomach of plunging through space.

Then, within the same instant, there was nothing.

CHAPTER TWENTY-FOUR

Ryan

Ryan held on to a steel handrail in the lightly bucking and squealing subway car. The train barreled through the dark tunnel as strangers invaded his personal space, but he took no notice of them as he stared vacantly out the grimy window and into the flashing darkness. He was lost in thought. The night's sleep in Kristen's bed had been the most restful he had known in as long as he could remember. To think that such a warm experience had happened only one night after his nightmare returned was hard to grasp.

For the past year he had been naive enough to think he had at last escaped the torments of his past. But the nightmare—the memory—of that snowy forest had returned to him once more. In his mind, he could still smell the fires of the village burning, could still hear the shrill screams of children and parents parted.

Ryan could still see the look of fear and hatred in the eyes of those people, sentenced to die.

Yet it was only his familiar sharp gaze that stared back at him from the dirty Plexiglas. Ryan shook away the wintry chill of his memories as the subway brakes released a high-pitched scream, and an automated voice announced his stop. With hands buried deep in the pockets of his jeans, he pushed the past from his mind and paced through a station of fluorescent lights and grungy tile. He ascended a narrow stairway to the street, taking the steps two at a time, and emerged from the station into sunlight and chilly fresh air.

Manhattan's architectural exhibitionism bloomed overhead, and Ryan oriented himself by the towering buildings. Beyond the mirrored facades of skyscrapers, the day could not have been more clear, only a few sparse clouds nestled between the reflective high-rises. Ryan willfully focused on minutiae as he trod through Midtown in the direction of Times Square and the Marriot Marquis. The workload in his classes had reached a lull, and his weekend schedule at the library along with few assignments due early the following week hardly seemed daunting. Aside from Professor Hilton's class, his semester was humming along at nearly a 4.0 pace, more than high enough to allow some self-satisfaction.

He was worried for Kristen. There was an odd hope within him that gravitated around her. She was nothing like the brilliant minds from his home—so utterly convinced of their own brilliance and their grim practices. Young, beautiful and endearingly awkward Kristen was the hero that he could never be, and her words were more powerful than anything he could ever shoulder himself. She was a glimmer of what once was, so long ago and far away, and what its future may have been had it not been ripped away.

But in his heart, his feelings for Kristen were far simpler than that.

It was difficult to imagine how she must be feeling as she prepared to stake her future on the vicissitudes of the media's whim. Her selflessness filled him with a hopeful feeling, as it was a characteristic he was not entirely unfamiliar with. Sacrificial altruism was a path chosen by few. Ryan only hoped it would work out better for Kristen than it had for himself.

A street corner vendor had set up shop in the shadow cast by a tall financial building, and Ryan stepped in line to buy a drink. The few waiting customers rummaged hastily in their pockets for bills and coins as they procured their hot dogs. A tiny television blared beside the disheveled cashier, and as he ordered a bottle of water Ryan noticed the news was still airing live from the plane crash in Albany.

"Some shit, huh?" the cashier grunted with an accent Ryan could not place.

Ryan opened his water bottle and passed over a dollar bill. "Do they know what happened yet?"

"Not a clue. Heads up their asses."

Ryan looked at the man. "Maybe."

The cashier grunted and turned back to the television, lighting a cigarette with dirty fingers. Ryan continued down the avenue looking sidelong into the storefronts and lobbies. It struck him as remarkable; the ordinary fears people were forced to cope with in everyday life. With full knowledge of that morning's fiery crash, still travelers were boarding planes around the world.

People were more courageous than they gave themselves credit for.

Ryan took out his cell phone and saw a new message from Kristen, *I'm really glad you're coming.* The text brought a smile to his face as he negotiated past scaffolding and entered Times Square. Above him, glimmering billboards and revolving advertisements beamed down from all angles. Although Ryan would never admit it, part of him felt oddly alive every time he walked among the grand blinking billboards.

Only in a time of peace, of prosperity, could such trivial notions as fashion and celebrity hold such sway over society, and in that sense he was thankful for the overhead glamour. All things considered, there were worse things to worship than pop culture.

Gawking tourists and relentless street salesmen obstructed his way as he crossed congested intersections and came before the grand entrance to the Marriott Marquis. He tossed his water bottle into a gold-embossed hotel garbage can and took a deep breath of the agreeable autumn breeze. Beyond the street-level marquee, the hotel rose far overhead, its zenith indistinguishable among so many others of Midtown. Almost at once Ryan felt out of place with his untucked plaid shirt and jeans as he entered the opulent hotel lobby. Everything was elegant, from the detailed handrails to the sumptuous carpet. Ryan took the stairs up to the second floor, and ambled into the Lutvak ballroom. Hesitating inside of the doors, he stretched to his full height and looked out over the many rows of chairs and tables lining the huge space. The displays ranged from studies on viruses in Geneva to microchips in the Silicone Valley to extensive charts on radiation research in northern Japan. Ryan noted that the podium at the head of the ballroom was unmanned; he was early. He navigated the perimeter of the room and saw the largest congregation of people amassed by the Vatruvian cell display station against the far wall. Ryan meandered toward it, peering past some shoulders and watching a Vatruvian cell rotate slowly on a large laptop screen.

"Glad to see the demographic of suits and blazers didn't turn you away at the door," Ryan heard Kristen say, and turned to see her sitting down, her chin resting in her hands. A few looked at her strangely due to the irreverent remark, but Kristen did not seem to care. "Have you been watching the news?"

Ryan pulled up a seat next to her. "Seems like more of the same."

"Some hotel worker just announced the government has heightened national security," Kristen said. "Kind of freaky."

"I'm sure it's nothing too serious." Ryan watched a group of people and saw the man he recognized as Nicoli Vatruvia shaking hands with some old professor types. "Are you sticking to your plan?"

"I am." Kristen tapped the pen drive attached to the laptop nearest her. "I just put together a final slide that tells about the mice."

Ryan drew a nervous breath.

"It'll be fine," Kristen said. "It's what needs to happen. Professor Vatruvia told me we're presenting second on the itinerary, so I don't think I'll start our presentation for twenty minutes or so."

"Okay." Ryan nodded.

The amplified voice of a man standing behind the podium abruptly rose over the hubbub of the ballroom. "Hello, researchers from around the globe, and thank you for coming to this year's convention! We will be starting the day's presentations momentarily, so if everyone can find a seat, we'll get underway as soon as possible!"

Kristen sighed anxiously and clapped the laptop shut as Professor Vatruvia turned and beckoned her over. "Well, this is it," she whispered bleakly. "Wish me luck."

"Good luck," Ryan said. They looked at each other for one caring moment, and then Kristen turned to follow Professor Vatruvia.

Ryan rose from his seat and walked to the rows of seats by the rear of the ballroom. On the broad projection screen behind the stage, the title of the first presentation read: *Bovine Lymphocyte Formations.* He cringed at the subject and decided to visit the café downstairs and grab a coffee while he waited. Ryan swept down the main stairs, and found the lobby mostly unoccupied. Most guests were now up in the Lutvak Ballroom. After exchanging a pleasantry with the barista, Ryan stirred his steaming cup of French roast and raised his attention to a television screen propped beside the chalkboard menu.

The airplane crash in Albany had taken a secondary priority, and another evidently more important story was now holding precedent. Ryan noticed at once that the news anchors were failing to conceal anxiety behind their practiced on-camera guises. A flashing headline said the United States government was officially advising the country to be on guard. Ryan stared at the television as he stood alongside the few workers and patrons of the café. The broadcast suddenly cut to the president himself, standing behind a podium in the White House press room.

If the reporter's had looked worrisome, the President of the United States looked outright sick with angst.

"My fellow Americans. I will first affirm that the recent security advisory is not, I will repeat, is *not* a cause for panic or evacuation of any specific locality. Instead, the Department for Homeland Security and myself have collaborated, and decided to come forward with this advisory merely as a precautionary measure. Our decision to take this action was done only with the intention of having our national infrastructures prepared should a disturbance on American soil occur. At this time I cannot state what the cause for our concern is, but I assure you it will be made clear to the public the moment we have been given clarity on the situation. I do not want this message to be perceived as cause for alarm. Schools and public offices will remain open. Public transportation and airports will remain in service. I have issued assurances to my advisors that the honor and courage of our people will hold them grounded against fear or social unrest. To our citizens, I advise you to stay calm and vigilant. To our police, fire, and emergency responders, I advise you to be ready. You will be updated the moment we believe the cause for this threat to be pacified. God bless America."

An ominous quiet filled the lobby, where nearly everyone had seen the president's face above the blinking word *live* and stopped what they were doing to listen.

"What the hell?" a man on a couch beside Ryan murmured to no one in particular. Nervous talk broke out among the café workers and patrons. What should they do? Should they leave the city? Were they *safe*? Ryan stared at the television silently. It did not feel right. Terrible possibilities began to play in his mind. Unlikely possibilities. He quickly shook his head and forced out his irrational fears. Surely a terrorist had gone missing or a threat had been made. Still, he did not like it, and assorted worst-case scenarios filled his imagination.

He thought of Kristen, upstairs by herself.

The reporters were beginning to speculate upon a connection between the Albany plane crash and the president's announcement as Ryan reluctantly turned away and began to trudge back up to the convention. He was halfway up the main stairs when he heard a cry from the lobby. Turning, he saw people pushing against each other to get in front of the television, several of the women with hands raised over their mouths in horror. Ryan stared at their frightened faces, uncertain what could possibly have captivated them so completely. Slowly, nervously, he put one foot in front of the other and descended back down the wide stairs.

Ryan froze in place when he saw the television.

The words flashing on the screen could not be possible. An icy dread filled his being.

BREAKING NEWS: CHICAGO UNDER ATTACK

Above the blinking headline, a reporter was standing in the middle of a horrible scene. Men and women were running hysterically in every direction, and the scene was obscured by dust in the air. The camera was faltering, and moving about like a home video. Beneath the news reporter, the street shook as though an earthquake was ripping through the scene, indiscriminate roars and crashes nearly drowning out all other sound. The reporter was pressing one hand against her earpiece and with the other holding the microphone against her mouth, screaming into it as loudly as she could, though her voice could barely be heard.

"Chicago is under attack! The entire downtown area has turned into some sort of . . . of *warzone!*" the reporter screamed, the microphone pushed against her lips. She was stumbling, and the camera could barely stay on her. "We have *no* idea what is attacking the city, but it feels like . . . like . . . bombs are going off in the buildings! We don't"— a terrible booming sound overwhelmed her voice. Whatever it was caused her to crash against a local news van as she screamed— "WAR."

"What is happening?" Ryan asked with an unusually hollow and croaky voice.

A man in a polo shook his head slowly, his face turning pale. "The . . . the buildings are collapsing?" the man said, more as a question than a statement.

Ryan said nothing; he wanted to swallow heavily but his mouth and throat were dry. He took a step closer to the large television and squinted at the frantic broadcast. The shattering carnage on the screen was like nothing he had ever witnessed. He began to breath heavily, uncertain of how to act. Hundreds of thousands—maybe even millions—of people were being killed. Placing a clammy palm against his forehead, he had to steady himself as he embraced the terror.

"It doesn't seem like missiles," the man in the polo said.

"No," Ryan muttered, his eyes unblinking and the color leaving his own face. "They don't know?" Ryan repeated and stepped directly in front of the television, intensely scanning the chaotic camerawork of the Chicago streets. A number of people loudly objected from behind him, but Ryan was too distracted to hear.

The atrium of the broad skyscraper behind the shouting news reporter suddenly exploded outward, instantly engulfing her and the cameraman in a grayish cloud of debris and mangled steel. CNN's broadcast went ominously blank, before cutting back to the studio. The two newscasters behind the desk each seemed momentarily unable to speak despite the teleprompter. They simply stared at the camera at a loss for words.

Ryan felt nausea rise in his own stomach.

"I—we . . . remain uncertain what is happening in Chicago," one of the newscasters stammered in a detached tone. "We received some . . . startling . . . footage from a freelance cameraman in Chicago. What it depicts . . . what it depicts speaks for itself. We have no explanation . . . as to what it is. I must warn you, what you are about to see is very alarming."

The broadcast cut to an entirely normal-looking Chicago on an ordinary-looking drizzly day. The digital time signature on the recording evinced that the video had been taken just minutes ago. A video camera was recording the narrow vista between two rows of gigantic skyscrapers drenched with whipping rain. Two men were discussing the best angle for their shot, their voices rising over gusts of wind.

"Jake, we need to get across the street. In this diffuse lighting, we should focus on the closest buildings. The far ones aren't going to be clear anyway 'cause of the fog."

"But what about if we took the shot from that build—" the other man stopped and hissed, "What the *hell* is that?"

There was a fumbling noise, and the camera jerked to the side. It came to rest overlooking several skyscrapers across the street. Above and between the dark forms of the buildings, a stormy cloud cover loomed.

"What in holy hell?" the first man exclaimed.

There was an odd dark spot in the sky just over the spire of one of the skyscrapers. The camera focus shifted, going from blurry and rushing past clear to blurry again. It then readjusted slowly, and with it so too did the dark object over the building. Against the silhouette of murky clouds, an unmistakable man was floating in the sky.

Ryan's hands began to tremble uncontrollably.

The man, the freakishly huge man, hovering high in the storm turned in the air and darted through the sky, piercing straight into the side of one of the skyscrapers. A moment passed, then the skyscraper let out a great shiver, the roof collapsed inward, and the whole building fell out of the camera's shot.

The several people watching the broadcast around Ryan gasped, unable to understand.

Ryan blinked at the image several times, his whole body beginning to shake uncontrollably. "Oh no. Oh no," he muttered as he placed his trembling fingers against his brow. "Oh no."

Stumbling to the side, Ryan crashed onto a suede chair, his legs barely able to keep him upright. "Not here. Oh, please not here. Don't do this to me."

The man in the polo and one of the café workers stared at him, puzzled by his reaction. He looked up the stairway to the doors of the Lutvak ballroom, to where Kristen was. How could he leave her in this place? Beautiful, radiant Kristen left to fend for herself against the horrors of his past. He could not bear to think of it. She could not meet the truths he knew. The thought of it made him want to die with pain. On the television, another skyscraper crumbled to ruin. As it fell, he made up his mind at once. Ryan knew he would never forgive himself for abandoning her.

"How did they find us?" Ryan murmured. He thought of his father. He thought of his teacher. They were the only two who knew about this place. "How did they possibly find us?"

One of the baristas looked taken aback. "What on earth do you mean?"

"Get out of the city!" Ryan suddenly yelled as loudly as he could. "Get out, all of you. Don't think—just run! Tell the people in the convention to get out! They're going to kill everyone."

Ryan sprinted out of the Marriot Marquis and crashed out onto the street. People were everywhere, going about business as usual. Ryan turned again and again on the sidewalk, looking up to the skyscrapers, utterly unsure how to act. His stomach lurched, the familiarity of the city he loved and the people he knew churning up piping emotion.

Around him the news of downtown Chicago's destruction was visibly spreading through the crowds of Times Square like an outbreak of plague. He darted his attention around the congested intersections with growing panic. Here and there people were beginning to shout into cell phones. New York City was on a countdown to bedlam. The image of a giant man crashing into the Chicago skyscraper was seared into his mind as it undoubtedly was in everyone's, though he alone knew the depths of the malice. Ryan turned in agony, his breath unsteady as he paced back and forth on the sidewalk. He looked upward, but saw only brilliant blue. The afternoon weather was a stark contrast to the grimness of Chicago. There were no dark forms above the buildings.

Ryan took off in a dead sprint up Seventh Avenue. He ran straight out into the street, tearing through the lanes of beeping traffic. His eyes were locked skyward as he raced up the avenue. Just as he ran past the biggest digital billboard screen of Times Square, he watched it transition from a bright red Coca Cola can pouring into an ice-filled glass to the gloomy Chicago news broadcast.

Evacuate. The historic and unparalleled martial order would be issued to New York within minutes, he was sure of it. With it would come an anarchy unrivaled in history. Ryan weaved between honking taxis and shouting drivers, his gaze locked skyward as he sprinted toward his dorm, toward his locked trunk. In his peripheral vision, a number people were running toward the nearest subway stations. Others were hurrying along the adjacent streets, perhaps toward the eastside bridges leading off Manhattan. The sound of beeping cars grew louder—in some way more frenzied—as radio stations were no doubt beginning to issue Emergency Alert System messages. The growing panic surrounding the people he had come to love was as palpable as the onset of a biblical storm.

If this day was to be their day of reckoning, of apocalypse, then it would also be the day the human race would embrace him in all of his immeasurable power. Deep down he had been waiting for this moment his entire life, and he was ready to meet his destiny and repay it for the things he had seen.

With an iron determination, he cast aside his masquerade and exploded from the sidewalk of Seventh Avenue.

CHAPTER TWENTY-FIVE

Vengelis

"Stay away from me," Madison said as she painfully inched and crawled away from Vengelis on scraped elbows.

Shattered glass from the nearby pizza shop's front window was scattered around her on the sidewalk, and in the middle of the intersection the ruins of the eighteen-wheeler smoldered and smoked. Vengelis regarded her pitiable retreat with a look of silent disapproval, as if her display of pain was shameful and inappropriate.

"You made a promise. Let's get moving," Vengelis said without a trace of warmth.

Madison seemed not to hear him. She pulled a thin glass shard out of her thumb and placed her hands on her forehead. Blinking dizzily, she tried to piece together what had just transpired. Vengelis's eyes widened with disbelief as he saw tiny shards of glass had hewn narrow cuts on her palms, and her elbows were bleeding where they had grazed the cement of the sidewalk. He was taken aback at how delicate she was; the human form was impossibly fragile. How could they even survive in vessels so frail and anemic?

People collected cautiously around the wreckage, and lines of beeping traffic began to spread up and down the avenue. It looked as though the destroyed semi had driven full force into the side of a mountain. The rear of the truck's mass had accordioned on top of itself from the frontal impact. It had been loaded with wooden pylons of soda, and hundreds of cans sputtered and rolled across the street in a growing puddle of fizzing drinks.

"W-what are you?" Madison said.

Vengelis took a step closer and held out his hand to help her up, changing his expression from a look of disdain to a mask of neutrality. On some level he recognized that he had just shattered everything she knew to be real. Surely some of his race's strongest had similar reactions when they first witnessed the shock and awe of the Felix.

"I am a Primus," he said simply. "Now get up."

"I . . . don't . . . understand." Madison looked back and forth from the fizzling wreckage to Vengelis.

He continued to hold his hand out to her. "I wouldn't expect you to understand. But now you are breaking your promises. Get up."

"P-please, leave me alone." Madison winced from a pain in her hip as tried to rise from the sidewalk, and fell back into the shattered glass.

"You *asked* me to stop that truck. I'm sorry you underestimated my capabilities, but a deal is a deal, and now you need to help me."

"Help you? Help you? How could you need my help?"

"You will lead me the Marriott Marquis, right now. It was the second part of our agreement. Stand up."

"Are you going to kill me?" Madison asked with growing sobriety.

Vengelis kneeled down to her, and she recoiled nervously away from him. He smiled sympathetically at her reaction. "Right now, at this very moment, you are the safest a human has ever been. Now come. Get up."

Madison looked up at his outstretched hand. People around them cowered back, all of them too alarmed to speak to the familiar and yet terrifying man before them. Sirens screamed from close by, and an ambulance appeared through the parting traffic at the other end of the intersection. Two paramedics in blue uniforms hopped out of the doors and gaped at the extraordinary accident.

"Come on," Vengelis said. "Authorities are on their way and I don't want things to escalate here. That display was not . . . subtle."

Madison looked up at him, her mouth frozen in an expression of turmoil. Then she suddenly snapped her mouth shut and her eyes came into focus as if she was awaking from a daydream; she took a deep breath, and reached up to take his hand. Vengelis lifted her into a standing position as if she were a child that weighed nothing at all.

Madison stared at him with trepidation. Her hair was awry, her arms were dotted with scrapes, and her white pants were marked from the ground. "Do you promise you won't hurt me?"

"As long as you do as I say, I promise no harm will come to you. That is, assuming you hold true to your promise. Now, where is the Marriott Marquis?"

Madison looked up and down the avenue with feeble rotations of her head. Her face was as gray as the sidewalk, and she was clearly still in shock. Her hands shook as she brushed herself off with clumsy motions. "It's . . . it's that way. Midtown." Madison pointed down the avenue toward the tallest buildings many blocks to the south.

"Come on, then," he said.

"No." Madison flinched as she leaned tenderly on her left leg. "No way. Just leave me alone . . . please. I don't want anything to do with this, or you."

A police cruiser barreled into the intersection followed by a monstrous fire truck, both with lights flashing and sirens blasting. The crowd of onlookers grew with each passing second as people exited the surrounding buildings to get a glimpse of the grisly spectacle.

"I can't ensure your safety if you aren't with me. If you want to guarantee your well-being, you will come along with me. Otherwise, you will be another face in this crowd to me and my men."

Madison shifted woozily. Vengelis thought she might pass out, but she did not. He turned aside and peered over the heads of the crowd in the direction she had pointed, thinking he could lift off the sidewalk and fly in that direction. But there were countless buildings, and he did not know which one was the Marriott Marquis. It would be too much of a risk not to bring a local to show him the way and help him through any exigencies that might arise.

"What are you?" Madison turned back breathlessly to the smoking wreckage as they walked. "What . . . the hell. . . are you? That isn't possible, that isn't re-motely possible."

"*That* was nothing." Vengelis shook his head with a note of contempt. "A small glimpse at most."

As they hurried down the busy sidewalk, he noticed Madison's strength and cognition began to return. Soon she was walking normally. After a few blocks, she abruptly pulled away from his grasp and stood her ground. "I need some answers. Right now."

Below his calm face, a fiery anger was rising. "What do you want to know?"

She looked at him with a dubious and scared expression. "Um, how about *everything*? What the hell is going on?"

"I told you, I'm on an errand." He grabbed her and continued forward. Walking in the other direction, an unkempt teenager wearing headphones and reading something on his phone brushed shoulders with Vengelis and bounced backward, falling to the ground heavily. As Vengelis stepped over him, the kid held up his broken headphones and shouted something with a spit-filled fury, but neither Vengelis nor Madison acknowledged him.

"Why are you here? Is the errand to like, I don't know . . . kill everyone?"

Vengelis said nothing; he looked down the long avenue at the tall glass buildings on either side. He cringed at the thought of what Hoff and Darien must be doing to the similarly flimsy buildings in the other city, each of them following his command.

"*Well?* I think that's a perfectly reasonable question," Madison said.

"No," Vengelis muttered with little interest. "I'm not here to kill everyone. I couldn't care less about you people."

"Then why are you here?"

Vengelis drove his hand into his armor and pulled out the *Harbinger I* remote to see if Hoff had tried to make contact with him, but the Lord General had not. Vengelis opened Pral Nerol's Felix report and held the screen out to Madison. It was a labeled diagram of a Felix cell. Madison's eyes narrowed and she slowed her step to look at the image.

"What is that?" she asked.

"That, more or less, is my question as well. There's a convention of your scientists at the Marriott Marquis. I will put that question before the smartest of your race."

"I don't understand . . . what is that thing?"

"Enough!" Vengelis waved a hand. "Take me to the Marriott Marquis."

Madison was about to press the issue when the avenue transitioned into Times Square. Vengelis noticed that what she saw took her aback. Sprawling several blocks before him, a multitude of people was frozen in place on the sidewalks, their faces upturned to the giant screens and live-action billboards that hung among the tall buildings. Lines of cars and taxis were parked in the middle of the street, the drivers and passengers leaning out their windows and staring agape at the huge screens. As Vengelis and Madison approached the subdued crowds, the billboards were still out of sight; they could not yet see what had so completely captured seemingly the entire city's attention.

"What the hell is going on?" she murmured, looking out across the countless frightened faces in dismay. Knowing exactly what was going on, Vengelis suddenly reached down and took Madison by the arm and quickened his pace, knocking people out of the way before him.

"They must have begun," he said.

"What? Begun what?" Madison was forced to break into a jog in order to keep up with him.

"Which building is it?" Vengelis demanded, his tone harsh.

As they pushed through the transfixed pedestrians, Madison turned her head and strained to look up at the giant screens. Vengelis noticed her trip, nearly falling, as she saw what was being depicted on the billboard screens. Each one was flipping from colorful products and celebrities to a single unified news broadcast. Within moments, all of the billboard-sized screens were flashing the same breaking headline:

CHICAGO UNDER ATTACK. HUNDREDS OF THOUSANDS FEARED DEAD.

It was a live video feed from a helicopter, and the camera moved wildly as it recorded a broad landscape shot. Underneath a harsh gunmetal sky, a city skyline was barely identifiable. Gray-brown dust formed a thick blanket over the area. Giant plumes of black ash and smoke rose into the low clouds.

"Oh no . . ." Madison said. She would have fallen to her knees if Vengelis had not yanked her upright.

"I don't have long!" Vengelis said. "Which building is the Marriott Marquis?"

"You . . . ordered?" she said through short breaths.

"Yes." Vengelis glanced up at the screens. The destruction was having the exact effect he had hoped for, but time was no longer on his side. The convention would be cancelled any second, and a citywide evacuation would begin within minutes. People would begin migrating out of every major city—that is, if they had any sense whatsoever.

"But," Madison gasped.

"Which building is the Marriott Marquis?" Vengelis suddenly screamed at her and throttled her body.

Madison's head hung droopily by her shoulder, her eyes still trained with dread on the screens. The broadcast was now zooming in on random spots in the dust-filled massacre. It was unmistakable; the buildings in the heart of Chicago were being utterly destroyed. Gasps and terrible cries broke out from the crowds watching the feed alongside them. Hands reached up and covered gaping mouths and eyes unwillingly watched with sick disbelief. A number of panicked voices began to break the anxious silence around them. People started aggressively pushing bystanders aside as they made for the subway. Vengelis watched the escalating panic with no pleasure, only a hope that the scientists would be encouraged by the dread he was now witnessing. He heard a man alongside them mutter that it could not be terrorists, and a young girl holding her father's hand ask him if they were safe in New York.

All at once, as though practiced in a chorus, the screams rose. Like the crescendo in a brutal symphony, Times Square began to surge and thrash, the very cement beneath their feet shaking from the unified wail of fear. Madison's face went pale, but she held her ground against Vengelis.

"You ordered that attack!" she screamed over the crowd.

"Yes, I did. Where is the Marriott Marquis?"

"How *could* you?"

Vengelis pulled her close to him, inadvertently lifting her clean off the ground. His face was mere inches from hers. "WHERE IS THE MARRIOT MARQUIS?" he shouted in her face. "If you do not tell me right now, I'm going to leave you here to die with the rest of these people! You can be another name-less face in this hysteria. And believe me, if I don't get what I want, this city will get it just as hard as the one you are witnessing now. I have to get to the con-vention *right* now or all of this will have been for nothing!"

Madison's face twisted with conflict. She breathed heavily and looked from the images of the carnage in Chicago to Vengelis's enraged gaze. A man in a flannel shirt pushed into Madison's back as he sprinted toward the subway. She fell forward, narrowly missing another man who was shoving through the crowd with his messenger bag swinging wildly at his side. A stampede had be-gun.

Vengelis had succeeded with the first part of his plan. He had successfully lit the spark of pandemonium, and soon the entire world would be crackling and roaring with it. By sundown of that day no one would be safe—from either Vengelis or the ubiquitous mobs of terrified people.

Submission was already his.

"The Marriott Marquis is right there at the corner of the block," Madison said, at last, opting for survival and pointing a finger to the tall glass hotel. "You're a monster," she added.

"That is a matter of perspective," Vengelis said. He broke into a run toward the entrance to the Marriott Marquis, Madison sprinting along beside him on her own volition. They pushed through the front doors into a lushly carpeted lobby. Vengelis looked around with a panicked confusion. A few dozen people huddled around a television mounted in the lobby coffee shop. It was showing the same broadcast as the giant screens of the street.

"What is this?" Vengelis asked as he looked up into the countless floors. He hadn't been anticipating further complications. "Where are the scientists?"

"This is the lobby." Madison said distractedly, approaching the vacant conci-erge desk. "There!"

A computer screen had the day's event schedule displayed. Among others was written: *ICST Science Convention: Lutvak Ballroom, 2nd floor.* At once Vengelis was off, moving fast. Madison had to race to keep up with him, breathing heavy as she trod the rich carpet. He tore up the stairway and fol-lowed an arrow to the ballrooms. The white double doors of the Lutvak ball-room were closed, and he let out a long uneasy exhale as he approached them.

Vengelis pushed the heavy doors open and stepped in.

A presentation was underway. There was a pretty young woman on the stage talking to a crowd of a few hundred people sitting quietly in rows of chairs. A projection screen hung behind her above the center of the stage. At the top of the screen was the title: *Columbia Vatruvian Technologies Research*. Vengelis fell back in horrified disbelief as he turned his attention to the screen. He saw something there that resided in his nightmares. With numb hands he pulled out the *Harbinger I* remote and connected with Hoff.

"Yes, my lord?" Lord General Hoff's voice shouted faintly over crashing on the other end.

"Drop what you are doing and get to New York immediately." Vengelis looked down at his remote and turned his gaze from Pral Nerol's report to the projection screen overhead. On the stage in the front of the ballroom, rotating in three-dimensional perspective, was an unmistakable Felix cell.

CHAPTER TWENTY-SIX

Kristen

Kristen stood behind the podium preparing for her lecture, her fear of public speaking vastly outweighed any dread she felt toward her precarious location in Times Square during a heightened national security alert. She stared out at the few hundred people in attendance as prickly nerves tumbled through her body and left her feeling empty and exposed.

Kristen turned to Professor Vatruvia, who was sitting beside the podium in all of his glory, waving to people he recognized in the crowd. She resented his polished *60 Minutes* guise; it concealed the deep reserve of reckless ambition he had just below the surface.

A convention worker signaled for Kristen to begin, and she anxiously moved the cursor of the laptop and clicked the play button on the slideshow she had prepared with the additional slide on the Vatruvian mice. That one slide would bring their research crashing down. How would Professor Vatruvia's self-satisfied expression transform when he saw the slide? An enormous high-definition image of a Vatruvian cell came to colorful life on the projector screen behind her, and the ballroom filled with inspired applause. A few piercing whistles sounded from the ocean of eager faces. She often forgot the degree to which the Vatruvian cell was the coveted vanguard of the scientific world. Kristen nodded in acknowledgement of the applause and felt color rise in her cheeks. The numb sensation traveling through her body reminded her of how she felt before the curtains were drawn back in her third-grade class play. She had been Martha Washington. Standing paralyzed behind the podium, Kristen felt as though she was still a terrified eight-year-old wearing a white bonnet. All of her degrees and accomplishments did nothing to overcome the sudden deluge of self-doubt. She took a deep breath, her pulse nearly choking her vocal chords.

"Thank you. Thank you very much," Kristen spoke into the microphone and listened to her own magnified voice carry easily across the ballroom. She thought it sounded nasally. The first words were always the hardest. "I would first like the thank the ICST organization for allowing our research team the privilege of presenting our work here at the convention. It is a great honor to be among so many prominent researchers." She took a deep steadying breath, and the room fell so silent she could hear the whir of the laptop in front of her. "I am Kristen Jordan, and I work with the genetics of the Vatruvian cell. I've been a part of the Vatruvian cell research efforts alongside Professor Vatruvia since the project's very beginning. My primary area of study has been specific to the deconstructing of biological cells' genetic structure and the reconstructing of viable synthetic variations."

Kristen kept her eyes locked on the rear wall of the ballroom, avoiding eye contact from the politely nodding heads and prying eyes of the front rows. Ryan was out there somewhere, and though she could not hope to find him among all the faces looking at her, that knowledge gave her reassurance. At least one person in the audience would have her back when she told them of the mice. She realized, thinking of Ryan and only Ryan despite the crowd, that she was falling in love with him.

"Though we have made tremendous progress recently in our research, I will start by first providing a basic overview of the Vatruvian cell since its earliest developmental stages over a year ago." Kristen's breathing was becoming less constricted, her words less labored and her voice beginning to feel like her own again. "When Professor Vatruvia first contacted me with a proposal for a cutting-edge research endeavor, we spoke of discovering a means to create a truly synthetic cell. Well, from there on . . . the sky has been the limit."

The irksome ringtone of a cell phone sounded from the audience, but Kristen ignored it. "As I'm sure you all know, what we ended up with was something slightly more complex and elegant than even we could have expected."

Two more cell phones rang, and then a third. Their owners fumbled to silence them as their inane jingles played for the ballroom to hear. But there was something far stranger than the few chirpy ringtones breaking the polite silence of the crowd. The very ballroom itself seemed to be faintly pulsating with vibrating plastic. Countless cell phones that had been appropriately set to silent were vibrating in pockets and handbags. The abrupt surge of telecommunications was inexplicable, and in a way unsettling. Why were so many people being reached all at once? Kristen only hesitated for a moment before clearing her throat. She was about to continue when she noticed the double doors in the back of the room burst open. Her eyes lingered on the doors as a bizarrely out of place young man and woman walked into the ballroom. Not wanting to get distracted, Kristen quickly averted her gaze.

"What we were able to do in the earliest stages was—to put it simply—create never before seen proteins that. . . ."

Kristen's attention was magnetically pulled back to the young man and woman as the room continued to buzz with cell phones. For a moment she thought the strange young man was Ryan, but she quickly thought the better of it. He was strikingly good-looking, even from across the ballroom, though he was dressed in a peculiar outfit. From her distance, Kristen thought it might be a costume. He was staring at the image of the Vatruvian cell on the projection screen behind her in what appeared to be a mingling of amazement and dismay. Kristen forcefully moved her attention away from the young man and cleared her throat once more.

"What resulted was a functional cell that operated similarly to a biological cell, but was comprised of an entirely fabricated genetic code that included our own alterations. From there—"

Kristen at last stopped altogether and threw her hands up in irritated exasperation. A number of things were happening. The room was now echoing with a throng of cell phone rings so consistently that she could barely think. The young man in the bizarre attire had moved to one of the side emergency exits and seemed to be barring the door shut behind the backs of the seated audience. The doorframe was making strident creaking sounds, and some heads turned in the back row to see what he was doing, but the cell phones distracted most of the audience's attention. At the same moment a hotel manager was waving an arm to Kristen as he hastily approached the stage and jogged down the center aisle.

Kristen looked from the manager back to the mysterious young man in the back, who was now moving to another emergency exit on the other end of the room, and seemed to be barring that door, too. The woman he was with had sunken into an empty chair in the rear row and buried her face in her hands, appearing to be distraught over something.

"Excuse me, miss," the hotel manager called out to Kristen.

Every face in the ballroom turned to him in surprise. He came onto the stage and motioned for Kristen to step aside. As she did so, she saw the strange young man now closing the main double doors to the ballroom, and barring them last. Kristen glared at him uncertainly and raised a finger to point at him, but all eyes were on the hotel manager.

"If I can please have everyone's undivided attention." The manager took the microphone as Kristen stepped out of the way. "We have been informed that the city of Chicago is under some sort of attack. The federal government has issued a national state of emergency, and has advised the evacuation of every major city. Our concierge staff will remain downstairs to direct people to the proper evacuation routes should they require any assistance." His words had an immediate effect on the audience, which erupted into an appalled uproar. The manager raised his voice over the upheaval and yelled into the microphone. "We are postponing the convention, and closing the hotel until further notice. If you have belongings in one of our rooms, we assure you the room will remain locked, and your valuables safe, until the hotel reopens. We are advising all of our guests and employees to calmly and orderly exit the hotel and make your way out of the city."

Kristen watched as the bizarre young man stepped away from the main double doors and began to walk down the center aisle with an explicit manner of command. There was something extraordinary about him, and as the hotel manager made his announcement, Kristen's gaze fixated on this stranger; he looked out of place, incongruous with the ballroom and the situation. The moment the hotel manager finished his announcement the mysterious young man abruptly raised his arms into the air.

"Everyone get back to your seats!" the young man called out, but no one seemed to hear him aside from Kristen. He brought his attention to the stage and stared directly at her. Not knowing what to think, Kristen held his gaze as he approached the stage. The audience around him was frenzied, taking no heed of his demand. People were moving to the exits only to find them barred shut. Shoulders clogged at each set of doors, and people began to shout across the ballroom to each other as they realized they had been locked in. Kristen heard indiscriminate shouts about bent steel door handles and frames that would not budge.

Someone was shouting, "Trapped."

The young man stepped onto the stage, his eyes steadfast on Kristen. His glare roused fear in her. The young man seemed immune to the rise of panic that had now taken hold of the audience and her. Where everyone else was beginning to run and shout, he was silent and methodical in his approach toward her. Kristen raised a hand and pointed at him, as if somehow to draw the attention of security. He did not fit in. She felt that the hysteria beginning to claim the confined Lutvak ballroom was provoked by this stranger; he seemed the deceptively composed eye of a storm they did not quite understand. The young man walked straight to the podium and came to a stop just before her, regarding her curiously.

Kristen looked the strange man up and down in unreserved bewilderment. Her first thought was that he was impossibly handsome, and after a moment she decided *impossibly* was precisely the right word. There was something inherently off with his appearance. The young man should have looked absurd, and yet there was something jarringly authentic about him. He was wearing ornate and seemingly ancient raiment that evoked images of Julius Caesar and Alexander the Great. Although his attire looked eccentric and outlandish, it also looked very genuine: elaborate materials of obvious craftsmanship that were certainly not sold at a Halloween gag store. Though to what possible purpose or meaning his garb and severe expression represented, Kristen could not guess.

"Hello," he said to Kristen, his voice barely audible over the now shouting audience.

Kristen took a slow cautious step away from him. There was haughtiness to his tone she found unsettling in contrast to the rest of the room's fright. The young man placed a hand adorned with an enormous crimson ring on his hip. Kristen noticed his arms were sinewy and muscular, as though the lean muscles and tendons in his forearm had to struggle for room underneath his skin.

He motioned to Kristen. "Tell these people that if they do not shut up, I will turn this room into a slaughterhouse."

Kristen swallowed, unable to form a response. She did not understand.

The disparity between his stately appearance and the savageness of his words was disquieting. Kristen's cheeks turned beet red and she took another step away from him, nearly falling into Professor Vatruvia, who was still sitting in a folding chair beside the podium.

"Sir, this behavior is highly inappropriate, especially at a time such as this." The hotel manager shook his head with disapproval at the peculiar young man. He leaned into the microphone. "Security can you please come up front here and escort this man out of the hotel."

The armored stranger's gaze had not lifted from Kristen for a moment. Behind the young man's back, a group of security personnel stopped trying to wedge open the barred doors and hurried to the stage. Kristen was thankful to see them coming. Her fear under his watch was inexplicable. She should have been laughing at this foolishly dressed stranger, yet something she could not be certain of was holding her back.

"Who are you?" the man demanded, oblivious to the rest of the ballroom.

"Who are *you?*" Kristen shot back.

He stared at her expressionlessly. "I am Emperor Vengelis Epsilon."

His statement was met with a moment of stifling silence.

"This isn't the time or the place for some immature prank." Professor Vatruvia stood from his chair and glared at the newcomer, Vengelis Epsilon. "Very poor form, young man. Not the time or the place."

The man calling himself Vengelis ignored him. "I need to speak with you. Now." He was still looking only at Kristen.

"Please do as he says! Do *whatever* he says!" the woman Kristen had seen enter the ballroom alongside the handsome psychopath was now hurrying down the aisle. Everyone in the audience had by now risen from their seats. But with nowhere to exit, all eyes were beginning to watch the peculiar drama unfold up by the podium.

As the beautiful young woman ascended the steps to the stage, she called out directly to Kristen. "Give him whatever he wants!"

"I need you to tell me everything you know about the technology you were just discussing," Vengelis said. The coolness of his features flickered with a wild anticipation as his gaze bore into Kristen.

"Now wait one minute!" Professor Vatruvia said. He stepped between Vengelis and Kristen, placing a firm hand on Vengelis's shoulder. Vengelis slowly and reluctantly drew his gaze away from Kristen and looked at Professor Vatruvia. They were about the same height, but the stark contrast between their appearances was staggering: the arresting splendor of this Vengelis Epsilon next to Professor Vatruvia's corduroys and beige sport coat.

"Don't, Vengelis." the beautiful young woman said.

Vengelis knocked away Professor Vatruvia's arm and grabbed him by the throat. Professor Vatruvia's neck and cheeks turned a dark shade of purple crimson and he choked and flailed in agony.

"What the hell are you *doing*?" Kristen demanded with incomprehension, at last finding her voice.

The security men shouted and hustled to the stage. Kristen watched in shock as the young man lifted Professor Vatruvia into the air by his neck. Her mentor gurgled and desperately pointed his feet to find footing, but the toes of his loafers only groped at the wood. Vengelis stared at him emotionlessly for a moment before turning and hurling him into the rear wall of the stage. Professor Vatruvia's body was thrown backward, and his shoulder blades hit the hard wall with an awful smack; the exposed supports behind the drywall splintered loudly from the impact.

Kristen immediately recognized the peculiar young man's strength as unnatural and recoiled in panic and disgust, holding her arms out and aligning the podium between her and the strange man. The hotel manager stood and gawked, a dark stain running down the front of his trousers.

Vengelis turned to the impending security guards, and Kristen dashed over to Professor Vatruvia's side, kneeling down to him in repulsed disbelief. He was unconscious, his head limp in her hands and his eyes dilating blankly at the ceiling. Kristen wheezed with fear as she looked away from his face and turned to the confrontation between the mysterious man and the security guards. There was a hardened NYPD officer leading the group of three Marriott Marquis security personnel. The cop must have been in the room before the doors were barred, and the hotel security guards followed uneasily in his wake as he approached the stage. There was a no-nonsense look about the officer, and Kristen could not have envisioned a more fitting person to intercede this Vengelis figure.

"Get on the ground now!" the heavyset cop bellowed, reaching a thick-knuckled hand down and unclasping the holster to his gun.

Kristen watched in disbelief as Vengelis gave the cop a scornful smirk and made no attempt to hit the ground. The cop pulled out his handgun and pointed it straight at Vengelis's chest.

"*Stop*! Oh god! Don't fight him!" the beautiful young woman pleaded. "He's with the people who are attacking Chicago! He'll kill you all!"

"I don't know about all of you, but certainly you," Vengelis said, staring down the barrel of the pistol and speaking only to the cop.

The cop shifted his stance uncertainly, his shoulders squared with the gun. He had surely never witnessed someone elicit such staggering confidence while being held at gunpoint. Kristen found herself unable to speak as she kneeled by Professor Vatruvia and watched the stand off. Dark blood was beginning to soak through Professor Vatruvia's blazer. Kristen moaned and pressed her index finger all over his neck to find a pulse, but could not find one. Her fingers were numb, her surroundings fast becoming overwhelming.

"I suppose I have to make an example of someone. It might as well be you," Vengelis said to the police officer.

The cop pushed his gun toward Vengelis threateningly. "The nation's on high alert, kid. I won't hesitate to shoot your ass if I have to. Get on the goddamn floor and put your hands behind your head before I blow you away."

Vengelis inclined his head with a sarcastic expression and took one step forward. The cop fired a round straight into his chest. The room grew dead silent as the tinny burst of the gunshot echoed across the walls and vaulted ceiling. Kristen waited for this bizarre Vengelis to stumble and collapse but instead he shrugged and shook his head, entirely unharmed. The cop hesitated for a moment, and then unloaded four more rounds straight into his midsection. Vengelis stood entirely unfazed as the stage filled with a sharp sulfur smell from the gunshots. Five mangled bullets fell smoking to the stage at Vengelis's feet.

As though the very gravity had shifted in the Lutvak ballroom, the hundreds of attendees in the audience all flowed and pushed against the far wall, pressing and heaving at the blocked double doors in an attempt to get away from the demon on the stage, yet the firmly secured doors held strong against their efforts.

"No!" the beautiful woman called.

Vengelis took another step forward, and the cop fired another round, this time straight into his face. Another bullet hit the stage floor as Vengelis ripped the handgun out of the cop's hand. The man tilted his head and stared at the empty bullet shells at his feet in astonishment. "W-what are—" the cop said.

Vengelis grabbed the officer by his belt and the scruff of his neck and spun, heaving the man across the entire ballroom. The cop's body soared flailing above the display tables and connected high on the opposite wall, falling limply onto the very shoulders of the pushing and recoiling audience. An unspeakable splatter of gore was left high above the crowd, where the body had bounced against the crown molding.

The room instantaneously filled with heated screaming and bawling terror. The sound of the tumult was horrible as Kristen hopelessly and frantically gave Professor Vatruvia something that resembled CPR, though she had no idea what she was doing. She saw Vengelis glance back to check on her location before turning to the guards that had been standing behind the cop. Kristen looked up at his back with a perplexed expression. Why was he so interested in her?

"Are you satisfied yet?" Vengelis said to the trembling security guards, none of them even armed with guns. "Or do I need to kill more of you to prove that I am God?"

Kristen felt nausea rise. She thought of only one thing, escape. While Vengelis was turned to the security guards, she rose and dashed off the stage, sprinted past rows of abandoned chairs, and dived headfirst into the standing audience. She hastily slithered and squeezed her way past a number of tall men and tried to blend in with the mass. The shoulders surrounding her were a comfort, now she was one face in a crowd. She lurched and swayed, nearly being taken off her feet as the crowding audience pressed and shoved around her.

"SIIILLLLEEEENCCCEEEE!" Vengelis Epsilon's voice tore over the ruckus of the room.

Miraculously, the room fell silent almost at once. Evidently the audience feared their supernatural guest more than they clung to hysteria. Kristen held her breath as her powerfully beating heart thumped again and again against her ribcage. She ducked to stay out of his sight, and even pressed the side of her face into the shoulder of a middle-aged woman's blue cardigan.

He had been shot six times and was not dead. A bullet had bounced off his face.

They could have been blanks. Kristen kept telling herself that. They *could* have been blanks. But there was no way she could logically explain how he had thrown a grown man across the ballroom. Kristen suddenly realized she was shivering from head to toe, her extremities growing cold.

"Come out," Vengelis's voice rang emotionlessly across the subdued ballroom. "Now."

Several hundred voices remained dead silent, and only the sound of pushing and shuffling feet rose from around her. She could hear the woman behind her and the man next to her breathing. They were as horrified as she was.

"Girl! I know you are still in here. Come out."

Kristen pressed her eyelids shut and trembled silently. She could actually see her heart beating like a sledgehammer through her shirt.

"I will ask you nicely only this last time, girl. Then I will kill a person in this room every *second* until you grow the courage to show yourself."

It was as though the voice of Lucifer himself was singling her out and beckoning her from the masses. Kristen became suddenly concerned that she might pass out. She felt dizzy and lightheaded with a sense of overwhelming dread and public humiliation. The terrible sounds of men and women whimpering in fear enveloped her from all sides. What the hell was going on? What could he possibly want with her? Kristen tried to anchor her mind with the things she knew; yet she knew nothing. The entire convention was trapped in the Lutvak ballroom with some sort of . . . Kristen could not seem to bring herself to guess what he could be. Where was Ryan? Was he with her somewhere here in the panic of the ballroom? Kristen prayed he would not try to protect her and get hurt.

"Not brave enough?" the voice of Vengelis called. "So be it."

"N-n-no! Please! Don't hurt me! N-no!" a man cried out from the stage. Kristen knew it to be the manager whom she had just been standing alongside. He began to beg and yelp, the otherwise silent and frightened ballroom echoing with the sounds of his frantic struggle. "Oh god, no, please not me!"

"I'm here!" Kristen heard her own voice suddenly shout, though it was barely recognizable to her. She blinked down at her sneakers in resignation.

The few people standing in front of her hastily moved out of the way. Kristen pushed past the shoulders of the audience and revealed herself.

CHAPTER TWENTY-SEVEN

Kristen

With wobbly steps, Kristen Jordan emerged out of the trembling crowd and stood to face Vengelis Epsilon. The scene in the room was dream-like despite her willful effort to focus on the things that were concrete. Help was coming. The entire nation was on alert, and it had something to do with this person calling for her. Help had to be on the way.

The baffling Vengelis was standing on the stage, holding the hotel manager in the air by the collar of his shirt. Vengelis's body was not even in a tensed position, and his arm held the husky man clean off the ground with seemingly no effort at all. Kristen could feel the fear coursing from the audience behind her. The beautiful young woman sat on the stairs leading to the stage with her hands wrapped round her knees. She was looking at Kristen emphatically, and Kristen saw she had scrapes on her arms and hands.

"There you are," the man calling himself Vengelis said. "Come here."

Kristen stood her ground and looked up at him carefully. He raised the hotel manager farther into the air. The poor man was being strangled by his own necktie, his face turning purple as his lips gasping for breath.

"What do you want?" Kristen called.

Vengelis turned to the young woman on the stairs.

"Madison. Explain if you will."

The beautiful woman's—Madison's—face flushed upon being addressed. Although her attractiveness matched that of Vengelis, Kristen could tell by her unconcealed fear that Madison was not with him. There was a traumatized and demoralized look to her that said more than her words possibly could. Despite her appearance, her voice was surprisingly steady. "He just wants our coopera-tion. If you do what he says, I don't think he's gonna hurt you."

"To that I will hold," Vengelis said. "Now come here. I want some clarifica-tion on both *you* and the presentation you were giving."

"Drop him first," Kristen called.

Vengelis gave her an oddly approving expression and released the manager at once, who collapsed with a clatter onto the stage and rolled into a fetal posi-tion. Kristen moved to the stairs and torpidly ascended the steps past Madison up to Vengelis. The manager violently hacked and wheezed from the stage floor. Terror was pumping through her, and she looked with disbelief at the body of Professor Vatruvia in the corner. She could feel hundreds of pitying eyes burning into her back as she crossed the stage, but no one from the audi-ence volunteered to speak up against the manifest nightmare standing by the podium.

"Well?" Kristen asked with a soft voice, now much closer to the mysterious man than she wanted to be.

"Who are you?" Vengelis's tone was peculiarly suspicious.

"Kristen Jordan."

Vengelis stared intently at her for a long moment. She watched his eyes move slowly from her jeans to her hair to her glasses. "Were you the one who came here on the *Traverser I*?"

His bizarre words passed over her head and into the open space of the ball-room.

"*What?*" Kristen said.

Vengelis looked suddenly dangerous as he took a step closer and lowered his voice to a whisper.

"Are you one of Pral Nerol's researchers pretending to be a human?"

"Please—"

"Tell me the truth or I'll kill you where you stand."

"Please." Kristen took a pace back. "I have absolutely no idea what you're talking about."

Vengelis reached out and grabbed her by the chin, squeezing her jaw be-tween his thumb and forefinger. "Then how do you know of Felix technology?"

Kristen's mind screamed in agony and humiliated indignation. The pain of his grip was beyond comprehension; it felt as though her jaw was about to crumple like a ground eggshell and tear away from her skull at the same mo-ment. She was in the clutches of a maniac.

"Wha'...is...'elix?" Kristen gasped, her eyes wide.

"You tell me!" Vengelis seethed. "It's the technology you were describing so enthusiastically as I entered. How did you find out about it?"

"I . . . *created* . . . it . . . wit' . . . him." Kristen darted a shaking finger to Professor Vatruvia's body.

Vengelis released his grip at once and Kristen fell against the podium heaving for breath and rubbing her chin forcefully. She glared up at Vengelis with a scathing hate that surprised even her. "You killed its creator. And it's called Vatruvian cell technology, not Felix. I'm just a goddamn assistant, you psychopath," Kristen panted, her eyes welling against her will from the enduring pain of his grip.

Vengelis considered her words for a long moment as he scrutinized her face for honesty. He raised his attention to the Vatruvian cell on the projector screen. His body language was perplexing, and his face looked as though he was in nearly as much confusion as Kristen—which was no easy feat.

"*Vatruvian* cell . . . ?" he muttered.

Kristen was at a loss for words. She felt separated from the rest of the ballroom, let alone her life five minutes previous. His hesitation concerned her, made him more dangerous and unpredictable. Perhaps she would be the next person thrown across the ballroom. For what felt like an eternity, Kristen stood perfectly still, afraid to even move and remind him of her presence. The three-dimensional Vatruvian cell rotated on the screen, silently captivating his total attention. The sight of it enraptured him, as though the image held dominion over his mind.

At last Kristen could take the silence no longer. "Who are you?"

"I already told you my name." His eyes did not lift from the projection screen. "What is that?"

"A Vatruvian cell. That one in particular is a bacterium. Well, it looks like a normal bacterium but it's really a—"

"Machine," Vengelis said.

Kristen paused in surprise. "A machine? I don't know if I would call it that, but it's a cell we constructed in a laboratory."

Vengelis slowly drew his attention away from the screen and turned to Kristen with an attentive expression. "You created this . . . this cell?"

"Among others, yes."

"How could you possibly be capable . . ." Vengelis murmured to himself, but quickly silenced his own tongue. "How? How did you create it?"

Kristen shrugged. "Lots of research. Genetic engineering and computer programs mostly."

"And you're familiar with its conception? You understand how it operates?"

"Certainly."

Vengelis pulled a strange contraption with a large screen out of his pocket and began to operate it in a manner not unlike a tablet or cell phone. For a fleeting panic-stricken moment Kristen thought it might be a bomb, but quickly realized it was not. After a few adjustments, he handed the device to Kristen.

"What is this?" Kristen asked, taking the contraption but keeping her attention on him. The bizarre device now in her hands was not helping her understanding of what he might be. He had referred to himself as God to the security guards, and yet he was using a technological device. That seemed paradoxical and suspicious to her—Kristen doubted gods required touch screens.

"Read. It's been translated to English," Vengelis said. "I will provide you with no predisposed impression. Read it, and then you can tell me what it is."

Kristen looked at the screen, her brow furrowing at once, as she read through the familiar yet foreign sentences.

Operation Felix Rises
Nerol, Pral; Trace, Argos; Loh, Cintha; et al.

Our research aims to investigate the complex tissue structuring potential of the recently discovered Felix cell. The Felix cell is a highly anomalous artificial form that mirrors the physiology and structure of a biological cell. Recombinant Felix cells were imbued with Primus genetic sequences with the intention of producing a synthetically derived Primus entity. Potential alterations of complex muscular-skeletal system physical traits resulting from the aberrant and anatomically enhanced Felix cells are unknown, but likely to match the Primus genetic sequences used as templates. It is predicted that the Felixes will exhibit Sejero traits, though to what degree is currently unknown.

Kristen Jordan's brilliant mind began moving a mile a minute. So much could be inferred from the single paragraph that she had to slow herself and read it again very carefully. She forced herself to read it again and again, trying to commit as many things as she could to memory.

At last she looked up and squinted warily at Vengelis. The cogs of her intellect were beginning to pull her out of the belief that perceived him as some sort of god. Whatever he was, he was not a god. He was trying to appear as such, but he was not. Whoever this Vengelis was, his origin was clearly based in knowledge, in science. Kristen held the proof of it in her hands, though she was uncertain if this revelation helped her plight in any way.

"Well?" Vengelis asked, barely able to hide that he was breathing fast in anticipation.

Kristen shook her head. "Well, what?"

"Can you help me?"

"Help you?" Kristen asked. "In what sense?"

"Do you understand what Felix technology is?"

"Yes. I'm fairly certain this Felix cell that"—Kristen glanced at the screen—"Pral Nerol mentions, is the same thing as Vatruvian cell technology, though I could be wrong."

"Unbelievable," Vengelis said. "When was it created?"

"Umm. About a year ago now."

"Is anyone else here familiar with the technology?" Vengelis asked sharply.

Kristen looked to the audience pushing against the far end of the ballroom. Some men were heaving and shoving at the barred doors. If they were in her research lab uptown someone might be able to contribute, but she certainly was not going to endanger anyone she knew. Kristen turned and saw the inert body of Professor Vatruvia at the rear of the stage and forced herself to look away at once. It would be cruel to invite anyone else into this predicament.

Kristen shook her head.

Most of the eyes in the ballroom were watching them on the stage, but she felt in a secluded world, encompassed only by Vengelis and the threat of his power. He had thrown a grown man hundreds of feet. Bullets had deflected against his chest and face and fallen to the stage like nothing at all. Kristen was mentally sprinting through any and all logical explanations, but coming up with absolutely nothing to explain what she had just witnessed.

"You," Vengelis said to the hotel manager still curled on the stage at his feet. Vengelis nudged him pitilessly with his foot. "The broadcast that's playing on the billboards outside. Chicago. Can you get it to play on this screen in here?"

"I-I don't know," the man wheezed.

"Let me reword it. I want the footage of Chicago playing on that screen. Now."

The man scrambled to his feet and Kristen stepped out of the way, allowing him to the podium. She felt as though she and the manager were being held at gunpoint; though in truth they were being held by something worse—something evidently impervious to guns.

Vengelis turned to Kristen. "Can you tell me anything about what you just read."

"Well," Kristen spoke slowly, "assuming it is the same as the Vatruvian technology I know, that abstract glossed over a dozen dissertations and several thousand pages worth of content. That aside, I am familiar with the subject."

Whoever wrote the report she held in her hands clearly had a greater grasp of Vatruvian cell technology then she did. Even in the brief introduction to the article, it was obvious the researchers were beyond the stage of Professor Vatruvia's team. However, that did not mean Kristen failed to understand what she read. She had been able to surmise more than a little bit of information from the loaded sentences.

Three particular references, the only true variables that differed from basic Vatruvian cell technology, had caught Kristen's eye: Felix, Primus, and Sejero traits.

Felix was clearly interchangeable with Vatruvian. If these Vatruvian, or Felix, replicate entities were created using people like Vengelis as genetic templates, Vengelis and his people thus had to be biological entities: a species known as Primus. That fact was irrefutable. Just as the Vatruvian mice in their cages uptown had been created using biological genetics as a template, so too must any Vatruvian identity. Beyond the obviously shattered ethical boundaries brought up in the scientific summary written by a one Pral Nerol, there was one question that stood out above all others to Kristen. There was one thing alone she did not understand, and therefore the crux of her remaining confusion.

"What are Sejero traits?" Kristen asked.

Vengelis shifted and failed to hide the surprise at being asked the question so directly. "I need you to figure out what everything else means. The Felixes are what concern me. I have no questions about Sejero genetics, they are irrelevant."

"Sejero *genetics*?" Kristen's gaze narrowed. "What does that mean? The article already made reference to Primus genetics. I'm assuming that is what you call yourself, a Primus?"

"Yes."

"Well, if that's the case, then what are Sejero genetics?"

Vengelis visibly thought over the question, and Kristen recognized at once that she had pinpointed something he did not want her to know. He was staring at her uncertainly when the large vaulted windows overlooking Times Square suddenly crashed down on the ballroom floor. Kristen turned to the clatter and watched with blank dismay as two gigantic men flew into the room. They were wearing the similar strange attire as Vengelis, and greeted the young man who had at first introduced himself to her as emperor with dramatic salutes. Kristen was immediately unsure which attributes were more terrifying, the fact that these beastly things could fly, or their gargantuan size and unnatural muscle. They each seemed to be nine feet tall, and more muscle bound than the bulkiest body builder Kristen had ever seen. They would have looked like grizzly bears standing on hind legs were it not for their humanlike faces.

The ballroom was roused into a tantrum anew at the sight of the two grotesque goliaths. Vengelis evidently seemed unbothered with the uproar for the moment. He held a commanding hand up to the behemoths, indicating for them to wait, and turned to Kristen.

"If you try to run away again, I will kill every person in this room, and you last. You are mine now."

Kristen could barely hear him. She felt a renewed fainting wave splash over her as she gawked at the two giants standing by the shattered windows. "What the hell is going on?" she mumbled as Vengelis turned away from her and approached the giants, his face stern.

"*Grazil-ta liriko Shicago?*" Vengelis called out to them.

Kristen looked up, startled by his abrupt switch to a language she had never heard.

The two giants each nodded, and Vengelis looked satisfied.

"*Pezca rez iliam ta. Rakool fahresk.*" Vengelis beckoned them with a finger, and paced back to Kristen. The two lumbering giants followed him across the ballroom, their footfalls shaking the panels beneath her soles. She thought their faces were wild and feral where Vengelis's was regal and composed. Vengelis seemed pleased by her queasy reaction. "Kristen Jordan, I would like you to meet Lord General Alegant Hoff and Royal Guard Krell Darien."

Kristen's lips were as white as paper. She said nothing, for fear of throwing up if she opened her mouth even slightly.

"We're going to make this very simple for you, Kristen. These two soldiers you see here are what attacked the city of Chicago. They do not feel even a semblance of compassion or remorse for your people. To them, their actions in Chicago were equivalent to stepping on an anthill, nothing more. At my slightest whim, they will destroy another city in minutes. You, Kristen Jordan, will help me with what I need, right here and right now. If you do so, these two won't have to destroy this city, or others. All I ask is for your cooperation. It is as Madison here said: all I'm asking for is compliance. That is the truth, and it seems perfectly fair to me. Does it seem fair to you?"

Kristen nodded her head a quarter inch, still captivated by the sheer size of the two giants. Even though they were not standing on the stage, they were still at her eye level.

"Good." Vengelis turned back to the giants and waved them to the window. "*Jinrak ezkeesh lorr mischka.*"

Both of the monsters turned and sprinted across the ballroom, the large chandeliers swaying and chiming from their heavy steps. They then leapt straight out of the windows into the open air, and instead of falling down to the street, ascended upward past the window frame.

"They . . . you . . . fly?" Kristen mumbled.

"Yes. But that is just one facet of our power. *Sejero* power. However, it isn't my wish to talk about Sejero genetics, I am here to discuss Felixes."

"Genetics allow you to fly, allow those *giants* to fly? That's not possible."

Vengelis snapped his fingers in front of Kristen's face and her head started violently. "I am not here to argue possibilities or impossibilities with you. We need to talk about the Felixes."

"You actually created them?" Kristen said, her pale lips barely moving and her attention still on the empty window frames. "Vatruvian replicates based off your own genetics?"

Vengelis nodded gravely.

"Evidently, wherever you come from doesn't place much stock in morality."

"Evidently." Vengelis nodded with a trace of sorrow. "But now it is up to me to deal with them."

Kristen thought about the glowing blue eyes of the mice in their cages. It was going to require a lot of insight and speculation to shed any light on the Felix replicates mentioned in the report he had given her. She thought back to Cara William's stress tests of the Vatruvian cells.

"The Felixes are resilient, strong," Kristen ventured. "More powerful than you."

Vengelis turned up to the projection screen, his eyes looking heavy. "Don't speak to me of power."

Kristen turned to where he was looking and saw that it depicted what was happening in Chicago. She forced herself to look away at once; it was too terrible and overwhelming. The hotel manager had evidently been successful in turning on the news broadcast, but he now lay wheezing on the stage. The giants had been too much for him.

"You did that?"

"Yes," Vengelis said at once. "The two soldiers you just met did, under my command."

"Why?"

"Simple, really. Submission. I gave the order so the scientists here would help me, though I never could have imagined Felix technology would actually *exist* here. In a sense I'm reeling as much as you are."

"*Are* they strong? These Felix replicates?" Kristen asked quietly.

"Yes. Incomprehensibly." Vengelis sighed as he watched the news report of Chicago with an expression that conveyed a hint of being overwhelmed himself.

"And their eyes?"

Vengelis froze and she noticed his chest constrict. "Their eyes . . . you know of their eyes? How?"

"I've seen them," Kristen said. "Though not on the face of a human. The man who you just killed—my boss—created Vatruvian mice."

"Mice . . ." Vengelis trailed off.

From beyond the empty windows a series of deep resonant clanging sounds echoed from far off, and the hint of a distant crowd's high-pitched roar drifted faintly in the wind. Kristen turned for a moment to the windows and back to Vengelis. On the screen overhead, a leaning skyscraper in Chicago at last fell to its side, and the audience in the ballroom momentarily transitioned from whimpers to wails.

Vengelis roared for them to be silent, never taking his gaze off Kristen. "I have told my two men to destroy any bridges leading off this island so we can have all the time in the world for our discussion. With one word from me, they will shift from simply toying with your people to outright massacring them. Millions of people can die at your whim, right here and right now. Or you can do as I tell you and ensure that every one of them stays safe and sound and protected from my men."

Kristen's nostrils flared, and she nearly responded hotly, but quickly composed herself and tried to respond as lucidly as possible. "So what is it exactly that you are asking of me?"

"*Asking* of you?" Vengelis raised his eyebrows. "I am not asking you to do anything. I am ordering you to show me how to defeat these Felix machines."

Kristen found herself unable to respond she was so afraid. Try as she could to stay calm, panic was rising in her stomach. How could she possibly describe how to destroy something she knew nothing about? She knew the genetics and molecular construction of Vatruvian cells, not how to *kill* a Vatruvian entity replicated off of an enigma that was obviously beyond the grasp of modern science.

Vengelis was looking at her with unmistakable hope, which Kristen knew was not good, for she now understood his question. Kristen also knew that—with Professor Vatruvia dead on the stage—she was the only person capable of answering it. And she knew she would not be able to.

CHAPTER TWENTY-EIGHT

The Lord General and Royal Guard

The sun reflected against their Imperial First Class armor and shimmered off the buildings below, the noon radiance contradicting the dark nature of their charge. Hoff and Darien reached the last skyscraper lining the southern tip of Manhattan, and before them the end of the city met with the swelling gray waters of an open bay. On the banks surrounding the bastion of skyscrapers on the narrow city-island, dense populations extended as far as the eye could see. Where earlier in the morning the two soldiers had embraced boundless woodlands and rolling hills and fields, now they were witness to the grand kingdom of man: sharp angles, towering monoliths of austere glass and concrete. A mirage of smog hugged the horizon and spread across the region.

Two rivers extended up each side of Manhattan, and a few prodigious bridges connected the main island with the adjacent lands. Even from his distance, Darien could see the nearest one spanning the eastern waterway—an enormous and dignified suspension bridge—was congested to a standstill with evacuees seeking refuge outside the city limits. Surely they were the survivalists, the smart ones, leaving the city merely as a precautionary measure after what they saw happening in Chicago.

"Vengelis told us to seal off the island. Let's separate and move up each side of the city," the Lord General called, and pointed to the east. "I will take the river to the west. You go up the eastern river there, and bring down any bridge connecting the city to the mainland. I'll meet you up north."

"Okay." Darien nodded.

The two soldiers turned from one another at once and soared northeast and northwest up the expansive rivers surrounding Manhattan.

...

Sam Larson pressed hard on the steering wheel of his Acura, more out of exasperation than as a command to the Taurus with Connecticut plates idling in front of him. The sound of his horn was drowned out in the resonance of puttering cars that sat at a dead stop along the Manhattan Bridge.

Twenty minutes ago, as Sam had hastened out of his office on William Street and made for his car, he had felt certain that if—god forbid—something did happen in New York, he would at the very least beat the traffic out of Manhattan.

Sam's situation could not have been better, given the circumstances.

It was by chance that he had happened to drive his car to work that morning and swallowed the agonizing parking bill. Furthermore, it was by shear happenstance that Sam had been absentmindedly clicking the refresh button on *The New York Times* website for stock quotes when he saw the breaking news of the Chicago attack. Straightaway, it had not felt right as Sam read the bizarre headline. Preferring an approach of prudence, he stepped out early and stopped at a sandwich place near the parking garage while the broadcast was still speaking of a *single* skyscraper falling in the Windy City.

The moment the second skyscraper fell, his pastrami was in the trash and he was hastily pulling his car out of the parking garage and through the intersections toward the Manhattan Bridge.

Despite his seemingly good luck and quick thinking, Sam was forced to slam on his brakes as the lanes atop the bridge abruptly clogged to a halt the moment he crossed over FDR Drive. After several minutes of creeping along, he found himself utterly gridlocked, suspended a hundred feet over the East River and staring up past his sunroof at broad cables and naked steel girders of the bridge and blue skies beyond.

The Billboard Top Forty radio station he normally listened to was at the moment covering what the media had tentatively dubbed, The Devastation in Chicago. Sam listened in growing disbelief as the anchors stressed that this was no nine-eleven; this was no earthquake. This was something infinitely more terrible and catastrophic. The anchors described the video footage as unspeakable, as apocalyptic. Hundreds of thousands were feared dead. The word *war* was repeated over and over, and it filled Sam with a very poignant kind of dread that he was not accustomed to.

Who was responsible for the attack? What was it? How did it begin and end so abruptly? Were other cities in danger? Were other countries in danger?

No one had any answers.

Special correspondents and advisors were pointing fingers at everything and everyone from Al Qaeda to North Korea to the United States government itself. One evangelical correspondent even mentioned the End Times and The Second Coming of the Messiah. Sam swallowed at the man's words, and ran his palms nervously around his steering wheel.

A ring tone sounded over the radio program, and Sam pulled out his cell phone.

"Hey, Dad."

Sam pressed his horn again. He was thankful to have the towers of Manhattan in his rearview mirror, but not at all happy about his bridge-bound location should New York be next on the terrorists'—surely, they were terrorists—hit list. Though he was not truly concerned for his immediate safety, it was more of a negligible lingering sort of trepidation in the far recesses of his mind.

"Sam! Have you been watching the news?" his Dad asked, surely sitting behind the desk in his office in Stamford, a pile of paperwork in front of him and his phone balanced against his shoulder. "Oh my god. Chicago."

Sam nodded. "I know."

"Where are you? I want you out of the city right now." His father's voice was stern, his tone filled with concern.

"I'm already on my way out now. I'm sitting in traffic on the Manhattan Bridge."

There was a pause. "You're getting out of Manhattan by *car*? Are you crazy?"

"No—I'm not crazy. I'm at the front end of the traffic. I got a head start."

"*Head start?* Sam it took people *days* to get out of the city after nine-eleven. The moment you're off that bridge, pull your car over anywhere and get to a commuter rail station."

"Dad, New York isn't even in danger. You're being a little drama—"

"Sam! Mom and I will pay for the bill if your car gets towed, I don't care. Promise me you'll get on a commuter rail at the next station you see and get as far from the city as you possibly can. I don't care if you have to go all the way up Long Island."

"I . . ." Sam raised a hand in exasperation and pressed hard on his car horn again. "Okay, fine, Dad. I promise. I'll call you when I know where I'm headed."

"Okay. I love you, Sam."

"I love you too, but you're being really dramatic here. Chicago is a thousand miles away."

Sam ended the call with a roll of his eyes and turned his radio up just in time to hear a woman say something about New York City. Every hair on his body rose. He reached out and turned the volume knob to full.

"We have received word of a possible incident starting in New York City just minutes ago." Sam felt his intestines turn to liquid as the broadcast continued. "Though at this point the unconfirmed claims of an attack on New York remain just that: unsubstantiated. There are pockets of civil unrest being reported across the nation in nearly every major city from Los Angeles to Miami. But there is no cause to believe that whatever assaulted Chicago will spread."

The radio station continued to stress a lack of any reliable information as Sam stared out his passenger-side window to examine the Brooklyn Bridge. It looked to be in no better condition than the one on which his Acura was now parked. He could see lines of cars and a dozen or so semis waiting in similar traffic. Giving up with his car horn, he stared at the rear bumper of the Taurus before him, propping his elbow against the door and resting his chin in his palm as the minutes dragged on.

The chilling words of the broadcast echoed through Sam's mind. It did not seem possible that terrorists could plant bombs in so many buildings. What could cause that level of destruction? Sam lifted his head up when he noticed a woman open the driver-side door of a Subaru a few cars ahead and step out of her car. A truck behind him beeped. The woman was staring southward in awe, the scarf wrapped about her neck blowing in the open air. Her passenger got out as well, standing and staring in the same direction downriver. Sam looked from car to car as more people opened their doors, exited their vehicles, and gazed southward. He was reluctant to match their stares, knowing what lay in the direction of their attention. They were all looking at the Brooklyn Bridge. A sudden terrible pang of nausea rose in the back of his throat. Fearfully and slowly, Sam turned his eyes downriver.

"Oh *shit*," he moaned in a terrible whisper.

Sam pulled at the handle of his door and stepped out onto the pavement of the bridge. He was taken aback by the gusty wind that forcefully and loudly whipped about his face as the indicator alarm chimed familiarly from his open door. Staring in disbelief down the East River, a queasy pallor began to fill his features. He watched as the Brooklyn Bridge visibly rocked, swayed from side to side, and then collapsed into the devouring water of the East River. Countless toppling and tumbling cars crashed down against the surface of the water and disappeared into the veritable abyss alongside the loose rubble and cables. The sounds traveling across the open water from the calamity were unspeakable.

Sam was suddenly pushed forward against the hood of his car as a man sprinted by and knocked him out of the way, followed by another, and another. People were abandoning their vehicles in the middle of the Manhattan Bridge and moving on foot across its length toward Brooklyn. Within seconds everyone had collectively weighed the value of their lives versus their cars, and at once Sam left his Acura idling. He became one face in a horrendously crammed marathon across the top deck.

The events that followed the abandonment of his car all seemed to happen very quickly, though with a remarkable degree of clarity to Sam's conscious mind.

Sam did not allow his thoughts to slip into a panic, or—for that matter—to think anything at all. On the contrary, he focused on pumping one leg in front of the other as he bumped elbows with other sprinters and wheezed in the chilly Atlantic air. Perhaps it was a primal mechanism of composure in the face of imminent death. Perhaps it was raw adrenaline. Regardless of the cause, the lucid awareness of his mind felt extraordinary—almost euphoric.

There was no screaming or shouting among the moving crowd, save a few individuals. It was not as his imagination or as Hollywood would have pictured such a rush. There was only the panting and huffing of running. The majority were simply too preoccupied with pushing forward to shout out.

Then Sam stumbled and nearly tripped as the pavement beneath him lurched. Pinging sounds came from above. He steadied his feet and looked skyward to see a thick steel cable of the suspension bridge sailing through the open air, snapped free from its heavy load. The visible horizon of Brooklyn's skyline shifted to a forty-five degree angle with the bridge underneath him. His orientation in space became jarred. Something hard hit him in the left hip. Sam heard a deep popping noise, and he looked down with incomprehension at the rear bumper of a Honda that had slid due to the sudden incline of the bridge. It had crushed his pelvis and pinned his lower half against the side of a Volvo. There was no pain. He heard a crumbling of pavement—or perhaps it was the pulverized bones in his legs—and a deep sound of yielding iron.

At once he was thrown upside down, his world moving in slow motion. He was falling. Sam tumbled and spun through open space, and his vision rotated between grayish swells and white-capped crests to the crystal blue sky. As he fell closer and closer to the unwelcoming water, his mind could not, would not, comprehend what would happen upon impact.

Plooosh.

Cold. Dark. Hell was not blistering and fiery; it was this. The icy river clutched at his helpless body, pulling him deeper, swallowing his life and extinguishing the fire in his heart. Countless watery and gurgling screams—his own one of them—filled his ears like dreadful whale calls in the blackness.

Then there was nothing.

...

Vengelis had specifically told them no theatrics, so Darien flew north up the span of the eastern river loosening cables and ripping out load bearing rivets on the several bridges. He turned and watched each monumental bridge waver and buckle before unceremoniously collapsing with a mighty splash into the river to an orchestra of shrieks—both man and steel. The span of choppy water steadily narrowed as he made his way north, and as he knocked out several smaller bridges, Darien soon recognized the conspicuous form of the Lord General flying above the rooftops to his west. With a last glance down the now unobstructed, albeit trouncing waterway, Darien veered up to meet his fellow Imperial First Class.

"All set?" Hoff called as he came into earshot.

"Yeah," Darien said. "Should we head back to Vengelis?"

"Please," Hoff glared at him contemptuously as they came to a halt, "I'm sure he won't have difficulty handling himself, and if he does all he has to do is call for us on the remotes. I spent way too much time stuffed in that goddamn *Harbinger I*. I'm enjoying the open air."

Hoff brushed some crumbled cement from his shoulder and soared past him, and Darien hastened alongside. "For the life of me I don't understand what we're doing."

The Lord General said nothing, but looked back and forth across the enormous now secluded city that sat imperial and proud under a crown of navy skies. A colorful park blotted in autumn hues spread out before them, its colorful stands of trees and paths enclosed on all sides by dense buildings. On its south end, the park gave way to the tremendous skyscrapers in the center of the city. Yet below the impressive spires and broad impassive facades, the teeming avenues and streets were seething with anarchy. The sounds of the felled bridges had carried like a herald of carnage across the rooftops. There was an enormous exodus northward, and countless heads and shoulders of the rushing stampede hid the very asphalt of the streets and sidewalks. It appeared as though the denizens of New York believed their city to be next on the list of destruction, and a riot seemingly five million strong was permeating through the city, a blood curdling mutiny upon civilization.

In the crowding blocks and intersections, anything that could be picked up was being lugged and heaved through glass panes of storefronts. Men and women were running out of retail shops with armfuls of electronics boxes and lumpy heaps of new clothing. On other street corners, people were congregating and shouting at regiments of police officers armed with broad plastic shields. The rioters were flinging debris at the organized lines of pushing police. The paltry riot squads were overtly fighting a losing battle. Despite the faint pops of rubber bullet rounds and the whooshing hisses of cloudy tear gas, they were incapable of pacifying the sheer scale of havoc that was growing exponentially around them.

"What are they doing?" Darien asked.

"Their system is breaking down. They're panicking," Hoff said as he ran the back of his hand over his nose. A wafting smell of pungent tear gas had lifted in the breeze and rose to greet them, proving only a mere annoyance against their resoluteness.

"When the Felixes attacked, we fought them to the last man—to the last child. Now we're attacking these people and they seem to only want to fight each other." Darien was watching the revolution below in wonder.

"Our race was founded on discipline. Theirs . . ." The Lord General watched a group of men overtake an armored police officer and begin to beat him to the pavement, kicking and beating at his outstretched arms. "Who can say?"

Darien began to grow ill at ease, sickened, as of one watching livestock in a butcher house struggling desperate and dumb against the sudden awareness of the inescapability of their plight.

"A house of cards," Hoff muttered, marveling at the conflicting panorama of tranquil skyline and surging street level. "Just a tap and its innards of nothingness show."

Darien nodded silently.

Hoff then descended, soaring southward down the avenue east of the park. His skyward swoop went unnoticed by most of the bobbing heads of the migration. A few upturned eyes saw his flight and proceeded to trip over their feet and fall in their momentary bewilderment, instantly vanishing underneath the thundering of feet. Hoff came down and landed powerfully in the center of the pushing mob, looking impossibly enormous between two abandoned cars. The men and women closest to him drew back in disbelief, causing the subsequent runners to trip over them and fall. Beside Hoff, a dozen or so beautiful horses were harnessed to ornate carriages. The horses began to rear and buck as they saw Hoff and felt the raw hysteria of the crowd. Frothing at the mouth, their hooves clapped against the pavement and they dashed in every direction, several of the carriages overturning and knocking the poor beasts to their sides as they screeched and neighed.

The Lord General's face was stoic as he looked down into the sea of horrified souls. The people were no different than the horses. They knew. The faces of the men and women illustrated their comprehension. In some instinctual way they understood he was not one of them; this nine-foot-tall giant had something to do with the destruction. The people in the front recoiled and backed away from him on all fours. Yet still the pack pushed them forward, pushing them toward the Lord General of the Imperial Army.

From overhead, Darien saw there were thousands of people pushing up the avenue toward them. The men and women in the front continued to flop and claw about, hoarsely screaming for everyone to get back. But the mob was incapable of comprehension, and foot by foot they were pushed yelling in horror toward Hoff. The rhythmic thumping of helicopters descended from above, the pilots and cameramen all stricken with terror. The camera lens was locked on the growing hysteria in the streets. It was locked on Hoff.

One of the terrible giants was in New York.

Darien was watching Hoff's callousness with growing unease from far above when something suddenly caught his eye. An object seemed to blaze for a moment across the clear sky with impossible speed. He looked west, but whatever it had been was already gone. Darien glared uncertainly, scanning the sky and squinting between the rooftops and towers. After a pause he slowly withdrew his attention back to watch the Lord General in the avenue below.

Hoff leaned over and picked up a red Jeep that sat idling beside him. The owner had left it running, and the radio was still playing music, though it was impossible to hear against the riotous surroundings. He held the car over the ground as though it weighed nothing at all, the steel frame wrenching under the unusual weight displacement of his grip. Hoff spun in place to gather momentum, firmly grasping the undercarriage, and released the car. The car shot out of his hands as a projectile going straight into the crowd. It careened and bounced high into the air, plowing a grisly path through the densely packed men, women, and children. There was nowhere to move, nowhere to duck or get out of the way. Finally the barely recognizable car came to a stop outside a torn-down pizza shop awning. The mangled hood spurted blue crackling fire, and with a whoosh of air the gasoline tank caught fire, burping flames onto the trapped bystanders.

The sadistic interior of his soul reared its hideous face, and Hoff smiled at the slaughter. He leaned down to pick up another car to bowl through the crowd. The mob now had its priorities straight, and there was a distance between its ranks and the mysterious giant. The people in the front row were trembling and gasping as though the very sight of what they had just witnessed had knocked the wind out of them. They held out their hands, pleading and crying out for him to not kill them, *please* not to kill them. Hoff regarded their display with scorn. He picked up another larger car and began spinning in place to throw strike two.

BOOOOOOOOOOOM!!

At first it was unclear what had happened. The street—the entire city—rattled as though a meteor struck the pavement between Hoff and the mortified crowd. The impact was deafening, and a shockwave of cloudy debris kicked up, obscuring the chaos of the street in dust. The intersection fell into a still silence, all uncertain what had just occurred.

"What the hell?" Hoff whispered as the dust slowly settled back to the ground. He let the car he was holding fall with a jangle to his feet, the windows shattering.

A young man was standing in front of the motionless mob. The avenue was cracked in a wide crater around the mysterious young man's feet. Hoff blinked several times at the strikingly familiar sight. He was looking at one of his own. It was a Primus of obvious Royal descent clad in flawless Imperial First Class armor that glinted in the sunlight. A long threadbare crimson cloak shifted slowly in the cool breeze behind the strange young man, and underneath the shadow of the cloak's hood, a pair of sharp eyes bore into him with cold fury. The Lord General stared at the face of a ghost, an apparition of an unspeakable event long forgotten. Darien silently descended, landing beside Hoff and examining their mysterious guest, who was decked in Imperial First Class armor, uncertainly. Hoff and Darien embraced an undimmed vision of the grandeur of Sejero champions of old, befitting the very depictions on Sejeroreich's War Hall. The newcomer's expression was murderous, and his fists were clenched as he smoldered with rage.

A phantom. An exile. As ever before, Gravitas Nerol stood alone.

The people on the street sensed the sudden uncertainty, perhaps even fear, in the monstrous faces of the mammoth god-destructors. The enmity between the lone young man and the two giants was palpable, the power of their stand-off emitting an electric charge. Men and women, complete strangers, looked from one another to the pair of giants to the surreal young man with feeble misunderstanding. Then, one by one, they began to move behind the cloaked man that had descended from the sky, or was it from the heavens? Just as they could perceive the danger of the giants, they knew—somehow, someway, in some visceral sense they could tell: this one was on their side.

This god was here to protect them, and for the first time in history, humans rallied helplessly behind a higher being—they rallied behind the last son of house Nerol.

CHAPTER TWENTY-NINE

Gravitas

For a long moment it seemed as though time stood still as the intense standoff persisted. From the bewildered bystanders to Gravitas to the two giants, all characters seemed unwilling to break the profuse silence. In their immoral clamor, the depraved hyenas had awoken the sleeping lion, and now he stood before them. At the head of countless scared faces, Gravitas Nerol waited for the two Imperial First Class soldiers to break the hush.

The two giants looked back at him, standing shoulder to shoulder, each with an equally mystified expression. The mangled Jeep that had been thrown was crackling and sizzling on the sidewalk, emitting an acrid stench of melting plastic and upholstery. In the corner of his vision Gravitas was aware of a helicopter thumping over the trees of the park and recording every second of the standoff, the sound of its presence barely perceptible over the roar of the panicking masses in the streets and avenues.

At last the slightly larger of the two behemoths stepped forward, his leg the girth of a tree trunk. Gravitas could see from the insignias on his armor that he was high ranking, not an average grunt of the Imperial First Class ranks.

"Do you remember me?" the giant soldier asked, his voice baritone and harsh.

Gravitas looked at him with repulsion. Over the years he had almost willed himself to believe the soldiers of the Imperial Army were not as monstrous as his memory would have him believe. He let out a frustrated and pained sigh, and for the first time in many years he spoke his native tongue.

"Yes. I recognize you, General Hoff." Gravitas spoke slowly, and drew his gaze to the other, younger, giant. "I don't know you."

The closer soldier nodded his grotesquely thick neck and placed a hand against his broad chest. "It's Lord General Hoff, now. This is Royal Guard Krell Darien. I must say I was not expecting to see you again . . . Nerol."

To this, the other warrior, Darien, looked from Gravitas back to Hoff with an incredulous expression. "*This* is the Nerol warrior? *How?*"

"Quiet. Stay on your guard, he is no ally," the Lord General growled, not taking his eyes off Gravitas. "What are you doing here, Nerol?"

Gravitas raised his arms to his sides, and his crimson cloak shifted in the cool air. "This is my home, and you have come unwelcomed."

"Anthem is your home," Hoff called back. "Your people need the help of a soldier such as yourself in this dark hour, assuming you are even half as powerful as you were on Orion. Come, we must speak with you."

"No," Gravitas shook his head definitively. "This is my home, and these are my people. And you are correct, they do need the help of a soldier such as myself. The troubles of my vile native race are not my concern. I am ashamed of my connection to you. Nothing more."

The Lord General was obviously holding back anger as he reached his hands out imploringly. "Emperor Faris has been murdered. His son Vengelis Epsilon wears the Blood Ring now. I suspect he will pardon you of the charges made against you by his father if you come with us willingly."

"Faris is dead?" Gravitas repeated. "Good. My only wish is that it could have been by my hand. I don't know his son, but I would imagine he is hiding in true Epsilon form on the throne in Sejeroreich and letting others bloody their hands in his name."

"My, don't we have nerve." Hoff shook his head, his expression unreadable. "No, Nerol, the high Epsilon is not in Sejeroreich. It might interest you to know that he is here on Filgaia. As such, I entreat you to not act imprudently here."

Gravitas felt his heart rate quicken as this truth crashed over him. If the Epsilon Emperor was on Earth, there were surely hundreds and hundreds of soldiers with him. Gravitas swallowed hard, recognizing at once that his fight would not be a winning one. It would now simply be a matter of how many he could kill before exhaustion set in. He tried not to give in to desperation or panic as he clenched his fists.

"I will be sure to assassinate him for this disgusting treachery."

Darien suddenly joined the conversation, his deep hearty laughter echoing off the buildings around them. Yet as he laughed, Hoff remained steady, never blinking his attention away from Gravitas. Gravitas examined each of their body language, hoping one of them would surrender something to indicate which of them was more powerful.

"You think you can defeat Vengelis Epsilon?" Darien called out with amusement.

"Think? No. I'm quite certain of it."

"Well, you may get your chance to challenge him. He's in this city as we speak."

Upon hearing this, Gravitas immediately turned to the mob of people cowering behind him, careful not to take his eyes off the two giants, and roared out in English, his voice barely carrying over the tumult of the surrounds. "Get out of the city! Now! *Swim* if you have to!"

The mob did not need telling twice.

As though his words had the effect of a starting whistle, bedlam erupted around the three otherworldly warriors. Men and women scattered. As people rushed by him, Gravitas saw that some were clutching the hands of petrified children and pulling them practically off the ground as they fled the bizarre standoff and joined the thundering stampede of an exodus. He tried to phase out his surroundings, to focus on his actions; he could not allow himself to consider how much Ryan Craig's world would never be the same—at this moment these people needed Gravitas Nerol. Hoff smirked cynically at Gravitas as the plaintive horror rose to a deafening pitch around them, as if the terror was proving some sort of point he was trying to make.

Gravitas narrowed his gaze dangerously at the giant Lord General. He knew the mindset of these soldiers. They saw this display of fear only as a pathetic weakness. The evacuation around them was due to a lack of resolve, the lack of will to fight as mere cowardice despite their incomparable superiority, even the carrying of children was scorned as a coddling indulgence to these deluded minds. The two soldiers before him had likely never been the recipients of a kind act in their entire lives, never been shown the keystones of morality, fortitude, and respect. Since birth these giants had been used and manipulated by those more powerful to be mere blunt instruments—unthinking weapons of war. Despite the awareness that it was not entirely their own fault, Gravitas realized he truly hated them for their ignorance. He also realized Hoff would not be the first Lord General to fall before him.

If the emperor himself was indeed in the city, it did not bode well for his chances. The emperor never came along on extraction operations. What possible reason would he have to come all the way here? Gravitas shook the thought from his mind. It did not matter. The new emperor would fall unceremoniously alongside his brutish ranks, or Gravitas would die seeing it attempted. Gravitas calmly untied the knot to his cloak and let it fall to the pavement. This was about saving these people, but as his cloak shifted to rest against the ground,

Gravitas knew it was also about revenge. He was finished with words. As the cloak fell from his shoulders and revealed the ornate glimmering Imperial First Class armor he had been given when he was sixteen, he cast aside the cautious intellectuality of Ryan Craig and allowed the raw adrenaline, the sheer competitiveness, and the absolute fury of his warrior side to spill through him.

"I would be following them if I were you. Run and hide like these pathetic fools. I've beaten sons of Royalty before. Skinny, small, like you are," the Royal Guard Darien called. The giant began to pull out a ship remote from within his armor, perhaps to call for reinforcements.

This, Gravitas could not allow.

Without a trace of warning Gravitas erupted toward him with dizzying swiftness. Before Darien could even flinch, Gravitas buried his fist into the giant's face with a connection that reverberated through the city like a crack of resounding thunder. The Royal Guard launched backward as though he had been shot out of a cannon, tumbling and flipping down the length of the avenue. The ship remote fell clattering to the pavement and the screen shattered at Gravitas's feet.

Gravitas Nerol turned to the Lord General of the Imperial Army.

"You don't want to do this. There is too much you need to hear, Nerol!" Hoff warned, talking fast. "Sejeroreich lays in ruin!"

"And now so does Chicago because of you!" Gravitas said, "And this city is doomed too if I don't intervene, is it not?"

"You don't understand!" Hoff spat.

"Stop talking and fight an equal for once, coward."

"*Coward?*" Hoff screamed, his face turning beat red. "Bronson Vikkor was my mentor you little *snake!* I'm going to enjoy beating you to death in his honor."

"You're soft from preying on the weak," Gravitas said with cold fury. "Come. Try to rival a fellow predator."

The general gnashed his teeth in ugly rage and rushed with a blistering fierceness toward him, his footfalls shaking the pavement. At the same moment Gravitas saw in his peripheral vision a recovered Darien barreling up the avenue toward him and casting cars out of his way with huge crashing impacts, blood running in a thick stream from where his fist had connected with the giant's cheek.

Better their attention on him than the city, but Gravitas was all too aware of the many years since his last actual spar. He was sure to be rusty. In the split second of their approach, Gravitas exploded into the air, the force driving downward from his legs making spiderweb cracks in the pavement around the intersection. He soared upward into the brilliant cerulean sky, the two soldiers hounding in his immediate wake.

Higher and higher Gravitas drew them away from the streets and people, until far below the very island of Manhattan had shrunk to the size of his hand. As they drew near, Hoff accelerated past Darien, twisting his midsection and cocking his right arm to launch a wild punch. Gravitas steadied himself, floating alone against the outline of the sky. His mind transported his consciousness to a day long since past, and he felt once more as if he were with Master Tolland on Mount Karlsbad. Hoff's speed was genuinely impressive for his size, and the swing was powerful enough to inflict serious damage. Gravitas remained absolutely still as the giant charged him. The enormously bulky fist was a hundredth of a second from his face when Gravitas's body snapped into a swift dodge. Hoff's fist met nothing but air, and his momentum caused him to shoot straight past Gravitas.

Darien was close behind, also pulling his arm into a punch. With a piercing crack Gravitas shot toward him. He launched a knee soundly into Darien's gut, stopping the giant in his tracks and brutally taking the wind out of him.

Gravitas reached out and wrapped his fingers around the Royal Guard's thick neck and squeezed, exploding forward and thrusting Darien back-first toward the city far below. The wind whistled in their ears as they plummeted toward the ground. The city whirled in his vision as Gravitas spun round and round, seemingly with the intention of impaling the goliath's back on the narrow spire of one of the tall buildings. Darien tried desperately to free himself from the grip of the livid fighter on top of him, but Gravitas's grasp was as unyielding as his rage.

Gravitas was holding him responsible for a lifetime of pent up anger and frustration.

As the two plunged toward the city, Hoff caught up with them and skillfully wrapped his huge arms around Gravitas's head in a chokehold. This only added to their aerodynamic instability, and the three Sejero warriors flipped and rotated in a free fall, limbs and bodies tangled and interlocked in excruciating positions. Hoff's rocklike bicep, the size of a trophy winning pumpkin, flexed forcefully into Gravitas's exposed neck between his collarbone and chin, pressing into his bare windpipe and jugular. In immediate panic, Gravitas realized the mistake of his anger. He would be unconscious within moments.

As they descended spinning and falling through the air, Gravitas desperately lifted one of his squeezing hands from Darien's neck and formed a fist. He swung upward blindly at Hoff's face, but the enormous arm around his neck prevented full extension of his strikes. He could not find his target as black dots began to fill his field of vision. He quickly changed strategy and began to maddeningly strike elbow after elbow into the general's exposed ribcage, all the while still clutching Darien by the throat and pushing him downward with his left arm. At first the elbow strikes did not weaken Hoff's iron grip, but after six or seven lethal blows Gravitas heard a number of Hoff's ribs crack loudly. Hoff roared in pain and released his hold. As the enormous Lord General rolled off Gravitas, Hoff reached out and tried to savagely claw at Gravitas's face. It worked, and his huge fingers palmed Gravitas's jaw and pulled him away from Darien.

The three quickly recovered and halted in space, falling into readied positions. They were not in the high atmosphere above the city anymore, and the tall roofs reached upward, not far below their hovering feet. The sounds of the streets rose to greet them.

"So, I guess even one-on-one duels have fallen to the wayside nowadays," Gravitas said through heavy breaths. "Honorless bastards."

To his surprise, Darien—without a semblance of a verbal comeback—charged him this time, thrusting a kick at Gravitas's midsection. Gravitas spun out of the way, turning just in time to duck below another one of Hoff's incoming fists. By nothing but sheer practiced reflex, Gravitas lowered his shoulder and flexed his arm tightly against his side, blocking another monstrous blindside kick from Darien. Though the properly sustained kick inflicted no injury to him, Gravitas was punted in a soaring arc across the sky of the city from the rocking blow. To Gravitas's surprise, he soared straight past the thrashing rotors of a helicopter. From the open side door, the black lens of a camera along with a cameraman and pilot watched the aerial brawl in vacant disbelief.

"Get out of here!" Gravitas roared to the helicopter as the two giants tore after him.

Gravitas watched Hoff veer from his direct path and fly straight through the spinning rotors, surely just to anger him. The narrow steel shattered against the Lord General's body, and Gravitas held up a forearm as long blades of shrapnel shot out in every direction. The helicopter fell from the sky, twirling and spinning out of control toward crowded streets.

Gravitas darted down after it, but Darien got in his way. The giant lost his senses and launched a furious and uncontrolled punch at Gravitas's face. Gravitas took advantage. He dodged his head to the right, and Darien's right fist passed just above his left shoulder. Gravitas then turned his body, jutting his own right shoulder upward into Darien's armpit. In the same movement, Gravitas reached out and grasped Darien's extended arm. In one swift downward yank, Gravitas twisted Darien's arm so that his huge palm faced upward, and brought it down forcefully against his own slender shoulder. The giant's elbow hyperextended viciously. Ligaments and tendons stretched and tore apart; the bones connecting at his elbow separated with a loud pop. Darien's face took on the sick pallor of a child that has fallen from the top of the jungle gym, and he let out a terrible expulsion of air. He was in too much pain to cry out or scream. The Royal Guard simply fell in shock toward the city, his right arm flopping limply.

"What the hell is wrong with you?" Hoff screamed as he stared at his falling comrade in disbelief.

Gravitas said nothing. Instead, he silently watched Darien fall, taking careful note of where the giant was going to land in the maze of skyscrapers. He would finish him off after he was through with the Lord General. Below them, the crashed helicopter smoldered in an intersection.

Hoff panted for breath as he watched Gravitas. His enormous shoulders were held at a tender angle, and he was failing to hide winces from the several broken ribs on his right side. He made a grunting noise as he pressed a hand against his ribs. "You really think you can defeat us?"

"You're already defeated," Gravitas called, still watching Darien plummet between two rows of buildings.

"I'll tear you apart!" Hoff snapped.

Gravitas turned to him humorlessly. "Then do it."

The Lord General clenched his fists in an obvious attempt to swallow the incapacitating pain in his side and his growing panic. He did not try to reach for his remote to call for help, which Gravitas guessed was the result of his pride. Instead, Hoff lunged toward Gravitas. Their arms met and they grappled violently with one another, pushing back and forth, to and fro, across the brilliant blue skies over the spires and gravel rooftops.

"It was stupid to lock arms with me!" Hoff grunted heavily between breaths. "Y—you may be quicker than me. But I'm certainly stronger than you! Vengelis Epsilon *himself* avoids grappling contests with me."

Gravitas focused on not losing control of the situation. The Lord General's arms were six or seven times the girth of his own, and Hoff was indeed remarkably strong. For a time Gravitas refrained from using his full strength against the general, and even allowed Hoff to push and pull him through the air. Gravitas was hoping to trick Hoff into thinking his strength was less than it really was, though he was careful not to allow himself to fall in danger of any precarious hold.

Then, just as Hoff began to grow overconfident in his superior strength, Gravitas, quickly summoning his total power into one movement and pulled downward on Hoff's enormous arms. The giant fell forward awkwardly. Gravitas then ripped his arms back and swung a powerful punch at the giant's chin, connecting brutally.

Hoff's huge head rolled from the blow.

Gravitas then spun, rounding on the general and launching a kick straight into his side, precisely hitting his already broken ribs. Hoff let out a wide-eyed howl and arched his back in agony. Gravitas leapt at the opening, and leveled a punch into the exact same spot, and another, and another. The Lord General's side was bleeding profusely from the beating. Hoff fell toward the city, his upper body locked in a painful and immobile condition.

The fight was over.

For a time Gravitas watched Hoff fall, and longed to show him mercy, to extend to this oblivious soldier a sympathy that he had never given to another. Then he thought of Kristen Jordan's beautiful face and felt a smoldering fury seep out of his very heart. This Lord General, this soulless and thoughtless monster, would have stripped her of her life without the slightest hesitation. All of her brilliance, all of her hopes and dreams and all she might yet come to be would have been devoured by this grotesque man's hunger for conquest. His crimes ran too atrocious for forgiveness. And so Gravitas exploded down toward the plummeting Hoff. With the full gathered momentum of his approach toward the free falling general, Gravitas reached back to full extension and launched a killing blow straight into Alegant Hoff's liver. Hoff made a gasping gurgle sound, and his body lurched toward the buildings below.

Gravitas then turned and accelerated toward the southwestern end of the city, where Darien had descended into the assemblage of shimmering skyscrapers.

CHAPTER THIRTY

Vengelis

Vengelis stared at Kristen Jordan silently. He examined her closely, methodically weighing out her potential value. She was tapping a sneaker nervously against the stage and drumming her fingers along the side of the *Harbinger I* remote. Behind her glasses, she was reading Pral Nerol's report with a mingling of apprehension and wonder. Vengelis was still not entirely convinced that Kristen was not in fact one of Pral Nerol's researchers—a Primus—living incognito on Filgaia. But if this young woman was a Primus, she would have recognized the heir to the Epsilon throne enter the ballroom and consequently faltered during her presentation when Vengelis arrived. Yet Vengelis had distinctly seen Kristen notice and disregard his initial entrance. Beyond that, he had felt the delicateness of her jaw when he had grabbed her by the chin. It had taken a conscious effort to avoid inadvertently crumpling it with a mere squeeze of his thumb.

No. Kristen Jordan had to be a human, but how?

How were humans—by their own capacity—also on the cusp of Felix technology? It did not seem possible that a civilization so inferior to the Primus in every other aspect would be on an equal ground in this one solitary scientific respect. Vengelis had to admit that he was as perplexed by her existence as she no doubt was by his. They were each enigmas equal in kind, one physical, one cerebral.

Kristen drew a steadying breath and let it out slowly, and when she lifted a hand from the *Harbinger I* remote to massage her chin, Vengelis saw she was trembling.

"What do you mean when you ask me to show you how to *defeat* these Felixes?" Kristen asked cautiously, lifting her gaze from the remote.

Her question jarred Vengelis from his thoughts, and her tone stoked irritation in his chest. She was beginning to look increasingly worried, and it bothered him. "You need to tell me how they can be unmade. Tell me how I can disassemble them."

Kristen's expression showed a lack of understanding. "I know Vatruvian technology on the scale of the cellular level. You're referring to these . . . Felixes . . . as though they are some sort of army?"

"Yes."

"I don't understand. How many of them did this scientist create?"

"The number of Felixes is irrelevant. The question is how I can destroy one of them."

"Well, you're mentioning Felixes in the plural, so I will assume you people created more than one," Kristen said. "But are we talking about some sort of, like, *legion*, or a few?"

"We created four."

"Four?" the answer visibly took Kristen aback. "*Four* Vatruvian humans—or Primus or whatever you are—were cause for you to come all the way here?"

Vengelis nodded, in disbelief himself. "Yes."

"Well, what do . . . hold on." Kristen glanced back at the remote in her hands. "What do Pral Nerol and his researchers have to say about it? I really think you should be talking to them, not me."

Vengelis scratched his chin, pondering how much he should risk telling her. He did not trust Kristen Jordan. The young woman before him was obviously intelligent; her exceptional intellect was on par with Pral Nerol and the greatest minds of his own people. He could see in her eyes that she was putting pieces together, attempting to solve the puzzle of how he and his men were flying through the sky, throwing people across rooms, and ripping down skyscrapers. The growing glint in her eyes was unmistakably her mind trying to establish how her notion of reality was so obviously deficient. Kristen was not a sheep who would curl up and write him off as a god. Instead she would use her mind and figure out what they were, perhaps by tricking him. She was proof the humans were not as archaic as he had believed even hours previous.

Vengelis broke it down simplistically in his mind. Felixes, or creations of modern Primus science, brought about the fall of the Epsilon empire. The humans were capable of replicating the Felix technology on their own accord. By logical correlation—in this one respect—the humans were equal to the Primus. It was then possible as an *equal* race, however obscenely unlikely, that the humans could pose a genuine threat to him. The key factor missing in their hypothetical equality was, of course, Sejero genetics.

Yet Kristen Jordan's very first question had gone straight to Sejero genetics. In a few mere sentences Kristen had been able to pinpoint and question the source of his tremendous power. There was cleverness to match intellect in that mind, a combination that made Vengelis uneasy.

"Well? What does Pral Nerol think about it?" Kristen asked.

Vengelis knew if he told her the Felixes destroyed his world, Kristen would think it possible for humans to fend him off, perhaps with the very Vatruvian technology she was capable of manipulating. That could not be risked. He decided to err on the side of caution and keep her in the dark about the broader picture of the destruction of Anthem.

"Nerol is unable to answer my questions."

"Okay," Kristen said, skeptical toward his reticence. "There are four Vatruvian entities created using your genes as architecture. That is the situation?"

"Yes."

"And the creation of these entities has forced the *emperor* of these people to travel to a different world in the hope that a scientist there would be able to help them? And all this has been done without simply asking the creators of the technology what should be done."

Vengelis held her gaze and said nothing. There was a hint of sarcasm in her voice as she said emperor that he did not like, but he let it slide. He needed to start making headway in unraveling the mystery around the Felixes, and he was certain she could help if he allowed her to continue without intimidating her.

"Well," Kristen looked at him with doubt. "The best I can do is to tell you what I know about the technology, and how it might relate to your situation. Though I will be the first to admit my knowledge is limited."

"I'm listening."

"I don't know how familiar you are with the technology itself."

"Then explain it carefully."

Kristen drew a deep breath. "Well, okay. Just recently we discovered a peculiar phenomenon of Vatruvian cells; it was a trend that may shed light on your situation. There is something inherent in their artificial conception—the very molecules of their fiber and being—that allow Vatruvian cells to be stronger than the natural cells they are modeled after."

Vengelis's face turned severe, but this was not a surprise. "Continue."

The noises of a hysterical uproar traveled in with the breeze through the shattered windows where Hoff and Darien had entered the ballroom. It sounded as though the entire city was trembling under the throes of havoc and struggle. Voices could be heard like gales in a storm outside, and there were clamors not unlike a battle. Kristen turned her attention to the noise and stared in disbelief out the windows. Vengelis leaned forward and snapped his fingers again to get her attention. She brought her gaze back to him and raised her voice uncomfortably over the mayhem.

"O-one of my colleagues first noticed the unexpected trend in a bacterium during stress testing of one of the Vatruvian cells."

"The unexpected trend?" Vengelis asked. "What do you mean?"

"Yes. Well, the results were . . . bizarre. You have to understand that all Vatruvian technology, or in your case Felix technology, aims to accomplish is a mimicry of natural cells. The end goal is to imbue biological elegance upon an entity created in the lab. But what we found during stress tests was that, in fact, a Vatruvian cell bacterium was *more* resilient to inhibiting variables than the natural cell it replicated." Kristen paused. "Do you understand what I'm saying?"

Now it was Vengelis's turn to shift uncomfortably. He drew his attention to Madison, and saw she was listening intently to their conversation from the side, though she was staring out the windows toward the outside racket. He wondered if their feelings were similar to when he descended on the burning Municera and felt the pit rise in his stomach. Kristen and Madison were surely far from inured to the degree of destruction that was being brought down around them.

"Do you understand?" Kristen repeated. "What I mean to say is that a Vatruvian cell is able to live in environments that would destroy a normal cell. The specific example I was told was of a Vatruvian cell bacterium functioning in an environment far beyond the heat threshold of its biological version."

Vengelis nodded, glaring at the stage floor. "Okay."

"I can only speculate what kind of other superiorities would surface in larger organisms or tissue structures. As far as I know, we have not done stress tests on the Vatruvian mice."

As he listened to Kristen, the perilously beautiful face and gleaming sapphire gaze of the Felix woman he fought over Sejeroreich seared across Vengelis's vision like a ghastly specter. He placed his fingers on the healed gash across his cheek, remembering the gaping hole it had been, and he shivered. The shudder did not go unnoticed by Kristen. She cast him a measuring gaze as if to guess what was going through his head.

"By all means, speculate," Vengelis said, quickly composing himself.

"Well, if the artificial cells that comprise a Vatruvian entity are superior to biological cells, it can be assumed the tissues of the entity will also be superior." Kristen shrugged and looked again to Pral Nerol's report on the handheld screen. Her lips articulated a few of the words as she scanned through it. "The scientists who performed this research were clearly also aware of this occurrence. They even mention its possibility in the synopsis here: *Potential alterations of complex muscular-skeletal system physical traits resulting from the aberrant and anatomically enhanced Felix stem cells are currently unknown.*"

"I know," Vengelis said, frustrated.

"Look, I've told you all I can based off the information I have." Kristen exhaled. "I'm sorry if it wasn't helpful."

"No," Vengelis said. "You need to tell me more. I will not leave until I am shown *specifically* how to destroy a Felix."

"I don't understand. You said yourself that you're a god. Just . . . I don't know . . . pull them apart. Kill them."

Vengelis knew it was a trap. He was certain her concern was not in the strength of the Felixes, and how could it be? The Felixes were imaginary to her. No, Kristen's concern was instead on the strength of the baffling humanlike being standing before her. Kristen had her own agenda, her own race's self-interest, in this conversation. Ultimately, he did not hold it against her, and part of him even admired it.

"I told you the machines were constructed using the genetics of my people." Vengelis looked away from her, the admittance of his defeat hard to voice. "The Felixes appear to be as superior to my race as your Vatruvian bacterium cell was to its natural counterpart."

Kristen nodded. "I don't doubt that."

"Then I will ask you this: how would a natural mouse go about killing one of your Vatruvian mice?"

"I would say, based off of my colleague's data and what you have hinted about these Felixes, a natural mouse couldn't kill a Vatruvian mouse. The Vatruvian would be too superior."

"But we aren't dealing with mice, are we?" Vengelis said. "How would a *human* murder a Vatruvian human?"

"Well, that's a completely different situation." Kristen said in a matter-of-fact tone. "Humans can wield weapons capable of creating far greater force than their bodies alone can produce. The firing of a gun created by a natural human would still kill a Vatruvian human."

Vengelis nodded gravely. "And if the template species—the natural cells themselves—upon which a Vatruvian replicate has been created, are more powerful than any weapon? If a Vatruvian entity was created using the cells of a life form that was impervious to any technology or weapon of science? What then?"

Kristen paused as the panic of their surrounds pushed in on the bubble of their conversation.

"Then, somewhere out there, there are synthetic organisms more powerful than gods." Kristen's eyes began to widen in sudden comprehension of the gravity of Vengelis's situation. "And they are called Felixes."

"Do you now understand the task I'm asking of you?" Vengelis said.

"I—" Kristen stumbled. "How can I possibly tell you how to destroy these Felixes when I don't even know what *you* are, let alone them? It isn't that simple! That's the very intent of Vatruvian technology—vast complexity."

"I don't know how you'll do it, but that is your task. And if you can't succeed, I will begin a genocide that will leave a gaping and disfiguring scar across your civilization's memory. That is, if they don't do it themselves." Vengelis nodded to the rising sounds of unrest filtering from outside.

"You can't," Kristen said. "You're asking the impossible!"

Vengelis reached out and forcefully yanked the *Harbinger I* remote out of Kristen's hands. She fell forward and looked up at him with a fierce aversion. Vengelis decided she was going to need some motivation. If a technology could be made, it could be unmade. That was Vengelis's position on the matter, and he was not about to stray from it. To suggest the Felixes were indestructible was to suggest his civilization had reached its end, and that was not an option. There had to be a way. It was a matter of ingenuity, and this young woman obviously had ingenuity aplenty. Kristen just needed help coming around to the severity and actuality of her plight; she needed to have as much depending on her efforts as he did.

Like him, Kristen needed the fear of destruction driving her labors.

Vengelis pressed the transmit button to connect with Hoff and Darien. He would order them to begin destroying the city from the south portion of the island upward. The building Kristen, Madison, and he now occupied would be the last remaining structure in a desert of ruin if necessary. He waited a long moment, but received no answering transmission from their end. Again he pushed the button on his *Harbinger I* remote with growing irritation.

There was no response.

"Hoff! Darien! What the hell are you two doing?" Vengelis held the remote close to his face for a long moment, expecting to hear Hoff's deep voice.

Yet nothing came.

At last he let his arm fall to his side in bewilderment. What could they possibly be doing? Faint tremors of angst traveled through him. Now was not the time for unforeseen complications.

"Wait. Whatever you're about to do, wait." Kristen said, seeming to guess his intention. "I will try to help. I really will. But you are going to need to tell me more about what you are. You can't simply demand results and expect them to appear. I need more information to work with."

"What do you need?"

"Well . . . first, we need to discuss your power. You and those giants . . . how are you so strong?"

"We simply are."

"You have the power to destroy cities. I think it's safe to say we have established that." Kristen looked up to the live broadcast of a devastated Chicago on the projector screen and trembled, but continued. "Does that power reside in *you*? Or are you and those two giants wielding some sophisticated weaponry or technology that I can't see or, I don't know, is somehow beyond my comprehension?"

"We don't brandish smoke and mirrors, if that is what you're asking. The power you have witnessed is raw, corporal; it is within us. Technology itself is archaic and ineffectual when compared to my people's innate power."

"So you are telling me your strength—whatever its scale may be—is inherent? You were born with the ability to destroy cities with your bare hands and sustain gunshots to the chest?"

Vengelis nodded.

"That doesn't seem possible. You were . . ." Kristen looked at him uncertainly. "*Born*, right? You have a father and mother, et cetera? You aren't some advanced experiment—or a machine yourself?"

"No. Everyone of my race, to greater and lesser degrees, was born with this power."

"How?" Kristen asked as her face filled with awe.

Vengelis said nothing.

"So this extraordinary strength is contained in your genes. That's the Sejero genetics referenced in the report, I take it?"

"Yes, that is safe to say."

"If you want me to help you, I need to know everything about Sejero genetics. They are the only concept referenced in this research synopsis that are a mystery to me."

The statement seared an opening of fury into Vengelis's consciousness so overwhelming that he nearly reached out to throttle her by the neck. She was casually demanding to know everything about the source of power—the very lifeblood—of his race. Kristen Jordan was nonchalantly asking for a simple explanation of the Sejero strength which waylaid the merciless technology of the

Zergos: an alien race so powerful, cold and cruel that should the two become acquainted, the human civilization and all of Filgaia's natural world would only know a single fleeting moment of horror and flame before they were gone. The lack of decorum was astounding, and the insult to his illustrious inheritance nearly too much to bear.

"Sejero genes," Vengelis said, closing his eyes and holding back his fury. "Are what separate me from you. They give rise to unlimited power. If life itself was first sparked out of some dead primordial sea, then its grand pinnacle is the power within me. A power over all else."

Kristen waited for him to continue, but when he did not, she furrowed her brow. "Well then, one thing is absolutely certain. If the Sejero genes are a part of your race's genome, then the Felixes certainly retain the traits as well."

"Yes, well—"

As Vengelis spoke, a distant screeching sound followed by a distinct explosion sounded from somewhere in the city. Kristen's eyes widened in distress and Vengelis returned her look with a slightly confused expression. He looked to the windows, suddenly aware that Hoff and Darien never responded to his call.

"Stay here," Vengelis murmured. He turned and walked across the shattered glass on the floor to the air drifting in through the windows. Pulling the *Harbinger I* remote out of his armor, he looked up and down the long avenue of tall buildings and billowing flags in the direction of the curious explosion. His order to Hoff and Darien had been to cut off the bridges. The sound of the explosion was of an airplane or helicopter crash. Vengelis raised the remote to his mouth. "Hoff! Darien! What are you two doing? What was that explosion?"

No response.

Vengelis glared into the distance above the teeming frenzy of the avenue. He turned back into the ballroom, his agitation growing. The pathetic manner in which the gawking audience was now staring at him suddenly kindled infuriation, but he quickly quelled it. He steadied himself and calmly walked back onto the stage.

"What was that?" Madison asked him.

"I don't know." Vengelis shook his head.

"Look. There's nothing I can do for you," Kristen said with an unruly tone. "There is nothing anyone can do. If there isn't a technology that can inflict damage to your flesh, then there certainly isn't a technology that can damage Felix flesh."

"There are a few hundred pages to Pral Nerol's research document." Vengelis handed the remote back to Kristen. "By all means, you may begin reading it in its entirety."

"But that's not going to change anyth—"

"Enough!" Vengelis snapped. "And you better *hope* you don't succeed in convincing me there is nothing you can do."

"I-I . . . okay. I'll read through it, but it's going to take awhile."

"I'm not unreasonable. Take your time, I wouldn't want you missing any minute detail."

"So, for the record, you are looking for a structural weakness? A physical deficiency of the Felixes you can personally manipulate? Something along those lines?"

"Now we're on the same page. Yes, that's exactly what I seek."

Kristen looked like she was about to protest, but evidently thought better of it. Instead, she brought her gaze down to the *Harbinger I* remote and began reading the translated report. Vengelis let out a deep breath and leaned down, taking a seat at the end of the stage. He quietly watched Kristen read Pral Nerol's report as he mindlessly polished the Blood Ring and pondered his plight. He longed desperately to be away from this primitive and underdeveloped place. The notion of a world without Sejero blood was disconcerting to him. The men and women surrounding him lacked any sense of higher order and balance. They didn't even *try* to defend themselves against him; they just acquiesced. Vengelis was ashamed to even share so similar a likeness in appearance to them. When the Felixes attacked his world, children rallied for the cause, standing against the Felixes alongside the strongest of the world's warriors. He turned to the audience to see that most of them were now simply weeping into cell phones.

"Needless to say, you should be thinking out of the box," Vengelis said, more to himself than anyone else.

"Yeah. Thanks for the tip," Kristen said sarcastically and looked up at him for a moment with a scathing hate. Vengelis held her gaze until she looked back to the remote. He turned to Madison, who said nothing.

After several strained minutes passed, Kristen seemed to be well into the research paper's introduction when the remote in her hands crackled with an incoming transmission. She looked up to Vengelis, but he was preoccupied with his thoughts. He was thinking about Master Tolland. Was it possible that his teacher—and perhaps Pral Nerol, too—knew of this Vatruvian technology? Did Master Tolland know Vatruvian technology existed on Filgaia, and send him here for that reason? As logical as that seemed, it could not have been possible.

There had been no correspondence between Anthem and Filgaia in four years, since Pral Nerol's ship made the one-way journey. Master Tolland could not have known. The more Vengelis thought about it, the less sense it all seemed to make.

"Um. There's something up with this thing. It's making noise," Kristen said to him.

Vengelis sat up straight. "What?"

Another static filled noise came from the small speakers of the remote.

"E-e-emp." A voice spoke.

Vengelis leapt to his feet and ripped the remote from Kristen's hands. He pressed down on his transmission button. "Come in!"

"Emp . . . Venge . . . Vengel—" The unmistakable voice of his Lord General Hoff moaned unsteadily.

"Hoff!" Vengelis said. "Why have you not checked in? I've been trying to reach you and Darien! What the hell is going on out there?"

"I . . . I d-don't . . . " The Lord General's words came in short labored breaths. "Darien . . . defeated."

"*What?*" Vengelis said.

"I—d-dying . . . *he* . . . killed . . . m—"

"Who?" Vengelis shouted furiously. "Hoff what the hell are you talking about? What is going on?"

"I'm s-s-sorry, my lord. I . . . can't . . . breathe. . . . "

"Speak! General Hoff, I order you to speak! What has happened to you?"

A long silence ensued. Vengelis stared expectantly at the small remote. Kristen and Madison quietly watched his body language and listened to his foreign words with a concerned lack of understanding. Then, Lord General Hoff's final crackling transmission came through with a hacking, terrible wheeze followed by a death rattle.

"N-N-Nerol. Nerol is here."

CHAPTER THIRTY-ONE

Vengelis

Vengelis held the remote close, glaring at the stage floor as he tried to wrap his mind around the impossibility of Hoff's words. A sensation of frustration and alarm traveled down the length of his spine. After a prolonged moment of stillness, he suddenly shouted, fully knowing there would be no response.

"Pral Nerol is dead, Hoff. The Felixes killed him in Municera. He's *dead!*"

Another silence.

"What is happening?" Madison asked him nervously.

Vengelis held up a stern hand to silence her. Madison and Kristen exchanged a look of subtle concern at his abrupt volatility. Vengelis thought back, recalling the video feed of Nerol's death in the Municera laboratory when the Felixes had been awakened. Vengelis watched the male Felix, Felix One, kill the old scientist. Or had he? Vengelis's face contorted with concentration as he racked his memory in an attempt to recall every minute detail of Pral Nerol's laboratory video.

"Should I start reading the report again?" Kristen asked.

"Be quiet," Vengelis said, desiring only silence. He held his hand across his forehead and closed his eyes, trying to focus on visualizing the video he had watched so many times aboard the *Harbinger I*. It came back to him vividly. After the Felix had awoken on the steel laboratory table, the machine had proceeded to kill one of the assistants and the warrior Von Krass. Pral Nerol had hit the security alarms just before the video feed went black.

Pral Nerol had *not* been explicitly murdered.

Everyone who had subsequently watched the feed had assumed it, but there was no footage of it. The old man Nerol could still be alive, though it was tremendously implausible. Municera had been utterly leveled, and everyone in the city slaughtered. Vengelis recalled the heat and stench of the burning city with unpleasant clarity. When he had burst through the cloud cover, he had thought the once metropolitan and sparkling Municera to be a vision of hell, destruction incarnate. If Pral Nerol had somehow managed to escape the city, surely the old man would have presented himself in Sejeroreich to aid in Anthem's defense? And even if Vengelis was to make the assumption that the Felixes somehow spared or overlooked Nerol during their rampage, it still did not explain why Pral Nerol would be on Filgaia or how he got there. It also failed to explain why he would have a motivation to murder Hoff and Darien, or, for that matter, how the aging man would even be capable of defeating two of the strongest soldiers in the Imperial Army.

One thing was certain: if Pral Nerol was alive and on Filgaia, he was going to pay dearly for the slaughter he unleashed upon Vengelis's people and proceeded to flee from. There was no choice; Vengelis knew he had to investigate this at once. He turned and looked to Kristen and Madison, who each looked troubled by the sudden severity of his expression.

"I have to leave for a moment," Vengelis said, his voice distant.

"What?" Kristen asked.

"Something has come to my attention. I need to check on it immediately."

Kristen's gaze flickered momentarily to the shattered windows and street beyond. Vengelis glared at her, guessing her intentions of escaping the moment he was not there to hold her and the rest of the convention.

"If you try to escape and slip into the evacuation out of this city, my solution will be to indiscriminately slaughter the migrating masses. Do you understand me, Kristen Jordan? If you choose to take your chances and flee from this room, you will be gambling with millions of lives—including your own."

Vengelis reached out and pulled Kristen close to him by the collar of her shirt. "That means *stay*. It's a command a dog can follow. Let's hope a scientist can, too."

"Fine," Kristen said, straining her head away from him in disdain. "God! I'm not going anywhere!"

"Where are you going?" Madison asked.

"I need to check on something," Vengelis looked out the windows and began to walk toward the empty panes. "You have no excuse not to be here when I return. If the doors to this room are pried open and you two are ordered to evacuate the building by some sort of authority, refuse them. This ballroom is in the only safe building in the city, and—for now—I would like to keep the both of you alive. If you leave, your lives will be in jeopardy. I should be back in a minute."

With that, Vengelis turned from them and accelerated through one of the tall window frames and into the open air and sunlight of the street. There were crowds raging everywhere along the avenue. With all routes off Manhattan destroyed, the would-be evacuating masses were festering and boiling over. Under the imposing overhead displays depicting a decimated Chicago, chaos alone reigned.

Floating over the street, Vengelis stared at the screen of his *Harbinger I* remote and tracked the linked remotes of his Lord General and Royal Guard. Darien's was not being detected anywhere, but Hoff's was blinking from several blocks to the north. The dot of the Lord General's remote remained ominously stationary as Vengelis stared at it indecisively. He ignored the multitudes on the streets and flew north a few hundred feet above the avenue, periodically looking down as he moved toward the flashing location of Hoff's remote. Vengelis did not know which was more concerning, the stillness of Hoff's blinking dot or the total absence of Darien's.

Vengelis soared past a lofty office tower, his lithe reflection moving swiftly across the darkly mirrored windows. A peculiar sight met him from below, and he straightened as he looked down upon the scene of the street ahead. There was a crowd of people huddled around a shadowed mass on the pavement. Vengelis looked back to the monitor in his hand. The flashing location of Hoff's remote was directly where the circle of people had gathered. He glared and cautiously moved forward, his attention darting about the surroundings.

Men and women pressed and crowded around the motionless mass, and as Vengelis neared, he saw it was a prostrate body. With a stunned breath he recognized the unmistakable glint of Imperial First Class armor. It was the lifeless body of Alegant Hoff. Someone had killed his Lord General. Vengelis glared down at his fallen subordinate before quickly raising his vision and squinting sharply into the bright skies all around him. There were just clouds, steel spires, and the wind. The attacker had left in a hurry, whoever it was.

Nerol. Why had Hoff said it was Nerol?

Vengelis descended and touched down on the pavement beside the bruised and bloodied corpse of his highest-ranked general. There was an upsurge of screams and trampling of feet behind him as the men and women watched him descend from the sky. Vengelis stood beside Hoff and looked at him expressionlessly for a long moment, unable to keep his wits afloat in the growing confusion. He glared at the giant's battered backside as he kneeled down to his motionless body and saw the Lord General's armor was cracked and broken in places. Someone had fractured his ribs. Vengelis ran his fingers down Hoff's back and saw evidence of a brutal liver strike—the killing blow. He frowned and let his hand rest on Hoff's lower back. Whoever assaulted him had done so with technical and practiced precision.

People were shouting, though Vengelis was so lost he took no notice of the insurgence encompassing him. With both hands, he reached down and rolled Hoff over on the pavement, pushing the giant Lord General onto his back. Below the thick bristles of Hoff's heavy moustache, a streak of red-brown blood spread across his wide chin and neck. The Lord General's lifeless eyes stared vacantly into the sky.

"Nerol couldn't have done this," Vengelis murmured under his breath and shook his head. Whoever did it was strong, very strong, and certainly not an old man.

A prickly feeling rose on the back of his neck and Vengelis turned, once more searching the brilliant sky above him. He half expected to see the grim outline of a woman floating between the two tall buildings and smiling down at him with blonde hair and blue glowing eyes. Vengelis quickly shook the notion of Felixes from his mind and grabbed hold of Hoff's enormous forearm, pulling the Lord General onto his own shoulder and easily lifting off the ground and ascending gracefully to the top of an adjacent building. He let Hoff's body rest against the backside of a stone ledge. One more Primus life claimed without any semblance of validity or commemoration by this nameless struggle. The last Epsilon placed a hand on his Lord General's shoulder and allowed himself a moment's silence before lifting back into the sky.

Vengelis was actually surprised at the anger he felt over this crime. He tore off the rooftop and flew high into the air over the city, scanning the entire surrounding area. His gaze traced the horizons of endless blue ocean to the east and flat meadowlands to the west. The bright roof of the world was dotted only with the scattering of thin clouds. He looked into the expansive and empty horizons and decided that whatever killed Hoff was surely still in the city, so he brought his gaze back to the rooftops of Manhattan.

Vengelis found himself in a dilemma.

On the one hand, it was his desire—no, his responsibility—to determine what killed Hoff and where Darien was. On the other, it was unbelievably dangerous to leave the one and only sliver of a hope he had at defeating the Felixes, Kristen Jordan, unattended to. He looked down and carefully scanned up and down each avenue and street below. Noxious black smoke rose from one intersection, where the mangled wreck of a helicopter smoldered into the pavement.

Where the hell was Darien? Surely he had fought alongside Hoff against their enemy? Vengelis pulled out his *Harbinger I* remote again and scanned for a location on Darien's remote. The monitor flashed, *no readings in proximity.*

As Vengelis glared at the message, something caught his attention momentarily above the city to the south. It had been nothing more than a dark dot against the light blue backdrop of the sky. He snapped his head up and stared intently in the direction of the movement, hair blowing across his forehead in the breeze. In his peripheral vision he had seen something soar above the buildings and rooftops.

Without another moment's consideration, Vengelis pocketed his remote and erupted toward the collection of skyscrapers to the southwest.

CHAPTER THIRTY-TWO

Gravitas

Floating against the strong winds blowing above the rooftops of Manhattan, Gravitas Nerol carefully scrutinized the streets and avenues of Midtown for any sign of the incapacitated Royal Guard. Gravitas was certain he had seen Darien fall somewhere into this nest of towers, though he was quickly realizing it would be impossible to discern the giant amid the raging disorder and floundering mobs far below. The wounded giant was probably resting in an alley, or perhaps hiding within an office building, his arm hanging maimed and loose at his side.

Gravitas had no doubt the Royal Guard would be calling for reinforcements, though after the slaying of the Lord General, the city would be swarming with Imperial First Class ranks within minutes, regardless of one Royal Guard's call for help. But the fear of more giant soldiers was not anywhere near the culmination of Gravitas's trepidations. The notion of an Epsilon in the city was a larger concern than even a hundred members of the Imperial First Class or Royal Guard ranks. Gravitas could not bring himself to believe what the huge Lord General had told him with that snide and gloating smirk.

The son of Emperor Faris could not be in New York City.

One of the more modern and arabesque buildings under his feet abruptly caught Gravitas's attention. Unlike the main entrances to the other skyscrapers, the pale stone sidewalk outside the front of this glass tower was absolutely deserted. Not a single person was entering or leaving through the huge central doors. Instead, the ant-sized shoulders of suits and blouses were pouring out of a few constricted emergency exits on the side of the building in single file lines. Gravitas glared suspiciously at the incongruity of the bare sidewalk in front of the building. The slow and congested evacuation through the emergency exits contrasted greatly with the torrent of evacuees pouring out of the main entrances in other office buildings. The workers were unmistakably avoiding the main foyer of the building, and there were very few logical explanations.

Gravitas dived down through the open air, passing floors of the surrounding buildings as the sidewalk grew larger and larger in his vision. He landed with a sharp thud and briskly pushed one of the heavy glass doors open and stepped into a huge domed lobby.

The awareness that he was in the abandoned foyer of a national bank barely registered to him as Gravitas surveyed his surroundings. The entire lobby, from the floor to the high ceiling, was carved out of pearly white luxurious marble. To each side there were rows of golden elevator doors, and before him a magnificent sprawling stairway led to the floors above. The big reception desk stood unattended, and several phones were off their hooks repeating faint busy signals. Gentle violin music traveled through the near silence around him, and yet rising over its placid ambiance Gravitas could hear the labored breathing and strained wheezing he had been expecting. The painful moaning and whimpering of an overgrown giant was coming from behind the reception desk. Gravitas paced forward unhurriedly, his steps echoing across the polished marble. He walked around the desk and looked down at the source of the heavy baritone panting.

"So this is the storied courage of a Royal Guard?" Gravitas said to Darien.

The giant soldier was sitting down behind the desk and cradling his limp right arm in his left hand. Beside the Royal Guard were several bodies of people who had been unfortunate enough to be behind the desk when he had burst into the lobby. The giant soldier rolled his head to the side and looked up at Gravitas with a sudden start, beads of fevered sweat covering his face.

"Leave me alone!" Darien cried out and recoiled away from him against a file cabinet.

"Not a chance," Gravitas said coolly.

The massive soldier actually began to plea, looking up at Gravitas from the marble floor. He begged between pathetic sobs. "I was only following orders. What was I supposed to do? The emperor himself ordered me. Please, show mercy! You were in the Imperial Army once! You know that commands have to be followed."

"Not always," Gravitas said, his eyes tired.

"Please!" Darien moaned in agony and hugged his injured arm against his chest. His forearm was hanging loose, attached by nothing but skin. The effect gave his arm an odd rubbery quality. At last Darien fell silent and let his chin fall to his chest. "Then just *kill* me and get it over with, you goddamn traitor."

"You call me a traitor as if it were an insult," Gravitas said.

Darien made a repulsively disapproving face and let out a hacking cough, though no intelligible words came from his mouth.

"Let's go." Gravitas reached out and grabbed him by the nape of the neck, dragging him on his back across the floor. Darien bellowed in pain, and lashed out with his good arm and his mammoth legs. His heels came down and connected with the floor, cracking the solid marble loudly. He kicked straight through the reception desk, sending sundered marble along with folders and papers across the lobby. Gravitas ignored his struggle as he easily pulled Darien, flailing and sliding with a squeaky sound of skin on the polished floor, across the lobby and out the main entrance.

A gathering of onlookers formed almost immediately as an odd-looking young man pulled a gigantic man out of the investment banking building by the scruff of his neck.

The display of weakness by the Imperial First Class warrior within his grasp only added to Gravitas's wrath. Here in Darien was a man so imperceptive that he had never even considered being on the other end of the equation. Here was a person so convinced in both his omnipotence and his perspectives, that to perceive of anything else resulted in the childlike transformation these people were now witness to. There was, perhaps, a time and place where Gravitas would have given Darien clemency, but not today. This day the wounds of this villain's intrusion ran too deep; today Gravitas was begrudgingly answering the roll call of executioner. Darien was too dangerous to be left alive among these people, and there were others like him to hunt down before the day was through.

"I'll do whatever you want! Please!" Darien begged and sobbed.

Gravitas cast him down on the sidewalk. Disbelieving people watched from all around. Some had seen the images on the news of the two deadly giants. Many were pulling cell phones out of their pockets to take a video of the bizarre scene unfolding before their eyes.

"Nerol, please—*please*—show me some compassion. For god's sake not in front of them!" Darien breathed, his face mortified with embarrassment.

"Were it not for my interception of you two and your genocide, everyone in this city would be dead!" Gravitas screamed down at him. "You dare attempt to slaughter so many souls and then ask to be shown compassion? You dare?"

"I'm sorry . . ."

"If you really are sorry, good. But that doesn't excuse you for your actions. You are broken beyond repair."

Gravitas turned to the growing cluster of shocked spectators, who seemed unsure whether he was friend or foe. Closest to him was a group of teenagers standing beside the hood of a recently abandoned Toyota. They could not have been older than high schoolers. One of the girls in a pink hoodie was shaking from head to toe and being held up by two of her friends. All of their faces were overflowing with fear.

"Mortal!" Gravitas roused himself and roared in English to no one in particular. His voice carried across the disbelieving onlookers as he moved his gaze from face to face, every camera phone recording the display. "These giants— though very powerful—are mortal! They are like me. We are not deities, or the agents of any god or devil. There is nothing, *nothing*, magical, religious, or supernatural about us. We are simply more advanced! We are in every way as fallible and foolish as any of you. Do not despair and give in to anguish, for not all of our race are as coldhearted as those who have attacked Chicago, and justice will be brought upon them. You are not alone in this fight."

Darien flailed violently on the ground. Gravitas reached down and grabbed him. He pulled the behemoth up to an unsteady standing position, and pushed him against a street lamp that bent behind his shoulder blade. Darien leaned into the iron and wheezed heavily.

"Y-you stupid little . . ." Darien gasped. "V-V-Vengelis is going to slaughter you."

Gravitas stared at the grotesque Imperial First Class soldier, and again spoke in English, this time just to Darien.

"This is for what you would have done to Kristen Jordan." Gravitas lowered his voice even more. "This is for what you would have done to Ryan Craig."

Without another word, Gravitas cocked his right fist back, ready to execute Darien with one final killing blow.

Just before he uncoiled his strike, a sudden and distinct popping sound emanated from the sky to the north. Gravitas instantly recognized the noise as a rupture of the sound barrier, and for a split second his eyes widened in surprise as he turned his face to the direction of the sound.

CRAAAACK!

A strike like nothing he had ever felt in his life connected with Gravitas's face. His world rolled back, and he felt himself lift and jettison across the street. Gravitas crashed headfirst straight through a building and his body erupted out the opposite end. His back skipped brutally off the pavement of the street beyond. He reached his arms out to steady himself, but his fingers clawed right through the pavement and he flipped backward, smacking into another building and crashing through the exterior wall. Like a wrecking ball he rolled across the first floor of an office building. Desks and cubicle partitions were hurled and thrown in every direction as the veritable typhoon traveled across the office floor.

At last Gravitas's stunned body came to rest, sliding to a stop on his back. Gravitas stared in shock at ceiling tiles and a faintly whirring vending machine. His ears rung and his vision filled with blinking colors. He shook his head and looked dizzily past his legs at the tunnel of destruction his body had bored. An unobstructed path like the trail of a meteor led to where he had stood a moment previous; even cars had been tossed aside by the force of his body.

It felt as though something immensely heavy was forcefully pressing down on his face. Gravitas placed a shaking palm across his cheek and pulled it away to see startlingly bright red blood on his fingertips. His cheek was cut below the eye. Gravitas could not remember the last time he had seen his own blood, and he stared at it in wonder. Whoever hit him was immensely strong, stronger even than Master Tolland.

As he looked at his blood stained fingers, Gravitas knew he had just become acquainted with an Epsilon. He unsteadily rose to his feet and oriented himself with a shake of his head while wiping his bloodstained hand brusquely on his armor. He was not concussed, just rattled. The wind had been knocked out of him, and his breathing was uneven.

There was no other option, no space for reservations or second thought. He had to be victorious.

The warrior side of Gravitas, the animal side, closed its eyes. He transcended into a steadied and practiced concentration. He inhaled stability and exhaled doubt, he inhaled focus and exhaled insecurity, he inhaled strength and exhaled weakness. Powerfully and deeply his chest heaved again and again, each time his breaths becoming stronger and more furious. He allowed himself to absolutely seethe, and he let rage claim him.

At last he exhaled, and when his eyes opened there was a searing fire burning behind them. The entire office seemed to explode as Gravitas Nerol erupted like a raging bull, and charged back through the tunnel.

This was the fight he had waited for his entire life.

CHAPTER THIRTY-THREE

Vengelis

Vengelis watched with a wary expression as the mysterious warrior clad in Imperial Armor reeled backward from his punch. The man's body crashed straight through the building across the street and tumbled out of sight beyond. Deep ringing echoes from the massive strike traveled up and down the avenue of tall offices like the deafening crack of a whip.

The people on the street corner instantaneously scattered, cupping their ears from the sound of the blow and bowing their heads to the pavement. Vengelis remained perfectly still and ready. As the dust cleared, he could see straight through the wrecked building and into the street beyond, where his unknown aggressor had slid and disappeared into a trail of rubble leading into the building one block over.

Vengelis's eyelids shook, not in fear, but in concentration, as he stood at the ready over the wheezing and whimpering Darien. Whom had he just hit? No one was strong enough to defeat Hoff and Darien at the same time, save for a few Royal soldiers.

"M-my lord. I'm . . . s-sorry," Darien gasped by Vengelis's feet. "Thank god you're here. My . . . my *arm!*"

"Shut up," Vengelis whispered, his voice cold and callous. His eyes were still locked on the burrowed tunnel of carnage.

"H-he's . . . like you, my lord. Nerol s-son. Royal . . . blood . . . *trained* . . ."

A hushed moment passed where, perhaps just in Vengelis's focused mind, the entire city block seemed to become still with a pulsing medium of apprehension. Then, the muffled supersonic popping sound Vengelis had been waiting for sounded from the loose debris two blocks over. Vengelis grimaced uncertainly as the mysterious young man sprinted back through the tunnel and charged toward him. His eyes suddenly widened in stunned shock as he realized his antagonist's astonishing speed almost before it was too late. Vengelis had barely enough time to raise his forearms to shield his face before his attacker was within striking distance.

The strange warrior unleashed his own equally powerful strike upon Vengelis. The mighty fist smashed into Vengelis's crossed forearms with a pulverizing strength like Vengelis had never before felt, save perhaps against the Felixes. Vengelis's arms flew to his sides in absorption of the punch, and he staggered backward several steps, nearly falling onto his back. Behind Vengelis, the shockwave of raw energy that traveled past the mirrored windows from the blocked punch had a bomb-like effect on the outer wall of the office building. Darkened panes of glass shattered outward all the way up to the fiftieth floor. Millions of tiny shards fell from the lofty heights like torrential sparkling raindrops in the sunlight, chiming noisily against the pavement and upon the two warriors' impervious shoulders.

The two young men stared at each other wordlessly through the cascade of silvery glass. Not crude and ungainly like most Primus soldiers, the two idols each stared at a strikingly similar manifestation of their own Sejero purity. They were young and lean, relatively thin of shoulder, with striking looks.

They were equals in kind.

Vengelis glared at the dark-haired stranger. The young man was within a year or two of his own age, and perhaps an inch taller than he. He was clad in Imperial First Class Armor, yet Vengelis could not place his face. Vengelis would have considered him a human imposter if not for the startling pain that throbbed through his forearms from deflecting this young man's strength. Although this stranger's cheek was bleeding, Vengelis could not believe how little damage his punch had done.

Yet even in the midst of his total confusion, and the pins and needles in his forearms, Vengelis's face remained a portrait of cool. His calm countenance veiled even the slightest indication of his pain or rising bewilderment. Vengelis watched as the stranger's eyes fixated momentarily on the Blood Ring before returning to meet his gaze.

Vengelis at last broke the silence, his voice carrying over the shimmering shards of glass that fell seemingly from the heavens.

"Who are you?"

"Ryan Craig," the enigma replied.

Vengelis looked doubtfully to his Imperial First Class armor and shook his head slowly.

"No, you aren't. What's your name?"

There was a long silence between them, interspersed only by Darien's guttural moaning from the pavement.

"My name is Ryan Craig," the stranger said. "Though there was a time when I was called Gravitas Nerol."

"*Gravitas* Nerol?" Vengelis repeated, glaring at him disdainfully. "What?"

"You might know of my father, Pral N—"

"Of course, I know Pral Nerol," Vengelis said. "But you're lying. Pral Nerol's son is dead."

"Then you must believe in ghosts to be speaking to me."

This statement left Vengelis speechless for a moment, but he then shook his head in stern disbelief. "Pral Nerol's son died in space during the Orion campaign. I remember reading the report. It was the transport accident; he died with Bronson Vikkor."

"And yet here I am."

"Here you are . . . and quite riled up it would seem." Vengelis frowned as he regarded Gravitas Nerol, coming to the conclusion at once from the radiating pain in his forearms that this stranger must be telling the truth. "I take it you're the one who traveled here on the *Traverser I*?"

Vengelis saw a flicker of confusion pass across Gravitas Nerol's face at the mention of the ship, but he merely nodded. "Yes."

"Why? What the hell have you been doing here?" Vengelis looked about the glass-strewn intersection and frightened faces hiding underneath anything and everything against the killing rain of glass. "You're the son of Royalty for god's sake."

"I have been living. Your father banished me from Anthem upon my return from Orion."

"What are you talking about? Upon *what* return from Orion?"

"When the transport arrived on Anthem, Emperor Faris banished me for—"

"You're lying," Vengelis interjected, frustration and contempt growing in his voice. "I have never heard of my father banishing anyone—let alone the son of a Royal family."

Gravitas shrugged. "Believe what you will. Your father exiled me for killing Bronson Vikkor. I find it strange that your general, Hoff, knew of this, and you do not."

Vengelis flexed his wrists forcefully to dissipate the throbbing in his forearms. He then rolled his eyes impatiently and, unexpected even to himself, reached out to shake Gravitas Nerol's hand.

"I don't have time for this. I am the emperor now, and I pardon you of whatever petty war crimes you committed in the past. There are more important matters at hand. You're the son of Royalty, and our race needs a pure bloodline such as yours during this desperate hour."

"These are my people," Gravitas ignored Vengelis's outstretched hand and looked to the nearby humans shrinking away from them. "And it is to the cause of their desperation that I will rise."

Vengelis glared at Gravitas with growing distaste.

"Look around you. Do you see the Imperial First Class with me? Do you see the Imperial Army razing every city on this archaic globe and the ranks of the Royal Guard standing by my side? It was just three of us—two now because of your recklessness. I will only ask once to take my hand and help us in—"

"Leave," Gravitas Nerol said, his voice rough and furious. "Leave this place now, and never return. *I* will only ask *you* once."

"Excuse me?" Vengelis smirked, though his nostrils flared in rage. His outstretched hand fell to his side as he let out an arrogant chuckle. He shook his head and regarded Gravitas Nerol with amusement and condescension as the strange Royal son held his ground. "Are you threatening me?"

"If I must."

"All right," Vengelis nodded. "We can go down this path too. You did murder my Lord General after all."

"Put him down like the savage dog that he was, yes."

Vengelis raised his eyebrows. "Not much sense of honor for the son of a Royal family."

"You speak of honor after ordering the slaughter of innocent people?" Gravitas asked.

"That word you just said," Vengelis held up a palm, "I'm entirely unfamiliar with it."

Gravitas Nerol inclined his head. "What word?"

"In-no-cent," Vengelis enunciated each syllable slowly with a grave and humorless look. "I only know of its synonym. Weak."

"You sicken me."

Vengelis shrugged his shoulders. He had been right to come investigate Hoff's dying statement that Nerol had been on Filgaia. The concern that Pral Nerol was here or that the Felixes somehow traveled to Filgaia had now dissipated. It was time to end this trivial exchange. Remnants of his people were surely hiding hopelessly in the ruins of Sejeroreich and every city of his empire, and a scientist capable of helping him was within his grasp. He needed to get back to Kristen Jordan as swiftly as possible.

"Look, Nerol, I don't have time for this ridicul—"

"Leave!" Gravitas shouted.

Vengelis sighed. With a wave of his finger he motioned to the stream of blood trickling down Gravitas's cheek. "I think you have something on your face."

For a brief moment Vengelis thought Gravitas Nerol was going to punch him right then and there in response to the slight, but he did not. Instead, to Vengelis's disappointment, Gravitas lifted weightlessly into the air above the pavement and motioned Vengelis upward.

"Follow me."

"Venge . . . he's . . . unbelievably . . . strong . . . b-be careful!" Darien rolled over on the pavement and sputtered the words through a hacking cough.

Without taking his upward gaze off Gravitas, Vengelis followed him.

Gravitas Nerol rose into the sky alongside a slender skyscraper, and Vengelis ascended steadily in his wake. Once the height of the surrounding buildings fell away beneath them, the son of Pral Nerol accelerated southward with a boom, soaring high over the city and into the broad gusty autumn skies above the bay to the south of the island. Vengelis glared at the backside of Gravitas distrustfully. He did not know what to make of this Nerol, but he followed willingly in his path regardless.

The two foreign titans left Manhattan behind and flew southward high over the cold white-capped navy waters of the Upper Bay. The influence of their immense presence was evident everywhere below, and yet the two dark dots in the sky received the attention of none. The waters underneath them were crowded with a convoy of boats and watercraft of every description. With the bridges destroyed, it seemed to Vengelis that the evacuation of the city was taking the form of water transport. Yachts with brilliant sails splashed side by side with hulking rusty barges and cargo boats. All were answering the call of the evacuation. Vengelis disapproved of the futile solidarity. It was only by his prudence that they were still alive and able to evacuate the city at all, and yet here they were—fleeing from his discretion.

After a moment or so, Vengelis turned back toward the city and saw the vast and glinting grandeur of Manhattan—along with the building in its center that contained his one and only hope—shrinking away under a brilliant dome of sky.

"This is far enough!" Vengelis called to Gravitas.

Gravitas reluctantly pulled to a stop in midflight and rounded to face him. Vengelis looked all around them, from the densely packed roofs and spires crowding the shores in every direction, to the bright cloud strewn skies, to the crowding waters below. They had plenty of room on all sides to act as their arena, and he suspected it was not by accident.

"Let me guess," Vengelis called. "This was a precautionary measure against harming them?"

"It was, yes." Gravitas shouted over the winds that blew across the water. "That, and to bring our duel out into the open so this world can watch as justice is brought against you."

"Ah, justice." Vengelis nodded. "So tell me, Nerol, is it the worship of these people that drives you? The total adoration of an entire race, you playing the role of shepherd to their little flock? Do you get off on knowing these oblivious fools think you're God?"

A visible wave of rage passed across Gravitas's face as the wind pushed and pulled at his unyielding shoulders.

"They've never known of my existence. I've lived as one of them since I left Anthem. But if they are to play witness to foreign powers of torment—*gods* in their eyes—then I'll be damned if they don't get a glimpse of foreign forces of good too. They deserve to know there is balance."

"Balance!" Vengelis belted out scornfully. "Spare me. You and I both know there is no balance. There is strength, and nothing more."

"Either way, I know where I am on that scale. And right now my strength stands equal and opposite you."

"Fair enough," Vengelis called. "You see, *Gravitas* Nerol, thanks to your father's recent actions, your family has the blood of a genocide still dripping hot from its hands. So this little endeavor of yours into justice can't hurt the now heinously stained legacy of the *noble* Nerol family."

Darkness passed across Gravitas as foghorns and dinghy bells sounded dimly across the open bay. "What are you talking about?" he shouted.

"Well, I may be responsible for the death of many people today. But your father . . ." Vengelis shook his head and took some enjoyment from Gravitas's suddenly anxious face resultant from his ominous tone.

"What about my father?" Gravitas demanded.

"Your father is responsible for the destruction of our entire race. Soldiers, women, children, it didn't matter. Nothing was of consequence to Pral Nerol in all of his intellectual fortitude. Holocaust will be the last legacy of family Nerol, if anyone even lives to tell of it."

"You lie! My father hated your empire, but he would never have involved himself in killing innocent people."

"Believe what you will. I thought you would like to know that little bit of information before you died. The Nerols, their genocide, and the creation of the Fel—"

"Get out!" Gravitas roared, his voice carrying across the waters and the gray urban horizon. The very atmosphere surrounding Gravitas seemed to rupture and disintegrate in disbelief of his power, and he charged toward Vengelis. With a matching inundation of rage caused by nothing but the sheer audacity of Gravitas Nerol's overconfidence, Vengelis, too, exploded forward with a matching ferocity.

For a splintering second, as the two Herculean dark dots bore down upon one another across the sky like two blazing missiles, it seemed as though time stood still. Only the deep rumbling roar of the two gods' speed could be heard above the din of the bay and its strands of shores. And then,

KRRRRGGGHHHH!

The mortified upturned faces in the overcrowded vessels directly below the collision surely thought a bomb had detonated overhead. The incomprehensible crash knocked people straight off their feet and sent them careening across the slippery decks, and, in a few cases, off their very boats and into the cold swirling waters. People on the barges and sport boats screamed to one another and frantically threw out life preservers and floats; all were temporarily deafened from the impact. From the nearby crowded shores, all eyes turned in dread to the source of the terrible crash over the bay. It sounded as though the very world had split in two.

Though they had each intended to throw a strike at one another, in their blind rage and combined speed, Gravitas and Vengelis instead collided straight into one another in a collision of limbs like two bullets meeting in space.

The colossal impact was blinding. Vengelis barely even realized that he had ricocheted off Gravitas and careened to the side. His head spinning and his vision filling with throbbing pain, Vengelis flipped and rotated through the air. He had completely lost control of his bearings. An overwhelming sting radiated from above his forehead. Vengelis pressed his palm as hard as he could onto his swelling scalp and desperately tried to shake away the disorientation as he plummeted through the sky. After many moments of wild freefall Vengelis realized that instead of exchanging punches, they had inadvertently rammed heads like two charging bucks.

With horrified shock, Vengelis felt a thin stream of hot blood drip past his pressed palm and trickle from his hairline. The blood passed between his eyebrows and ran down the right side of his nose. As it moved past the corner of his lips and off his chin, he could taste its salty bitterness.

Vengelis focused on not panicking. As his vision returned, he saw that Gravitas Nerol was in a similarly discombobulated state, and had nearly fallen into the water of the bay far below. Gravitas was hovering unsteadily a few dozen feet over a giant barge with a greenish camouflaged hull; his face, too, was glistening with blood.

Vengelis watched, his mind filling with insane anger and indignation, as Gravitas shot back up toward him.

CHAPTER THIRTY-FOUR

Kristen

For some time Kristen's gaze lingered blankly on the empty row of windows from which Vengelis had so casually flown out. A feeble portion of her mind held on to the wish that she was dreaming, and would soon wake up in her warm bed. But that collapsing enclave of a notion was rapidly giving in to the certainty that all of this was very real.

Kristen wearily approached the rigid and bent body of Professor Vatruvia and leaned down to check his pulse again. His neck felt stiff against her fingers, and she could find no trace of a beating heart. Beside him on the stage floor, his glasses were broken, both of the lenses cracked down the middle. It was hard to recognize him without the glasses on his face. Kristen wordlessly pushed them into the front pocket of his blazer. She was still in shock. All of this was too much to take in, and Kristen would have thought herself drugged were it not for the anchoring sobriety in her mind.

The strange plane crash in Albany, the heightened national security level before the attack of Chicago, the glimpse of dread upon General Redford's face as he had been informed of flying men moving across the country: all of the pieces fit into place. It was a *War of the Worlds* in true H. G. Wells fashion, with mighty men and their fists instead of towering tripods and their technology. Kristen could not decide which destructor was more unsettling. Of one thing she was certain. Despite the seeming familiarity of Vengelis Epsilon's face and language, he was as unrecognizably cruel as any nemesis of fiction.

For the moment Kristen allowed herself to languish in self-pity as she pushed her palms against her closed eyelids, half sitting, half collapsing onto the end of the stage and letting her sneakers dangle off the edge. She searched the faces of the audience for Ryan, but could not see him. Had he not been in the ballroom when Vengelis barred the doors? A desire to cry rose like a bubble in her throat as she looked in vain for him, but Kristen held it back sternly.

She had to hold on to courage, to logic.

Now with no treacherous otherworldly fiend forcing them into the corner, the audience of professors and researchers began to grow louder and bolder with each passing moment. Yet despite their prestigious educations, their panicked questions of *how* or assertions of *impossible* were no more intelligible than the rising screams in the streets beyond the broken windows. A macabre live news broadcast was still playing on the large projection display above the stage. The program had now split in two, with half of the screen showing an ash-covered news reporter stumbling through the devastation of downtown Chicago, and the other half depicting an aerial shot of the East River littered with floating detritus of bridge remnants and half-sunken windshields.

Madison joined Kristen's isolation at the end of the stage and sat down beside her. Kristen wanted to ask Madison why she had been with Vengelis when he entered the Lutvak ballroom, but she could not stir up the words.

"Do you think he's telling us the truth?" Madison asked her after some time.

Kristen shrugged and cleared her throat, her voice cracking. "We have no way of knowing."

"Yeah."

"Although." Kristen ran her hands over the knees of her jeans, "If Vengelis's true intention is to conquer the world—and based on what we've seen, I do believe it's within his capability—all of these theatrics and specific demands seem rather pointless."

Madison nodded. "That's what I was thinking."

"So, I guess I'm not sure. His actions lead me to believe he really does need our help. That said, I do think he's partly lying, or at the very least not giving us a full picture of his intentions."

"What do you think those machines, the Phoenixes or whatever he called them, did to his world?"

"Felixes."

"Yeah, Felixes."

"I can only guess," Kristen said. "If the Felix technology and Vatruvian cell technology really are one in the same, and if my limited knowledge of the Vatruvian cell is accurate, then the Vatruvian replications are definitely more powerful than he is. But I don't understand what *he* is."

For a while Kristen said nothing and merely listened anxiously to the profound roaring struggle of the city outside.

"I don't understand it," Madison said. "I saw Vengelis run face first into an eighteen-wheeler to prove his strength. Face first. You wouldn't believe the impact. The truck was demolished. I mean . . . demolished. His shoulder . . . flesh and bone . . . crumpled the steel like it was made of paper. Then there's what happened in Chicago. I mean, for god's sake they can fly! None of it is possible."

Kristen shook her head sternly. "According to our laws of science, our constructed reality, it isn't possible. But science is based in observation of the world around us, and in that sense, our witnessing of their power proves it to be irrefutably possible."

"But flying . . . ?"

"I would imagine a higher civilization's technologies are always first perceived as unattainable or fantastical when first witnessed." Kristen looked at Madison intently. "Imagine explaining to someone from the Dark Ages not only what the moon in the night sky really is, but that man has walked—hell, played golf—on its surface. So I'm not dealing in any absolutes here, I'm trying to keep my mind as open as possible. Modern knowledge might be able to provide no answers, but *science* can. Vengelis said their extraordinary power is inherent, that it lies within their genetics. If that's true, then mechanisms of science bestowed that power there. There is nothing impossible or supernatural about them, they are simply foreign to us."

By the windows in the far corner of the ballroom, a small group of scientists had given up on attempting to pry open the blocked doors or sinking into a folding chair and fruitlessly lamenting their situation. Now, wearing white undershirts and tank tops, they were roaming the ballroom and collecting any heavy shirts or blazers people were willing to give up. Two men were tying the arms of the various articles of clothing together to form a makeshift rope. Kristen immediately recognized they were planning to climb down to the street from the shattered windows; they would rappel out of the ballroom.

But where were they hoping to escape?

Together, Kristen and Madison hopped off the stage. Hands buried in the pockets of her sweatshirt, Kristen cautiously stepped across the shattered glass and approached the broad windows overlooking Times Square. She leaned against the window frame and looked out on the city as cool air touched her face. With the breeze came a shiver and a vision that shriveled her soul. Neither she nor Madison could come up with words as they looked out upon the avenue.

New York City was unrecognizable.

If Kristen had thought the dreamlike roar of the riot rising from the streets below was unsettling, the sight of the vast sea of people under her second-floor vantage point was outright nauseating. Midtown looked more like a despairing third-world refugee camp than a metropolitan hub. People were crowding shoulder to shoulder across the entire width of the streets as far as the eye could see, their bodies pushing and leaning in an attempt to move toward the north. The very cars lining Broadway and Seventh Avenue were buried under the cover of humanity, and provided the appearance of rising swells and undulations in the crowd. With nowhere else to occupy their bodies, people were standing on the depressed hoods and caved in roofs of abandoned cars and taxis. Some had even climbed atop street lamps, where they perched with hands held to their foreheads peering northward into the endless bottlenecked multitudes. The first floor storefronts looked looted and mangled. Restaurant and retailer signs hung dangling by wires, and broad awnings were tattered to shreds.

Individual police officers, firemen, and SWAT members were scattered here and there throughout the crowd, their gear lost and their uniforms serving no better purpose than costumes against the incalculable horde of the Manhattan populace. Kristen watched a young man about her age wildly swinging a thick riot shield with the words *NYC SWAT* over his head, the shield now a mere relic of what it once symbolized.

The sheer mayhem was a sight Kristen never could have conjured up in her most vivid dream, for no imagination could fully capture the breadth of this terror. Her legs went weak, her stomach raw. In this hysterical screeching sea of humankind before her, there was no foothold, no niche upon which the enforcement of civil obedience could cling. Words such as order, law, restraint, and authority were all merely indulgences that perhaps had held a place in the city earlier that morning. But such reassurances held no sway over a million-strong mob.

"Dear god," Madison muttered from behind her.

Kristen turned back into the ballroom to see that people from the audience were gathering the courage to move from the rear of the room and look out the windows. They, too, were staring with awe at the collapse of civilization occurring below. At the other end of the windows, shouts began to rise from their ranks as people were demanded to part with their blazer or fall coat so as to add another link to the makeshift rope. Kristen turned shamefully away from a scuffle between two PhDs over a heavy twill sports coat, and saw Madison was looking across the Lutvak ballroom to a navy banner that had been draped across the far wall.

The banner read: *ICST The Future of Man.*

"These people are the future of man?" Madison asked scornfully, indicating the two grown men who were now wrestling across the carpet. "Give me a break. Why do they even want to make a rope? Look outside, there's nowhere to go! We're trapped."

"Yeah." Kristen unwillingly brought her attention back to the miserable sight of Professor Vatruvia up on the stage floor.

"You . . . knew him?" Madison asked.

Kristen nodded slowly.

"I'm sorry."

"He was my boss." Kristen cleared her throat in a detached manner. "Somewhat ironic that Vengelis killed him before they had a chance to speak. He murdered the very man he was aiming to exploit."

"Yeah."

Kristen turned to Madison. "Why were you with Vengelis?"

Madison let out a long fatigued exhale and shrugged her shoulders. "I don't even know. These men attacked me at my work. One had a knife. And then Vengelis came out of nowhere to help . . . he must have been in the crowd. For the life of me I can't imagine what he was doing there."

"Strange," Kristen said.

"He told me New York wasn't safe, and he said all the insane things he later proved without explanation to everyone in here. I thought it was a joke at first, some weird reality TV prank or something. Then he hit the truck. He wanted me to show him where the Marriott Marquis was, so I brought—"

Krrrrghhh!

An immense clapping noise suddenly emanated from outside their building in the far distance. Everything—even the ruckus of the avenue outside—immediately fell quiet. The boom had been loud enough to silence the entire city. Kristen was unconsciously locked in stunned eye contact with Madison, both of their mouths agape. They stared straight through each other's gaze, both straining to listen to the dead silence that now pressed down upon them.

Krrrrrrrgggghhhhhh!

K-K-K-K-Krrrrrrrrghhhhh!

The sounds were eerily reminiscent of a violently intense thunderstorm, though somehow different and unearthly. The cracks were sharper, louder, and more pronounced than a roll of thunder, with a less drawn-out rumble. They were unmistakably the sounds of tremendous impacts, though not of pushing clouds in the lofty ceiling of the atmosphere. The crashes were so loud that it sounded as if the very tectonic plates of the planet were splintering apart, except the noise came from the sky to the south.

Then, as quickly as the strange overhead crashes had begun, they ceased. A long hush ensued, filled only with nervous glances and apprehensive breaths. Then the masses awakened. The crashes, or explosions, or whatever they had been, were the last traumatic nudge necessary for the multitude filling Times Square to reach its final tipping point. An earthquake began to shake the very floor of the ballroom as the avenue outside erupted into a unified and earsplitting wail of stampeding dread. If the masses had been a downtrodden sea of humanity minutes previous, now it was a violent maelstrom of thrashing limbs and screaming faces. The roar of men and women coming in through the open windows was equally as alien to Kristen's ears as the crashes in the sky; the communal roar was a calamitous requiem for the fallen order of their world.

KRRRRGGGHHHH!

The loudest bang yet reverberated from a point directly over their heads. It was as though the center of the storm had shifted to sit above them. A descending torrent of fire and brimstone would have been an appropriate counterpart to the thunderous crashing, yet only clear afternoon sunlight spilled onto the floors through the tall windows. Kristen, along with everyone in the ballroom, visibly flinched and stooped in shock with her arms raised above her head. For a moment she thought she was dead—that the hotel had collapsed down on them. This louder series of cracks sounded from just above them and shook the walls of the ballroom. The chandeliers rattled and swayed against their brackets.

"What is happening?" Madison shouted.

Kristen shook her head, her hands raised to cover her ears. "Don't know!"

"Do you think it's Vengelis?"

Kristen's eyes lingered uncertainly on the ceiling tiles as the booms rattled over and over again from somewhere far above the Lutvak ballroom. She could not bring herself to envision what could possibly be generating the decibels shaking the world around her, though she knew it had to be related to Vengelis.

Madison winced. "It must be him!"

Kristen felt paralyzed. She had seen it on Vengelis's face—something had concerned him. Whatever it was had forced him to leave, and Kristen did not like the idea of what that might entail. Something that concerned Vengelis Epsilon would surely prove to be a concern to her as well.

An upsurge of fierce bangs sounded from the clear skies outside the windows. Instantly the clamor became deafening, and the floor shook violently beneath their feet. Kristen was forced to her knees, and Madison grabbed hold of the windowsill, barely able to stay standing. Her chin tucked to her chest and her hands pressing against her ears, Kristen's painful scream went unheard even to herself.

CHAPTER THIRTY-FIVE

Gravitas

It was the mingled sounds of fever pitched shouts rising from the barge below him that snapped Gravitas out of his incapacitated condition. His mind came to attention, and his body steadied itself from freefall just before he crashed straight through the barge's rusty deck. The entire bay spun round and round in his vision. The dreary water and the bright blue sky were barely distinguishable from one another. His eyes seemed unable to focus on anything. At once, the spires of Manhattan, the wharfs of Brooklyn, and the shores of New Jersey swirled and revolved.

In his daze he squinted at three blurry Statues of Liberty standing side by side across the bay, all three raising a green copper torch into the Atlantic sky.

Gravitas could feel warm blood running down his head from above his right temple. He moved his jaw back and forth and blinked the stars out of his vision as he cursed his recklessness. The fight had just begun, and he was already concussed. He trained his gaze on the unsteady horizon and tried to focus on ridding the growing daze in his consciousness. Wind touched a clammy sweat on his cheeks and brow, and he forcefully quelled the rising queasiness in his gut and turned to search for Vengelis Epsilon. As he raised his head, Gravitas could feel the stream of blood change its course and run behind his ear and into his armor.

The dark form of Vengelis was thankfully easy to identify contrasting against the clear sky overhead. He was visibly moving back and forth unsteadily. Gravitas latched onto one hope: that even if Vengelis was stronger than he—

which had yet to be determined—Gravitas would prove tougher than the Epsilon. Without a second thought, Gravitas erupted upward at Vengelis with a swerving wobbly charge.

As Gravitas accelerated toward Vengelis, he could hear the Emperor of Anthem scream in unintelligible infuriation. Instead of repeating the same careless stroke once more, this time Vengelis Epsilon held his skyward position and readied himself for impact. Gravitas flexed his midsection and forced his dizzied body into a ferocious swinging kick at Vengelis's side.

But Vengelis was too quick.

The Epsilon turned his body to the side, flexing each of his arms together. Gravitas's uncoiled shin connected powerfully, not with tender ribcage, but with Vengelis's iron biceps. Just as the deafening ring of the impact boomed across the immensely populated shores of the bay, Vengelis pulled up his forearms and grasped Gravitas's leg like a vice.

"Got you!" Vengelis said, his face furious, and launched himself forward while holding Gravitas's leg in his arms. Gravitas flung his free limbs outward and teetered to maintain his balance as he was pushed backward, reeling across the sky in Vengelis's grasp. Salty moisture from the bay touched his face as he frantically considered his next move. Gravitas steadied his upper body as best he could to deliver a swift punch to Vengelis's exposed face. But the moment he did so, he was shocked to feel Vengelis skillfully figure four his legs around his own trapped hamstring and attempt to put Gravitas in a heel hook that would tear every tendon in his knee within seconds.

Gravitas recognized the subtle beginning steps of the submission move as though it were a sixth sense. He had defended the specific maneuver Vengelis was attempting every day for half of his childhood, though the fact that this Epsilon knew how to execute such an intricate submission was deeply unsettling. It was not the kind of move taught by the Imperial First Class.

The figure four had been one of Master Tolland's favorite moves.

Knowing the only functioning counter quite well, Gravitas twisted his body in a tactical position, keeping his knee at a protected angle as he stretched and grabbed Vengelis's exposed ankle. Gravitas rolled his own upper body around, swinging Vengelis by his now vulnerable foot.

Yet Vengelis, too, seemed to know counters, and Gravitas was even more surprised as the Epsilon expertly rolled his entire body in a sleek motion and freed his foot from the grasp.

The limbs of the two Sejero sons untangled, and Gravitas and Vengelis spun free in the gusty air. They faced each other in astonishment, each regarding the other in equal bewilderment and breathlessness.

"A heel hook counter," Vengelis called. "Impressive."

Gravitas stretched his knee out gingerly and shook his head in disapproval of his own carelessness. The fight had been a moment from ending, and his leg snapping in two. This would be no uncouth Imperial First Class fistfight. Vengelis Epsilon knew how to handle himself.

"I'm impressed, too. You almost got me with that leg lock. Almost. Ready to give up and leave yet?"

Vengelis smirked.

"Just leave," Gravitas yelled, exasperated. "No one will know you retreated."

Vengelis shook his head. "Can't."

This time it was Vengelis's turn to charge. He accelerated and launched his fist into a punch, which crashed into Gravitas's quickly raised arms. Without hesitation, Vengelis wound up and swung out again in an attempt to breach through Gravitas's defenses. At once, the individual blows transitioned into an indiscernible flurry of stinging strikes against Gravitas's raised arms and midsection; Vengelis cycled between face and stomach hits, forcing Gravitas to flex his abdomen as hard as he could and fall back into total defense. Each sustained impact of fist on forearm or elbow against gut sent a disproportionate boom echoing and rumbling across the chaotic waters of the bay and through the city to the north. It was as if the very world around them was in total submission to their power, incapable of shielding itself even against the mere sound of their struggle.

After barely sustaining Vengelis's initial explosion of strikes, Gravitas lowered his guard and began returning blows. And so the two Royal sons engaged in a turbulent back and forth exchange while involuntarily moving northward back toward Manhattan. They pushed and pulled at each other violently, each trying to get the upper hand of momentum as they moved miles across the open water. With a roar and a sudden surge of strength, Vengelis pulled a few feet away from Gravitas and savagely swung out at him, catching him directly in the face.

Gravitas felt the knuckles snap against his exposed nose.

Seeing a first genuine window of opportunity, Vengelis lurched forward in an attempt to bombard Gravitas with an overwhelming barrage of strikes. But once more Vengelis underestimated him. His right fist missed terribly as it flew past the space Gravitas's cheek had inhabited a moment previous, and Gravitas buried a blind knee directly into his stomach. The air audibly deflated from Vengelis's lungs like a popping balloon, and he staggered back. Gravitas took no delay in his follow up. He sunk three brutal fists into Vengelis's unprotected face before Vengelis rolled his body to the side and slipped out of the way.

They turned to face each other once more, and Vengelis gaped blankly at Gravitas as blood surfaced and spouted from the swelling wounds on his cheek and nose. Deep crimson droplets of pure Sejero blood dripped from his face and were carried away in the sea breeze; each drop a preternatural jewel of immeasurable power and magnificence eternally lost. Vengelis watched the blood fall off his own face, and Gravitas knew his mind; surely the Epsilon viewed the drawing of his own blood as an unspeakable crime. Gravitas floated poised and ready as Vengelis turned from his own falling blood to meet his gaze.

Gravitas's stomach was tender from his sustained blows, and the lake of dizziness in his head was getting deeper. He knew now without a doubt that he had sustained a concussion, but he also knew that he stood alone between this man and a complete domination of everything he held close. There was a singular line in the sand—or in his case, the sky—standing between Vengelis Epsilon's selfish rage and the fragile hopes of billions. He alone could champion that deserted line, and it had to hold. His expression hardened to steel despite his condition, and Gravitas shook the throbbing from his forearms.

They had somehow managed to move back over Manhattan, and both of them looked down, panting and heaving, toward the churning disorder of streets below. Gravitas prayed the government and the media had noticed his presence; that they realized the implications of the thundering occurring *above* the city and not within, that where Chicago fell in minutes, New York still endured. Yet in the streets he now saw, there was no such optimism, no silver lining, for the countless horrified souls he looked down on.

"Look what you've done!" Gravitas shouted. "In one day you've ruined thousands of years of social evolution. You've *ruined* an entire civilization on a whim."

Vengelis heaved for breath and spat blood streaked spit into the wind. "Please. They'll be fine. Our ancestors managed, didn't they?"

"We're gods to them. Gods." Gravitas groaned in fatigue. "Do you understand? Can you grasp the magnitude of your actions, as a god? By our decency we could have generated a movement of goodness unparalleled in their history. We could have given them everything that was not given to us; *hope* in something *greater!* Where Anthem met only apocalypse at the hands of a higher species, we could have given them a bright light, we could have been the example for their future. It was within our power to protect them from the horrors our people had to endure. It was our responsibility to protect them. And instead look down at them now, look at what you've done to them. You've taken any belief they held in morality by the reigns and ran it straight into the ground!"

"I don't give a damn about them! My responsibility is to my own people—to Anthem! Do you think I am so imperceptive that I don't see your perspective? Don't flatter yourself! You don't need to explain it to me; they are words I already know. But your point of view is selfish. You hint at responsibility, but you know *nothing* of it. You've never led men. And you've never had anyone depend on you to be hard when it's so much easier to be soft. Do you see this ring?" Vengelis held up his hand. His knuckles and forearms were purple and beginning to swell from the blows he had already delivered and received. The Blood Ring glinted on his finger in the afternoon sunlight. "This ring means I don't have the luxury of being philosophical! This means I *alone* can save my race—*our* race—from oblivion. So spare me your naive accusations. You are playing the roll of ill-conceived guardian to these simple people, and that's fine. Win and you'll be their hero; die and you'll be their martyr. But you and I both know there is another existence, another point of view, a greater race—your race—that sees you as the traitor, and me as the hero. I'm here to find a way to save my people from ruin, and nothing, including some one-dimensional fool, will stand in my way."

A silence fell between them, punctuated by sounds of the indiscriminate riots below.

"Your move, then," Gravitas called. "Because I'm not going anywhere until you are either off this planet or dead. I won't let one race be sacrificed for the good of another."

"You know what your problem is?" Vengelis said, a broad stream of blood now rolling down his face. The wind whipped at their shoulders and the roar of the chaos erupting in between the buildings below nearly drowned out his voice. "You're unwilling to acknowledge the simple truth that life is cold and merciless."

"Whatever allows your diluted mind to justify a slaught—"

Gravitas suddenly choked and hitched as a gigantic arm, moist and sticky with cold sweat, wrapped around his neck and placed him in a textbook chokehold. His eyes widened in stunned and horrified panic, and he knew at once that it was Darien's arm.

The giant Royal Guard had evidently found some inner courage and overcome the pain of his dislocated elbow. With wide and welling eyes, Gravitas realized that Darien must have risen from the pavement and snuck up behind him. Had Vengelis merely been keeping him distracted with their words? Had he been smugly watching as the giant snuck up on him?

Darien floated sturdily behind Gravitas, his one good arm wrapped securely around his windpipe and his gargantuan legs wrapped around Gravitas's lower half like constricting snakes. Darien's massive head was pushing against Gravitas's shoulder, and he whispered to Gravitas in a hoarse voice, "Got you now."

In front of Gravitas, with blurring vision as blood pooled behind his eyes and asphyxiation began to claim him, Gravitas watched Vengelis smile miserably.

"Wow," Vengelis called appreciatively. "Darien, you have proven yourself a worthy soldier. A true Royal Guard—our people would be proud."

"You . . . got . . . it," Darien wheezed through gritted teeth.

"As I was saying to you, Nerol," Vengelis continued. "You are unwilling to accept that life is cold and merciless. Take your current plight for instance. Here you were, rising—quite impressively—in an attempt to save people who, if they knew of your existence, would only fear and plot against you. Look how fate has repaid you. As we speak you are being strangled to death by a vastly inferior soldier with the knowledge that I will kill many more of the people you were trying to save if I deem it necessary."

Gravitas heaved and pushed at Darien's arm, but it felt like an immovable object to his quickly weakening arms and legs. He swung his head back and forth in hopes of headbutting the giant's nose and kicked his feet back in hopes of kicking Darien's groin. Not wanting to underestimate him, Darien was holding nothing back, and squeezing his neck as hard as he possibly could. Gravitas could feel the giant's entire body shaking from the hold. In his fatigued and concussed state, Gravitas knew he was powerless.

Vengelis came closer and raised a palm to his own scalp, dabbing the blood stoically and rubbing it between his thumb and index finger.

"Anticlimactic isn't it?" Vengelis murmured introspectively, though loud enough for Gravitas to hear. "I've been in your position, you know, Nerol. The exact situation you're in right now, though against far more terrible and pitiless enemy—the true enemy. I remember the feeling of consciousness slipping into black as your whole world descends to ruin around you; the overwhelming feelings of both resentment and inadequacy rising like vomit. Atrocious, isn't it?"

Gravitas flailed and thrashed at Darien, but found him unyielding to any counter. He could feel Darien's hot breath touching the side of his face as the goliath panted and shook with exertion. Gravitas stared at the blurry Vengelis with a burning hate. He tried to call out, to swear furiously at Vengelis Epsilon, but found himself only able to make a gagging sound as he frothed at the mouth. His vision became darker by the moment, and Vengelis's description of his sentiments proved quite accurate.

Vengelis looked at the interlocked bodies of Darien and Gravitas and shook his head grimly.

"You are a powerful warrior. You have proven yourself, and you deserve a seat among our forefathers. But—regardless of what some might say—I am a man of principles, and I am afraid ours are simply not compatible."

Without another word, Vengelis burst forward, launching toward the restrained Gravitas. With no way of defending himself, Gravitas knew it would be a killing blow. Gravitas shut his eyes, and for a fleeting moment he thought of a dream that was Anthem, was Orion, was Earth, and the hopes they all once had.

KRRRRGGGHHHH!

Gravitas's left ear felt like it exploded inward as a definitive collision echoed across the rooftops of the city. Eyes still closed, he felt a twitch move through Darien's bicep and forearm. The giant's arm then completely let go from his neck. As the pressure released from his windpipe, Gravitas gasped for breath and opened his eyes. Vengelis was floating silently a few feet from him, staring below them with an unreadable expression.

Lowering his gaze to where Vengelis was looking, Gravitas saw Darien, his facial structure unspeakably mangled, plummeting lifelessly toward the streets of Midtown. He turned back to Vengelis and watched as the Epsilon stared wordlessly at his soldier's body as it fell among the skyscrapers.

With his one chance at a killing blow, Vengelis had chosen Darien.

"I—I can't . . ." Gravitas coughed and hacked as he massaged his reddened neck. "I can't . . . believe—"

"Don't," Vengelis said, his tone more a request than a command, as he drew his wearied and bruised gaze away from the falling body of Darien and met Gravitas's stare. "Just don't."

CHAPTER THIRTY-SIX

Kristen

The skyward crashes expelled any chance the Lutvak ballroom had at regaining its composure. Much like the open avenue outside the tall windows, the boulder of rationality within the ballroom had been tipped over the precipice; now it rolled out of control with seemingly no end in sight.

"Maybe we're winning," Madison said. "Maybe the Army or—or the Air Force is fighting them."

Kristen shrugged, her hands intertwined against the belly of her sweatshirt. "It's possible, but I seriously doubt it. I think it's safe to say Vengelis and his people are powerful on a scale beyond our reasoning."

They were standing in the sunlight near the windows, their attention turning from the unspeakable madness out in Times Square to the news broadcast on the projection screen above the stage that was now reported failing infrastructures and widespread rioting in every major city in the United States. Every so often an Emergency Alert System message would disrupt the CNN studio. It advised people to stay in their homes, to lock their doors, to think of their own survival.

Still there was no sign of Vengelis.

"I know what you said about us not being able to comprehend technology of a more complex people," Madison said slowly. "But Vengelis and those giants *aren't* technology. They're people. How can people be so strong?"

Kristen acknowledged that Madison had a point; it did not seem to make any sense. Vengelis had told her technology itself was inferior when compared to his inherited abilities. The nature of his power was inescapably far more complex than anything she knew, but that did not mean it could not be understood.

"He said their power was derived within their heredity, that it's in their very genome. Sejero genetics, he called it. He was hesitant in discussing it, guarded, like he didn't want to reveal too much to me."

"You would really want to know more?"

Kristen turned to Madison skeptically. "You wouldn't?"

"Well, yeah, I suppose I would. But as you said, it's technology beyond our reasoning. What does it matter?"

"That's exactly what I'm not so sure about." Kristen stared expressionlessly across the arguing researchers in the ballroom. "What if it isn't so much *advanced* technology as it is a *foreign* technology?"

"It's not technology at all," Madison insisted. "Those monsters brought down the buildings in Chicago with their bare hands. I cannot bring myself to believe that's the result of technology."

"Maybe," Kristen said. "But think about it. An ant can lift something five times its body weight over its head, and drag something twenty-five times its own body weight. That would be equivalent to, say, a human lifting something one thousand pounds clear over her head with ease, and dragging around something that weighed over five thousand pounds."

Madison rolled her eyes. "Yeah but—"

"All I'm trying to say is that disproportionate body weight to strength ratios do exist, even here. So does flight, along with any number of the other things we've seen them do today, albeit not on their scale. But evolution works by fostering diversity, and it isn't a directed force. Vengelis's people have obviously found a way to tamper with genetics and expand their possibilities on a grand scale."

"How could they go about doing that?"

"I'm not sure. I've spent the majority of the last few years figuring out how to replicate genes, not figuring out how they came to exist in the first place."

At that moment, a windowpane beside them shattered, and Kristen recoiled in alarm. A heavy yellow pedestrian crossing sign clattered to rest among the splintering shards of glass, its frayed wires hanging out of its exposed innards. It had been wrenched from the side of a lamppost and thrown up through the window. Within the ballroom, the entire audience partook in a singular self-pitying bawl of torment, as though the infiltration of the violent unrest into the Lutvak ballroom was an inevitability.

"Are you okay?" Madison said and pulled Kristen away from the glass smithereens now strewn across the floor.

"Y-Yeah." Kristen ran her gaze and shaky palms over her body to check for cuts. The heavy yellow box had missed her by a foot, and the window had shattered at her feet. Powdery specks of pulverized glass were clinging to Kristen's shoes and the bottom of her jeans like little diamonds. Beyond that, the shattered pane had done no damage to her. *Don't Walk* was still flashing in flagging letters on the crossing sign.

Kristen felt a strange swell of heartbreaking sorrow as the flickering words on the sign guttered out and disappeared. What chance did the architecture and unity of the civilized world have against the peril of such supreme adversaries? Maybe it was the initial shock of her quandary waning, or a sudden realization of the worldwide implications of the events occurring around her. Regardless of the cause, the sudden sadness for the vulnerable integrity of her world allowed her mind to focus on the bigger picture.

"Maniacs. I swear they're going to cause more damage than those giants did to Chicago," Madison said, and turned to the window farthest from them. Some of the audience members were lowering their improvised rope out of an opened window and tying the other end securely to the leg of a heavy table.

"Where are you planning on going?" Madison called out to them.

"Anywhere!" one of the men yelled back. "We're not waiting for that goddamn demon to come back, and the Emergency Alert Broadcasts are saying for people not in safe locations to make for the Hudson River."

Kristen cautiously approached the window to get a glimpse of the street below, taking care to keep herself protected behind the broad framework between the windows in case any more projectiles were sent her way. The crowds outside actually seemed to have pacified slightly, and many of the people crowding around the abandoned cars and ruined sidewalks were not partaking in the anarchy. Instead they were staring skyward and shielding their eyes from the sun's glare. They were pointing in disbelief into the sky between the tall buildings.

"What are they looking at?" Madison asked behind her as she, too, approached the open window.

"I don't know."

They exchanged an anxious glance, and, after scanning the people below for any throwing weapons, Kristen leaned out the window. She craned her neck and squinted up past the long height of the glinting Marriott Marquis. Something was falling through the bright sky. It was the unmistakable shape of a body falling silently from the heavens. The body was gargantuan, its hulking limbs hanging loose in the air. Kristen stared up at the falling being. Although it was plummeting in freefall, the body had a surreal and tranquil look to it as it descended silently toward the earth. Then she saw the familiar glint of armor. It took only a moment for Kristen to recognize the slowly spinning and rotating form.

"Well? What is it?" Madison asked.

Kristen looked back into the ballroom, her expression bewildered. "I don't understand. It's—"

A strange thud sounded from the intersection outside and rose over the hubbub of the riots. The impact was reminiscent of a slab of meat smacking down against a butcher's block.

"What the hell was that?" Madison frowned and stepped forward as Kristen also turned back to look out the window.

A little ways down the avenue, prostrate and still against the pavement, was the body of one of the giants Vengelis had introduced to Kristen. It looked as though in the last moment, the people in the body's trajectory had managed to move out of its path. A generous width of pavement separated the massive corpse and the surrounding circle of dismayed bystanders. Kristen could not bring herself to comprehend the sheer size of the man—if the giant could indeed be called a man at all. The grotesquely thick legs and arms took up nearly half the street, and the mass of his unmoving chest and midsection was analogous to the girth of the cars adjacent to his lifeless body. The giant's neck was angled in an unnatural position—as though his spine had been snapped—and it looked as though every bone upon his bloody face had been broken.

"What . . . the . . . hell?" Madison breathed, horrified, as she looked down at the body. This sentiment seemed to be the consensus of the avenue below, as everyone seemed to take a momentary respite in order to stare at the monstrous body and then turn to look into the sky.

Kristen stared, her mouth hanging open. "I have no idea."

"Is he dead?"

Kristen shook her head numbly as she looked at the corpse. "I don't know. I think so, right?"

"I don't understand," Madison said. "I thought they were invincible? We must have figured out a way to kill them!"

"I'm not so sure."

"We *must* have figured out a way."

Kristen could not look away from the beaten giant. She did not know what to make of this, and she recalled the trace of fear that had claimed Vengelis before he left them. "Vengelis said they were invincible to our technologies."

"Well, clearly he lied!" Madison said.

Kristen strained her eyes to see the giant's mortally wounded face. The mangled features looked more like it had received a blunt trauma impact, like it had been bludgeoned. "I can't imagine what could have done that damage to him," she said. "It looks like he was beaten to death."

"Kristen," Madison exhaled. "Look."

Kristen hesitantly moved her attention away from the giant body, and she immediately noticed every face in the avenue was staring into the sky. Their upturned expressions made her suspect that whatever it was, it would not prove heartening. Resigning herself to whatever she was about to see, Kristen threw back her head and looked skyward.

Just over the skyscrapers, which cast shade over Times Square, there hovered two dark figures. Kristen squinted at the two dots against the bright blue sky. "What are those?"

"They look like people, don't they?"

"It's Vengelis," Kristen said.

With the undivided attention of the entire city block, the two moving figures suddenly shot toward one another and collided.

KRRRRGGGHHHH!

At once, Kristen and everyone else registered what the thunderous crashes had been: a battle between titans was raging over the city. The realization did not have a pacifying effect on the crowds below, but Kristen could not take her eyes away from the two darting figures above the buildings as she winced with each deafening boom caused by their impacts. She was all but certain that one of them was Vengelis, but who was the other? It was not a giant; the sizes of the two forms looked similar.

"It has to be Vengelis," Madison gasped.

Kristen nodded.

"But who's the other one?"

"I can't imagine."

The ballroom rattled and shook from the brawl overhead. Back and forth the two bodies soared across the sky, disappearing and reappearing behind the mirrored sides of the skyscrapers. Kristen could barely follow their movements, and quickly lost track of them.

"Oh my god!" Madison suddenly shrieked. Kristen looked to where she was pointing and saw that one of the figures had been thrown straight through the top floors of a skyscraper up the avenue. Like a bullet, the dark body pierced a narrow hole through one end of the building and erupted in a pluming wreckage of rubble and dust out the other end. Kristen pulled back from the window frame and slumped down against the wall, feeling dizzy as the blood drained from her head. What they were witnessing looked so unreal, so impossible, and yet even as she tried to steady her breathing she could hear bits of the falling rubble hit the street some way up the avenue.

"It's okay. I think the building is going to hold!" Madison called over the rising cries engulfing them.

Kristen tried desperately to control herself as she looked up and watched the rampant chaos unfolding around her. At the far end of the room, men and women were frantically clambering over one another to grab hold of the makeshift rope of clothing and rappel awkwardly down the side of the building to the street. The news broadcast on the projector screen was depicting footage of the gaping hole upon the side of the building just to the north of them, with the word *live* blinking in big letters. Kristen could see the Marriott Marquis among the other skyscrapers in the background of the broadcast. They were in the center of a warzone. The storm of screams rising from the street was now so shrill that Kristen could barely hear her own thoughts. She raised her head and peeked out the window to see the corpse of the dead giant on the pavement. It was as though the corpse was magnetically charged, and repelling the people nearby. They understandably kept their distance, in fear that the monster would awaken at any given moment and start rampaging through the avenue.

"We can't . . ." Kristen said to no one in particular, her voice drained out by the shouting. She interlocked her hands on top her head. "We can't be powerless like this. We can't be defenseless."

"Who could Vengelis be fighting?" Madison shouted into Kristen's ear, her eyes still staring intensely out the window.

"This . . . this can't happen." Kristen unsteadily rose to her feet and looked at the body of the giant. A not quite tangible idea was beginning to surface in the back of her mind. "Sejero . . ." She murmured, unheard.

"What if this building collapses?" Madison asked as she recoiled from the terrified insurgence outside the window. The researchers were now pouring down the makeshift rope, obviously concerned of the same threat. "What if the hotel isn't safe? Kristen what should we do?"

"Listen!" Kristen shouted and grabbed Madison by the shoulder. "We're not safe!"

Madison looked at Kristen as if she had uttered the most apparent exclamation imaginable. "No kiddin—"

"I mean, we, as a world, are not safe!" Kristen screamed at the top of her lungs directly into Madison's ear. "Whoever, and whatever the hell they are, they've already proven they don't give a damn about us. Do you know what happens when two societies clash and one is inferior?"

"I—" Madison could barely hear her.

"The lesser society gets wiped out!" Kristen screamed. "Whether it happens in a day or a hundred years—they get *wiped out!* We won't be able to survive against them! We won't endure, in my heart I know we won't!"

"I've noticed!" Madison yelled.

"We—as a race, as an entire way of life—are *doomed* if we can't figure out a way to stand our ground!"

"Yes, I realize this!"

"Listen!" Kristen stepped closer to Madison, the gathering audience by the windows pressing against them on all sides. "I—I have an idea!"

Kristen turned back and strained to look at the bloodied giant. People were pouring past the huge body, not daring to go near it. She then turned to Madison and shouted into her ear, "We have to get down there!"

"What?"

Kristen sprinted across the ballroom, moving from table to table madly pushing laptops out of the way and throwing papers and exhibits off of the assembled display tables as she frantically searched for something. Any box she found she upturned violently, spilling the contents across the floor.

"What the hell are you doing?" Madison demanded as she followed her.

"Looking for something!"

"Why?"

"Because," Kristen called as she ransacked a bovine lymphocyte display table. "What's the need to *understand* a technology if you can *copy* it? We may only have one shot at this!"

"What do you mean? What are you talking about?" Madison shouted, trailing Kristen in confusion.

At last Kristen opened a small cardboard box and glared triumphantly at what she had been looking for. She reached into the box and pulled out an empty glass slide. It was a simple tissue slide, two thin pieces of glass that were clear against her fingers. Kristen carefully placed it back in the case as Madison called out more questions. She jogged to the Vatruvian cell table and picked up her backpack, placing the box with the glass slide inside and throwing the bag over her shoulder. She tightened the straps around her shoulders and turned to Madison with a rising look of passion.

"I'm going to get a sample of their blood."

"What?"

With the fear that the Marriott Marquis would collapse any moment, the researchers were now simply jumping out of the windows of the Lutvak ballroom and onto the heads of the crowd below.

"I may not be able to understand Sejero genetics, or even the most fundamental aspects of their strength. But if I can get their DNA, if I can get a sample of their genetic code, I can try to replicate their power."

"Replicate their power with what?"

Kristen's face hardened, and she cast Madison a sobering look. "The Vatruvian cell."

CHAPTER THIRTY-SEVEN

Vengelis

Vengelis watched Gravitas rub his fingers over the enormous dark red marks left by Darien's arm on his neck. Tiny capillaries had ruptured under Nerol's skin and left deep purple blotches. Together the two of them lingered over the clustered rooftops and spires in a momentary respite from their struggle.

"You killed him for trying to help you?" Gravitas called to Vengelis over the roar of the streets.

A gust of wind touched Vengelis's face and he could feel its presence thicken the blood running down his cheek. The thumping of his pulse was sending surges of pain past his forehead to the back of his skull and down his back. It took all of his willpower not to visibly wince from the sharp pain. He was encouraged by Gravitas's battered state, but he was in no better condition.

"Darien had no place interfering in a fight beyond his abilities," Vengelis said.

"So you killed him?"

"I'm a man of principle, Nerol, even if you choose to believe I'm simply a tyrant. I have the courage to act on my convictions; a trait in which you and I are evidently alike, I suppose."

"The only thing you and I have in common is that neither of us belong here, and very soon one of us won't be."

Vengelis smirked despite the pain coursing through him.

"Your troops are gone. You are alone. Once again I offer you the choice to leave," Gravitas said. "Go back to Anthem and forget this place exists. It's a win-win: this planet can return to life as normal, and you can return to your throne."

A dismal and rumbling laugh emerged from the bottom of Vengelis's chest and spilled out of him. "You think those crude fools Hoff and Darien had any effect on my chances of survival—or yours? Don't insult our power, Gravitas Nerol, you're a son of Royalty."

"I take no pride in my power, and neither should you."

"Spare me," Vengelis said. "It was the power of our blood that allowed for our race's survival. If it weren't for the Sejero strength you seem to be so ashamed of, our ancestors—along with all of Anthem's natural life—would have been used as mere fertilizer for the Zergos, our entire history and existence blown to oblivion in a day. Instead we—*we*—rose up and defended our world. I would think you would exercise your Sejero gifts with a greater degree of respect. I mean for god's sake you've spent the last four years pretending to be one of them. How can you live with yourself? You slander and turn your back on all your ancestors fought and died for."

"*My* ancestors!" Gravitas shouted and pounded a finger to his own chest. "Fought for the cause of those weaker than themselves. They protected a fragile world from a gross enemy that was otherworldly and ruthless. Today I believe I follow in their footsteps."

Vengelis's mouth fell open. "How dare you compare me to the Zergos, Nerol. You go too far. How dare you! You are nobody, a pathetic nobody hiding from his gifts and his responsibilities. Nothing but a stale, conventional fool filled with the opinions and platitudes of weak men," Vengelis said, his face turning red. "Men too weak to act. I am emperor, Nerol. And I need to act now, not for my own whimsical interests, but for the good of my people. I alone can do this, or my—*our*—existence will fall."

"The people here have an expression that might interest you, emperor: 'With pride comes the fall.'"

Vengelis looked down at the riots below. "A lot of good that logic is doing them today, these noble savages of yours."

Gravitas made to say something else, but Vengelis had heard enough. He darted forward and drove a fist into Gravitas's quickly raised forearms, then swiftly raised a knee to block an irate counter kick from Gravitas. Once more the very atmosphere began to tremble as their strikes detonated over the rooftops of the city. Here and there a blow would slip past one of their nearly perfect defenses and cause brutal damage.

Vengelis had never experienced anything like it. His heart rate had never been so high, even in the most vicious of his spars and duels. The feeling was foreign to him. He was no longer breathing, but instead was sucking in gasping inhalations: his quick breaths matching the racing pace of his heart. In the brutal swapping of blows, Vengelis reached and exceeded his threshold of exhaustion. They each became blind with rage and ferocity.

Vengelis tried desperately to keep his mind lucid and not give in to his frustration. A slip up against an opponent like Gravitas Nerol would end the fight. Though no intelligible words crossed Vengelis's tenacious mind, his conscious was going ballistic with frustration and bewilderment. It was true that Nerol was Royal blooded and not some half-bred giant. But even in his early teens Vengelis had brutally demolished many Royal fighters who had been overconfident enough to challenge him. He had easily cast all of them aside as amateurs, vastly inferior to his overwhelming strength, speed, and resolve.

How was Gravitas Nerol so strong?

Then, as Vengelis began to come around to the mortal danger he was truly in, it was Gravitas that made the first blunder. Surely as exhausted as Vengelis, Gravitas missed his target—the tendons in Vengelis's right knee—with a powerful kick. His leg swinging at nothing but air, Gravitas staggered forward in space, losing his balance and tumbling forward for a single breath.

Vengelis did not hesitate. The moment Gravitas's body slipped unintentionally forward, Vengelis raised a left fist, sending it barreling into Gravitas's chin. Gravitas's head rocked back from the blow, and as it came forward again, stunned and discombobulated, Vengelis's right fist came up and caught Gravitas on the cheek. He could feel bone break against his knuckles. Vengelis then grabbed Gravitas by the arms and launched his hips into him as he spun around with all his might. Roaring with exhaustion, Vengelis released Gravitas and sent him spinning through the air.

Gravitas's body careened straight into the side of a skyscraper as Vengelis instantaneously dropped his hands to his knees and wheezed over and over again, his lungs barely able to supply his brain with enough oxygen to maintain consciousness. Below him the people roared as bits of maimed skyscraper fell from the sky. A wide cloud of gray-white dust rose into the blue skies from the opposite side of the building, where Gravitas exited the structure.

Vengelis thought he was going to pass out from the exertion.

Gravitas's cheekbone had broken. The fight was over—it had to be over. No one could continue fighting with a broken cheekbone. Again and again Vengelis's mind repeated this encouraging thought as he gasped for breath. Vengelis held his hands out and stared at them as he panted and heaved. The rough skin around his knuckles and the joints of his fingers were agonizingly scraped and split. Drops of blood fell from the gashes on his face and landed on his forearms. He noticed how closely the shade of the Blood Ring matched that of his actual blood.

As the peaking adrenaline abated, Vengelis shifted the focus of his gaze beyond his hands and into the chaos of the city below. Now was not the time to give in to the limitations of exhaustion. He lethargically pushed himself forward and circled around the glass skyscraper through which he had propelled Gravitas. There was a broad chunk missing from the side of the building near its top, where Gravitas's body had obviously made its exit. The wind had diffused the kicked up dust, and the gaping hole provided an architectural cutout of the building. A few exposed stories were visible, and the lofty wind blew through the office levels. Nestled between each floor and ceiling, exposed steel supports, sparking wires, and heating ducts hung loose. Gravitas's body had connected with one of the giant vertical steel support beams of the tower, and Vengelis saw it was bent precariously. The immense skyscraper looked as though it might collapse any second.

A flicker of concern grew at the thought of what Kristen Jordan and Madison might do if they saw the skyscraper fall, but he drew his attention away from it nevertheless. He had to establish Gravitas's condition before he worried himself with anything else. Wincing from his injuries, Vengelis turned from the gouged skyscraper to survey the skyline and then down into the crowded streets as he searched for Nerol. Surely Gravitas had retreated, or was hiding.

Not readily seeing his adversary, Vengelis anxiously oriented himself in the city. The apex of the Marriott Marquis was below him, which was a solace. The sounds rising from the city were increasing in pitch, and Vengelis vaguely realized he was easily within plain sight of the teeming masses on the streets below. With an exasperated curse at his situation, Vengelis spit in an unsuccessful attempt to rid his mouth of blood. Slowly and shakily, he descended past the bright windows of the Marriott Marquis to get back to Kristen Jordan. He leveled off outside the second-floor windows—where he was met by the blood curdling screams of the mob just below—to see a line of connected articles of clothing hanging out of the ballroom. The rope of shirts and jackets was shifting in the wind, its end touching the pavement of the sidewalk.

His heart rose into this throat. If Kristen Jordan escaped . . .

Vengelis's face twisted with a sudden wrath and he shot in through a window. His eyes darted to the stage, then to the strewn-about chairs and desks. The doors were still barred shut by his doing, but the ballroom was nearly deserted. His mouth hung open, he turned from the rear wall to the front stage.

Kristen and Madison were gone.

Vengelis turned to the half dozen people huddling by a corner window. They were scrambling to get away from him, some even crawling to hide under a display table.

"Where did the two women go?" Vengelis shouted.

One man who was caught unaware turned to him, his face suddenly drenched in dismay. The front of the man's pants immediately became wet with urine. If Vengelis's presence had terrified the ballroom earlier, his now bloodied and beaten face was the finishing brushstroke required to paint him as the arch-fiend himself.

"P-Please, I don't—"

Vengelis lurched forward unsteadily and gripped the man's face with his palm, ramming him backward and burying his head and shoulders into the drywall. "WHERE ARE THEY?" Vengelis screamed, but when he released his hand the man's body fell to the floor unconscious.

Vengelis turned to the others, but it was obvious even in his rage that they did not know where Kristen and Madison went. A few had fallen to their knees and were begging. Others took their chances and simply turned and leapt out the open second-story window. Completely disregarding any semblance of civility, Vengelis turned and exploded out of the Marriott Marquis, his body crashing through the crown molding above the windows and taking a broad chunk of the ballroom ceiling with him. Dust from the crumbled wall of the hotel gathered and caked to his wounds as he moved into the open air of the street. He jerked his neck up and down the crowded avenue as he scanned the thousands of heads.

Vengelis had told Kristen and Madison he would demolish the entire city if they ran away. Why would they run? Why would they test him like this? They were gambling with millions of lives. Their gall astounded him. Were they really going to force him to follow through with such a threat?

In his heart Vengelis was not certain if he even had the remaining strength or will to do so. He glared down at the makeshift rope that billowed out of the Lutvak ballroom. All of the exits within the ballroom had been barred shut. Kristen and Madison had to have used the rope of jackets to get out. Therefore, their two heads were somewhere in the packed crowd below. Frustration began to overwhelm Vengelis as he frantically looked down on the faces of the endless people in the crowd and scanned for the two he would recognize.

If what Kristen Jordan said proved true—that there may be no way to defeat the Felixes—what would he do? Vengelis forcefully pressed the idea from his mind as he realized there was no way he would be able to discern two individual women in the midst of the bedlam sprawled out beneath him.

Taking no notice of the pointing fingers and skyward shouting faces, Vengelis rotated back and forth in space as he stared up and down the extensive vista of the avenue. He considered screaming for them to show themselves, but his voice would have no chance of carrying over the uproar below. He could not believe how many people had taken to the streets, surely hundreds of thousands—maybe a million. The jolt to the skyscraper seemed to have jarred the confidence of the people who had decided to remain safe in the raised sanctuaries of their buildings. Now the already clogged riot was growing exponentially by the moment as people poured out from the various towers.

A deafening shudder of shrieking steel and a pinging of loosened bolts echoed down from far overhead. Vengelis turned upward to see the skyscraper Gravitas's body had damaged visibly pitch and lean treacherously to the side. The terrible sight was met with a chorus of hoarse screams from the masses. Vengelis looked up to the disfigured upper portion of the skyscraper, then his gaze moved around the skies over the buildings. Where had Gravitas gone? Could he have knocked him out? It was possible, but Vengelis would have felt much more comfortable knowing Gravitas's condition for certain. He began to move forward slowly, continuing to scan the mob in an attempt to find Kristen and Madison.

A strangeness in the masses suddenly caught Vengelis's eye some way down the avenue. Several hundred yards from him, there seemed to be an imaginary fence holding back a ring of people. In the center of the open pavement, positioned grotesquely, was what Vengelis immediately recognized as Darien's dead body. As Vengelis drew nearer to his fallen Royal Guard, he saw the abandoned circle around the corpse was not entirely empty.

There were two people leaning down to Darien. Vengelis began to fly faster, and as he neared, he recognized Kristen and Madison. Vengelis's mangled face narrowed in confusion, and he accelerated forward unsteadily. Kristen Jordan was kneeling down to Darien. Coldness poured through Vengelis's veins, and with a sudden pale terror in his face that matched the people below, he saw what she was doing. Kristen was collecting a sample of what she knew to be Sejero blood.

Vengelis had not considered the horrendous possibility he now saw unfolding before him, and he exploded toward Kristen with all of his remaining might. He knew at once what she was attempting. All of the pieces were set, the knowledge and capabilities aligned.

Kristen was going to create Felixes.

CHAPTER THIRTY-EIGHT

Kristen

The riot beat against them as Kristen and Madison slipped down from the makeshift rope and clumsily crowd surfed to the sidewalk. They stayed close as they pushed through the crowd of Seventh Avenue. In the lead, Kristen drove past the currents of people and toward the mammoth body she knew lay to their south. They navigated the unruly sidewalk, littered with everything from broken benches to dented vendor kiosks and cracked cell phones. Here and there injured people lay curled on the pavement, crying out with their arms raised over their faces to fend off buffeting feet. Kristen held Madison's forearm tightly as they pushed forward.

After what felt like an eternity immersed in this chaos, Kristen wedged through the last pair of shoulders and stumbled into the wide empty space surrounding the behemoth. Kristen stared at the giant dead body, eyes wide with anxiety. Now up close and personal with the malformed corpse, she identified with the people who had given it a wide berth. It looked as though a big game kill had been left in the middle of the avenue.

"I really don't think this is a good idea," Madison yelled over the uprising surrounding them as she looked with disgust at the hulking carcass.

Kristen hesitated, overwhelmed by her surroundings. Beside them, a group of men had stopped a Ford with Maryland plates that was attempting to plow a path through the avenue. They pushed it back and forth on its tires, trying to flip the sedan over. Behind the tinted windows and locked doors, Kristen saw a family.

"It will only take a second," Kristen called out numbly. Diverting her eyes from the horror around them, she walked determinedly to the dead body. She slipped off her backpack and kneeled beside the giant's still shoulder, marveling at the sheer size of the strange man. Resting lifeless against the pavement, Kristen could not even venture a guess as to how much this person weighed.

"We're going to get a blood sample and then get back up to the Lutvak ballroom as fast as we can. We'll get there before Vengelis returns."

"And what if he realizes we left while he was gone?"

Kristen looked up to Madison as she unzipped her backpack. "Then we're in trouble! But we don't have a choice. This could be our only shot to get a sample of their blood. I guarantee they'll be sure to retrieve this body before they leave. And that's assuming they *do* leave!"

"What does it matter?" Madison shouted.

"Because." Kristen took out the thin glass tissue slide and wiped it down with the sleeve of her sweatshirt, her eyes nervously locked on the sky for any sign of Vengelis. Beside them, the Ford finally flipped, and the group of horrible men whooped with excitement. The indiscriminate sounds of anarchy and disorder surrounding them made her cringe. She felt as though she was immersed in the middle of a parade or sporting event gone horribly wrong. Kristen had never thought a crowd could be so coldblooded, its impulsiveness so chilling. "Vengelis said their power is derived from their genetics. With a sample of this blood, we can map their genetic code and then delineate a blueprint of strength. We'll figure out what they are, and with that information decide how we can defend ourselves against them."

"I really think we should get back!"

"Look around!" Kristen motioned to the masses, to the flipped car. "What will we do without a means of protection? Nothing! This—what you see *right now*—will claim the entire world unless we can find a means to pacify this insanity."

Madison gave a fretful sigh.

"Take this giant here." Kristen carefully ran the slide along the giant's jaw line, smearing blood across the thin glass. "Who killed him? I have no idea. But it certainly wasn't by a human hand. Clearly Vengelis was lying to us. There's more to his story than he told me. The only thing we know for certain is that we are completely at their mercy. We have to use anything we're given to protect ourselves, and right now, we can get this giant's DNA and go from there."

"Okay, okay," Madison said. "Just please hurry."

A swell of screams rose suddenly from the crowds to the north. Kristen looked up and exchanged a momentary concerned glance with Madison before slowly rising from her kneeling position and anxiously peering over the people that sprawled up Seventh Avenue. The power to the city had either been shut off or severed, and the shade upon the city was striking as a cloud passed across the sun. For the first time Kristen noticed the electronic billboards overhead were now ominously blank, and the darkened storefronts and lobbies of Times Square appeared sinister in the afternoon light.

A sharp gnawing sound suddenly tore down the avenue from far overhead. Kristen elevated her gaze, and her shoulders drooped in woozy horror. To their north, beyond the spire of the Marriott Marquis, one of the massive dark skyscrapers looming down from the blue sky was visibly pitching.

"Oh dear god," Kristen murmured. "Please no."

"We have to go back that way," Madison called.

"I know."

Kristen held her breath. If the skyscraper were to collapse, all of its surrounds—Kristen and Madison included—would be immersed in the lethal wave of debris. Then, as the building began to steadily and perilously tilt into the open autumn air, it abruptly stopped. The mirrored windows hung in the wind like a grand modern rendition of the Leaning Tower of Pisa. The entire skyscraper—including the broad hole near its top—seemed to be teetering on the brink of collapse. But for the moment it held. The crowd stood motionless below it, in a collective unease that even the slightest budge would cause the building to thunderously tumble down onto them.

After allowing herself one shocked moment, Kristen turned and kneeled back down to her backpack.

"Kristen, let's *go!*"

"All right, all right. Just hold on. I—"

As Kristen spoke, the lower wall of the Marriott Marquis exploded, flinging loose mortar across Times Square. Kristen spun toward the noise, and her heart seemed to momentarily forget to beat. She recognized the source of clamor at once. Before a word could be spoken between then, Kristen and Madison watched as Vengelis Epsilon erupted out of the hotel and accelerated directly toward them above the crowd. Vengelis was covered in caked blood and dust, and his face looked beaten. Before Kristen even had a moment to consider their situation, he landed in the empty street before her, his feet splintering the pavement.

Kristen found herself even more confused as she beheld Vengelis's appearance at close proximity. His previously regal face was swollen and beaten. Kristen stood in shock as she held the blood-streaked glass slide. Vengelis's unsteady and swelled gaze moved slowly across the scene. He looked from the fallen giant, to Kristen and Madison individually, to the blood-streaked slide in Kristen's hand. His eyes narrowed wearily on the slide.

"Clever," he said, his voice hoarse.

"We thought the building was going to collapse. We weren't running away." Madison spoke quickly. "We were going to head right back."

Vengelis said nothing; he looked only at the slide Kristen held.

"Give it to me."

Kristen hesitated and rolled her fingers into a fist around the fragile slide. Vengelis looked up to meet her gaze and held out his open palm, his face oddly solemn. His hands were mangled and raw, his arms shaking with exhaustion.

"You have no idea the magnitude of power you are considering wielding so recklessly."

Kristen nodded grimly. "Says the man who wields it."

Vengelis considered her, the thoughts behind his beaten face impossible to guess. "Give it to me," he said.

Kristen opened her hand and looked down at the slide—the Sejero genetics—within her grasp. She knew exactly the enormity of power held in her hand: the power to defeat the man standing before her, the power of gods. With no other choice, Kristen sighed in submission and held the slide out to him.

Vengelis nodded sternly, his expression betraying a glint of compassion toward her idea. She noticed he did not seem overtly mad. He reached out to take the slide from her, and their hands reached toward one another to swap the blood sample. But in that exact instant, something happened that Kristen did not entirely understand. A flash of movement registered in her peripheral vision from the right side of the avenue. Then a tremendous impact occurred in front of her. In a transient sequence of her conscious vision, Kristen saw the image of a shoulder drive into Vengelis's side much like a tackle. It was as though a speeding car had hit Vengelis, except the force even greater.

Instantaneously, Kristen was lifted off her feet and a rush of air launched her backward into the door of the overturned Ford. Her back formed a gigantic dent in the passenger side door and shattered the window. Kristen slipped down off the car and came to rest on the ground, the side of her face pressed against the cold pavement and her ears ringing. The wind was knocked out of her, and her chest heaved futilely for breath as she blinked in shock. For a prolonged moment Kristen lay on the pavement, her mouth moving incoherently with confusion.

Something—someone—had hit Vengelis.

A firm hand took hold of Kristen's shoulder and pulled her shakily to her feet. It was Madison; she was helping Kristen up with one hand while clutching her own forehead with the other. Madison also had been knocked down, and her shoulder was scraped from the pavement. Kristen turned and marveled at the impression she had made in the side of the car door. She reached out and touched the indent. Her body must have hit it at a perfect angle, as she realized she did not feel any injury. Madison shook Kristen's shoulder violently, and Kristen turned to her as she mouthed something urgently and shook her once more in exasperation. She saw Madison's lips forming the words *let's go* over and over again. It took Kristen a moment to realize she could not hear anything.

The impact had deafened her.

Kristen lifted her arm and motioned to her ears. As she did so, she realized she was still holding the slide in her hand. She and Madison both looked down at the undamaged slide in disbelief. Kristen drew her gaze from the slide to the direction Vengelis had been launched. A gaping hole disappeared into the side of a storefront. Vengelis—and whatever had hit him—had gone straight through the side of the building.

Let's go! Madison's lips moved again in the ringing silence.

Kristen nodded. The clamor of the avenue was faintly audible, like the dull drone of a distant highway. Kristen turned around with a mustered resolve, and—whether by the concussive force of her crash with the Ford, or the actual quaking of the street underfoot—her world spun with vertigo. She stumbled forward a few steps and picked her backpack off the pavement, placing the slide in its protective case with trembling hands. Again, Kristen nearly fell over, and this time she realized it was not just her—the entire block was shuddering.

Come on! Madison pulled on Kristen's arm, and looked skyward to the towering buildings with an expression that revealed both awe and fear. Kristen, too, raised her attention to the sky. In her dreamlike quiet, she watched as two struggling figures brutally fought over the heads of the masses. The two juggernauts burst through the air, their evanescent movements barely visible to the spectators. To Kristen, it almost seemed as though the two battling forms were not moving at all, but instead were apparitions appearing suddenly here or there, and vanishing before her eyes had a chance to discern any concrete vision.

But their battleground offered evidence to their all too tangible struggle. Kristen turned slowly around as various floors of the towering buildings around her burst inward or outward with the impacts and accelerations of the two great beings. The two bodies surged back and forth among the skyscrapers, and each impact with the confining buildings had a wrecking ball effect on the towers. Loose debris, shattered glass, and huge fragments of concrete plummeted and ricocheted down into the crowd of upturned faces. Madison pulled again on Kristen's arm, harder this time. That was all it took to shake Kristen out of her overwhelmed daze. At once, Kristen averted her eyes from the battling gods and met Madison's expression with a fierce resolve.

The two young women turned and began sprinting up the avenue, the backpack containing the enigmatic Sejero blood jostling and bouncing off Kristen's shoulders.

CHAPTER THIRTY-NINE

Gravitas

Pulse, pulse, pulse.

Hammer strikes in the darkness, as though his heart had transformed into an instrument of torture. With each new beat, the flowing blood reawakened every nerve ending in his body. There was only the pounding throb of pain to his being.

Pulse, pulse, pulse.

Yet it was the exhaustion's influence that overwhelmed the hurt. Compared to the fatigue saturating into his very bone marrow, the pain was nothing; the pain was acting to ground him in reluctant consciousness. Were it not for the throbbing agony, his mind would have allowed him to sink into a paradise of nothingness.

But instead of passing out, and with an unthinkable force of willpower, Gravitas opened his eyes. Through his swollen eyelids, he peered into deep blue skies scattered with clouds. How long had he been dazed? Where was he? Where was Vengelis Epsilon? He blinked many times, and slowly turned his head to examine the sleek glass of a few nearby skyscrapers as they ascended stoic and impassive into the blue of the sky.

With a mournful sigh, Gravitas thought back to what felt like a lifetime ago when he had awoken with Kristen that morning, her fragrant hair wet from the shower and a pale morning sunlight across her smile as she lay next to him. The thought of her was painful to consider, and he nearly retched in misery as he quickly shook the sentiments from his mind and gathered his bearings. He was tangled up in the crumpled heap of a car. His upper torso had split through the roof, and the back of his head was resting at a strange angle against the tan leather of a backseat. Gravitas easily dislodged his shoulder from the malleable steel and sat up. There was a frenzied flood of people stampeding northward up the avenue, as if the car on which he had landed was afloat in a river of rioters. He could hear them bumping up against the car and scratching the doors as they passed.

Gravitas lifted a hand to place against his face and assess the damage, but he stopped before his fingers reached his cheek. The pain splitting across his face was beyond words, but his condition did not matter. He was conscious; the fight would continue. Without a second thought, Gravitas abruptly lifted himself out of the remains of the car and accelerated into the air. He was insensate and drunk with fatigue, and he veered to the side, inadvertently grazing into the side of a skyscraper. His shoulder cleaved a broad gash into a dozen stories of sparkling windows. Gravitas dazedly cursed his indiscretion and continued to rise more carefully, halting above the tall buildings to survey the streets below and locate Vengelis Epsilon.

A tearing noise rose against the sounds of the city, and Gravitas turned to watch the building his own body had maimed begin to tremble. The supports were yielding, and he watched with a pleading expression as the broad tower began to pitch to the side for a moment. Gravitas reluctantly drew his gaze away from the teetering Midtown skyscraper, as it looked like it would hold for the time being. He focused on finding Vengelis, and his efforts did not take long. As he peered down into the city, he watched one of the lower floors of the Marriott Marquis burst outward and expel thick rubble across the square. Penetrating out of the dusty upheaval, he saw the glint of Imperial First Class armor. Gravitas discerned the Epsilon accelerate down the avenue and toward the fallen body of the Royal Guard Darien. Gravitas's swollen eyelids narrowed as he noticed the apprehension, perhaps even panic, in Vengelis's excessive speed. Vengelis veered down Seventh Avenue as if his life were on the line, and came to a landing beside the gigantic corpse of the Royal Guard.

Without hesitation Gravitas erupted downward, the sound of his approach drowned out in the welter of the streets. Vengelis's vulnerable side was facing an open intersection, and Gravitas descended with a swooping approach to mercilessly blindside him. It appeared as though Vengelis was preoccupied, or perhaps he had considered Gravitas defeated; either way he had left himself completely undefended as he stood by his fallen soldier. Gravitas barreled downward and pulled up at the last second, coming level to the street and sprinting as hard as he possibly could toward the emperor. His vision blurry, Gravitas watched Vengelis lift his arm out to someone, leaving his fragile midsection wide open for an ambush. Thundering up the street with all of the force his beaten body would allow, Gravitas lowered his shoulder and thrust himself forward with every drop of his remaining strength, plunging his flexed shoulder straight into Vengelis's ribcage.

The impact was ferocious. Gravitas could hear a number of Vengelis's ribs crack from the impact. Together the two bodies—Gravitas on top of Vengelis—reeled across the street and crashed through a plate-glass window into a deserted five-star restaurant. Weakened by his injuries, Gravitas simply pushed forward, pumping his legs one after the other. He drove Vengelis backward, his shoulder buried into the tender space below Vengelis's armpit.

Vengelis let his own body fall underneath Gravitas and flipped him over with a heave. Gravitas's momentum carried him booming through a hostess table with a discharge of splintered wood. He rolled across the restaurant in a calamity of tablecloths, shattering plates and silverware.

"You don't quit, even when you're beaten!" Vengelis screamed hoarsely. He rose to his feet on the mahogany floor, wincing from his ribs.

Gravitas grunted and ripped a white tablecloth from his body. He ran straight at Vengelis, swinging out with a right fist. Dodging his head out of reach, Vengelis sent his knuckles up into Gravitas's stomach. The blow sent him straight through the ceiling, and Vengelis ascended after him. They interlocked arms and began to wrestle through the walls and ceilings of the building. Floors and walls crumpled and disintegrated around them, the structures yielding to their bodies without the slightest resistance. Gravitas reached down and grabbed Vengelis behind the knee, pulling Vengelis's left leg into his grasp and pushing his shoulder into his stomach. Vengelis fell backward; their two bodies smashed through drywall and mortar and out into the daylight of the city.

Vengelis swung his fist and caught Gravitas behind the ear. The blow forced Gravitas to relinquish his hold on Vengelis's leg, and sent him careening through the air and into a billboard. Back and forth across the open street they fought, even Gravitas now disregarding the massive damage he was inflicting to the buildings around them. Concrete and steel broke against them like porcelain. There was not a trace of defenses now between the two of them. Every swing from either one of the Sejero warriors struck its mark as they exchanged blows like wild animals. Gravitas could barely see, and his limbs felt like they were filling with hot lead. He was beginning to even forget whom he was fighting or why.

With an obvious last-ditch effort, Vengelis buried a fist into Gravitas's stomach with gathered strength. Gravitas hunched over, but at the same time came up with a wild uppercut.

It hit home.

His fist caught Vengelis square in the jaw. Vengelis fell back, and his body crashed into a window behind him where it did not move. His legs were left dangling out the broken window, but his upper torso was inside the building. Vengelis lay stunned for a moment before pushing himself up onto his elbows.

"Do you give up?" Gravitas blurted.

Vengelis spit to the side and stood up shakily in the thirteenth-story window frame, his head lolling. He murmured something that sounded like "Kristen," though Gravitas thought he might be delirious himself and hearing things.

"Fel—" Vengelis coughed up blood. "We . . . Felix."

Gravitas could not do anything but pant for breath. His spinning vision was filled with stars. He was too spent to think anything at all. The two of them stood before each other, each neither defeated nor victorious.

KRRRRRCH!

A strident tearing sound echoed suddenly across the rooftops of the city, drowning out the clamor of the anarchy below. Gravitas drew his blurred vision away from Vengelis. He strained to look up the long crowded avenue. High over the heads of the clogging masses migrating northward, the wounded monolith of a skyscraper shuddered and screamed in tenors of yielding iron and failing steel down into the streets of Midtown. Gravitas felt a terrible desperation as he turned his gaze from the massive skyscraper to the droves of people bottlenecked in the congested intersections below. The collapse would swallow them whole. Thousands were about to die an unspeakable death. The fight was over; Gravitas doubted either of them now had the power remaining to perform a coup de grâce on the other.

KRRRRRCH!

The sound filled the city: another support failing. Gravitas shut his eyes, his upper body rising and falling with heaves for breath.

"You . . . deserve . . . death . . . " Gravitas said to Vengelis through his split lips.

"I . . . know," Vengelis murmured and stumbled to a wall for support. "Brought . . . Felix. N-never could have known . . . "

A new kind of sound carried down to them from atop the tilting building. It was the sound of floors collapsing. Gravitas turned to the skyscraper and watched as the roof and the top floor caved inward. The base of the building gave way, and the bottom floors began disintegrating into rubble. He moaned in wearisome desperation and turned away from Vengelis Epsilon with determined finality.

"Don't you dare. It . . . it is hopeless," Vengelis murmured, his jaw hanging open by his shoulder as he regarded the falling tower with a muddled gaze. "Don't even think about leaving."

"We're finished," Gravitas whispered.

"Nerol! No!"

Without another word Gravitas rushed up the avenue toward the falling superstructure, weaving unsteadily through the air with his final scrap of strength and leaving Vengelis astonished and alone in the lofty recess of the empty window.

CHAPTER FORTY

Kristen

Tears of despondency and dread welled in Kristen's eyes as she sprinted up the quaking avenue beside Madison. Entering the migrating riot was an immersion into a world with no rules, a scene entirely distant and alien to the life with which Kristen was so familiar. Man's carefully sewn and timeworn fabric of compassion, kindness, and morality was ablaze and scorching to nothingness before her eyes, leaving only caustic despair in its wake.

In fleeting sidelong glances Kristen beheld unspeakable atrocities. Curled on the pavement, a trampled and broken body of a young teenager, her sneakers twitching from the kicks and stomps of the mob. Marching out of an electronics store, a man balancing a stack of brand new laptops in his arms. Parents desperately holding infants and toddlers into the air to keep them from being swallowed up, while futilely begging for someone to help them.

A drear of chalky dust obscured the afternoon sunlight as the dreamlike conflict between Vengelis and his nameless foe pervaded straight through the towering buildings on all sides, sending wreckage plunging down into the crowds.

Ahead of Kristen and Madison, the disfigured skyscraper leaned diagonally over the intersection at a treacherous angle. Kristen stared agape into the dusty sky at the countless teetering windows overhead. The building blocked the warm autumn sunlight that splashed upon the rest of the city, and cast an ominous dark shadow across the block. The air felt suddenly colder in the chill of the building's shadow. Deadly debris fell from the lofty heights into the narrow chasm of the avenue. Kristen had never felt as small and frail as she did under the eclipse of the vast skyscraper. It was a sensory overload, and all the while the same word repeated over and over in her mind: *war.*

As they ran, Madison gripped Kristen's arm tight. They were in this together, and Kristen was glad not to be alone. Madison was strong and fast, and Kristen could barely keep up.

In the middle of the swarming intersection, a hulking black-and-green camouflaged army tank was stationed in the shadows below a set of drooping unpowered traffic lights. The austere tank contrasted starkly with the rest of the posh storefronts. Around the tank, a ring of indomitable Marines was stationed at attention, all shouldering enormous black assault rifles. The guns were pointed outward at the stampede. The men looked ready to fire upon the pressing riot at the slightest provocation. Standing on the hood of the armored vehicle, a soldier with black boots was shouting into a megaphone. You could see the panic in his eyes: he had prepared himself to serve in distant lands, not in the beating heart of America.

"The bridges on the east side of the city have been demolished! Don't try to evacuate east! I repeat, do not try to evacuate over the East River."

Kristen and Madison slowed to a jog to listen to the man. The magnified voice barely carried over the uproar around them. He waved his arm to his right, Kristen's left.

"Make your way to the west side of Manhattan. The Holland and Lincoln tunnels *are* still operational! There is an evacuation effort underway across the Hudson! Shelters are being erected along the New Jersey side of the river. Please remain calm! But get to the Hudson and out of the city as quickly as possible!"

"Let's go!" Madison shouted and made to turn west up the clogged street.

"Wait!" Kristen called, and she forced her way through a few shoulders to get closer to the Marines. She waved to them vigorously as she shoved people out of the way.

"I need to talk with you!" Kristen screamed, her voice scarcely audible amid the riot.

The soldier standing mere feet in front of her made no acknowledgement of her presence. He stared coldly past her, the barrel of his gun pointing directly at the chest level of the mob, at Kristen.

"For god's sake, *look* at me! I know what they are!" Kristen raised an arm and pointed a finger to the sky and the gaping hole upon the top floors of the leaning skyscraper looming overhead.

The soldiers could have passed for statues. They stared blankly down the sights of their guns.

"Where is General Redford?" Kristen shouted. "I need to speak with someone who is in command here! Hello?"

Madison caught up to her and attempted to pull her back by the shoulder. Kristen forcefully shrugged off her grip and stepped forward furiously. "This is too important!

One of you needs to be a responsible human for one goddamn second and listen to me! I have in my possession a technology of *theirs* that needs to be taken to safety! Listen to me!"

"Miss, step back right now!" the man with the megaphone roared down at Kristen.

"I need to speak to someone in charge," Kristen shouted. "Please! I have a sample of their DNA—the DNA of the people who attacked Chicago and are in New York now!"

"Step back!" the man roared into the megaphone.

"No!"

"Come on, Kristen." Madison pulled again at her shoulder, but Kristen held her ground.

"No! I have in my possession their *complete* intact genetic code! It has to be taken to safety out of the city!"

The soldier with the megaphone was not having it, and he glared down at Kristen with obvious disbelief. He raised the megaphone to his mouth and was about to assert a threat, when an enormous oak desk fell from the tenebrous sky and landed directly on the shoulder blades of one of the Marines standing in the circle. The soldier's body crumpled to nothing in an instant, and the heavy desk burst into a few dozen fragments and splinters against the hard street. There was a subdued moment as all the bystanders gawked at the space where the man had been standing a moment before. Kristen and everyone around her slowly raised their heads into the opaque and shadowy sky.

The immense skyscraper leaned down upon them like a tremendous tree about to fall with a catastrophic crash. The darkened windows of the tower hung over the intersection and depicted a grand portrait-like reflection of the riotous avenue. It was a stunning refracted mirror image of the insanity, like a nightmarish portrait in a still lake. All along the length and width of the great structure, bits of office furniture slid across uneven floors and crashed through the thick panes of glass, falling freely into the crowd in which Kristen stood. The skyscraper trembled and hitched. Shattered glass and bits of the superstructure fell through the open air, and iron supports shrieked deafeningly. The structure had transformed into a horrendous monster, ready to ravenously devour them all.

The building was going to collapse any second.

Immediately there were no words, save rasping screams. The reaction was animalistic: a herd of prey running from a gargantuan primordial predator. Kristen pulled her gaze away from the dreamlike overhead reflection. Madison stood in a stunned silence as she stared up the length of the collapsing skyscraper. Reaching out, Kristen pulled her by the shoulder and Madison snapped back into reality. Kristen looked to the Marines, perhaps to jump aboard their tank, but they had all thrown their duty aside and joined the growing charge westward up the confined street. Kristen felt her own legs suddenly thrust forward, and she followed the fleeing crowd in a dead sprint, her backpack jostling against her shoulders.

Adrenaline pounded through her arms and legs. Kristen ran faster than her feet had ever taken her; she ran for her life. All around her people fell and stumbled, instantly disappearing underfoot. Side by side, Kristen and Madison hurdled over obstructions and clawed on all fours over the abandoned cars and taxis, disregarding the bruises and deep gashes they got on their way.

BOOOM!

The collapsing skyscraper roared at Kristen's heels, rumbling through the pavement and sending reverberations up through her knees. She could not comprehend how many people were about to die—including herself. As the street lurched and cracked beneath her rushing feet, Kristen turned her head and raised her eyes to catch a glimpse of the impending avalanche of cement and steel. The roof's spire was caving downward upon itself. The windows along the top floors shattered in unison, exploding outward in great waves.

In her momentary distraction, Kristen's ankle caught the curb and she fell forward, crashing onto the sidewalk and skinning her palms. Heavy feet kicked out and stomped on her arms and legs as the multitude sprinted past. A familiar hand reached down to Kristen and she desperately grasped hold of it as she raised her other arm to shield her face against an incoming boot. Madison pulled Kristen upright with all her strength just as a heavyset man collided into both of them. Kristen and Madison were sent heaving to the side. Kristen's back came to a sliding stop on the hood of a car. All she could do was simply stare in resignation at the impending doom. It was too late, and happening too fast; she was about to die. The building was collapsing directly onto her.

Her thoughts blurred into an obscure mosaic of emotions as her world untethered itself from all the things she had once believed. She was scared and fearful for everyone around her, so soon to depart the things they loved. But mostly Kristen felt alone. She wanted to bury her face against someone and give up, to entirely surrender, if only to find some small sanctuary as she died. A heartrending longing to be with Ryan in some faraway place surfaced deep within her. Kristen hoped in that moment he had somehow managed to escape.

The looming skyscraper encompassed her entire vision. One by one, the bottom floors began to flatten and disintegrate with cataclysmic booms. Kristen's body bounced off of the hood of the car from the tremors. A tsunami of cement dust erupted from the base of the building, and then a massive cracking rupture splintered down the center of the entire superstructure. For a fraction of a second Kristen watched the main section of the skyscraper lose its reinforcement and fall inward as if imploding. Then a wave of gray-black dust and ash detonated downward like a pyroclastic volcano eruption. The cloud of destruction thundered and discharged down upon her. Kristen screamed in terror and sucked in one last breath while covering her face from the thick noxious flow as it inundated her world. She shut her eyes tight and held her breath as the powerful rush of poisonous dust blew past her skin and buffeted her hair.

The dense wave of death consumed her. Kristen rolled and writhed as specks of cement pelted and stung her body. In her blind torment she felt her body slip off the hood and land hard on the pavement. Her vision became a shifting black kaleidoscope from the lack of oxygen, and her chest heaved and burned for air. She held her breath with all her might. The thick dust accumulated on her firmly shut eyelashes and eyebrows like snow. At last, Kristen could stand it no more, and her body forced her to take a gulp of the toxic air. She opened her mouth and, by no will of her own, sucked in a deep inhalation. The breath sent biting particles to the depths of her lungs. It felt as though she had been pepper sprayed. She hacked and coughed and violently gagged in an attempt to expel the awful toxins. Nestled in her position between two cars, Kristen felt as though she were trapped in a trench being bombarded with mustard gas.

She braced herself.

But almost at once she felt the dust cloud dissipating rather than thickening. Her coughing was lessening in severity, and the burning in her throat was calming. The dust was not drowning her. She did not hear what she expected— the impact of the plummeting skyscraper parts against the ground. Kristen flopped onto her back on the ash-covered pavement and shook the accumulation from her face, her eyelids still locked tight. Rubbing her eyes and wiping off the cement dust and plaster before opening them blearily, she stared in wonder all around her. A pall of dust blotted out everything. She looked upward into a swirling blizzard of dark gray snow. A blanket of the sawdust-like material covered her sneakers to her head, along with every other surface of the street. But it was not the layer of ashy dust, or Madison recovering beside her that caught Kristen's attention.

They were still in the shadow of the skyscraper.

Through the diminishing storm of dust, Kristen could clearly see that the top of the tower had collapsed inward fifteen or twenty floors. The tiered apex of the building was nowhere to be seen. The bottom portion of the skyscraper was gone, disintegrated into nothing. Kristen realized it had been relocated to everywhere around her, pulverized to ruin. Yet despite the structural damage, the vast majority of the building stood prominently intact. Kristen gaped in confusion at the gigantic standing facade. It held true with no foundation and no supports, as though it were floating in space.

"Kristen," Madison's voice was hoarse.

Kristen breathlessly turned to her. Madison was also covered in the dust. Around the two of them, hundreds of other powder-covered people also stared up at the building.

"Look," Madison said.

Kristen matched Madison's gaze, and looked halfway up the length of the broad structure. There, clearly evident in the jumble of huge gnarled steel garters and rivets was a man. Impossibly bent iron supports bent and stacked atop his shoulders like a car wrapped around a tree. The man was holding the entire skyscraper—and all of their lives—on his shoulders. It was the most alien and impossible sight Kristen had ever imagined. Her chin trembled, and she began to cry at the overwhelming display of strength. Vengelis was right; Kristen had not witnessed their true power. There was no refuting it to the hushed and awed crowd of pale faces surrounding Kristen and staring upward; they were in the presence of a god.

With great effort, Kristen drew her welling gaze from the unreal vision.

"Madison!"

"Y-yes," Madison was transfixed with the sight above them.

Kristen pulled at Madison's shoulder. "We need to go, *now!*"

Madison nodded, drew her gaze away from the grand vision, and together they began running westward through the dust cloud and away from the balancing skyscraper.

CHAPTER FORTY-ONE

Vengelis

Vengelis stared dazedly at the backside of Gravitas as he soared northward, his tattered Imperial First Class armor growing smaller in the distance and finally disappearing into the cloud of doom that was billowing from the falling skyscraper. Suddenly alone in the shadow of the afternoon, Vengelis slumped against the side of the broken window and watched an unhinged billboard sway back and forth across the avenue. He tried to compose his body and his mind but found himself unable. His broken ribs made even breathing a painstaking struggle, and when he tried to make a fist, he realized his forearm and most of his knuckles were broken.

Strange calamitous noises echoed across the city from the falling skyscraper, and a developing dark cloud expelled from the streets around its base. Gravitas was holding up the building, Vengelis had no doubt about it. It was an unspeakable insult. Gravitas had turned his back on him, as though he were no longer even a threat. Bitter hate brewed in Vengelis's chest. It was Gravitas's fault the skyscraper was in danger of collapsing at all. Inflicting damage to the buildings of New York had never been a part of his plan. Gravitas's rashness was to blame for the failing skyscraper, and yet here he was acting as though he were the decent and respectable one between the two of them. Vengelis could not believe how much he hated the Nerols, father and son both.

"Who do you think you are?" Vengelis screamed unsteadily to no one, his voice hoarse. "Nerol! We're not finished!"

The roar sent spasms of pain up his side, and Vengelis let out a constricted exhale with a grimace. He hacked and spit up bloody phlegm, unable to guess how many ribs must be cracked. His body was broken, but he was too overwhelmed with rage and exasperation to acknowledge it. Mumbling to himself, Vengelis reached into his armor and pulled out the *Harbinger I* remote. Things were spiraling out of control, and the situation had escalated more than he could have possibly imagined. Vengelis could not wrap his mind around why he and Gravitas Nerol were so evenly matched. On top of that, somewhere in the craven multitude far below, a scientist capable of manipulating Felix technology had Sejero genetics within her grasp. In their unfathomable hubris, the humans were going to bring about their own destruction.

And it was undeniably his fault.

Vengelis looked down to the glowing display of the remote and commanded the *Harbinger I* to lift off and head to his location. It was time to cut his losses. He stashed the remote back into his dinted armor and peered around the afternoon with shaky vision. The buildings that rose around him were in shambles. It looked as though gigantic bullets had riddled them, structural damage from his fight with Gravitas.

Hoff and Darien were dead. They, too, had joined the fallen ranks of the rest of the massacred Imperial First Class. So much death and destruction, all in the name of some mysterious cause that now seemed vain and futile. He was the last one left.

How had it come to this?

Vengelis lifted from his position against the side of the building and pushed out into the open air, rising unsteadily and flying northward up the avenue in the direction Gravitas had gone. A fine dust hung in the air, catching the rays of sunlight. Traveling listlessly above the oblong shadow of the leaning skyscraper, the dust added striking contrast to the daylight and the shadow.

Vengelis felt wayward and grieved at the cruel cards dealt to him by fate. To this world and their narrow scope, he was the villain, and he resented it deeply. He was another victim, like them, doing his best given the circumstances. Vengelis longed more than anything to be back on Anthem. Even the killing fields of Sejeroreich would suit him.

Taking his time while approaching the leaning skyscraper, he pulled to a stop above its caved in roof. Below him was a peculiar sight: the bottom portion of the colossal building was gone, vaporized by the incalculable force of the upper building's collapse. Yet the rest of the structure seemed to hang in the open air as though it were immune to the laws of physics and the longing hands of gravity. A wide radius around the base of the building had been decimated by the momentary collapse, and a few blocks in every direction were covered in powdery debris. Vengelis descended into the thick dome of dust rising from the failing building and surveyed up and down the length of mangled windows and exposed floors in search of Gravitas Nerol.

It did not take long to find him.

About halfway up the superstructure, conspicuously pressing his shoulders into the side of the building, was Gravitas. Vengelis found himself hating Gravitas more than anything as he watched his struggle against the collapse, more than even the Felixes. It was this fool's father that had caused this mess, and now the son had the indulgence of taking the high road at his expense. Vengelis's face showed no reaction as he slowly descended in front of Gravitas. He lingered in space before him and stared at Gravitas for a long mocking moment.

"Really?" Vengelis croaked.

Gravitas said nothing. He glared at Vengelis with a scathing aversion. His entire body was shaking with exertion and his face was trembling and deep red under the impossible load. Steel beams four feet in girth were stacked and bent around his neck and shoulders, their rigidity turned pliable in comparison to the Sejero shoulders upon which they wrapped.

"And this accomplishes what exactly?"

"You . . . said . . . you . . . have . . . principles. . . . " Gravitas gasped feebly. "So do I."

Vengelis blinked with contempt. Far below them, the two Royal sons engrossed thousands of ashen dust-covered faces. A cold gust of wind blew by them, and Vengelis could see the strain in Gravitas's expression as he kept the building upright against the wind's push on the entire side of the superstructure.

"And the principles represented here are what exactly?"

Gravitas shook his head a quarter of an inch from side to side. "One's that require . . . no explanation."

The building shifted loudly from far above, and the thick beams bent deeper around his shoulder blades. Gravitas sunk a few feet, failing under exhaustion and the incomprehensible load. Vengelis descended with him, and peered up the length of the shadowed windows, having to turn his neck upward to see the maimed spire looming far overhead.

"Let go. This is over," Vengelis said. "Listen to reason."

Gravitas buried his chin into his chest and heaved himself upward several inches. Vengelis saw him watching the crowd that had now begun to flee from the base of the building.

"Let go!" Vengelis shouted.

Gravitas did not budge, and Vengelis smoldered with fury.

"As we speak, a scientist within this city is unwittingly playing architect to this entire world's destruction. That includes all these people. I know you think of them as innocent, but they aren't . . . no one with intelligence ever is. They are brilliant and conniving, and will stop at nothing to secure dominion over their way of life. Just like we did. So know this as you hold that building on your back and spew your would-be logic at me: all you have done today is assure their self-destruction. After your strength wanes and you fail under the load of this building, I will destroy this city. I have to, in order to stop them from bringing about their own end. I will raze this city to save their world."

Vengelis awaited a response, but nothing came.

"I can give them salvation from an extinction," Vengelis said with a tone of finality. "It is all I can give them, and it is more than we received."

"Annihilation." Gravitas exhaled.

"What?"

"Annihilation is all you can give them. That is all Sejero strength has ever been able to give. For all of its grandeur, our blood knows only destruction."

Vengelis looked past his feet to the intersections below. Insect-sized people were fleeing from the base of the tower, some limping with injuries, others laboriously dragging the wounded away from the teetering tower.

"What are you talking about?" Vengelis said.

"We were born out of atrocity. The Sejero were created during the Primus race's darkest hour, and in the wake of their creation the Primus race has never advanced forward. We were born out of apocalypse, and that is all we have ever provided. We've mired our beliefs in truths that aren't so, based our worldview on certainties that were never intended by the natural order."

"There was necessity to our creation."

"There was desperation. Terrible desperation," Gravitas gasped. "Our bloodlines were created to protect, *only* to protect. Our power was derived from a need for good. And yet all we have managed to do is obliterate."

Vengelis waved a dismissive hand. "Had it not been for the Sejero, Anthem would have been swept into destruction. What good did the natural order of things do for us, then, when our entire world was covered in mushroom clouds and killing fields?"

"The blood of the Sejero vanquished the Zergos invasion, yes. But the same blood—the same power—then turned on the morality of our own civilization and vanquished it, too, with equal force. The day we were given the strength of gods, we abandoned everything that made us men. What chance does sovereignty and morality have when the whim of a few unmerited individuals can deny them from all? When we stepped out of the boundaries of the natural world, our race might as well have been destroyed. Everything we once stood for, what the people down there still strive for, was lost forever."

Vengelis stared at Gravitas for a long moment. Nerol's body was beaten beyond recognition, his armor torn to ribbons and cracked throughout, his eyelids swelled to great fruits, and his nose and jaw were distended and bleeding profusely. The building pressed down on him with an unimaginable force, and yet he held obstinately against it, trembling with exhaustion. An obvious truth that had been staring Vengelis in the face since he first set eyes on Gravitas Nerol suddenly dawned on him. Its sheer obviousness crashed over him like a dousing of icy water. He bowed his head in shame of his own lacking restraint and reason. Vengelis had heard all of these sentiments before, many times over.

"You trained under Master Tolland," Vengelis centered his attention bleakly on the fleeing people and debris-covered pavement within the broad shadow of the building. "Didn't you?"

"I . . . Yes."

Vengelis slowly closed his eyes and shook his head in disgrace of his own imprudence. "So did I."

Gravitas looked up, both startled and affronted. "You lie!"

"You really don't believe me? After all you have seen of my fighting style and techniques? After this prolonged back and forth stalemate? Look at us both; we are equally beaten. Nerol, we are the same: students of the greatest teacher of our time."

"Master Tolland wouldn't . . . "

"Tolland *sent* me here, Nerol!"

"He would never do that," Gravitas's voice became enraged, his tone betrayed. "Master Tolland would have died before he sent a slaughterer to this world."

"Come with me, Nerol. Come back to Anthem and turn your values into realization. You seek to defend those weaker than you from death. Anthem lies on the brink of ruin! Cold and pitiless machines are ripping through our civilization. Our civilization, Nerol! Fight alongside me, and together we can defeat the Felixes. I know we can. The two grand sentinels of our world will return in a display of glory and splendor unparalleled since the fall of the old world and the rise of the Sejero!"

"Tolland . . . would never have wanted this. You've been here one day and you've already killed so many. Master Tolland would never have sent an Epsilon here."

"Nerol!" Vengelis's voice grew in feverish intensity. "He *did*. I didn't know you were here; you have to understand me. When Tolland told me of Filgaia, it was in the midst of Sejeroreich's fall. We were surrounded by madness. His words were drowned out in the carnage. I had to assume Tolland sent me here because of the humans. I had to push them! Each hour lost in this errand, scores of my people—our people—die. You must understand that?"

Vengelis tried to weigh Gravitas's thoughts. At last he spoke into the dusty wind. "Come back with me, Gravitas Nerol. Come back to Anthem and save your people."

Gravitas said nothing. The steel supports pushed and gnawed against his shoulders, and he sunk several feet.

"Return with me to avenge a dying race," Vengelis pleaded. "Return to become the champion among equals that you are!"

Gravitas looked up, his face was severe and his eyes were bloodshot from his strain. His tone was harsh. "*No.*"

"You must come with me."

Gravitas shook his head. "If I return, and we together destroy your machines, if all that you hope for comes true, it will only lead to the second rise of oppressive rule. How long will it be until the next Yabu race, the next human race, is bent to our descendants' will? No. We were given our shot . . . we failed."

The momentary rise in color suddenly drained from Vengelis's face. His lips went white with fury. "I will only ask once more."

"Save your breath. I won't willingly let go of this building. Upon my shoulders rests the faith of an entire spectrum of existence. I will not forsake it to misery and despair. As a martyr I can provide for them a cohesion that may hold their society in tact. So go on; kill me. Then return to Anthem and die yourself. In time the horrors we have seen will be forgotten."

"And there will be no changing your mind on this?"

"None," Gravitas said.

A moment of silence fell between them, each with expressions pained and miserable.

"Very well," Vengelis said. He knew what he had to do, it was clear to him now. "I thought Master Tolland sent me here for human scientists, but now I see I was wrong. He did not send me here for the humans at all. He sent me here to retrieve *you*, to recruit your help. Master Tolland knew that together we could defeat the Felixes."

"He . . . never . . . " Gravitas gasped.

"If you will not come back to help me save my people, so be it." Vengelis leaned in close to Gravitas, their faces a foot apart. "But I will not aid you in helping yours either. Make no mistake, Nerol, the Felixes will be created; the people down there fear us too much, and their dread will push them to create terrible things—things that will shock this world like nothing you can possibly imagine. You will be forced to embrace what I have seen, to feel the horrors I have felt, and only then will you understand my actions today. When you look into their blue gaze you will realize your mistake."

"I . . . " Gravitas sunk several feet, the building hitched, and he screamed out, his strength failing.

Vengelis watched sadly as Gravitas Nerol's strained body began to steadily sink against the weight of the skyscraper. He wondered, watching the tears of hopeless exhaustion fall down Gravitas's cheeks, if perhaps the strength of the Sejero had at last waned against the ages. With a terrible moan, Gravitas Nerol's strength failed. He slipped backward and was swallowed by the nest of mangled steel. At once the building collapsed inward from its own unsupported weight. The entire superstructure plummeted past Vengelis in a deluge of carnage. Vengelis floated numbly in the sudden dousing of sunlight, staring vacantly into the empty space where the skyscraper had just stood. His mind was void of thought as a tremendous cloud of dust and ash bellowed and swelled upward in the skyscraper's stead.

As though it were a perfunctory task, Vengelis numbly departed the calamity of the fallen skyscraper and flew unhurriedly down the length of the avenue to retrieve Darien. Below him, the streets of Midtown were now mostly desolate of evacuees. Long shadows of the tall buildings were lengthening in the flagging afternoon sunlight, and the power outage across the city accentuated the abandoned gloom.

The giant Royal Guard was dead amid a demolished Times Square. Vengelis took hold of Darien by his rigid ankle and carried him into the sky, the giant's huge arms dangling free and reaching down to the streets. Vengelis hauled the enormous body up to the rooftop where Hoff lay, and cast the loyal soldier he himself had killed alongside his departed Lord General.

A muffled beep sounded from the *Harbinger I* remote, indicating that the ship was near, but Vengelis ignored it as he gazed regretfully across the city to the endless lands to the west. The adrenaline had abated its pacifying hold on his broken body, and he could not believe the hurt that now coursed through him. He limped in agony to the ledge of the roof and gingerly lay down on his back far above the evidence of his inflicted pain and misery far below. His body was encompassed with pain, but as he turned his head and looked past the nearby spires and into the broad horizon, he felt only anguish.

For the first time in as long as he could remember, Vengelis allowed his eyelids to shut, and he simply stopped caring. Allowing the defeat to drench over him, he listened to his own labored breaths and stared to the serene clouds in the far distance.

It had always been Gravitas Nerol.

The purpose of Master Tolland's intent had not been hidden from him either; he had known from the beginning that someone had traveled to Filgaia on the *Traverser I*. But how could Vengelis have known it was a warrior equal to himself? How could he have known there *was* an equal to himself? He hated the Nerols: one, the bringer of ruin, and the other, a self-proclaimed saint, each equal in their ignorance. He resented Master Tolland and his cryptic orders. He despised Kristen Jordan and her negligent courage.

The throes of destiny had cast him as the herald of genocide. In his misery and desperation he had lashed out and extended the bloodshed to a blameless people. A large part of him knew he should chase down Kristen Jordan and Madison and tear the sample of Sejero genetics from their grasp. But there was no practical way of finding them without drawing out the slaughter, and he could not bear any more blood on his hands. Vengelis decided to pass the compass of fate, to place it in the hands of another lost navigator. A mighty gift had unintentionally been given to the people far below. How they used this offering would be up to them—he only hoped Kristen Jordan would prove more cautious than his own people.

Vengelis could not bring himself to grasp the true enemy, cold and callous: the Felix. In the midst of his hardships, the true enemy had been shrouded. As he looked across the cityscape, he was filled with a great sadness.

Everything he once had was lost.

His expression hopeless and distraught, Vengelis pulled the Blood Ring off the swelling knuckles of his finger. He looked at the brilliant ring for a long heartbreaking moment, its lustrous scarlet hue against the ruin of the streets below. What valorous achievements Sejero strength had ever achieved in legend and myth had long been overshadowed by the brutality of this ring's history.

Vengelis reached out over the ledge of the building and turned his palm, letting the Blood Ring slip from his hand.

CHAPTER FORTY-TWO

Kristen

Side by side, Kristen and Madison ran steadily up along the length of the chilly shadow cast by the teetering skyscraper. Plaster and dust spilled off their hair and clothes and billowed behind them as they jogged past shattered storefronts and overturned cars. They were two faces in the indiscriminate mob, though the mass was noticeably diminishing as they crossed the intersections westward and put distance between themselves and the high-rises of Midtown. Out of danger from the collapsing skyscraper, they each still ran as fast as their dust-filled lungs would allow.

A loud rumbling thundered from behind them, and at the same moment the shadow of the skyscraper abruptly vanished. The grand building fell, its lashing supports crashing and hurdling into the heart of Manhattan. Rising from where the skyscraper had stood, a dark pillar of dust ascended high over the city. The cloud of wreckage that sprawled into the sky and surrounding streets, the one of which Kristen and Madison had been so nearly a part, seemed to touch the very ceiling of the clouds. Kristen turned and watched the churning plume in wordless awe. They were now well out of range of the devastation, but she took a few stunned steps backward on the trembling street. The back of her thighs touched the side of a police car, and she leaned back against it and watched the dreamlike cloud of destruction unfurl across the otherwise glittering autumn cityscape.

"Those poor people," Madison said.

Kristen's eyes reflected the ruin, and she quietly said, "Unforgivable."

The sentiment of the people pressing around them was not that of total relief, but certainly that of momentary appreciation for their narrow escape from a grisly death. They were leaving Midtown behind, and their growing distance from the towering skyscrapers placated the fear of an imminent death. Together, Kristen and Madison turned their backs to the towers of the city with a sense of final resolve, and continued at a steady trot toward the Hudson River.

"Someone shouldered that entire building. We both saw it." Madison spoke over the moving crowd as they fell in step. "If it wasn't Vengelis, who was it?"

"I don't know, but I don't like it."

"You don't like that someone saved your life?"

"That's not what I meant," Kristen said. "It's just that, well, I thought I had a grasp on the situation in all of this insanity. Now it looks like things are more complicated, which begs the question: what was Vengelis hiding? And that makes me scared."

Kristen reached a hand back and rested it against her backpack, where she felt the boxy form of the slide case through the nylon fabric. The case felt secure, undamaged. Somehow she had made it out of the disaster with the Sejero blood in her possession. They jogged wordlessly along the street, breathing the clean air deep down. Kristen's chest still felt fiery, the channels of her lungs razor sharp and inflamed. There were cuts and scrapes all over her body from the barrage of falling debris that had engulfed her, and her right ankle was tender from being twisted.

The crowd before them parted as the westward street met with the Hudson River, and they saw the full extent of the grand exodus off Manhattan Island. Kristen had never seen so many people in her life, and could not even venture a guess of their numbers. Countless men and women in military uniform were ushering the endless masses toward the river's edge. Sprawled out for miles and miles along the glistening cement strands, the grayish choppy water of the Hudson was swarming with ships. Though most of the boats were flying Navy and Coast Guard colors, there were also countless private yachts and heavy commercial vessels carrying anyone and everyone across the comparatively narrow body of water. Many of the boats were weighed down to the very brim with refugees throwing buckets of bilge from the sides, hulls lingering inches above the water.

Kristen paused to take in the momentous panorama, but the surrounding migration quickly pushed her forward. Turning to catch a glimpse of Manhattan, Kristen observed that the crashes and reverberations seemed to have died away with the felling of the giant skyscraper. The world was no longer trembling at the mercy of higher beings. At their backs, the city seemed eerily still, empty, and silent. The growing dome of dust that so nearly claimed her was being carried across the skyline in the cradle of Atlantic wind. With a mesmerized shake of her head, Kristen turned back to the riverside.

Pangs of anxiety began to flutter in her stomach. Her intellect alone controlled the fate of a technological creation unparalleled in the history of science—a truly *foreign* marvel. An undeniable truth faced her exhausted mind. If she chose one of the paths laid out before her, the name Kristen Jordan would be synonymous with Vatruvian cell technology, with the genesis of the enigmatic Felix.

The Felix.

Kristen buried her face in her dusty hands as indecision and doubt claimed her. The form of the destiny held within her backpack was obscured in boundless unknowns. Ruin and torment lingered from every angle. Would the idea taking form in her mind be mankind's grand salvation or inexorable peril? A large part of her wanted to shatter the slide of Sejero blood against the street or cast it into the Hudson, to abandon all thoughts of so compelling a notion. The power within her grasp was inconceivable, far too much for any one person to bear alone. But deep down Kristen knew it was not her decision to make.

"It's going to be okay," Madison said, seeing her inner torment.

Kristen looked out over the river and the crowding boats. Was this to be the future—the next hand dealt to humanity by the capriciousness of the fates: fear and desolation, subjugation and displacement? She could not selfishly destroy the Sejero blood to the torment of her world. With a sudden charge of gathered assurance, Kristen took a deep stirring breath. "You're right. It is going to be okay." At once, Kristen pushed to the nearby company of Marines standing by the river. "Hey! Hey! We know what they are; we have their weapons! Please!"

The nearest soldier, a man in his forties with an exhausted expression, held up a disinterested hand to her as he waved people onward to the boat launches. "Please continue toward the river and get in the lines to board one of the transports. We advise only boarding the Navy or Coast Guard ships. If you choose to board a private vessel, you do so at your own discretion. Just keep moving forward!"

"We need to talk to someone in charge!" Kristen shouted, her hair blowing in the wind. "We have vital information on the people attacking us! We were just in the Marriott Marquis where one of them held us captive!"

The soldier looked to Kristen with a thoughtfulness that surprised her. "Ma'am, look around you. Every single person you see is telling us they have seen something or know something about them. Now please, mind your *own* safety and board one of the designated crafts over the river. If what you say is true, then take it up with authorities once this mess settles down and you are out of harm's way."

"We didn't just *see* them," Kristen insisted. "We talked to them. Their leader explained to us what they are."

The soldier gave them a discerning look and raised a walkie-talkie to his mouth, but before he could speak, Kristen saw someone she could not believe. She stared past the Marine in disbelief for a stunned moment, and then lunged herself forward, nearly knocking him over.

"General Redford!" she screamed at the top of her lungs as the Marine grabbed her by the backpack. "General Redford!"

Kristen could not believe it. General Redford was walking beyond the line of soldiers, flanked on either side by a dozen men in uniform. The general stood a full head above the rest of his soldiers, and was issuing orders into a heavy military phone.

"General Redford!" Kristen shouted. "I need to talk to you! They came to the Marriott Marquis! They came to the convention! They held us hostage! Please!"

Hearing his name, General Redford turned to her and glared distantly for a moment, trying to place how he recognized her. His expression then lightened in familiarity. "Kristen Jordan?" he said, bewildered. "Let her through, soldier."

The Marine stepped aside at once and allowed Kristen to pass. Kristen grabbed Madison's arm and pushed through the line of camouflaged shoulders and machine guns.

"Bring the F-thirty-fives over the city one last time to remind people we're still here, and then ground them." General Redford spoke into a phone. "Yes, that's right. Ground them. They're doing no good. Fuel them up and be ready." He beckoned Kristen over to him as he hung up the phone. "I'm glad to see you made it out, Kristen." He placed a hand on the shoulder of one of the soldiers standing with him. "Lieutenant, please see that Miss Jordan here is brought aboard a transport right away."

The young soldier nodded. "Yes, sir. Please follow me, miss."

"Wait, wait!" Kristen said. "General Redford one of them came to the Marriott Marquis!"

"I beg your pardon?" the general's phone was already ringing again.

Kristen blurted out her words. "One of them . . . the people doing all this to New York and Chicago. He called himself Vengelis Epsilon, and he introduced us to those giants! He locked us in the convention ballroom and said they would destroy another city if I didn't help them."

General Redford was taken aback. "One of them was at the convention? I don't understand."

"They came here for Vatruvian cell technology."

"They . . . Vatruvian cell?" General Redford turned and faced her, his expression stern. "I don't understand. Where is Dr. Vatruvia?"

"He killed him."

"He?"

Kristen sighed shakily, aware of how insane she must sound. "Vengelis Epsilon."

"Vengelis Epsilon?" General Redford glared down the crowding riverbank. "Dr. Vatruvia is dead?"

Kristen nodded. "Vengelis Epsilon, the man claiming to be the emperor of their people, killed Professor Vatruvia in the Marriott Marquis."

The phone at General Redford's side continued to ring as he allowed the gravity of Kristen's words to soak in. After a moment he shook his head and answered the phone, issuing a string of orders and military acronyms that went over Kristen's head. "Walk," General Redford said as he hung up, and turned to the riverfront.

Kristen and Madison did not need telling twice. They followed close behind him as they passed by regiments of rushing soldiers and jumbled lines of people awaiting their transports across the river.

"I don't understand," General Redford said, leaning down to Kristen. "You are certain it was one of . . . *them*? This is a matter of national—hell, global—security."

"Beyond any doubt. We saw him fly. If that isn't enough in itself, we also watched him throw people across the Lutvak ballroom and disregard gunshots that hit him straight in the chest.

"He destroyed an eighteen-wheeler with his bare shoulder to prove to me his strength." Madison piped in. "And then forced me to take him to the Marriott Marquis. He only cared about the hotel and the scientists that were there."

"Destroyed an eighteen-wheeler you say?" General Redford asked, his expression registering familiarity. "Come with me."

Kristen and Madison followed him up a narrow gangplank and boarded a small ship with a gray hull and a billowing American flag. Underneath the steel grate at their feet, the gloomy waters of the Hudson looked cold and unwelcoming, the surface choppy in the chill wind. Across the crowding river, the western waterfront was being stormed with a horde of evacuees. The length of the New Jersey shore was lined with recently erected tents. Vaguely, Kristen noticed the George Washington Bridge was missing in the north.

"We're doing the best we can, given the circumstances. It might not look like it now, but New York was the city best equipped for this level of catastrophe. Lots and lots of disaster preparedness and evacuation protocol." General Redford said, his tone professional, though his gaze looked beaten as he looked out across the countless boats in the river. "You wouldn't believe Chicago."

"Is it as bad as it looked?" Kristen asked.

"Worse," General Redford said. "Much worse. We tried to engage them over the city—those giants, or whatever they are. A single one of them wiped out an entire squadron of F-twenty-twos with his hands. Our most advanced missiles fizzled against their chests as if they were nothing at all; M-sixty rounds bounced off them like pebbles. We're putting up a losing fight here, if it can be called a fight at all. Right now the plan is to keep as many people alive for as long as possible. We started getting a lot of reports that there is conflict among . . . whoever they are. There are tens of thousands of witnesses, but no two stories are alike. We have hundreds of analysts sifting through the facts, but nothing's reliable yet. The one common trend in the reports is that there appears to be a divergence between them. You say you talked to one of them?" General Redford handed his phone to one of the men walking beside him and turned to Kristen, the breeze of the river ruffling his fatigues. "Tell me everything."

Kristen took a breath, and at once delved into all the tumultuous happenings that had transpired from the time she had begun her Vatruvian cell presentation earlier in the afternoon. Almost immediately, General Redford looked astounded. He called over an assistant to record every word spoken as their boat slowly made its way through the dense traffic of the waterway.

Against the clamorous backdrop surrounding them, Kristen told the general everything she knew. She spoke of Vengelis Epsilon and his apparent intentions; she explained the close relationship of the Felix research report and Vatruvian cell technology. As the boat pitched back and forth, Kristen described the two giants that destroyed Chicago and what she had inferred about the Primus race and Sejero genetics. Every now and then Madison spoke up and added something Kristen had overlooked. They were getting on with their account as the barge pulled away from its docking.

"I believe you," General Redford said as Kristen's telling came to the falling skyscraper and the person who saved their lives. He called over another assistant. "The reconnaissance images, please."

The assistant rifled through a leather suitcase and handed the general a manila folder with a classified stamp on the side. Flipping through the folder for a moment, General Redford pulled out a loose paper and handed it to Kristen.

"What do you see?" he asked.

It was a grainy printout of a photograph, the clarity of the image blurred with movement. There were two men who looked like they were falling through the sky, but after the day's events Kristen acknowledged that they were surely flying. They were striking out at each other and locked in struggle, their arms and legs obscured with sheer speed. Though the day had partially inured her to such representations, the captured image was nevertheless mesmerizing. They were alpha and omega incarnate, each of their allegiances equal in mystery. Only one of their faces could be seen in the image, and the other one had his back turned. Kristen tapped a finger on the handsome face and nimble body on the right. "This is the person we've been talking about. Vengelis Epsilon."

"The one in charge?" General Redford asked.

"Yes. We only met him and the giants who were under his command. I don't know who the person is with his back turned." Kristen glared at the backside of the mysterious man. "I don't know who he is, but I think he's the one who saved our lives."

"Yes, I don't doubt that." General Redford stared in awe at the picture. "We have no idea who or what he is, but we believe he's the sole reason the carnage of Chicago didn't spread. From what we've witnessed, it appears as though whoever he is, he's on our side. He overcame both of the giants above the city. The media's caught wind of him, too. They're already calling him our savior. People are beginning to suggest that he is some sort of . . . messiah."

"No," Kristen said, and met the general's gaze with an uncompromising look. "Neither of them have anything to do with religion, and the sooner that is ingrained into people's minds the better."

"I couldn't agree with you more . . . but with or without a religious perspective, this man *has* undeniably protected us."

Kristen stared at the nameless man's backside in wonder.

"He is the keystone," General Redford said as their barge lurched from contact with the western wharf and chains began to lower the gangplank. "We've tentatively decided that, for the time being, he is our ally. Considering none of our most powerful weapons succeeded in even scratching the giants, most of the world's governments have agreed to hold off on any radical counter measure until we can get in contact with him—or the faction he represents. But come, I'll have a trooper escort you to a missions operation tent. We'll need to have someone debrief the both of you."

"Wait, general," Kristen said, and looked sidelong at Madison, who nodded her onward. "There's one more thing."

"Yes?"

"Remember earlier today when we discussed Vatruvian cell technology and how it can recreate a given organism?"

"I . . ." General Redford blinked. "Yes, I recall."

"Well, it's not a hypothetical science to them. Vengelis's people did it; they created Vatruvian replicates of themselves using their own genetics. He said the scientists in his world gave rise to entities with the same immense power he and the giants exercised against us today. According to Vengelis, the Vatruvian entities they created are more powerful than themselves. He told me these Vatruvian creations set into motion all of this insanity."

"Okay," General Redford said, his expression showing a lack of understanding.

"You said none of our most powerful weapons wounded the giants. Well," Kristen took a deep breath and slipped off her dusty backpack, kneeling down to pull back the zipper, "I believe we do have a means of defending ourselves against them."

"I don't understand," General Redford said. "How?"

Kristen carefully pulled the slide from its protective case and held it up for him to see. The crimson stain of blood—of Sejero genetics—glinted in the sunlight, crude and bare. Beyond the slide held between her thumb and forefinger, looming high above the exodus, the great pillar of dust billowed southward across the vast skyline of New York, a curtain of darkness and doubt challenging the certainty of their world.

"We have their blood," Kristen said with anticipation and dread as she gazed exhaustedly at the slide and the maimed city beyond. "And with it we can defeat them."

"Sir," an assistant approached General Redford with another printed photograph. "The analysts just sent this image through the wire. It's the first reliable close-up of the man who saved the city."

The general reached out and held it in his hands for all of them to see.

Kristen's curiosity roused, she leaned over to look at the man who had saved all of their lives. Her expression froze. For a fleeting moment, she grasped the significance, the absolute enormity of who he was.

"That's . . . not . . . possible . . . " she heard her own voice speak. At last, her logic could take no more. Kristen felt her mind go blank, and she willingly passed out on the spot, her shoulders sinking into the nearby soldier.

ABOUT THE AUTHOR

S.L. Dunn is the debut author of *Anthem's Fall*, a novel he wrote amid the wanderings of his mid twenties. He has written while living intermittently in St. John USVI, Boston, Maine and Seattle. Raised on big screen superheroes and pop science fiction, he sought to create a novel that bridged a near-sci-fi thriller with a grand new fantasy. He currently resides in Seattle with his girlfriend Liz and their dog Lucy, and is hard at work completing the next book of the *Anthem's Fall* series. Get in touch and find out more at www.sldunn.com.

ACKNOWLEDGMENTS

There were many people who helped me create *Anthem's Fall*. For accepting the charge of beta reading early drafts, thanks to Debra Dunn, Evan Dunn, Liz Borgatti, Matt Sheridan, Jon Kalinoski, Chris McDermott, Andy Reed, Jenn Sherman, Adam Weiner, Rebecca Harris and Shane Armstrong. I'd also like to thank the steady handed editing of Anna Drexler and Amanda Triplett.

A few special thanks:

I had pretty much given up on *Anthem's Fall* when my girlfriend Liz encouraged me beyond all reason to continue my pursuit. I can say without a doubt that this novel would still be an out of sight file on my laptop had it not been for her support.

For encouraging me ever forward in this "authoring" endeavor, I thank my Mom. As I write this section, a particular memory comes to mind. I remember reviewing weekly vocabulary words for my Language Arts classes on the morning commute to middle and high school. I think of all those commutes, along with all of the library and book store trips, and I can't help but wonder if I ever would have discovered my passion for words were it not for all those fleeting moments that are so easy to overlook in hindsight.

Made in the USA
Charleston, SC
20 May 2014